W9-AZE-888

VIGILANTE
POLITICS

VIGILANTE POLITICS

CJ Houy

Vigilante Politics
© 2017 C.J. Houy. All rights reserved.

No part of this book may be reproduced in any form or by any means, electronic, mechanical, digital, photocopying or recording, except for the inclusion in a review, without permission in writing from the publisher.

Published in the USA by:
CJ Houy

ISBN 978-0-9992187-0-9

Printed in the United States of America

Book & cover design by Darlene Swanson • www.van-garde.com

VIGILANTE POLITICS

PART ONE

Senate Inaction

CHAPTER I

Thursday, August 3rd

US Capitol

A loud, guttural *buzz* pierced the quiet. In the pitch-black room, one of six tiny amber lights glowed on the base of a mahogany and gold antique clock. Startled by the sound, he jerked his head up from the couch and stared. He lay there, watching, waiting. *Come on, one more light. Please let this be a quorum call.* The buzzer continued its long, unbroken racket, signaling that a roll call vote had begun. "God damn it. I've got to go vote."

He paused for a moment and softened his tone. "Sometimes you can't catch a break. We were supposed to have an hour. Well, we better get down to business." He stood up in the darkened room. "What's the latest on the Chinese?"

Rebecca DeLaurio rolled over on the couch. Pushing up onto her elbows, she shimmied back and forth, pulling her dress straps over her shoulders. Sitting up, she grabbed a pack of cigarettes from the coffee table. The flash from her lighter illuminated the room for an instant. It revealed her thin oval-shaped face aged gracefully by the years—shoulder-length, jet-black hair, large brown eyes, rouged cheeks, and olive skin. The telltale lines from smoking and stress provided the only clue she was no longer an ingénue or thirty-something.

She offered the pack to the shadowy figure before her. He waved her off. She exhaled smoke toward the ceiling in the politically correct manner ingrained by a long career in Washington and spoke in a calm, authoritative voice. "It's going better than we ever dreamed. Everything's working precisely as you planned. The money comes right to me, and I funnel it into the campaign like any other contribution. The staff believes it's from the Asian-American PAC, but they aren't asking a lot of questions."

He paced back and forth across the plush carpeted floor, his smile growing as she spoke. *This is terrific. Far easier than I'd ever imagined.* He turned back to Rebecca. "Now you're absolutely sure no one else knows what's up. This has to remain our secret."

"Not even Harry. He's focused on this a-hole opponent and getting to the election without mistakes. He is just," she paused to exhale, "grateful for my efforts." She paused again. "I hope you realize I could help you on this in the future too."

He nodded. Her description of the Republican candidate Anton Keakaua Keahole and talk of the future made him smile. He checked his zipper and straightened his tie, hoping he didn't look too rumpled. *And to think, this might be all I need to get over the top.* He leaned over, squeezed her now-covered breast, and pecked her on the cheek. "We're all grateful, dear, but I'll have to take a rain check. God damn votes. You never know what's going to happen in this place anymore."

"I'm headed back to LA tomorrow to snatch more cash, so that rain check's going to have to wait a few days."

"More cash? That's great." He smiled, grabbed his coat, and walked out the door and down the corridor toward the Senate chamber.

CHAPTER II

Dirksen Senate Office Building

Paula picked up the phone on the first ring. "Appropriations, Paula Means speaking."

"Paula." Immediately she recognized the deep, melodious voice of Senator Ken Mitsunaga of Hawaii. "I just got to the cloak room. What's this vote?"

She pictured him sitting in one of the four cloakroom phone booths set aside for senators. He would be impeccably dressed, his salt-and-pepper hair neatly in place. "Senator," she said. "It's a Brown amendment. It links Asian campaign donations to a conspiracy to buy influence in the upcoming election. You've opposed this witch hunt since Parker raised it last spring." She added the explanation knowing it wasn't necessary.

"You say Brown offered it?"

"Yes, sir. Of course, Parker's behind it, but he got Brown to offer the amendment."

"Well, Brown's retiring. This way Parker can't be labeled a racist by Asians. How'd he get it on this bill? What's it got to do with Financial Services Appropriations?"

"Nothing, sir, but he offered it as a second degree to an amendment that the majority leader wants. So, we're stuck.

5

The leader won't drop his amendment, that's for sure. You're going to have to vote on Brown."

"And, that's all he wants. He wants to force us to vote for questionable campaign funding and use it against our guys in November. Anyone speak in opposition?"

"The chairman did, sir. Said it doesn't belong on this bill. Then he moved to table it."

The senator chuckled. "Jackson's a sly one, tabling it to kill it off before anyone can get worked up debating it."

"The chairman's staff is saying he can get about twenty Republican votes to agree with the 'unrelated amendment' tabling move. Your side will need thirty-one if you're going to kill it."

"What's the whip count?"

"It's close. I talked to Bankhead's people, and they aren't making predictions. Most of your Democratic colleagues are nervous. They've all taken money from the Asian-American PAC, and they're afraid of attack ads on the issue."

"So they'll vote in favor of the amendment. I suppose that's easier than giving back the money. Hm . . . mm. What's Keahole saying?"

"He hasn't said much, sir, but Harry says his folks are watching. They'll be ready to pounce as soon as you vote."

"Let 'em pounce. This is an awful amendment. It charges and convicts people without any regard for the rights of the accused. Sure, if it's accurate, they ought to be hanged by their thumbnails. But this isn't the way to do it. This is America, not Putin's Russia."

"Yes, sir."

"Sometimes you've got to do what's right and take your lumps. This won't buy Keahole the ten points he needs to catch me—maybe in South Dakota, but not Hawaii. Let me know if we get a better vote count. And Paula, you better start collecting some old speeches and get a copy of the Bible. If Jackson can't kill this thing, I may be out there speaking for a long time. And ask Susie to send some comfortable shoes over to the cloakroom. I could be on my feet for hours."

"OK, sir. Boy, I hope you don't have to filibuster. That'll kill all our bills until after the election. But I'll call Susie and put some stuff together in case you need it."

"Thanks, Paula."

"Thank you, Senator."

Paula hung up, kicking herself that she'd thanked him, a silly nervous reaction even after all these years. She stood up and arched her back. She ran her hands through her long blonde hair and deftly knotted it in a ponytail. At five foot seven, she was tall enough to grab the top of her bookcase and stretch out. Being hunched over her computer all day killed her. *I'm too young for backaches,* she thought.

She caught a glimpse of her profile in the mirror on the back of her door. She had to smile at the curvy girl with big, round brown eyes and rosy cheeks staring back. *At least I still look good. I might not have won that stupid Miss Teen Virginia contest, but I should've.*

She thought about the senator's call and chuckled. She'd known he'd call. Sure, she ran his defense subcommittee, and this didn't have anything to do with defense, but she'd become his expert on all things appropriations. She knew what he'd say, how he'd vote, before he called. But it was all part of the ritual. He liked having someone to discuss it with before he voted. She never tried to convince him to vote one way or the other, not that it would've mattered. He hadn't survived nearly forty years in the Senate without knowing how to vote on issues. The old bulls didn't need staff to tell them how to vote. If the staff gave them the background and reminded them of the facts, then they'd done their job. And Paula was one of the best at doing her job.

CHAPTER III

People's Liberation Army regional headquarters

Guangzhou, China

General Li Pen heard the fax begin to whir. As the message arrived, he grabbed it off his secure fax machine. *Damn the Americans' Yankee ingenuity. Nonetheless, what would life be like without secure communications?* The report was from the US, area code 213, Los Angeles. It had to be Agent Xian Huan Nod. He read the page aloud, "Received package from home and put to good use. More help required."

"More!" he shouted. *What could that mean? More ... money?* It wasn't like Agent Xian to be transparent in these communications. Yes, they were secure, but one could never be sure the NSA hadn't caught on. Any message sent from the United States to the People's Liberation Army regional headquarters was bound to be monitored by someone in the United States Intelligence Community.

He lifted up the phone and bellowed, "Get Yong-Li up here now." He slammed down the phone, stood up, and clasped his hands behind his back. Slouched over, he paced around the room, muttering to himself.

Within seconds there was a knock on the door. Major Yong-Li, his aide-de-camp, entered bowing. "Yes, sir."

"I have just received a note from America asking for more.

What could that mean? We've already funneled nearly $1 million to Xian. He can't be serious."

"Sir, American campaigns have become very expensive. In California, they expect to spend $1 billion in the next Senate election. You must have confidence in Agent Xian. He's the best we have."

"I know he's the best, but remind me again why I should be spending millions to bribe a congressman?"

"He's a senator, sir. And, you need him to protect your overseas companies. Remember last year? The Senate voted to deny you a contract to run the Long Beach port. In America, if one senator stands up and refuses to allow a vote on any issue, he can stop it dead—the filibuster. This investment guarantees that the next time the Senate tries to stop you from doing business in America, you can defeat them."

General Li Pen knew he was right, but that didn't solve the problem of where to get more money. He'd already wiped out the profits from his management of PLA's offshore investments. If he dipped into that pot again, the running dogs from Beijing might discover it. He couldn't go to the Party with a request for money unless he was willing to open his financials and explain what he was up to. That was out of the question. Those worthless, nouveau, communist, bourgeois dogs in Beijing would never approve.

"Send Xian another one hundred thousand dollars. I will find it somewhere. But, you tell him this is absolutely the last time. If I can't buy one senator with that, then we'll try another tactic to influence our friends in America."

Yong-Li bowed and excused himself.

The general sat down at his desk, unlocked a drawer, and pulled out a thin, black file. He flipped the pages and wrote down "$100,000 X."

CHAPTER IV

Wahiawa, Oahu

Twenty-four-year-old Technical Sergeant Amy Anderson sat twirling her red orphan-Annie curls with one hand. She downloaded the message from Yokota with the other and sent it off to National Security Agency headquarters at Fort Meade. She picked up her secure phone. It wasn't every day she intercepted an encrypted message between someone in Los Angeles and the People's Liberation Army headquarters in China.

"Sandy, this is Amy. I just got a strange one and wanted to give you a heads-up it was coming. I'd sure like to know what you find out."

Master Sergeant Sandy Baker hung up the phone as the message from the Wahiawa Regional Signal Operations Center arrived. He transferred the data to a Cray supercomputer to run the deciphering program. It wasn't going to be easy to break the code. Encrypted faxes were a lot harder to decipher than most secure voice traffic. But, their new software was working well. As he read the message, he noted that the fax was from an old Ricoh 2800 SFXT. *Cool, at least it's not from a state-of-the-art machine. That gives us a good chance. I wonder what they're up to.*

Within seconds, the Cray had done its work, and a message popped up on his computer screen. "English," he muttered, "that's odd. Not Chinese. It looks like a message from a college student living overseas. But what student sends encrypted messages to the PLA regional headquarters near Guangzhou?"

He copied the file and emailed it off to the duty officer. It was against "regs" to talk to Amy about it, but since she'd asked, and she'd given him the heads-up, and since it only looked like somebody's college kid in need of a few more bucks, he decided to fill her in. *What the hell. She's always helping me out. It's the least I can do.*

"Amy, it's Sandy. This is a strange one. The message is in English, and it sounds like a note from a kid asking his parents for more cash. It doesn't look like much, but I'll zap it back to you. You sure it came from the PLA?"

"That's what SIGINT says. You know most of that operation is remoted now, so we just get the data from the overheads. We don't have anybody on the ground to check it out. But Sandy, you ought to know better than anyone: computers don't lie."

She smiled thinking about it. Praising computers to NSA geeks was like telling Imelda Marcos that shoes were nice. "Thanks, Sandy." She hung up and waited for the fax to arrive. *Dear Dad, send money. That's a great idea. I ought to call home tonight. I could use a little extra cash.*

CHAPTER V

US Capitol

Senator Mitsunaga walked through the tall wood-and-glass doors onto the Senate floor from the cloakroom. To his immediate left, he could see the Democratic staff sitting on the back benches behind a low railing. It was known as the Byrd Cage. The former majority leader had insisted the railing be installed right after the Senate began live televised coverage. And, only shortly after, this newfangled intruder had captured an unfortunate incident—a mini-skirted staffer, going commando, sitting on the old, comfortable staff chairs directly behind her boss, the senior senator from New Jersey. While the good senator addressed the Senate, she gave an eyeful to the odd collection of C-SPAN junkies hooked on watching the daily workings of the Congress.

On the other side of the chamber, Republican staff were seated in their cage. In front of the railing, a group of freshman Republican members huddled around Senator Brown. They were the self-appointed watchdogs of the Senate. All were recent graduates of the House. They monitored appropriations bills to make sure their colleagues didn't do anything to upset their Tea Party supporters.

Near the front of the chamber, at the majority leader's desk, stood Chairman Sam Jackson, the feisty little fireplug from

Washington, looking ready to punch the next guy who spoke to him. He saw Ken Mitsunaga enter the Senate. Slowly he shook his head from side to side and gave him that classic frown that was almost a caricature since it looked exactly like the photo that *The Washington Post* liked to run of him—the one that gave him the appearance of being a mean SOB; the one he loved because it reminded everyone, not least of all his colleagues, that he was not a man to be taken lightly.

Senator Mitsunaga walked down the aisle and crossed over to Senator Jackson. "Where are we, Sam?"

"Ken, that jackass from Nebraska felt it was his civic duty to raise this. I tried my best to convince him this was not the right bill, but he doesn't give a damn. I sure am glad that son of a bitch is sticking to his stupid campaign pledge and retiring after one term. Not that it would've mattered. He's one of these guys who prove the rule that any idiot can get elected, but it takes skill to get reelected. And he certainly comes up short in that department. That asshole will be gone soon. For the good of the Senate, I just wish it already happened."

"Can you beat him?" Mitsunaga asked, already knowing the prognosis but also knowing Jackson would want to offer his assessment. Senator Mitsunaga had built his career by knowing when to ask for advice, or offer it, and when to allow a friend to share his views. Timing was everything in politics. His friendship with the chairman of the Appropriations Committee was one of the primary reasons Hawaii's economy was thriving even though his fellow Democrats were now the minority in the Senate.

"I can get about twenty votes, but you're going to need to get most of your guys to kill it. What's it look like?"

"The candidates are running scared," he said, parroting

Paula's words. "It will be close. So many of the fellas have taken Asian money; they're worried what your colleagues will do to them on the campaign trail."

"Hm. What are you going to do, old friend? You took that money, too. At least that's what my guys are saying."

"Of course I'm taking Asian money, I'm Asian, and many Americans of Asian ancestry support my candidacy. But it's all legal. Harry watches these things. I'm not worried." Senator Mitsunaga stiffened his back and narrowed his eyes. "But, this is a terrible amendment. We may as well hang the Asian-American leaders who are corralling the donations. This is vigilante politics at its worst." He smiled a crack. *Vigilante politics*, he was going to have to remember that one. It might make a good sound bite one day. "But seriously, Sam, if you can't table this, you know I'm going to have to filibuster. I can't let this pass."

Jackson nodded, then turned and frowned, spying Senator James Fillmore Parker of Nevada, who had just walked in. The group huddling in the back rushed to gather around him. He was their spiritual leader and the man they thought would be president in a little more than two years.

Senator Mitsunaga walked up to the front desk. He raised his hand, seeking recognition. When the clerk called out, "Mr. Mitsunaga," he motioned with a thumbs-up. The clerk nodded and spoke in a clear, emotionless tone, "Mr. Mitsunaga, aye."

Senator Jim Parker was straight out of Hollywood casting. He stood six foot two, square-jawed and broad-shouldered, with short gray hair, albeit thinning on top. He looked like the star athlete he had been in college. He ignored his colleagues and strutted down the aisle. "Jackson," he growled in a loud stage whisper, "What the hell are you doing tabling this?"

The chairman of the Appropriations Committee bristled and then blasted. "Jim, this amendment has no business on this bill. If we don't table it, somebody is bound to filibuster, and that'll kill the whole bill. We've got to finish this. We're not going to have our appropriations bills hung up again. I won't stand for it."

The chairman paused only for a rapid gasp of breath before charging on. "What the hell are you doing offering this amendment anyway? This is Financial Services, Jim. If you want to get a vote on this, get Chairman Wilson of the Rules Committee to launch an investigation or report a bill. I'll be damned if you're going to screw up my bills with this kind of shit. It's an election year, and we can't get bogged down like we did last time."

Senator Parker opened his mouth, but the chairman waved his finger at him. "The White House is just waiting for us to get caught up in stupid election year BS like this, and you better believe they'll stick it to us when we try to get out of here in early October. If you don't like it, bring it up on Tuesday with the leader."

Parker gaped, speechless after the tongue lashing from his senior colleague. At the back of the room, his cohort looked shocked, staring as their leader got an earful from "that old fart."

Parker spun around on his heels. He marched up the aisle toward the cloakroom. As he was about to leave, he turned and glared at Jackson. He waved his hand furiously at the clerk.

The clerk called out, "Mr. Parker."

Senator Parker shouted, "NO!" He turned and stormed through the double doors to the Republican cloakroom.

The clerk reported emotionlessly, "Mr. Parker, no."

After watching this spectacle unfold from the back of the chamber, Senator Mitsunaga returned to the well, the area of the chamber directly in front of the presiding officer's dais. He needed to win this one as much for his friend Jackson as for himself.

As each Democratic senator came in, he approached them. He explained why this vote was important to him. Senator Charley Johnson, the Democratic leader who was running for reelection and up by twenty points in the polls, said he agreed with Ken. But, he couldn't "take the chance." He voted "no." After that, the other twelve Democratic candidates also voted "no." Mitsunaga was successful in getting most of the other Democrats but lost two who were eying the presidential race in two years. He couldn't lose any more Democrats.

Longtime Kentucky Senator Tom Bankhead, the Democratic minority whip, came up to him. "How we doing, Chief?"

Mitsunaga raised his brows. "You asking me? You're the whip. I'm supposed to be asking you 'how we doing.' Sam Jackson says he can get twenty maybe. We ought to get thirty-one, but it's going to be close."

"Well, I'm with you, old friend." Bankhead grinned, his light blue-gray eyes twinkling. In a voice as smooth and rich as his home state sour mash whiskey he continued, "I didn't take any damn Chinese money."

"They wouldn't give an old swamp dog like you any." Mitsunaga laughed. "Besides, you aren't up, and they say you won't be running again anyway."

Mitsunaga knew that made Bankhead's decision a lot simpler. He also knew he was going to miss his old friend when he retired. Too many of the good ones, on both sides, were leaving. He, Jackson, and a couple others were the only ones left. The new crowd was full of young bucks who didn't seem to appreciate what it meant to be a senator. All they knew were the television cameras, the thirty-second spots, the tweets, and the best ways to embarrass an opponent.

The fifteen-minute vote had now run past thirty. The Parker-Brown forces had forty-eight votes—fifteen Democrats and thirty-three Republicans. Jackson had eighteen Republicans and thirty Democrats, a tie. That left three Republicans and one Democrat who hadn't voted.

Jackson grabbed two Republican members of the Appropriations Committee as they entered the chamber. Both voted "aye."

Republican Senator Redmond of North Carolina rolled into the chamber in a wheelchair. Jackson didn't even try to convince him. Redmond voted "no" and wheeled himself back out. The vote to kill the amendment was fifty ayes and forty-nine nays. It looked like they might pull it off.

The Democratic floor staff insisted that Senator Kauffman of Minnesota was on his way. Senator Mitsunaga had developed a good relationship with Kauffman, but he was unpredictable. He was also rabid on campaign finance reform. His zeal reminded some old timers of Bill Proxmire. In his last election, he stuck to his promise not to take PAC money. He managed to squeak back into office even though his challenger outspent him by a three-to-one margin. On its face, this looked like a vote over PAC money.

The vote had lasted thirty-two minutes. Jackson walked over to Mitsunaga. "Ken, how long we going to wait for Kauffman? You got his vote?"

"The floor staff says he's on his way. He's a reasonable fellow. We should be able to convince him."

"Let me call for regular order. We're way beyond the fifteen-minute time limit. We can cut off the vote now and not even worry about him."

"We can't cut him off, Sam. You know that wouldn't be right."

Jackson nodded reluctantly and headed back to his seat. It was the kind of thing the staff was always arguing for and the young bucks wanted to try. He and Mitsunaga weren't like that. It didn't make good sense to jeopardize a long-term relationship with any member by treating him shabbily on a single issue. In this place, you always had to think about the next vote, and the one after that.

Senator Kauffman arrived on the floor and Mitsunaga walked over to greet him. Kauffman listened carefully but shook his head. Mitsunaga looked over at the chairman, mimicking the Jackson frown. He shook his head slowly side to side. Kaufman raised his hand, voted "no," and walked out. A fifty-fifty tie; the motion to table the amendment would be defeated. It would be eligible for debate or filibuster. They'd lost.

The presiding officer asked, "Are there any members in the chamber wishing to vote or change their vote?" Senator Jackson raised his arm. The clerk recognized him.

"I vote, no," Jackson said.

The freshmen Republicans were ecstatic. They'd won, and the chairman had voted with them. As they patted each other on the back, Senator Parker stormed into the chamber. "What the hell are you cheering for?"

"We won, Jim. And Jackson voted with us."

"You fools," he growled. "That asshole is probably going to move to reconsider the vote. He must think that his good buddy Mitsunaga is going to turn someone. Didn't they teach you anything? Every vote in the Senate can be overturned. First, someone on the winning side motions to reconsider the vote. Then, if they change the outcome on a revote, you lose. Just watch. Jackson's going to fuck us."

"Why would he do that? Jackson's one of us."

"You stupid sons of bitches. Jackson's an appropriator. Haven't you heard the adage? There are three parties in Congress: Democrats, Republicans, and Appropriators. Those bastards always stick together. They don't give a shit about party loyalty. Not if it means messing up one of their precious appropriations bills. And Jackson and Mitsunaga are the worst. Those two motherfuckers always support each other. You watch. That old fart is gonna fuck us."

Senator Jackson sought and received recognition. He noted the absence of a quorum and walked off the Senate floor.

He knew just as well as everyone else that the rules of the

Senate required that a quorum, a majority of members, be present for business to be conducted. And, he knew equally well that it was rare indeed for a quorum to actually be present.

Most senators were too busy with meetings, hearings, or fundraising to sit on the floor. A handful were generally there to debate an issue or make a speech. Rarely, though, sufficient to constitute a quorum. But unless someone raised a point of order noting the absence of a quorum, the Senate was free to conduct business.

Chairman Jackson's timeless point of order check stopped the Senate in its tracks. Now they would either have to muster a real quorum or get the consent of all members present to rescind the quorum call.

The clerk began to call the role to ascertain whether a quorum was, in fact, present. The rules required it, even though, with five members in the chamber, the answer was obvious. The Senate would have to wait for the next move.

CHAPTER VI

Dirksen Senate Office Building

Sitting in her office, Paula watched the Senate floor on TV. The phone rang; it was John Silease, the Appropriations Committee majority staff director. "Did you see that?"

"Yeah," she responded. "Is he doing what I think?"

"I don't know, but he voted with the prevailing side and didn't table the motion to reconsider. This could be fun. You better stay tuned."

"You better believe I will." She hung up. God love Sam Jackson. The tabling motion had failed. Unless Jackson could overturn the vote, Mitsunaga would have to filibuster the bill on principle. The Senate would be stalled for days. That would kill Jackson's goal of getting all his appropriations bills completed before the election. She sure hoped Silease was right that Jackson was up to one of his tricks.

◆ ◆ ◆

The clerk moved slowly through the roll. Senator Jackson returned before the clerk reached Zachary, the last name on the roll. As speculated, Senator Jackson moved to reconsider the vote. Without any debate, the clerk called the roll again—this time for "yeas" and "nays."

As the vote unfolded for the second time, the Democrats voted the same. Sixteen supported and thirty opposed the motion to reconsider. Jackson had his twenty Republican votes, and Brown and Parker had thirty-three. No one had changed their vote except, of course, Jackson who was seeking the reconsideration. Twenty minutes passed. The count was fifty in favor, forty-nine opposed. The Republican floor staff was getting anxious. Senator Redmond and his wheelchair hadn't been seen.

Senator Parker stormed out of the cloakroom. He called over Mary Beth Anderson, the secretary for the majority. "Where's Redmond?" he hollered.

"I don't know, sir. His office hasn't seen him since the last vote. They don't think he's gone home, but they're not sure."

Senator Jackson rose from his chair. "Mary Beth, is he coming?" he asked, apparently innocently enough.

"We don't know, Senator. We can't find him."

Senator Bankhead, the minority whip, walked onto the floor and proceeded to the well. "What's going on? We've got a dinner tonight, and the leader promised to get these guys out by 7:30. You've got about ten more minutes. Let's get this over with."

As if on cue, the majority leader, Senator Howard "Jake" Jacobs of Louisiana, blew through the center doors thirty seconds after the minority whip. "Sam, whad'a ya'll got going on down here?"

"Leader, we're waiting for Redmond, but we don't know where he is."

"Mary Beth, where's Redmond?" the leader inquired calmly.

"We don't know, sir," she repeated for the third time, her exasperation plainly audible in her tone. "No one knows."

Jacobs looked at Jackson and the Democratic whip and nodded to the clerk. "OK," he said, "let's wrap this up."

The presiding officer asked if any other members wanted to be recorded. Senator Parker bolted out of the cloakroom. "What are you doing?" he demanded. "Redmond hasn't voted yet."

Senator Jacobs turned and looked up the aisle. "You got a problem, Jim? Redmond's not here, so we're gonna cut this thing off. We promised the minority we'd be out by 7:30, and I think we got one more vote. Isn't that right, Sam?"

"You're the leader, Jake, but I intended to move to table the amendment again."

"There you go, Jim. Now don't get all fired up; you'll get another shot at this. Besides, the strategy didn't work anyway. All their candidates voted "no" except Mitsunaga, and nobody's going to question him. We'll get 'em next time, Jim, but we need to move on now."

Parker's expression showed his barely-bridled frustration, but he just shook his head and stomped back toward the cloakroom.

The clerk announced the vote fifty to forty-nine; the amendment was up for reconsideration. The chairman moved to table the Brown amendment for the second time, and once again the vote was fifty to forty-nine. The amendment was dead.

As the other minority senators hurried off to dinner, Senator Mitsunaga headed back to the cloakroom. He picked up the phone and rang his old friend Jackson. "Thank you, my friend. You're the master."

"Hell, Ken, you would've done the same for me. I just hope you know what you're doing. That Parker's a sneaky bastard. I don't think you've heard the end of this."

"You're probably right about that. But, I can't worry about

him, not when he's questioning the integrity of my people. Besides, this won't hurt me in Hawaii. You know more than 40 percent of our state is of Asian descent. I'll be OK at home."

Jackson chuckled. "Good. I'm headed to Seattle tomorrow for the recess. I guess you're on your way home to campaign. You need me to come out and speak to the chamber or something? I mean you've sure helped me with the tribes and the union workers in Washington during my last election."

"Sam, you're always welcome in Hawaii. But frankly, we're so far ahead and Harry's sitting on so much campaign cash, I'm sure we'll be fine."

"OK, my friend, but say the word, and I'll be there."

Senator Jackson hung up the phone, a thoughtful look on his face; then he hit the intercom button. "John, we need to build a new road in North Carolina. Call Redmond's staff in the morning and get the details."

"Yes, sir," John Silease responded. Good old-fashioned politics, friends helping friends. "Sir, can I just say that was masterful."

"Say whatever you want, but make the call in the morning."

"Yes, sir."

John picked up the phone and called Paula. "Hey wasn't that terrific?"

"If he were here, I'd kiss him," she said. "Now that's the way this place is supposed to work. I'm a little surprised Redmond was the one your boss won over. What did it cost you? We opening a new shipyard in North Carolina? I'm for it, if that's the price."

"No, but I wouldn't be surprised to see us adding some money for a demonstration project on Highway 17." John chuckled. "Could be that new bridge over the sound that they want to connect to Corolla. The boss wasn't specific. But, I'm with you. It was about time he stuck it to Brown and Parker. We've got to get back to business, and that amendment would've killed the bill. I am a little surprised Jacobs went along. I didn't get a price tag for that."

"Well, we certainly thank you guys." Paula's voice grew more serious. "This is a big deal to the boss. He believes this is an attack on Asians, and I'm not sure he's wrong."

CHAPTER VII

Kahului, Maui

Chauncey Hayes exited the plane and headed to baggage claim. He snatched his bag from the luggage carousel but was stopped by a security guard at the exit. How could he forget? He had to prove his baggage claim matched his suitcase. *Full employment,* he thought and chuckled softly. The Hawaii welfare state: anyone who wants a job has one, albeit at taxpayer expense. *Oh well, if that's the price of paradise, I'll gladly spring for it because this time I'm back for good.*

After confirming with the airport security official that his suitcase did indeed match his baggage claim, he hustled to the curb to flag down the rental car shuttle bus. The driver opened the door. "Aloha, welcome to Maui. But relax, brah. No run. 'Dis bus wait."

Chauncey smiled and sighed at the laid-back culture and pidgin English of most of the service employees on the island. *Chauncey boy, we ain't in Kansas anymore.* He leaned his head toward the open window and felt the cooling trade winds blowing in off the ocean.

Chief Master Sergeant Chauncey Jefferson Hayes, at six foot two and 175 pounds, the trim and newly assigned technical director for the Advanced Electro-Optical Telescope Program, had arrived. He'd paid his dues, and now he had it made. He was to be one of only six air force military personnel assigned to the Maui Space Surveillance Site located on top of Mount Haleakala. His job? To get the new telescope improvements up and running. After years of dreaming and scheming, daydreams were about to come true.

Two summers ago, Chauncey had visited Maui as part of the Mitsunaga congressional delegation trip, or "codel." He'd driven two hours up the mountain to a groundbreaking ceremony for the new state-of-the-art telescope that Mitsunaga had rammed through Congress.

Chauncey had been the only member of the group who'd traveled by car. The rest of the delegation, even his boss, had flown up to the top in a National Guard helicopter. But as the low man on the totem pole, there hadn't been any room for him. It was truly ironic. He was the only one who had a clue what advanced electro-optics were and understood the significance of marrying the new adaptive optics package with the huge 3.67-meter telescope. Yet, he wasn't there to explain the increased resolution that the telescope would gain with the upgrade. He was there to carry bags, manage a reception room, and conduct the general drill of ensuring that the codel could get in and out of hotels and airports with the least hassle.

Three years of bag drags ensured he'd learned to do it well. But that trip, his first with Senator Mitsunaga, had been priceless. He went places and saw things that few enlisted personnel ever witnessed. More important, it had provided him a shot at his next career.

Over the ensuing two years, he plotted his strategy. He earned the boss's support by dedicating his every waking moment to the air force legislative liaison office for budget matters.

Perhaps more importantly, he curried favor with Paula Means. He had met Paula on that first Hawaii trip. The two hit it off. He learned right away she was not the typical ego-tripping staffer. Instead, she was as hardworking and smart as most of the others, but she seemed genuine. She wasn't that Hill phony, bootlicking for the boss, but bitchy or condescending toward everyone else. The first thing she said to him was, "Chauncey, my name is Paula, not *ma'am* or *Ms. Means*. If you can call me that, we'll get along fine."

From that moment, he knew they could get along. She wasn't like some staffers, demanding that he carry her bags, get her coffee, and perform other servile tasks. And Chauncy made sure Paula's requests got top priority. Her questions and requests to the department received responses as soon as possible.

He had the boss include him on each Mitsunaga trip—even the grueling three-day round trip to the Middle East on a noisy C-141 cargo plane. Funny how the *Washington Post* columnists ignored that trip when they called all overseas congressional travel "junkets."

It hadn't been quite as easy to get the boss to ask Paula to call the head of air force personnel and recommend Chauncey for the job on Maui. Sure Chauncey had all the right credentials. That didn't always matter in military assignments. But, after a few well-timed and not-so-subtle hints about his future goals, it worked. One call from Paula, on behalf of the good senator, encouraging the assignment, and Chauncey's orders were cut in less than a month.

And here he was, driving out of the rental-car parking lot and turning on Dairy Road toward Kihei on the south side of Maui.

It had been two years, but he still remembered the route to the high-tech park and the air force offices.

Just like at the Pentagon, Chauncey was going to be at the bottom of the food chain, beneath the Air Force Major who was in charge of the telescope and the captain, who ran the Maui High Performance Computing Center. Chauncey didn't care. He figured he had a year to get the telescope's adaptive optics running, and then he'd punch out. He'd be a catch to the on-site contractor as a tech rep to troubleshoot technical problems. He'd be forty and retired. He'd collect half of his sixty-five thousand dollar base pay with a lock on a seventy-thousand-dollar job at the telescope. Maui was expensive, but he'd sold the condo he bought in California twenty years ago when he first joined the air force—right before the huge rise in West Coast real estate. The profit would allow him to buy in the rainbow state. Prices had flattened in Hawaii because of the so-called "Asian flu," the downturn in Asian economies.

Thank God for the Republicans. He chuckled. *Their capital gains tax cut is going to pay off for me. Outside of NBA players, I might be the only high school-educated black male in America that benefits from that change.*

As the clouds surrounding the mountain parted, the sun reflected off the aluminum AEOS telescope dome. Paula had warned him that a few local zealots were calling this luminous reflection an affront to Hawaii and a blight upon the landscape. He laughed again. *Like she said, some of the locals will complain about anything.*

A few genuinely believed that a site as sacred in Hawaiian culture as Mount Haleakala was being desecrated by this monstrous fixture. Others just didn't want the military on Maui. Still, with the loss of pineapple and sugar plantations, most island residents welcomed the air force with its telescope, supercomputer, and Maui high-tech park. They understood this technology incubator could provide a future for their children. The Republican candidate for governor was campaigning on diversifying Maui's economy by bringing in high-tech jobs—even though when he served as mayor of Maui, he had done little except take credit for all Senator Ken's work.

The sign for Maui Research and Technology Park popped up on his left, and he turned up the hill toward the small, environmentally sensitive six-building industrial park that housed most of Maui's high-tech industry. He smiled widely, his brilliant white teeth a stark contrast to his black skin.

Home at last.

CHAPTER VIII

White House

Jack Ralston got up from his chair in his basement office and rubbed at his stubbled chin. "Holy shit, this fish is starting to stink." At forty-five, Ralston, the acting deputy special assistant to the president for National Security Affairs, was nearing the pinnacle of his career. His complexion was gray, his hair was thinning, and he carried fifteen more pounds than he knew he should—all the result of too much work and not enough relaxation. But he didn't care. It was worth it.

He was thinking about the Senate vote earlier that evening while reading an NSA report. On its face, the report seemed pretty innocuous. It truly seemed like it was some college kid asking for more money from home. But the NSA wasn't aware of any kids in LA whose dads or moms had access to secure PLA fax machines. *It sure sounds like someone is asking for money. It sure looks like it could be tied to our elections.* Just like Parker was insisting.

The Senate voted down an amendment on Asian money. Senator Mitsunaga, one of the leading recipients of Asian-American Political Action Committee money, helped orchestrate its defeat. No, it didn't look good.

He dialed the phone and spoke, "Madeline, is he available?"

"One moment," she replied. "Hold for Vice President Smith."

"Hello, is that you Jack? What's up?"

"Listen, Larry, I haven't told anyone else yet, but NSA just sent us a report. It might not be anything, but I think you might be interested. I don't want to say more on the phone. Are you going to be around for a while?"

"Yeah, I'll be here. Come on up."

Larry put down the phone, a frown on his face. Jack rarely called and never before he sent word up the chain. *Now that's loyalty. We're definitely going to be keeping him around.* He smiled as he pondered the president's idea of putting a few of Larry's guys in key positions two years before leaving office and supporting Larry's run for president. *I don't think he knows exactly what he's done, though. I doubt he realized people like Jack were going to talk to me before reporting to him. As much as I appreciate it, I won't be making that mistake when I'm in his job.*

Less than two minutes later, Jack Ralston walked in. The vice president—a man with thick black hair, chiseled features, and a wide smile—looked up at Ralston from behind a large oak desk framed by two brass lamps. Jack frowned and tossed a folder onto his desk. "I think you better take a look at this."

CHAPTER IX

Friday, August 4th

Georgetown

Rainy? Well, Fridays are workdays even if it's raining. Paula sighed as she pulled out of the garage underneath her townhouse. She turned her forest-green BMW onto P Street and headed east to Rock Creek Parkway. Once on the parkway, she accelerated to forty-five miles per hour. Even though the speed limit was only thirty, several motorists passed her. She hardly noticed the impressive view out her windshield as she drove under the Kennedy Center and around the Lincoln Memorial. Zoning out and focusing on the day ahead felt far too natural.

As she passed the Tidal Basin, she decided to drive along the National Mall instead of taking the Southwest Freeway. *Why not. It's Friday. Nobody will need me for a while.*

She wound around, slowing to the fifteen-miles-per-hour speed limit of Jefferson Drive. She drove past the Smithsonian Castle, the statue of museum founder, John Smithson, the Hirshhorn Sculpture Gardens, the Air and Space Museum, and the Native American museum. There it was, looming up ahead to the left of the Botanic Gardens: the Capitol. Even on a dreary, gray, rainy day, seeing it rising over the Mall still sent chills down her spine. She drove right up to the grounds and circled around. Hitting Constitution Avenue, she took a couple more turns and, after stopping to let the guards check her trunk, drove into the Hart Garage.

The route had taken ten minutes longer, but it was worth it. It put everything in perspective. She worked for the greatest institution in the world. She had the best boss in Washington. She absolutely loved her job, and why wouldn't she? Even in the minority party, she had a seat at the table when the half-a-trillion-dollar defense budget was divided up. She was making national security policy for the most powerful nation in the world. Her opinion mattered to every military leader in the country. So what if the hours were long and vacations were sacrificed? She didn't have a husband or kids that she was neglecting. She'd reached the top. What a life, and she didn't even need a raincoat. She grinned as she strode into the elevator and headed up to the office.

Coffee before office, she reminded herself. Exiting at the ground floor, she stopped for coffee at McSenate. *Or should they be calling it Dunkin' Sen-nuts these days?* She saw Justin Armor up ahead. *Oh, shit—a Senator Parker goon.* They were the thought police, out to protect America from waste, fraud, and abuse, if you believed Parker's frequent press releases.

"Hey Paula," Justin called out in a nasal twang. "What's all this about you guys planning to move the Statue of Liberty to Hawaii? You stole the battleship *Missouri.* Now I understand you want Lady Liberty too."

Paula stifled the urge to roll her eyes in disgust. Justin Armor had crooked yellow teeth and greasy hair. His disheveled clothes stretched over his short, fat body. She sensed he was ogling her as she paid for her coffee and started to walk away. She knew she'd regret it but couldn't resist. She spun on her heels, her long blonde hair whipping through the air.

"Sorry, Justin, but you got it wrong, as usual. We're looking for $175 million to build a Wahine Liberty on Ford Island in the middle of Pearl Harbor, not steal the one from New York."

You little shit, she continued under her breath. Typical Armor crap. She knew she'd better be careful though. That comment could turn up in *Roll Call's* Heard on the Hill as a rumor instead of the joke she had intended. Parker had lost his sense of humor, and most of his staff probably never had one. She turned the corner and headed up the stairs.

The phone was ringing when she walked into her office. She swiped it up. "This is Paula."

A voice replied, "Please hold for the attorney general."

Paula's mind raced. *The attorney general? What's she calling for? Must be Gitmo. What do I call her?* She googled how to address the attorney general.

"Hello, this is Maxine Marshall. Is this Paula?"

"Yes, it is, Madam Attorney General. What can I do for you?"

"Paula, I understand the conference committee on the Defense Appropriations bill will be meeting when the Senate returns in September. My staff tells me you're likely to prohibit the president from closing the military prison at Guantanamo Bay. Is that correct?"

"Well ma'am, it's impossible to say for sure, but that's the most likely outcome."

"I'm sure you know how important this is to the president. To be frank, we can't let you do that. We simply must close the prison. I'm sure you agree it has been a terrible black eye for the United States."

"Madam Attorney General, I agree it's a national tragedy. Even more important, Senator Mitsunaga agrees. But with all due respect, the administration doesn't have a plan it can sell to Congress. When you suggest moving the prisoners to military brigs like Fort Leavenworth, the Kansas delegation balks. Every politician with a military facility is fearful that you'll send the terrorists to his or her base. It's a classic case of NIMBY, you know, Not in My Backyard. It's killed support for your plan."

"Paula, speaking for the administration, I have to say this is unacceptable. The president has been trying to close Guantanamo for more than five years now. Congress has refused to act. Please let the senator know I'll be making a lot of calls on this issue."

Paula settled deeper into her office chair. "Madam Attorney General, I understand your frustration, and I share it. I first raised this matter with the White House after the Republicans retook the Senate. I told them your plan wouldn't pass. What the White House staff refused to grasp was that most senators don't support bringing known terrorists into the country. The best we can do is to keep allowing you to remand prisoners to other countries."

"That's been helpful, but I'm told Congress is likely to abolish that authority as well."

"Yes ma'am, the Defense Authorization bill includes a provision like that. But as long as the president says he'll veto that policy bill, I can assure you the Defense Appropriations bill won't include those restrictions. Chairman Jackson isn't going to send a defense bill downtown for the president to veto. Senators Mitsunaga and Jackson are partners on this. We'll get you a defense funding bill. We'll preserve the authority to send terrorists to prison in their home countries. But, if we include authority to close Gitmo, you won't get a bill. We don't have sixty votes to pass that bill, even if Mitsunaga could convince Jackson and the House to go along with it." Paula shook her head. "Heck, ma'am, with respect, no matter how hard you, and even the president, tried, we couldn't even get a majority of Democrats to support that. I'm truly sorry ma'am, but Jackson and Mitsunaga's plan is as good as it gets."

"Well, Paula, I can assure you the president won't give up trying. I know he'll veto any bill that abolishes his authority to remand prisoners to foreign countries. Look, I understand what you're saying about bringing prisoners here. We'll keep trying to build support for that. In the meantime, please let Senator Mitsunaga know I called. I'll get on his calendar when he returns to discuss this with him."

Paula ended the call and sighed. It wasn't every day she talked to cabinet officials. Deputies, sure. Generals, all the time. But she believed the cabinet level officials should talk to the senator. He was fine with her speaking for him to anyone, maybe even the president. But she never wanted to forget that she was staff. No one elected her. She took a sip of coffee. It was cold. *Where's the closest microwave again?*

CHAPTER X

Reagan National Airport

Senator Parker's voice came softly over the phone. "Bob?"

Senator Bob Wilson, the chairman of the Senate Rules Committee, leaned forward, grasping the phone with one hand. "Jim. What's up?"

Parker's voice was heated. "That vote last night stunk. I got a commitment from the leader that our committee can take this back up, at least. I want to hold hearings as soon as we get back in session on the fifth. This is a hot issue for our Democratic brethren, and I'm not going to let up."

"I hear you, Jim," Senator Wilson responded. He spoke slowly, allowing himself time to think, trying to make sure he didn't get Parker excited. "But, are you sure there's anything there? I mean they all voted with you, except Ken Mitsunaga. What good is this gonna do?"

"Bob, I'm telling you." Parker's voice started to rise. "This is a big story. We got a number of their guys in our sights. I can't talk about it on this line, but I've got it on good authority that this is going to bring them down. Hell, it might even rise all the way to the White House. We've got to act now. I'm a member of this committee, and Jacobs is with me."

Wilson took a deep breath and released it. "OK, Jim, I'll talk to my staff and see what they think we can do. But if you're talking about a major investigation, we won't be ready for hearings by Labor Day. That's only five weeks from now."

"Have your staff talk to Justin Armor on my staff," Parker said. "He has all the details of what the FBI has done, and he's conducted an independent investigation for me as well. We're ready to roll. I'll call you next week. Thanks."

The phone went dead in Senator Wilson's ear. *Guess I don't have a choice.* He shook his head. *Why did I accept this chairmanship? I thought it was going to be overseeing office space and parking. How did we get into campaign finance and Chinese money laundering?*

Wilson rested his head in his hands. *I could've stayed on the Aging Committee and not have to get linked to this and Parker. It sure sounds like a witch hunt. But, you never know; maybe he's onto something.* He lifted up the phone to call Missie Walsh, his staff director on the Rules Committee.

"Missie, this is Bob. Parker just called. He says the leader wants us to hold hearings on this Chinese money thing. I want you to talk to Parker's staff—Justine somebody—and find out what you can. They want to start this right after Labor Day. If it's going to have an impact on the elections, we have to do it then."

"Labor Day?" Missie's voice rang a bit unsure.

"I don't want you to get too bogged down on this. I don't think there's much there. The Justice Department declined to appoint a special prosecutor. Hell, the media hounds on judiciary won't even touch it. Nonetheless, we've got to go through the motions. Parker tells me he's got Jacobs's backing on this. You need to talk to Bankhead's people on the committee. I'll try to call Tom myself and let him know what's coming. But we might not want to try too hard to reach them, if you know what I mean."

Wilson frowned as he looked at the calendar. "I'm on my way to Bermuda for a couple of days. There's a Law of the Sea conference there. I'll check in with you next week. Oh, and Missie, I hope this doesn't screw up your plans for August."

Missie's voice sounded a bit faint on the other line. "Yes sir, don't worry about us, sir. We'll get right on it."

Missie set the phone down in a daze. She couldn't believe her ears. Hearings on Chinese money laundering beginning right after Labor Day? What did that have to do with Rules? Well, there went the Cape. Her husband and kids were going to kill her, but what could she do? That's life in the Senate. It wouldn't be the first vacation she'd missed, but it'd be the first time in August. August was sacrosanct. Unless you had to travel with the boss, it was the one time you could count on being free. Especially since the week between Christmas and New Year's was no longer safe. *And who the hell is Justine? He must mean Justin Armor, that little jerk detailee who's working for Parker. That's got to be it. Oh my god, I'm going to have to work with that despicable character for the next six to ten weeks. If only I were sixty, I'd quit today, get out of this circus, and start collecting my pension.*

She brushed her bottle-blonde hair out of her face and hit the speed dial for her husband's private line. "Jim, honey, we've got a problem. You won't believe what just happened."

CHAPTER XI

Dirksen Senate Office Building

The phone was ringing as Paula walked back into her office. The call monitoring device on the phone let her know it was from a cell phone but didn't show the number. She looked at the clock. It was 10:58 a.m. and Senator Mitsunaga was supposed to be boarding the plane right now. Could it be him?

As she answered, she knew immediately that she was right. "Paula, we didn't get a chance to talk last week about your recess plans. I hope you're taking some time off."

"Well, Senator, I haven't made any firm plans. I have about a month's worth of housework to get done. The IRS is going to lock me up if I don't finally file my tax return. And, I really need to spend a little time with my dog. He's been pretty lonely these past few months while I've been off marking up our bills. But, I can be in the office any day you need me."

"Actually, I was thinking maybe you'd come join me in Hawaii. I have an event on Maui next Monday night. I was wondering if we could go visit the supercomputer for a couple hours that afternoon before the fundraiser. I haven't been there for at least a year. What do you think?"

"Sir, I know they'd be thrilled to see you. I stopped in last April for an update before giving you recommendations for the defense bill. I think it'd be useful for you to see things for yourself."

"Could you get away this weekend and meet me there on Monday?"

Paula felt herself beginning to grin.

"Well, as long as I can get travel authorization from the committee. I'll need your signature on a letter requesting the trip."

"Oh, just write it up, and get Susie to sign it. I'll call her now and tell her to approve it. And Paula, thanks for changing your plans. I like you there when I meet with the guys. It keeps them a little more honest."

"Yes sir, thank you, sir. If I can get this arranged, I'll see you on Maui. Oh, what time should I tell them to expect you?"

"Let's see. How about 3:30 until 5:00? Then I can get to the fundraiser on time."

"OK sir, thanks again. I'll see you Monday."

"OK, goodbye."

Paula hung up the phone and called John Silease. "Hey, the boss just called, and he wants me to go to Maui. Is Jackson here to authorize a trip?"

"Well, actually, he took off an hour ago, but let's just say he can approve it from the air. Get us a letter, and we'll get it done. When are you leaving?"

"He wants me there Monday. So I'll need to fly Sunday, assuming I can get someone to sit with Bo. You and Janie need the pitter-patter of little footsteps around?"

"Gee thanks, Paula, but your pony had better make other arrangements. Our cats still haven't recovered from his last visit. I'll get your travel approved, but I don't run a kennel."

"My baby, tormenting cats? Ridiculous. But I hear ya. I'll get you a letter in the next couple of hours. Thanks, John."

CHAPTER XII

Maui

Chauncey Hayes began the long drive up Mount Haleakala. At 7 a.m., it was already a warm 75 degrees in Kihei, but he knew it would likely be only 45 degrees at best at MSSS. As he reached higher elevations, he closed his windows and eventually even turned on the heat. He chuckled. *This must be the only place in Hawaii where you need a heater in August.*

Chauncey reached the base camp and quickly made his way through security. He leaned his head into one of the eight coudé rooms where experiments were conducted using images from the telescope. Two Boeing technicians stood staring at adaptive optics black boxes, newly arrived from the mainland. The oscillators had been on the telescope glass for some time now, but the gizmo to drive them, the brains to tell it how to more clearly track light through the tiny particles in the atmosphere, was sitting here on the floor.

Chauncey tapped lightly on the doorframe. "What's up, guys?"

"Hey, Sergeant Hayes." Louis Leong, a native Hawaiian and recent hire for the Boeing Corporation, looked up with relief. "You got any idea of how this shit links up with the scope?"

Chauncey smiled. "Not a problem. You take the male part, and it goes in the female, like always."

Chauncey left the techs laughing and climbed the stairs up to the main control room. Dr. Frank Gordon, the senior engineer from Boeing, was staring at a display monitor.

Manny Kunio sat at the terminal, bashing keys frantically. "Look at this, Doc. It's freaking unbelievable."

"What you got?" Chauncey asked.

Dr. Gordon glanced over his shoulder at Chauncey and turned back to the screen. "It's the damnedest thing, Sergeant. Last night, we were doing an experiment for NASA. The 3.67-meter scope was targeting a meteor shower, west by northwest, toward Japan. Manny was watching the tape on playback to see if we got a good show, and he came up with something interesting." He nodded at Manny. "Run it again."

Manny clicked the mouse on two boxes, and up came a videotape image. "We recorded this for about forty-five minutes, based on NASA's projection. I was reviewing it at about three times its actual speed, and I thought I saw something at about eighteen minutes in."

"What time was that?" Chauncey asked.

"About 5:48 a.m. here, or 11:48 p.m. in Japan."

Manny turned the video on, and they watched six minutes of a meteor shower in silence before Manny said, "There, look off to the right. Do you see what looks like a star rising over the horizon? In real time you don't notice it among all the other shooting stars. But if you slow things down, you see it's the only one heading straight up. There! See. It seems to explode."

Manny stopped the video and backed it up. He narrowed the focus and ran the tape again. "There it is. It sure looks like something exploding. Could it be a missile launch?"

"Can you enhance the image?" Dr. Gordon inquired. "Let's

send it down to Jerry Loborio at the supercomputer and see what they can do with Adonis. In the meantime, turn on CNN to see if there's anything in the news about a satellite failure or missile launch by Japan." Manny nodded and started typing away as Dr. Gordon turned to Chauncey. "I wish the AO package was already installed. That would improve the resolution by at least five times, especially looking at that azimuth so low to the horizon."

"Have you heard anything from Colorado Springs?" Chauncey asked.

"Nothing," Manny responded without looking up from his computer. "You, Doc?"

"Nah," Dr. Gordon said. "The mainland guys only think about us here at the edge of the earth in February when they want to do a site visit."

Dr. Gordon and Manny exchanged glances, and Dr. Gordon picked up the phone. "Jerry, it's Frank. We're sending you some imagery to run on Adonis. It's from last night's meteor shower over Asia. We picked up something strange at 5:48 a.m. It looks like an explosion to us. Take a look, and if you have any questions, call Manny. He's the one who found it."

Jerry Loborio, the balding, fifty-something civilian director of MHPCC, put down the phone and walked into the lab. "Is Jeanine here?" he asked no one in particular.

"Over here," a voice called out.

He turned the corner around a tower of computers. He found the Reubenesque Captain Jeanine Lilly White leaning over with her head inside a computer rack. For a few seconds, he admired the view. Then he finally spoke. "Jeanine, Frank Gordon called. They saw something unusual in last night's collection. They think it might be an explosion, and they want us to see what we can do to sharpen the image."

She disentangled herself from the computer rack. "Sounds like fun. Let's take a look."

They left the computer equipment lab and moved into a much smaller room filled with computer terminals. Jeanine picked one out, logged herself on, and began searching for the new file. As it came up, they both watched the blurry image in silence.

Jerry muttered, "It might be something . . ."

Jeanine nodded. "Let's see. We take this file and mash it into here and hit this key. We click on that one, and bingo, we're running Adonis. It will take about 120 seconds for the SP-2 to spit this baby out, at least with the first crack."

In the next room, the IBM SP-2 supercomputer smoothed the image using the algorithm that Jeanine and UH graduate student Freddy Watanabe had written. The Adonis program was designed to take images from the telescope and, using the brains of the supercomputer, clear up any blurry images. Unfortunately, the Air Force Space Command had not identified any specific need for this technology, so the project had never gone anywhere. Yet, the program still existed because of Jeanine and Freddy's insistence, and they used their spare time to play around with it.

In two minutes, the computer had done its thing. Jeanine had programmed the computer to study the last few images of the event. The image came up with a clearer flash, but there wasn't much more to see.

"Well, that isn't worth a hill of beans," Jeanine said. "I've spent the last two years working on this, and that's all I get?" The disappointment was clear in her voice.

Jerry stood up straight, put a comforting hand on her shoulder, and sighed. "Oh well, maybe it wasn't anything anyway. It's so far away, Jeanine. We really shouldn't have expected Adonis to pick up anything."

"Damn it, Jerry, it's supposed to work better than this. If the image was a satellite or anything else in the inventory, it should have recognized it and built on the parts it recognized."

"Maybe the explosion spoofed Adonis. We haven't programmed any explosions into the package, have we? I'm sorry it didn't work out, Jeanine. I'll go call Frank and let him know we didn't get anything." Jerry turned and walked out.

Jeanine sat staring at the screen. *Could that be it? It didn't recognize anything because of the explosion? Was it the distance, or distortion in the atmosphere? Or something else altogether?* Jeanine sighed. *Or does it simply not work?*

Jeanine ran the original videotape again. *There's got to be something here.*

CHAPTER XIII

Honolulu, Oahu

Lieutenant General Al Gianini stood in his office at Camp Smith and stared out the window. He could see Diamond Head and the hotels of Waikiki to the southeast, Pearl Harbor in front of him, and the old Barber's Point Naval Base way out to the west. The view captivated him as it did everyone, from the natives who first sailed from Tahiti to the hordes of Japanese tourists deplaning from the never-ending 747's landing at Honolulu International Airport today.

Camp Smith was established during World War II as a hospital to care for wounded sailors and marines. By the time the hospital was completed, it was no longer needed. The Tripler Army Medical Center could care for all the military personnel and dependents on the island. Instead, Camp Smith became the home of the largest military command on the face of the earth: the Pacific Command. Its leader was the commander in chief of the Pacific Command, or CINCPAC to the military. Alberto Vincente Gianini, a crusty army veteran from Delaware, was the deputy commander, or D-CINC. He had enlisted after high school at the tail-end of the war in Vietnam, received a rare battlefield commission, and found himself a home and career. Now, some forty-plus years later, he was facing the stark realization that he had reached the end of his military service.

On his desk lay an official army notice. He'd been passed over for promotion. In a few months, he'd be a private citizen for the first time in his adult life.

He wasn't really surprised by the announcement. It was uncommon for the army brass in Washington to pluck a three-star from Hawaii for promotion. It was as if they felt being assigned to Hawaii was reward enough; some other less fortunate soul should get the fourth star. Then they'd be awarded the major command or key assignment in Washington that every general dreamed about.

The fact he'd been assigned a third year in this job was a sure sign his days in the army were coming to an end. Besides, as a former enlisted man, now already over sixty, his rise this far was itself unusual. Well, now he knew for sure. He'd called his wife to let her know. She was stoic, as he expected. He knew she'd be happy to have him home more. He knew she was hoping he'd find a good job, maybe in California near the kids. Yes, it was time, but for now, all he could do was stand at the window and stare.

His solitude was interrupted by a knock on the door and the entrance of his acting J-2, the intelligence chief.

"Sir, I'm sorry to interrupt, but I thought you should see this. The Joint Intel Center got this from the NSA folks at Wahiawa. You might find it interesting."

"What is it?"

"Sir, it's some signals traffic that we sent to Fort Meade, and their boys worked their magic on it. They aren't supposed to send us the decoded message, but our guys collaborate a lot, and they passed it back anyway. It looks like someone in the PLA is spending a lot of cash surreptitiously in the US."

"What's that?"

General Gianini grabbed the message and read it carefully. "Well, I'll be damned. What the hell do you think they're up to?"

"I don't know, sir, but there's been a lot of speculation about Chinese money coming into our election campaigns. And now we see this. I'd hate for it to be true, but it sure looks bad."

"Well, if your hunch is right, this could pucker up the political parties. You said we're not supposed to have this, right? I think we'd be a lot better off if we keep it that way and let the DC spooks deal with it. But let's not forget to tell the CINC when he gets back from Indonesia."

"Yes, sir. We'll let them worry about it."

CHAPTER XIV

Washington Dulles Airport

Rebecca DeLaurio entered the plane, turned left, and made her way to seat 1-C. *Thank God, not coach.* Seat 1-C was her favorite. It was right next to where Senator Mitsunaga always sat during the eight years she had been his principal assistant on the Select Committee on Indian Affairs. They must have taken seventy trips together, most to Hawaii to discuss native Hawaiian issues. But, they'd also met with dozens of Native American tribal leaders in New Mexico, Arizona, Washington, Idaho, Montana, the Dakotas, and even her home state of Connecticut. He was their champion, and she was his go-between.

When they traveled together, they sat together. Over time, she'd grown accustomed to flying first class, thanks to a mountain of frequent flier miles. They had grown very close, and she liked to think that he wanted her near. Though, deep down, she knew the more important issue was that he didn't want to sit next to a stranger and risk having to politely listen to the rantings of an anti-abortion zealot or animal-rights advocate or environmental do-gooder.

She had enjoyed her fifteen years in the Senate. Not quite a complete career, but more than two Senate terms, enough for the twelve-year pin and citation for service. Two years ago, she'd decided it was time to move on. With her ten additional years in the executive branch, she qualified for an early retirement package. She wanted to make money. She had grown tired of the travel, long hours, and uncertainty of the Senate schedule. Now, with her powerful friends and connections, she was cashing in.

Unfortunately, that meant back on an airplane again. This time to LA to raise more money for Mitsunaga. She had left his employ, but she hadn't left him. In many ways, he was still her meal ticket.

As the flight prepared for takeoff, she prepped herself for the task ahead. She would meet with the trustees of the Asian-American PAC to press them for more money. Sure, Mitsunaga was ten points ahead, but he wanted to win by twenty or more. He wanted to crush his opponent and prove that, even nearing seventy years old, he still had what it took to lead the Democratic Party in the state. Harry had been pushing her incessantly to raise more cash.

Oh right. Harry. I was supposed to call him.

She reached him on his cell. "Harry, I figured you'd be driving the boss to the airport. How many years have you been the chauffeur now? Fifty? I didn't know chiefs of staff moonlighted as Uber drivers."

A gruff voice responded, "That you, Rebecca? Where are you? Sounds like you're under a pillow in bed. Who you with, the gardener or the trash man?"

"Dream on, Harry. I'm on a plane, and from your comments, I'm guessing you already dumped Ken at the airport. You wanted me to call. Here I am, dear boy."

"OK, Rebecca. Where are we?"

"Like I told you yesterday, I'm on my way to the coast to snatch cash like you want, you old coot."

"How much?"

"How much you need?"

"Come on, Rebecca, stop kidding around. The boss wants to nail this guy before Labor Day. We got about four weeks to go, and he wants to hit the airwaves big between now and then. We need all we can get."

"I'll do what I can, big boy. Now be nice and say something sweet."

"Jesus, Rebecca. What's gotten into you? Just call me when you get back."

Rebecca leaned back into her seat and smiled. *Life is sweet.*

Harry, the silver-haired native Hawaiian, shook his head. He thought he'd seen everything, but times had changed.

This is crazy. We must've raised $5 million already. That's got to be enough. Forty-plus years ago when I quit my job as a bus boy to launch Ken's first campaign, we didn't have any money. I bet we didn't spend twenty-five thousand dollars on the whole thing. It's all about money and fundraising now. It seems that's all I do. Thank god for Rebecca–she's really come through.

He smiled out the window of his car. This Asian-American PAC was a great idea; he didn't know how she was doing it, but she'd raised around $1 million—her first time on a campaign, no less. But she couldn't have done it without the senator. Ken was one of the most effective spokesmen for Asian-Americans. God knew there weren't many in DC. It looked like the community had finally awakened to that fact.

CHAPTER XV

Los Angeles, California

Rebecca checked into the airport Hilton hotel, dropped her suitcase on the bed, and proceeded straight to the Golden Bear Conference Room. As she entered the room, she realized immediately she was the only non-Asian. All the heavyweights were there: Alan Fong, Johnny Chen, Myron Wong, Harry Matsuoga, and Susie Yshida.

"Well." Rebecca began a well-rehearsed speech. "That was a close one last week. I'm sure you're all fully aware we have our work cut out for us. The other side simply will not quit until the Asian community is persecuted. Despite there being no charges, no evidence, only rumor and innuendo, they are going to try to silence your voices. I don't need to tell you Senator Ken was critical in stopping this witch hunt. He deserves your support now more than ever. Now that he's thwarted their plans, they're sure to start after him."

"Rebecca," Alan Fong began, "I'm not sure why we are fighting this. We haven't done anything wrong. I think we should invite the IRS to examine our books. That would stop this today."

"Alan, I understand your frustration," Rebecca responded, already prepared with an answer. "But you have to trust me on this. We can't call in the IRS. Even if we could, it'd take them several months to review the books and go over the computer records. In the meantime, we'd be living under a cloud. The senator's opponent would jump on that. He wouldn't say we called for the review. Instead, he'd harp on the fact we were under investigation by the IRS. Politics is not like the judicial system. Politicians are tried by the media and are guilty until proven innocent. The election would be over before we had the chance to clear our name. No, Mr. Fong, I'm afraid that simply isn't a solution. We can't take that chance with Senator Ken.

"Now, what I'm proposing is we get back on the phones and see if we can get another contribution from our supporters. Myron, what about the Asian banking community here in California? They know Senator Mitsunaga is critical to keeping friendly relations with Asia. What do you think you can pledge from them?"

Myron Wong exhaled deeply and rose from his seat. He was the president of the First Pacific Bank, a mid-sized Los Angeles-based bank headquartered in Chinatown. Rebecca noted from his expression that he was not used to being called upon quite so publicly. She logged that away to remember for the future.

He spoke softly, "Rebecca, I can get you another fifty thousand dollars, I believe. We are holding an Asian-American PAC dinner at the Beverly-Wilshire Hotel tomorrow night. Everyone was told to bring their checkbooks."

Mr. Wong hesitated and glanced around the table. "But, this will have to be the last time. We have all given about as much as we can. Everyone in this community loves and has the deepest respect for the senator, but we have other charitable causes. Many of us have relatives still living in Asia, not to mention the need to care for the less fortunate members of our community here."

Rebecca noticed nods of understanding from around the table.

"I will get you this amount, but I won't ask my friends again." Mr. Wong made a slight bow toward Rebecca, then sat back down.

Rebecca was surprised by the frank nature of his comments but understood she had pushed these longtime friends of Ken very hard. It was time to soften her tone.

"Myron, that would be terrific. If we can get this last increment, say fifty thousand dollars from each of you, that should put us over the top. We can't give up now. The senator means too much to all of us."

Nods all around the table again. Rebecca smiled, glad to see the lightened expressions. "You should all know that his opponent, Keahole, is a skillful politician. His claims of direct lineage to the Hawaiian royal family make him doubly difficult to beat. We really can't do this without you. I am going to call Ken as soon as I leave here. Can I tell him the great news?"

They looked at one another, and finally each nodded affirmatively.

CHAPTER XVI

Hart Senate Office Building

"Hello, this is Missie Walsh. Is Justin Armor there?" she asked into the phone.

A moment later a chipper voice responded, "This is Justin. I've been waiting for your call, Missie." He dragged out the final *e* on her name in a nasal whine.

"What's this all about, Justin? Are we going to do a Salem witch trial and burn someone at the stake eight weeks before the election?"

"I like the way you think, Missie," again with the emphasis on the *e*. "That's just about right. When can we get together to plan a strategy?"

Oh my god, Missie thought, *this guy is serious. What have we gotten ourselves into? Senator Wilson's a good soldier. I'm sure he'll support the leader's plans to hold hearings, but we won't serve as an attack dog for the right-wing.*

"Well, Justin, I guess the sooner the better if we're supposed to start these hearings right after Labor Day. Are you free now?"

"I have a plane to catch to California. Can we meet Monday?"

"OK, let's meet in the cafeteria at ten. See you then."

Missie hung up the phone and placed a call to her Democratic minority counterpart, Skip Muldoon. She was well aware he'd already left on vacation. The voice that answered was Skip's. It was a recorded message saying he was out of the office and not likely to be back until the end of the August recess. She left a brief message for Skip to call her as soon as possible. She said that it was important, but didn't say why.

Missie sighed, shaking her head at the phone. She wasn't completely comfortable going ahead without getting a hold of Skip, but she rationalized it was probably for the best. This was going to get ugly. It would be easier to seek forgiveness than to ask for permission.

She emailed a quick note to Senator Wilson, stating that she'd left a message for Senator Bankhead's staffer and that he need not contact the senator directly. The email would go into the permanent log. It would serve to protect the chairman if he was confronted by an angry Senator Bankhead when he finally found out about the hearing. She estimated that would happen about twenty-four hours before the show trials began. Her note would leave no evidence that she knew Skip was unlikely to receive the message for three or four weeks.

She hated this part of the game—the deception required to push a party's agenda. But she needed to protect her boss from any accusation that he'd tried to keep the Democrats in the dark on this sensitive issue. She took a long, deep breath. She stood up from her desk, already regretting the planned meeting with Justin, the Inquisitor. Only two more years to retirement.

CHAPTER XVII

Saturday, August 5th

Washington, DC

Vice President Smith waved to the cheering crowd as he approached the podium, smiling broadly at his introduction as "the next President of the United States." Tall and trim at fifty-five, he looked the part. It was too soon to say, but he wouldn't deny that things certainly looked good. No one in the opposition seemed capable of mounting a serious challenge. All the likely candidates were either small-state governors or single-issue zealots, protectionists, flat tax advocates, or pro-lifers. Each appealed to a constituency but none to a broad-based coalition sufficient to challenge him. But, pundit projections at this stage were almost invariably wrong. Two years is a lifetime in politics.

His speech was before the Dot Com Workers of America, the country's newest union, and one that was multiplying in size weekly. It was his task to convince them that he was the only candidate who would protect their interests. He'd guarantee workplace protections while promoting future growth of their industry through internet advances, tax-free internet commerce, and improved satellite communication. He told them, as one of the founding fathers of the internet, his vision guaranteed their industry would continue to grow tax-free in the coming years. Since many of them were also part owners of their companies, they welcomed his message. When he noted that this campaign was going to be very expensive, he could almost see them reaching for their checkbooks and wallets to support this new protector. It was a beautiful thing.

He'd always loved fundraising. Some said President Hal Andrews chose him because, as former governor of New York, he could tap into more financial resources than any other candidate. Andrews hated raising money. Andrews was old-school, recognizing the need for money but never warming to the task of begging for it. Smith relished the practice of convincing donors to be ever more generous. It was like he kept his own scorecard, giving himself a point every time he got some fat cat or welfare mother to open up his or her wallet.

He suspected today's rally would top $1.5 million, not bad for a two-hour lunch including a ten-minute canned speech. It was taking candy from a baby, and it felt just right.

As he entered his limousine to return to the White House, Madeline, his personal assistant, handed him a phone. "It's Jack," she said.

"What's up, Jack?"

"Sir, is this a secure line?"

"It's the goddamn vice presidential limousine, Jack; it sure as hell better be."

"Yes, sir. Listen, our friends in California say they can get another two hundred thousand dollars from the AAPAC. What do you think? They are raising more money for Mitsunaga, and they figure you can tap into some of that goodwill. The only thing, sir ... remember that cable we saw?"

"Yeah, Jack, I remember the cable. So what? Nobody says there's any relationship. That was probably just a big mix up. Has anyone in the intel community made anything out of it?"

"No, sir. But Jesus, Larry." Jack Ralston's voice grew quieter. "If someone finds out you're taking money from the PLA, it'll blow your chances to smithereens. Do you really think it's worth it? None of those guys has a chance against you."

"Jack, how much are we going to spend on this election, $10, $20 billion? We're going to need every dollar we can get. You know that once the Republicans pick their guy, big businesses will begin throwing money at them. And, let's not forget the Christian coalition. Those guys will rally all the church-goers on the Sunday before November eighth. We've got to raise more money. Just make sure you bury the cable."

"OK, sir, you're the boss."

"Jack, don't worry. It's a coincidence; it'll be fine. And thank our friends for their efforts. Tell 'em we won't forget. Goodbye."

"Yes, sir, goodbye."

CHAPTER XVIII

Los Angeles, California

Rebecca climbed onto the airport shuttle bus outside her hotel. After checking in, she headed to the Red Carpet Lounge to wait for her plane. Seated in the corner drinking mediocre cappuccino, she was approached by a young Asian man, carrying a small paper bag, who bowed and sat down in the adjacent chair. Wearing ripped blue jeans and a Rolling Stones t-shirt, and sporting a diamond stud earring and black ponytail, he looked like many young, male Angelinos.

"Hello, Johnny, I was wondering when you were going to show up. You got what I need?"

"Ms. DeLaurio, it is good to see you again. My uncle sends his regards."

"That's sweet of Uncle Li. Now where's the cash?"

He chuckled. "That's what we Chinese love about Americans. You're always so eager to conduct business. How you get along with the Japanese, I will never know. You would do much better being allied with China. We are much more businesslike." His tone changed. "My uncle was not pleased with your request for more assistance."

"Life's hard, Johnny. If you want to play golf, you've got to pay the green fees. Let me put it this way. You've got a lot more to gain out of this than we do. General Li gets the right man voting the right way on the key votes to protect his offshore interests. We just get to sleep better at night knowing we can outspend our opponent three-to-one over the coming twelve weeks." She put down her cappuccino. "Now, I have a plane to catch. Have you got a package for me?"

"Ms. DeLaurio, we have acceded to your wishes, but this is positively the last time. We know your influence over Senator Mitsunaga. We have confidence he will be a valued friend to the People's Liberation Army, but this is now more than $1 million. This is the last time. My uncle wants to know when we might get to meet with the senator. Will he be visiting China in the coming months?"

"We're in the middle of an election, Johnny. We aren't traveling anywhere but to Hawaii, with stopovers to pick up cash here in California. When we win, then we can talk about a trip to the Middle Kingdom. In the meantime, tell Uncle Li the senator is grateful for his generous support. He looks forward to a close working relationship in the future. Mahalo and aloha." She stood up, snatched the paper bag, and walked away.

Xian Huan Nod, better known in Los Angeles as importer Johnny Wan, watched her as she walked away. *It's a good thing General Li Pen was not here to see that. I know the senator will do what we want; he is an honorable man, but Ms. DeLaurio would be hard to explain to the general. I hope she really understood this is the last payment.* Johnny looked around to see whether anyone had been monitoring their conversation. Satisfied that no one was, he stood up and headed for the exit.

Moments later, a disheveled Justin Armor walked over. He picked up the phone on the table next to where Ms. DeLaurio had been sitting. While pretending to make a call, he removed a small device from the receiver. He replaced the phone and scurried out of the lounge.

CHAPTER XIX

McLean, Virginia

Rebecca stepped out of the cab, tipped the driver handsomely, and carried her overnight bag up the stairs of her sandstone manor house. She thought for an instant how much she liked the house. Yes, it was awfully big for a single woman, but it was a symbol of who she had become: a rich lobbyist, campaign strategist, and now the largest fundraiser for her former employer.

Leaving the Hill had been difficult. Responsibility and power gravitate to the staff, especially if you work for a member as widely respected as Ken Mitsunaga. He had relied on her to take care of the day-to-day business of the Indian Affairs Committee. But, she'd never gotten over the shift from the majority to the minority. Her relations with the succession of three Republican staff directors hadn't been pleasant. Mostly though, Rebecca felt it was time to leave because she sensed others on the senator's staff were beginning to supplant her in the more important roles. Yes, she still traveled with him. Yes, they still shared a special relationship, but something had changed. It was time to move on.

When she told him she was going to retire, he'd been surprised, but hadn't asked her to reconsider, and certainly hadn't begged her to stay. He thanked her for all she'd done, promised to do all he could to help in her new career, and wished her the best. No gold watch, no tears. She'd felt a little betrayed, but clearly he'd moved on. Sure, there was the tribute from the senator printed in the *Congressional Record*. There was a retirement party in which a dozen senators and congressmen and at least a hundred lobbyists and staff stopped in to wish her well. Most importantly, she received a pension, indexed to inflation, that'd pay her about half her one-hundred-seventy-thousand-dollar salary for the rest of her life. She had nothing to complain about, and she knew it. Still, it left her angry, with an empty feeling that she couldn't explain.

In her first six months in the private sector, she signed up four clients, each paying her ten thousand dollars per month, a cool four hundred and eighty thousand dollars per year. Not all Native American tribes were poverty stricken. First, she bought the BMW and then the house. Her debts piled up faster than her income, but yes, she really liked the house.

CHAPTER XX

Sunday, August 6th

Makena, Maui

Paula walked into her room at the former Makena Prince Hotel, a medium-sized resort about fifteen minutes from the Maui tech park. The hotel had a special arrangement with the park, so Paula was able to get a very nice room overlooking the ocean and the island of Kaho'olawe at government rate. It was a gorgeous location on a spectacular island at the base of Mount Haleakala, hugging the Pacific Ocean. Paula threw her bags on the bed and stripped off her clothes, anxious to eliminate the clammy, stale feeling after eleven hours in planes and airports.

She turned on the bath and slipped on a luxuriously fluffy terrycloth bathrobe the hotel had laid out on the bed for its guests. She was surprised to hear a knock on the door. *Who could that be?* she wondered. Looking out the peephole, she saw Sergeant Chauncey Hayes sporting khakis, short-sleeved shirt, and casual loafers.

Opening the door, she said, "Well I'll be damned. I guess they'll let anybody into this place." She stood on her tiptoes, threw her arms out, and welcomed him with a big hug.

A startled Chauncey returned the hug and timidly followed her into her room.

"I heard you were coming to see us tomorrow, so I thought I'd stop by to say hi. I'm sorry to surprise you. I thought you might want company for dinner, and I hear Duke's Court has a new wine list you might want to check out. But, I can come back later."

At that point, Paula realized what he meant. She was standing there in a bathrobe. She had never even touched Chauncey before. Now here she was barely clothed and throwing herself at him. *Shit. What are you doing, Paula?*

"No, no, it's OK, Chauncey. She clutched the top of her robe, ensuring that she wasn't revealing much. "Dinner sounds great, but um, first I really need a bath or a massage after flying all day."

"Sure, let me come back in a half hour if that's enough time."

"You sure? What are you going to do in the meantime? There's no bar at this hotel, and anyway you wouldn't want to ruin your palate if we are going to check out a new wine list. Why don't you sit on the porch, or lanai as they say here?"

Chauncey shrugged. "OK, you're the boss." He started toward the glass doors.

Paula stuck her head out of the bathroom, "Hey, you better call for a reservation. Last time I couldn't get a table."

Twenty minutes later a clean, robed, and more relaxed Paula stepped onto the lanai. "We all set for dinner?"

"Well, yes and no. Dinner yes, but not for another forty-five minutes. That's the best they could do. So I ordered us this bottle of wine from room service. How was the bath?"

"Wonderful, but I still can't get the kinks out of my back. Maybe a little wine will loosen it up."

Paula poured herself a large glass, noting that it was a 2005 Bordeaux. "Gee, Chauncey, this stuff's pretty pricey, but it's a great vintage, if maybe still a little young. You get a pay raise moving to Maui?"

"No raise, but those senate codels ruined me. You guys always have fancy food and fancy wine. Well, maybe not in Afghanistan, but on most of your trips. I had to learn how to pick out the right wine. Yeah, it's a little steep, but I wouldn't want to disappoint you."

"Mmm, well this is delicious." She quickly finished her first glass and poured another. "So, how's the new job? Is it everything you hoped it would be?"

"It's only been a couple of days, but it's great so far. Everyone has been so nice, and Maui is spectacular. I rode my bike fifty miles on Saturday, mostly on the coast, taking it all in. I can't thank you enough for helping arrange it."

"I didn't do much. Besides, you earned it. You've been one of the most helpful liaison guys I've ever worked with. If you are half as good with telescopes as you were with helping us out, you're going to be a star here." She squirmed in her seat, twisting one way and then the other. "My back is just killing me."

"Don't take this the wrong way, Paula, but you want me to take a shot at loosening it up?"

Paula looked at Chauncey. "Oh gee, Chauncey, I don't know. What do you know about massage? It sure isn't anything like working on a 10-ton telescope."

"Hold on now, Paula, telescopes are delicate instruments, finely tuned with unique pressure points. They have to be handled with kid gloves. I'd say in comparison, getting the kinks out of an achy back is child's play."

Paula wondered if this was a good idea, but Chauncey was a good guy, and they had forty-five minutes to kill, and she really needed a massage. "OK Chauncey, I'm game, but this better be good." She drained her second glass, turned, and walked into the room. She threw the pillows on the floor and turned down the covers.

Chauncey came in as she was lying down, still mostly covered by her robe, but no longer wearing it. *Oh my god*, he thought. *Never in my wildest dreams did I think I'd be alone with a naked Paula Means. Down boy. Remember this is just a massage.*

Chauncey sat on the bed straddling her and lowered the robe down her back. He pushed her long blonde hair off to the side. Slowly he began to massage her shoulders, and she moaned approvingly. Her skin was flawless and silky smooth. His black hands were a stark contrast to her alabaster back. He worked his way down her back trying to reduce the tension brought on by sitting in a coach seat for eleven hours. He could feel her starting to relax and enjoy the sensation. "Paula," he asked, "would you like me to massage your legs as well?"

Paula, in calm comfort with the alcohol kicking in, answered with a sigh. Chauncey turned around and sat down again on Paula's lower back, hardly touching her. He reached down and carefully raised her robe so that her calves and most of her thighs were exposed. He was staring at perfectly toned perfection. As if handling the most delicate instrument, he lifted each leg and spread them to allow maximum room for massage. He began to soothe the tired and tense muscles in Paula's long, slender legs, beginning with her calves and working his way up to the tops of her thighs.

Paula was in a dreamlike state. It was after midnight in Washington, and she was feeling the effects of a long day. But Chauncey's hands were those of a master. She guessed he was right about working with delicate instruments. It was incredible. She began to sense a change in Chauncey's breathing as if he was beginning to feel the effects of all this touching as well. It felt too good to stop now. "Chauncey," she said, "could you do my lower back?"

Chauncey stopped, turned, and lowered her robe, exposing the top of her shapely behind, and began working his fingers deep into her soft flesh. She moaned softly and arched her back against him. He moved his hands lower and received the same reaction.

Chauncey could no longer contain himself. Alone with this beautiful woman that he both respected and admired, and who was melting under his touch, he was pleased he could satisfy her and also deeply aroused. Carefully, he climbed off her back and lay down beside her. He gently rubbed the back of his hand along her face and put one arm around her. He rolled her over on her back and began to caress her in a gentle massage. She reached one hand over to unbutton his shirt.

CHAPTER XXI

Makena, Maui

Paula awoke and realized Chauncey was lying next to her. The clock said midnight. *Six a.m. in Washington,* she thought. *Time to get up if I were at home. What've I done? How did I get myself into this one? Chauncey's a great guy, but this wasn't smart. What would the senator think? Actually, if those rumors about him were correct, he might be in favor of this. Oh shit, Paula, you've really screwed this up.* She got up and went into the bathroom. She put on her nightgown, grabbed a sleeping pill, and quietly headed back to bed, slipping in as silently as possible. After five minutes she was fast asleep.

Chauncey could tell by her breathing she had fallen back asleep. He didn't know if he should stay or go; if he should be happy about the wonderful experience they had shared, or embarrassed because he had taken advantage of this sleep-deprived and partially inebriated woman. Finally, he decided it would be best if he left instead of having them confront an uneasy morning together. He dressed quietly and tiptoed out of her room. Maybe they'd examine that new wine list another night, that is if she ever agreed to share a glass of wine with him again.

CHAPTER XXII

Monday, August 7th

Bermuda

"Missie, is that you? I can't hear much on this cell phone." Senator Wilson put down the piña colada and put a finger in his ear to try and quiet the sound of the surf in the background.

"Yes sir, it's me. I spoke with Senator Parker's staff, and we're going to meet later this morning. Oh, and I put a call in to Senator Bankhead's staff. Did you get my email?"

"Sure did. Thank you. Sounds like you've got everything under control. I can't hear very well here. You've got my number. Call me if you need anything, OK? And, Missie, tell Jim I'm sorry if this screwed up your vacation plans. Got to go now, bye."

Missie put down the phone and waited for Justin Armor's call. It was odd that he'd be in California for a weekend, but he was a weird boy. She wasn't going to waste much time thinking about it.

As the phone rang again, she had an awful, nagging feeling she was going to regret getting involved in any of this. Before she could say a word, he started. "OK, Missie, are you ready for some fun? I'll meet you downstairs in the cafeteria in five minutes."

Justin was waiting for her when she arrived. He grinned and seemed to check her out. She noticed his leer and involuntarily shivered in disgust. He looked like he just woke up after a rough night. His hair was greasy, his shirt was half-untucked, and he was wearing cheap khaki slacks that he certainly could have slept in. On the other hand, Justin usually looked like that.

"I just got back from LA, and I have all the information we need. I think it's better if you don't know all the details just yet. Let's plan on having a hearing on the Wednesday morning after Labor Day. We can get one of those mystery witness setups where the witness sits behind a screen. We can call her Jane Doe. This is only going to take one witness at one hearing to blow this wide open. I guarantee it. The Democrats won't know what hit 'em. Our guys are going to coast to victory in the fall. And, next cycle, the Democrats are going to lose the White House, too. All based on what I'll share with you right before the hearing. Got it?"

"Get what? What the hell are you talking about? In case you forgot, Senator Wilson is chairman. He decides who the witnesses are, and his staff does the legwork. Who do you think you are? You're not going to waltz in here and think you decide how the committee's going to conduct its business. I'm the staff director, and I make the recommendations to the chairman on the committee's plans. You got it?"

"Oh my goodness, Missie. Did I say something to upset you? I am so sorry. But let me tell you something, sweetheart. If you get in the way, Senator Parker will be telling the leader and ripping your dear chairman a new asshole. This is going to be done our way, and you better get used to it. You aren't back at Radcliff, honey. This is the big leagues, and you either lie back and enjoy it, or we'll blow right past you. And don't let your tits get in the way. Do you understand?"

It was Columbia, asshole, she thought as she carefully considered how to respond to this prick. She knew there were some Hill staff whom you couldn't cross, or they'd crush you. Some you had to worry about whether they'd be in a leadership position someday and crush you. And there were those who weren't likely to ever amount to anything. Looking at this hideous creature, she made up her mind.

"Listen, pal, I suggest you start thinking up a new game plan if you're planning to have a Rules Committee hearing. This ain't a fuckin' barnyard, and you ain't the cock of the walk. You understand? I'll tell you what. You do whatever the fuck you think you should be doing, and I'll wait until you get a better idea. In the meantime, I'd be thinking about how you're going to get a parking permit next year."

She started to rise, but stopped. "And, by the way, don't even consider asking for an extension on your detail from the Government Accountability Office. I don't think Chairman Wilson will be approving any for dear Senator Parker. Do you understand? And, why don't you take a bath sometime? Your stench is starting to affect the operations of the Senate."

Missie slowly slid back her chair, stood up, turned, and walked away.

Justin let out a high-pitched giggle, a cross between Woody Woodpecker and Pee Wee Herman. He ogled her as she left. *She's pretty round, but not bad for an old bag.* He was especially pleased that he'd got to use that line about keeping her tits out of the way.

CHAPTER XXIII

Kahului, Maui

Paula met Senator Mitsunaga at the terminal and led him to her rental car. She was just about at eye level with the dark-eyed senior senator from Hawaii, although he outweighed her by a good twenty pounds. On the drive to the supercomputer center, Paula asked the senator how his trip was going.

"Oh fine," he said, "this morning I cut a ribbon to open new military housing at Pearl Harbor. I don't know if you've seen it, but it's an incredible improvement over what the sailors had before."

"Yes, sir. You should be really proud of what you've done for them. The old housing was like a slum. I think the Pentagon figures if you're in Hawaii, you don't need decent housing. It's like they think military families are going to sleep on the beach. And I was told you were also going to stop by the university, UH?"

"I did. I talked to the dean about our Native Hawaiian Education Program. Do you realize that since we began funding programs for early schooling for the native population, we have tripled the number going to college? Dean Houston says that we've made real inroads in establishing the importance of education to that community."

"And tonight, is it Maui for a campaign fundraiser?"

"No, the fundraiser tonight is for scholarships for the local economic board's Women in Technology programs. Now granted, it's good for my campaign to be seen sharing credit for this program. But the real beneficiaries are the dozens of Maui school girls who'll receive college tuition. We're able to get all the big and even the little defense companies in the state to pay five thousand dollars per table to help."

"I've heard about it from the companies, but you know this isn't really charity for them. All the companies I've spoken to are eager to support the program because they need highly trained local college graduates to work for them. It's a win-win situation. And, you know sir, most of these companies wouldn't be in Hawaii if you hadn't steered programs this direction."

"I do my best." The senator smiled in appreciation.

At the Maui High Performance Computing Center, they were met by Captain Jeanine White and Jerry Liborio. The senator had met the captain on his visit a year before and, of course, was familiar with Jerry, who had been the civilian director of the center for years.

"So tell me, Captain White," the senator began, "are you getting accustomed to living in paradise?"

"It's beautiful, sir," she replied, "but I'm from New England, and I do miss the fall colors and the snow. But I love my work, and the people are very friendly."

"Snow? You can keep all of it as far as I am concerned. We get more than enough for me in Washington. But, I understand.

If that's what you are used to, I guess you could miss it. But not me. What about you, Jerry?"

"Senator Mitsunaga, I couldn't be happier. Good things are going on here, and we are starting to convince Washington of that."

"Great, and how's the telescope coming along?"

Captain White and Jerry looked at each other as a brief, uncomfortable moment passed before Paula spoke up. "Sir, that's really not their area. But we will have Major Lane and Dr. Frank Gordon joining us in about forty-five minutes to give you an update on their work."

"Yes, sir," Jerry added, "It's going well from what we hear, but we're not involved."

"Oh, OK. Well, tell me what's new here, then."

Jerry and Jeanine gave the senator and Paula a thirty-minute overview of their recent activities and a quick tour around the building. They made their pitch for additional funding to upgrade the supercomputer. It seemed to Paula they always wanted another upgrade. It was like they were constantly chasing some elusive goal that could be reached with just another terabyte. She understood upgrades were a fact of life when competing in the supercomputer marketplace, but it would be tough to convince the Pentagon that Maui needed more funding.

As they passed through the lab, they saw five technicians staring at a single monitor. "What are they looking at?" the senator inquired.

Captain White spoke. "Sir, we've been trying to identify an object that AEOS, oh sorry, the Advanced Electro-Optical System telescope picked up a couple of nights ago. We've been running our most sophisticated models on it to clean up the image, but so far we haven't found much. Would you like to see?"

Senator Mitsunaga shook hands with each of the technicians and then peered at the computer screen.

Freddy Watanabe gave a nervous cough and cleared his throat. "Senator Mitsunaga, a couple nights ago AEOS picked up this image while focusing on a routine meteor shower to the west. In the middle of the shower, we captured this meteor, or something apparently heading from our atmosphere into space. Then it appears to explode. Right there. We have tried everything we can to identify what it might be, but all our computer models have come up empty. It's a vexing problem, probably of no military value, maybe not even any scientific value. Still, it has us all scratching our heads."

Jerry turned to Mitsunaga. "Senator, this is Freddy Watanabe. He's a PhD candidate in computer science at UH and comes over part-time to work with us on our systems. He and Jeanine, Captain White, have been working on a way to enhance the images from the telescopes to get clearer pictures. It's been a great tool, although frankly, the air force doesn't seem interested.

"Freddy, pull up the space shuttle." Jerry nodded in Fred's direction. "Senator, several years ago, during a mission, the space shuttle lost some of its heat-protecting exterior tiles. No one was sure how bad the damage was, and NASA was preparing to use a risky unscheduled spacewalk to check it. But, when the shuttle flew past Hawaii, we were able to get this image. From the raw data, we couldn't tell much. But using the algorithms that Freddy and Jeanine put together, we could get a much clearer picture. As you can see here, we could tell there was minimal damage to the exterior of the shuttle. We figure we saved NASA millions, if not hundreds of millions, by allowing them to continue on with their planned experiments without delay or the need to conduct a risky spacewalk. We've been trying to use that technique on this mystery meteor or whatever it is, but so far we haven't found much."

The senator smiled and nodded throughout Jerry's explanation, and when Jerry paused, he said, "Fascinating. Well, keep up the good work, ladies and gentlemen. Thank you all very much."

"Senator," Paula said, picking up on the cue from the senator that it was time to move on. "I think we need to catch up with Major Lane now."

The group proceeded back to the briefing room where the team from the telescope, Major Lane, Dr. Gordon, and Sergeant Chauncey Hayes, was waiting.

"Senator Mitsunaga, it's an honor to see you here again–" Major Lane began.

"Well, what have we here. Chauncey? I didn't know you were on this trip," the senator interrupted.

"Sir," Paula started, reddening slightly, "Chauncey is assigned here as of last week. I believe I mentioned that to you."

"Oh yes, that's right. Well, Chauncey, welcome to Maui. I trust you're enjoying yourself."

Chauncey looked somewhat sheepish at the attention he was receiving. "Yes, sir, it's great to see you again, Senator. Sir, this is a great location and a great opportunity with the new telescope."

Major Lane tried to regain control of the meeting. "Senator, we are very glad to have Sergeant Hayes with us. While it's only been a few days, he's already proven himself to be a great asset here as we have gone about getting the telescope up and running. Do you remember Dr. Gordon, sir? He's the lead scientist from Boeing, which runs the space surveillance site here."

"Of course, how are you, sir? What can you tell me about that mysterious meteor shower we were watching?"

Major Lane looked at Dr. Gordon, who responded, "Unfortunately, sir, not much. It might just be an anomaly, but frankly, it looks to us mostly like a missile launch that exploded in space."

"A missile launch from whom? The Japanese? That's hard to believe."

"Senator," Major Lane interjected, "we don't know for sure. But based on the trajectory, we think it would've been launched from North Korea over Japan. But again, we don't know what it was."

"Goodness!" Senator Mitsunaga's eyes had grown wide. "What do you hear from headquarters on this, Major?"

"Nothing, sir. No one picked up anything like it. But sir, I understand we really don't have any assets monitoring the activity of the North Koreans on a regular basis. With the aging of some of our sensors, we focus almost all missile-warning attention on Russia and China. So it's possible that our guys, as good as they are, would've missed it."

The senator shook his head, concern clearly written in his expression. "Major, if you're right on this, it will change the landscape in Washington. I think the fellas will want to respond if the North Koreans are launching missiles with sufficient power to get them into space. That means they are only a step or two from having an intercontinental-range ballistic missile. Isn't that right?"

"Sir, we really don't have the information to say what this was. But all of us would be real nervous if the Koreans were that close to having an ICBM."

"Paula, what've you heard on this?"

"Sir, I can't talk about the classified National Intelligence Estimate here. But on an unclassified basis, I can tell you the most recent estimates predict the North Koreans are working on this type of technology. At the same time, virtually every expert speculates they're nowhere near ready to launch an ICBM. That should take at least another decade. It's hard to believe they'd all be wrong."

"It's happened before, Paula. No one thought the Japanese would attack Pearl Harbor. Remember the Maginot line? That was supposed to be impenetrable to the Germans. And, of course, 9-11. History is filled with well-meaning analysts and leaders misinterpreting intelligence."

"Yes, sir."

"Paula, I want you to take a copy of this tape back to Washington, and get the intel people working on it. Oh, and make sure Jackson knows about it. He is going to explode if he thinks the Koreans have Seattle in their sights."

Amidst all the discussion, Paula hardly had a chance to think about Chauncey. But when she glanced over at him, memories of the previous night came flowing back. He looked so different in a uniform. In legislative affairs, he had always worn business suits. Last night he was in island wear, at least initially. Chauncey noticed her stare. Their eyes met for a fleeting moment, but Paula looked away.

She looked at her watch and informed the senator they needed to be leaving if he was going to be on time for his event. The senator thanked them all. "Chauncey, you look sharp in uniform. Don't you think so, Paula?"

"Uh, yes sir," she stammered, hoping the blush she felt wasn't as apparent on the outside. Together, she and the senator turned to walk out.

"Paula, do you think they could be right about this missile launch?"

"Sir, all the data we have would say 'probably not.' But, as you said, we've missed these things in the past by focusing on the wrong cues. It'll sure change things if they're right."

CHAPTER XXIV

Tuesday, August 8th

Makena, Maui

Paula woke up at 5 a.m. It was 11 a.m. in DC, and she couldn't sleep anymore. As she stretched her back, she couldn't help thinking about Chauncey and the previous night. He hadn't called or stopped by. She wasn't sure if she was glad or sorry. It sure would be simpler if it were all forgotten, but that wasn't as easy as it sounded. With Chauncey stationed here, she was going to be seeing him at least two or three times a year. She knew she'd have to face the facts at some point, but today, she decided just to concentrate on defense projects on Maui and protecting the senator's efforts to bring high-tech jobs to Hawaii.

After a leisurely bath and breakfast, she started off to the high-tech park to visit the Pacific Disaster Center. At the door to a nondescript cinderblock building stood a short, fat, balding, very pale Johnny Taylor.

"Hey, Johnny, what are you doing here? You didn't need to come from the Pentagon just to see me."

Johnny Taylor, the Washington rep for the PDC, was decked out in aloha-wear and smiled broadly as they shook hands. "For the head staffer of Defense Appropriations, I'll go anywhere,

Paula. Plus, I haven't visited the site in three months. It's a good opportunity to do a mid-summer review and get ready for the coming fiscal year. That is, assuming you and the senator are going to fund us again."

"You're OK for this year, Johnny, aren't you? I thought you still had about $8 million."

Johnny grinned, and Paula laughed. "Hey, and isn't part of that money here just for that highly unlikely possibility the senator can't get you money next year?"

"We're taking good care of it." Johnny bowed.

"Good," Paula said. "Besides, you know the senator is committed to seeing this place thrive and hopefully become self-sufficient someday. Speaking of which, what are the South Koreans saying about buying products from you?"

"I'm glad you asked, but let's get you inside where we can both hear the pitch the staff put together."

He ushered her forward. "I got to say, though, this place is really coming along. They're doing some exciting work on disaster mitigation based on that sarin gas attack on the Japanese subway. We can model the best way to deal with chemicals released into the atmosphere by analyzing weather data that we're already collecting. We'll be able to tell emergency managers exactly how to respond. You know, we were real lucky in that incident. I can't talk much about it here because of the classification, but that would have been ten times worse if a couple things had gone differently. Next time you get a chance, come by the Pentagon, and we'll give you the details."

"Sarin gas attacks? I thought you were hurricane and tsunami monitors. Since when did you get into chemical warfare?"

"That's just it, Paula. The interrelationship between wind

patterns that we have been studying for typhoons and forest fires correlate directly to gas dispersion in an open-air environment. We saw some of that when we went back and looked at the Gulf War data. We have a couple of National Guard guys here working half-time on this project. We figure we can show the Defense comptroller gurus how it might benefit DoD and justify the funds you keep giving us."

Paula and Johnny entered an eerily quiet office. All the staff sat at their workstations, staring at computer screens. It wasn't impressive to look at. Yet Paula knew these technicians and engineers were designing models to study natural disasters. They'd spent the last decade putting together information management packages to ensure the data they collected could be provided instantaneously to emergency managers. So far, Hawaii was protected. They were beginning to branch out to the Pacific Islands of Guam and Samoa, in which there was substantial DoD interest.

"So, what's up with the Koreans?"

"Paula, if there is one thing you could do for us, it would be to allow us to sell our products to others. As you know, most government entities aren't in the profit-making business. They can't sell their services to the highest bidder. Some of the White House policy guys want us to give our services to our allies. But we figure, if we can sell them, we can pay for our costs and expand into other missions."

"What can we do? We don't have a lot of pull with the current administration. Senator Mitsunaga isn't quite liberal enough for most of them."

"Paula, what we need is legislative authority to create a public-private venture so we can sell our wares. We don't need the White House; we need Congress."

"Write it up, and I'll see what I can do. Our majority colleagues are a little squeamish about including new legislative provisions in appropriations conferences. They might like this one if we can legitimately argue it would save money. Just get it to me soon. I'm not promising anything, but perhaps we can slip it into the bill."

"That'd be great, Paula. It'd really help us out. How long are you here?"

"I'm flying to Honolulu this afternoon and catching a flight back to DC in the morning. It doesn't get back until about midnight, but it's the only one you can take heading east where you don't have to fly all night. Tonight I'm having dinner with the D-CINC, General Gianini; he's become a close friend after three years in the job. But I've got to get home. My Bo's anxious to see me; I haven't had much time for him the last few months."

"I know how that is. Sometimes it seems like we never go home from the Pentagon. I haven't seen much of my family recently either."

"Yeah, Potomac Fever: a bunch of delirious bureaucrats who don't know when to stop work. By the way, Bo is my eighty-pound yellow lab."

CHAPTER XXV

Honolulu, Oahu

Paula walked into the baggage claim area and was surprised to see Lieutenant General Gianini waiting for her. He was impossible to miss at six foot five and 245 pounds, clad in dress uniform with three stars on each shoulder.

"Good afternoon, sir. You didn't have to come meet me, but it certainly was nice you did. How's it going?"

"Hey, Paula, it's nice to see you again. I figured we can get an early start on dinner this way. Unless you're eager to get to your hotel."

"Oh no, sir. Dinner sounds great."

The general motioned to the Navy E-4 to take Paula's bags. Paula tried to resist, but recognizing that she would be countermanding the order of a three-star general, she acquiesced to the anxious young enlisted woman's earnest attempts to take her bags.

"So, General, you didn't respond to my question. Everything OK here?"

"I'm sorry, yes, things are going very well. Let me get this out of the way—in case you aren't aware, I'll be retiring in a few months. The army has decided it's time for me to go, and I won't fight it."

"Is that right? I think that's wonderful. You've been serving the country entirely too long; you and Midge deserve a break. I really mean it."

Al's half-smile said he knew what she meant but hadn't yet reconciled himself to his life post-army. He led Paula to the white Navy Sedan waiting for them and held the door for her, dismissing the driver as he did. Chivalry wasn't totally dead.

"So, sir, where are we headed?"

"Have you been to Germaine's? It's the hottest thing. Like so much of the food here, it's what they call Pacific Rim cuisine. It's really just dressed-up Chinese, but it's terrific."

"That sounds great." Paula glanced out the side window as the car began to move. "I hate to mix business with pleasure, but this has been nagging at me all day. Yesterday afternoon the senator and I visited the Maui supercomputer. We saw an image that the AEOS telescope happened to catch when it was studying a meteor shower over the Western Pacific. I don't want to be an alarmist, and this may sound crazy, but it sure as hell looked like a missile launch from North Korea. Have you heard anything like that?"

General Gianini turned to look at Paula. "You're saying you think you've seen film of a North Korean missile launch?"

"Sir, I don't know what it shows, but the technicians think that's what it looks like. I'll be damned if it doesn't look something like that."

"That's incredible, Paula. You have to understand this is extremely sensitive, but DC is reporting something similar. This is something you cannot repeat. But it looks like some folks in Washington are reaching the same conclusion based on other sources. The sense is that, contrary to every prediction, the

North Koreans have launched a two-stage missile, one that is potentially able to reach Hawaii or Alaska."

"What?" Paula shook her head. "But the Agency's saying the Koreans won't have anything like that for years."

The general nodded. "I know. But be sure you understand the sensitivity of this. Up to this point, no one has been sure, but if there's video footage, that's proof."

"Holy shit, Al! Sorry sir, but do you realize what this will mean on the Hill? We are going to be throwing money at missile defense from now until doomsday. This will give all the wackos the wherewithal to fight to the death for star wars."

"What's this Democratic Party crap, Paula? If the North Koreans are close to having an intercontinental-range ballistic missile, we have to do something."

"Right. Yes, you're right, I guess. Too many years fighting against right-wing polemics make some responses instinctive. In Washington, sometimes we get so caught up in politics and causes that we oppose something only because we don't trust the people who favor it."

Paula leaned forward and gently massaged her temples. "But seriously, we'll have to think hard about what the North Koreans are up to and the real threat associated with this new capability. If it's for real. Only then should we be making decisions about national missile defense. Besides, you're already working on a pretty decent capability to knock down any mean incoming stuff with the Navy's Aegis BMD program."

They made their way into the restaurant. General Gianini signaled to the waiters, who ushered them to a table overlooking Waikiki Beach.

Paula continued on the same track. "I mean, as I understand it, Al. Potentially, the navy could park an Aegis ship off Japan and knock down anything the Koreans and maybe even the Chinese could throw up. Isn't that right?"

"Paula, you can't ask an old army GI to tout the navy's alternative to our theater air defense and national missile defense programs. It simply isn't fair."

He sipped his drink, then grinned. "Even if it is true. I'm no expert in this area. But I've seen the simulations that are going on with the cruiser, *Lake Erie*, and the engineers at the Pacific Missile Range. It sure as hell looks like they are on the verge of discovering an antidote to ballistic and maybe even cruise missiles. I know the boss is convinced the navy's system is going to provide some awesome force protection for our ships at sea and perhaps any naval base or town for some three hundred miles. Can it do more than that? That all depends on the launch detection, the cuing, the angle of attack, and the speed of the kill vehicle. Let's just say, it's possible, but we won't know for several years."

"So, not to put words in your mouth, and certainly not for attribution, as we say in DC, you think someday we might have a credible missile defense which could provide homeland protection—let's not call it national missile defense for now—from our fleet of Aegis ships."

Al narrowed his eyes in thought. "With strategic disbursement of the assets, yes. It's starting to look like that might be possible."

Two waiters approached the table with several plates piled high with seafood, meat, and vegetables.

"What is this, sir? It looks great."

"I think you're going to like it. First is grilled sea bass with black bean relish. Second is a medley of wild mushrooms and lemongrass-flavored vegetables. Third is sweet-and-sour pork. But it's not like any you have ever had before."

"You know, Paula. There's this other thing . . . " Al stopped and shook his head. "Never mind. Enough shop talk. Let's eat."

Paula gave him a quizzical glance, shrugged her shoulders, and scooped up some mushrooms. "I'm starving."

CHAPTER XXVI

Tuesday, September 5th

Dirksen Senate Office Building

August had passed too quickly for Paula. Mitsunaga had been busy campaigning, and she scrupulously avoided getting involved in elections. He never even raised the subject with her. So after her quick trip to Hawaii, she had the month pretty much to herself. She'd taken the time to clean her house, and catch up on her personal correspondence, and finally pay her taxes after two extensions.

Bo was happy. She used the recess hours to take him to the park most mornings and spent the evenings on the couch reading and scratching his ears. She and Bo even spent the entire last week on the eastern shore, having a quiet getaway. But it was already the first Tuesday after Labor Day, the day when all the senators and congressmen return for the fall push.

When she walked into her office, she was greeted by a fourteen-inch stack of mail. *I guess somebody was working.*

Her answering machine signaled she had several messages waiting, and settling into her chair, she hit the replay button.

Most were the standard stuff, constituents needing help, lobbyists wanting meetings, and reporters wanting an off-the-record assessment of what the fall looked like for the appropriations process. The last message, however, was from Senator Mitsunaga. She immediately called his office.

"Hi Susie, this is Paula. How was your recess?"

"Paula, the senator's been trying to call you, but I think he's on the phone with Harry. Are you in your office?"

"I'm here, Susie. He's in the office already?"

"No, he's in the car, but he said he'd call back for you. I don't know what it is, but he seems to be on edge. You might want to stay off the phone, and I'll transfer him to you as soon as he calls in."

"You got it."

"Justin, where do we stand?" Senator Parker spoke loudly into the cell phone in his car.

"Senator Parker," Justin's high-pitched voice began, "it's all going just as you planned, and I must say, sir, it's a brilliant plan. Today at 11 a.m, the majority leader will announce that, in the interest of national security, he has granted authority for the Rules Committee to conduct hearings immediately and subpoena witnesses. Further, he will state that the Senate will not be in session on Wednesday until 3 p.m., to allow committees to meet. Chairman Wilson will meet today with the Republican members of the committee. He has a subpoena prepared for Ms. Rebecca DeLaurio. As soon as you and your colleagues agree, the chairman will sign the subpoena."

Justin's voice paused for a quick intake of breath before charging on. "At 6:30 p.m., an unsuspecting Rebecca DeLaurio will receive a subpoena at her home. At 7 p.m., Chairman Wilson will make a copy of the taped conversation available to Senator Bankhead. He'll then tell him that he's scheduled a hearing to begin at 10 a.m. the next day and inform him that Ms. DeLaurio will be appearing. She'll come to testify, and the rest, as they say, Senator, is showbiz."

"Good work, Justin, but how did you clear this with the leader already?"

"Senator, we didn't tell his staff much, just that we got the goods on a Democratic fundraiser and former Senate staffer. We told them it was critical that we be allowed to go ahead with sworn testimony immediately, or the witness might flee the country, as others in these scandals have done. We pointed out the extreme sensitivity, the national security implications, and the urgency that this be fully investigated before the upcoming elections. As you can imagine, the leader's staff was intrigued by the prospect that you had their guys in your sights, and they realize, of course, that they have no choice but to approve our request."

"That's terrific, Justin. How much does Wilson know?"

"Yesterday afternoon, I played the tape for his staff director, Missie Walsh. Her face went white when she heard it. Up to that point, sir, we had not had much cooperation from the committee, but that's OK. I can't really blame them. We told her to be ready for a hearing on Wednesday and didn't give her any more than that. As you instructed, sir, no one has heard the tape except you, me, and now Missie Walsh. I don't know exactly what she told the chairman, but it was enough to get the subpoena prepared and to get the 2 p.m. meeting set up. Also, sir, I'm FedExing a copy from you to the FBI director this afternoon, as we discussed last month. He should get it tomorrow, about an hour before the hearing."

"OK. When can we get together to go through the cross-examination we want to do with the witness?"

"I'm ready now, Senator."

"OK. I'll be there in about five minutes. Meet me in my office."

"Yes, sir."

Chairman Wilson welcomed Missie as she entered his office. "Listen, I'm sorry I screwed up your summer on a wild goose chase. So what's this diabolical plot that Parker's concerned about? Are the Chinese invading at dawn?"

"Mr. Chairman, I have to tell you this looks very serious. Senator Parker's staff played a taped conversation for me yesterday of a former Mitsunaga staffer receiving a campaign donation from an agent of the Chinese military."

"What the Sam Hill are you talking about? Ken Mitsunaga involved with the Chinese? Why, that's absolutely preposterous. I've known Ken for fourteen years. He is as patriotic and God-fearing as any man I know. What's Parker up to now?"

"Sir, I understand your skepticism. If I hadn't heard the tape, I would have said the same thing, but the evidence is very clear. Senator Parker has the majority leader's authorization for you to subpoena Ms. Rebecca DeLaurio, the former staff director of the Indian Affairs Committee and now fundraiser for Senator Mitsunaga. Senator Parker suggests you call a majority members' meeting for 2 p.m. today and request their unanimous support to subpoena Ms. DeLaurio to testify tomorrow morning at 10 a.m. Normally, I'd be reluctant to support something like this, but the evidence is so overwhelming, I must urge you to go along with Parker's request."

"Rebecca? I know Rebecca. We all know she and Ken are close, if you know what I mean, but I can't believe that Ken would be taking money from the PLA. That's crazy."

"Sir, the evidence is irrefutable. You have to go along with this. Parker'll be watching your every move. As much as it pains me to say this, you have no choice."

"Missie, you've worked for me for what ten, twelve years?"

"Yes, sir."

"Are you absolutely positive on this?" The chairman's wide-eyed look held a bit of desperation.

"Senator, I heard a conversation between a man and a woman. The man sounded Asian. He identifies the woman as Ms. DeLaurio. It sounds like Rebecca. She asks for money and notes that it's from a Chinese general. It couldn't be any clearer if we had the canceled check from the People's Bank in Beijing. Sir, I can't tell you how sorry I am to say this. I knew Rebecca a little. She always seemed like a nice woman, and I think the world of Ken Mitsunaga. He's one of the best Democrats in this whole body. Heck, sir, he's one of the best senators of either party, but the evidence is irrefutable. You simply must put the wheels in motion."

"OK, Missie, we'll do it your way. Call the offices, and tell the majority members we'll meet in the committee room at 2 p.m. I assume Parker will bring the tape. Do you have a subpoena prepared?"

"Sir, Parker's people insisted I prepare the subpoena and schedule a hearing for tomorrow. There's only one thing. We still have to tell Bankhead. Senator Parker wants to be sure the subpoena is served before you tell the Democrats. They suggest you tell him tonight and play the tape at that point. They also want you to get his assurance that Mitsunaga won't be notified in advance."

Chairman Wilson opened his mouth to speak and then snapped it tight.

Missie's look mirrored the sadness on his face. "As much as it pains me to say this, sir, they're probably right. If he's taking money from the Chinese, it's probably better for it to come out at the hearing. We can't let him try to influence Ms. DeLaurio before she testifies."

Chairman Wilson nodded, staring blankly down at the table.

"Sir, I want you to know how sad I am we have to do this, but I don't think we have any choice."

He nodded slowly. "OK, Missie, I'm sure you're right. I still can't believe it though."

◆ ◆ ◆

"Appropriations," Paula spoke into the phone.

"Paula, this is Ken. Is everything alright? I have this eerie feeling something's wrong. What am I missing?"

"Nothing I know of, sir. Everyone's just getting back today. There's nothing on the horizon yet. I don't expect we'll get serious on appropriations conferences for a week or so. And the Senate never does much more than our bills in September. So, I got to say, Senator, I don't see any problems."

"OK, but somehow, I feel something's about to happen.

Could you talk to Jackson's staff and see if there's something we might've missed? I'd appreciate it."

"Of course, sir, I'll call John right away. If there's something brewing, I'll let you know immediately."

"Thank you, Paula."

"Thank you, sir." *Damn, I did it again. Thanking him for absolutely no good reason.*

She shook her head and picked the phone back up.

"John, this is Paula. How was your summer?"

"Hey Paula, welcome back. I tried to get ahold of you last week to check in but only got your voicemail. Where've you been?

"I took some time off to clean the house, catch up on bills, and give Bo a little quality time. Relaxed on the eastern shore, nothing special. What about you?"

"Went to the Cape for the middle two weeks, back last week just in case. It was dead. Nothing going on."

"That's good. I got a call from the boss, and he wanted me to take your pulse. Glad to hear everything's quiet. Though, I don't suppose it'll last, especially with the election nearly upon us."

"Oh, I'm sure it will pick up. In fact, I already have twenty-five calls to return today, and it's not lunchtime. Good thing is, though, it won't last long. With the election coming, they'll be out by early October, so we only have one month of craziness to endure."

"True, true. Well, I'll let you get back to the messages. Let me know if you hear anything. See ya."

Paula put down the phone. *Everything sure sounds fine. Funny, though, because the senator's intuition is almost always on target.* But, if John Silease didn't know about it, chances were good there was nothing out there. It was September, appropriations conferences were the only item on the agenda. If anything else was up that might interfere or delay the completion of the year's business, surely the appropriations staff director would've heard by now.

Paula turned her attention to her stack of mail.

CHAPTER XXVII

Hart Senate Office Building

This was the moment Missie had dreaded most. Skip Muldoon, her counterpart, was on the phone. She had to let him know something was up. But she couldn't let on, yet, that the Capitol dome was about to explode and land right on top of him. She hoped he had a good summer because the fall was going to be a bitch.

"Missie?" Skip's voice already sounded annoyed.

Missie rushed through the next monologue. "Skip, how are you? You know I've been trying to get in touch with you. I've been emailing you, but the messages keep coming back. I thought your real name was Craig. How are you listed anyway?"

Her stomach churned as she spun her tale of how it was really all his fault that he was unaware of what was about to occur.

"But, Skip, I'm so sorry that we haven't connected. You won't believe what's happened. I'd rather not go into it on the phone. Senator Wilson wants to meet with Senator Bankhead about this personally. Can you come to his Capitol office around 7 p.m.? I'll save the details until then. But you should know that, at the direction of the majority leader, we'll be holding a hearing tomorrow morning. We're sending out notices and emailing the schedulers right now."

Missie sucked in a quick breath. "Listen, Skip. I got to run. The chairman's on the other line. Please give me a call if Senator Bankhead has a problem, but otherwise we'll see both of you tonight. Bye."

She hung up the phone and cradled her head in her hands. That was awful. Skip hadn't even had a chance to speak; he wouldn't know what to think.

She dialed the phone. "Marjorie, can I please speak to the chairman." After a moment, he picked up. "Mr. Chairman, I just notified Senator Bankhead's staff that we'll be holding a hearing tomorrow at Senator Jacobs's request. I told him you wanted to meet with Senator Bankhead personally at seven tonight to discuss this. But I gave him no details. To be safe, you might want to avoid the senator until then if possible."

"Well, I'm off to a fundraiser at noon. I have a speech downtown at two and expect to be in the steam room at four. We have the vote at six o'clock, but I can probably dodge Tom until seven. Oh, and thanks, Missie." He paused. "You should know I don't like this any more than you, but I don't see any way around it."

"No, sir, I agree. We'll just have to let this play out."

CHAPTER XXVIII

US Capitol

The key ingredient for the best reporters isn't writing skills; it's instinct. It does no good to write beautiful prose that no one reads because someone else scooped you three hours earlier. And in the era of twenty-four-hour news and instantaneous tweets, thirty minutes was an eternity.

Harris Ward, the longtime *Roll Call* reporter, was sure something was up. The rumor that the sleepy Rules Committee was holding a hearing on the first Wednesday after Labor Day was surprising enough. The inability to find a witness list was curious. But the fact that neither the committee's loquacious chairman, nor the ranking member, nor the staff director were available to talk about the hearing was unprecedented. Their communications directors all made the same excuse. They had just returned to town after the recess and simply didn't have time to chat for five minutes. But taken together it was clearly an interesting situation. The Rules Committee was never interesting.

As he had thousands of times before, Harris waited in the lobby outside the senate chamber—he'd catch Senator Wilson or Senator Bankhead coming off the Senate floor after the vote. Harris had been working the Capitol beat for more than thirty years. His once-blond hair was graying; his thin, nondescript face was masked by horn-rimmed glasses and a neatly trimmed beard. He'd seen hundreds of senators and congressmen come and go. Catching them in the hallway was part of the culture. Reporters waited at the door and pounced on interesting targets between the door and the elevator. Usually, it wasn't an unwelcome attack. Most members were happy to talk to the press, put their spin on an issue, and get their names in the *Post*, *Times*, or *Journal*. It was all part of the dance.

A few were unwilling to risk facing an obscure question that'd get them in trouble—those rushed through the lobby. Even the most press-friendly member would occasionally start a conversation with a colleague to avoid the press. That tactic didn't work if the dogged reporter kept following the senator as he or she walked through the corridors or rode the Senate subway back to their office. At some point, they'd be alone and couldn't avoid a question.

After a few years in the Senate, most members knew which reporters to be wary of—the ones who'd be looking for a gotcha moment. Usually this meant the young ones, eager to break their first big story. Their articles frequently had a catchy headline only marginally related to the details in the story. Harris was neither young nor hungry. He didn't engage in gotcha-journalism, but he could smell a story. When he caught the scent, he'd hound his prey until he got his answers.

The 6 p.m. roll call vote was underway as Harris waited off the floor. He saw no sign of either Wilson or Bankhead. From his vantage point, he couldn't be sure whether either had voted. But he could be pretty sure they hadn't entered the chamber through the usual door, the one closest to the subway. The vote ended, and shortly thereafter, the Senate adjourned. Still no sign of either one. How unlikely would it be that both senators missed the vote? Their offices implied they were back in town, although he hadn't specifically asked. With a hearing tomorrow, the chances that they weren't here seemed very remote.

He saw Skip Muldoon coming off the Senate floor and made a beeline in his direction. Skip saw him and turned to walk the other direction, but he wasn't fast enough.

"Hey, Skip, got a second? Harris Ward from *Roll Call*. I didn't see Senator Bankhead vote. Is he here?"

Skip kicked himself for getting caught. He knew he was stuck. If he said "no comment," that would only escalate the situation. Luckily, this was an easy question.

"Of course, he voted. He was in a meeting on the other side of the Capitol and used the other door."

"Was the meeting about tomorrow's hearing?"

Skip winced. *Damn it. The hearing.* He answered truthfully, "I don't know what the meeting was, probably leadership. I doubt it was about the hearing since I wasn't party to it." He knew he was getting in deeper but couldn't figure out how to extricate himself. The Senate had adjourned following the vote, so he couldn't insist he needed to get back on the floor. He didn't want to let on that his boss was about to meet with Wilson. And he didn't want to talk about the mysterious hearing that he knew nothing about. Of all the reporters to catch him, here was the one guy that usually knew more about what was going on in the Senate than the members.

"So, it's pretty odd for the committee to be holding a hearing right after Labor Day on such short notice. What's it all about?"

There it is. The question I can't answer. He's frigging right, of course; this is bizarre. His committee was having a hearing tomorrow. All he knew was the subject was campaign finance reform. He couldn't cry "foul" because he'd heard the month-old voicemail from Missie today when he finally checked his messages. He wasn't the only staffer that took August off and tried not to think about the Senate. *But, shit, on this occasion it's going to bite me in the ass big time.* And he couldn't tell Harris Ward any of that.

"Harris, the topic is campaign finance reform. It's something dreamed up by the majority leader. Sorry for the mystery, but they want to unveil the whole thing tomorrow and not before. They asked us not to say anything else, and Senator Bankhead agreed. So if you are looking for more, I suggest you find Chairman Wilson. Got to run."

It was only a little white lie. He couldn't say more because he didn't know more, but he certainly didn't want Ward to know that.

"That's just it, I can't find either the chairman or Senator Bankhead. Well, thanks for your time."

Harris knew he wasn't going to get a story filed today. He also knew that if Skip was that tightlipped, there was a pretty good chance he wasn't going to be scooped by any other reporter. But he was most surely going to be attending his first Rules Committee hearing since the committee looked at earmark reform a half-dozen years ago.

CHAPTER XXIX

Wednesday, September 6th

Hart Senate Office Building

The chairman's gavel brought the committee to order. The expressions from the faces on the dais made it clear this was a grave matter. There was none of the normal backslapping greetings that usually occurred at the first meeting following a long recess. Both sides kept to themselves, speaking in hushed tones. The Republican members had decided staff would not be privy to the details, only to the fact that this was a hearing on campaign financing. The only cheerful face in the room was Parker's. At the urging of Justin Armor, Missie had arranged for room SH-216, the largest and most modern of the Senate's many hearing rooms. She'd avoided the press entirely. Judging from the number of television cameras, someone had clearly let on that this could get interesting. Missie glanced to the side and caught sight of Senator Mitsunaga, second in seniority on the Democratic side. He appeared none the wiser, and her stomach clenched in anguished anticipation.

She groaned audibly as she caught a glimpse of Skip Muldoon glaring at her. It had been a tense meeting in the chairman's office the night before. Senator Bankhead had been justifiably outraged at what was about to take place. But the chairman had handled it extremely well. He'd let Bankhead and Skip listen to the tape, explaining that he'd just received it and only six people had ever heard it. The implications for Senator Mitsunaga did need to be explained, but the chairman had warned Bankhead that if anything was done to impede the investigation at this point, it would be very bad for all Democrats. He suggested Senator Bankhead call his other members together to discuss the implications without going into detail.

Bankhead had looked visibly shaken by the recording. Missie understood the feelings of incredulity and betrayal—how could he believe his friend and colleague was accepting money from the Chinese? But, like everyone else in the Senate, she knew he'd heard the rumors of the relationship between Ken and Rebecca. And she'd been raising money for him. He knew Ken was the leader in defending the Asian-American PAC. Sadly, it all fit together. Missie saw his hands tremble as Chairman Wilson handed him a glass of Kentucky sour mash. Bankhead had looked over at her then, but she welled up with tears and turned away.

The chairman hadn't even hinted that he, too, could hardly believe the evidence. But Missie could see his inner turmoil under the emotionless demeanor as he laid out the schedule. The meeting had ended coolly, formally—not cordially, but not acrimoniously.

Missie looked around the crowded hearing room and spotted Rebecca in the third row. Rebecca was sitting bolt upright in her seat, her jaw tense. The skin on her face was taut and pale, almost ashen.

Rebecca made sure no one could see it, but her hands were shaking. They hadn't stopped shaking since she'd answered her door last night and accepted a subpoena from the Senate sergeant at arms. She hadn't known what to do. She'd tried to reach Harry, but he didn't answer his cell. She was afraid to call the senator directly, and she wasn't sure what she would've told him. The summons didn't state why she was being asked to testify. Perhaps it was just the latest in the fruitless Republican efforts to attack the Asian-American PAC. Or so she'd tried to convince herself until she'd looked outside and seen the same two Capitol Police officers sitting across the street in their black SUV. As the hours passed and they remained on duty, her stress increased exponentially. Now she struggled to keep her breaths calm and even.

The witness list was being passed out to the staff and public. Harry almost jumped out of his chair when he saw it contained only one name—Ms. Rebecca DeLaurio. *What the hell?* He got up to approach the dais, but Chairman Wilson loudly banged the gavel and sternly directed everyone to be seated.

"Ladies and gentlemen, today we are presumptively holding this hearing on campaign financing, but it really is an altogether different matter. The true subject is trust. We are entrusted by you, as your representatives, to act on your behalf and that of the nation. Each of us takes an oath to protect and defend the Constitution against all enemies." His voice began to rise as he continued. "All enemies, foreign and domestic. I repeat: foreign and domestic. You send us your checks of five dollars or five hundred dollars because you trust us to represent your interests. We frequently say in this chamber, 'our word is our bond.' We say we won't do anything to jeopardize the trust you have placed in us.

"In the past twenty-four hours, this committee has come into possession of some most disturbing information regarding this sacred bond. Our witness today once worked for this great institution and now makes her living representing business interests."

Harry approached the dais and handed Senator Mitsunaga the witness list. The senator turned around in his seat and gave Harry a quizzical expression. Sweat was forming on Harry's upper lip, and he knew his expression must show something of his shock and concern. He'd served Ken Mitsunaga since his first political campaign more than forty years ago. He prided himself on never being surprised in this business, but this time he was completely in the dark.

Senator Bankhead sat with his eyes lowered. He had not requested an opportunity to speak, a privilege normally accorded the ranking minority member. Chairman Wilson hadn't volunteered one. To his credit, the chairman had decided to handle this matter as professionally and apolitically as possible. He felt he owed it to his Democratic colleagues, including the senior senator from Hawaii.

Ever the professional, Senator Mitsunaga turned back toward the audience. He remained stone-faced as Chairman Wilson introduced the witness.

Ms. DeLaurio approached the witness table and was met by Missie Walsh holding a Bible. The Chairman stood and raised his right hand, instructing Rebecca to do the same. Rebecca placed a trembling hand on the Bible and swore to tell the whole truth.

"Please be seated, Ms. DeLaurio, and state your full name and address for the record." Chairman Wilson sat erect behind the dais and kept his eyes fixed on her face as she answered.

"Are you a registered lobbyist?"

"Yes, sir."

"Are you active in fundraising?"

"Yes, sir."

"Are you familiar with the Asian-American PAC."

"Yes, sir."

"Have you actively sought donations from this PAC?"

"Yes, sir."

"For whose campaign?"

"Senator Mitsunaga's."

"Is it correct that you used to work for the senator?"

"Well not exactly, sir." Rebecca's taut expression lightened by the smallest amount. "I worked for the Indian Affairs Committee, on which Senator Mitsunaga served as chairman and vice chairman. But I never worked for the senator directly."

"Yes, of course. Excuse me. You worked for him in his capacity as chairman of the committee but not on his personal office staff. Since your departure from the Senate, have you served as a fundraiser for the senator?" The chairman gave her an encouraging smile.

"Yes, sir."

"Can you tell the committee, are you aware of any foreign involvement in the Asian-American PAC?"

"Mr. Chairman," Senator Mitsunaga interrupted, "we have been down this path before, and I must protest. This is just another witch hunt. Yes, Ms. DeLaurio is a fundraiser for me. Yes, she's sought donations from members of the Asian-American community. But I resent this accusation being pushed repeatedly by members of your party that money's coming from foreigners."

The chairman opened his mouth to speak, but Senator Mitsunaga charged on. "I'm sure you receive funding from your constituents. No one questions that. I believe you receive donations from companies that have interests in your state. Again, no one questions these. You have even received donations from the Friends of Animals league because of your exemplary work in the protection of endangered species. That's all well and good. Why is it, though, when donations come from Asians—people who don't look like most of you—you immediately contend that the money's tainted? This is racism, Mr. Chairman, and I'm shocked you would engage in it."

Senator Bankhead shot a frown over at his friend, as if to indicate this was not the time or the place for such outbursts. Senator Mitsunaga couldn't understand why his colleague hadn't already responded to these outrageous accusations.

The chairman's voice was grave and steady. "Senator Mitsunaga, you will have your chance to question the witness. But I am chairman, and I will continue with my questioning. You, sir, have no right to impugn my motives, just as those who are critical of donations from Asian-Americans have no justification to do so, unless it's proven that these funds are, in fact, tainted. We will determine that today. And I will continue.

"Now, Ms. DeLaurio, is it true that the funds you've raised from the AAPAC are actually from the Chinese government."

"Absolutely not, sir," Rebecca responded stridently, seeming emboldened by Mitsunaga's defense.

"Ms. DeLaurio, I remind you, you are under oath. Are you telling me you haven't accepted donations from Chinese nationals on behalf of the People's Liberation Army?"

Rebecca blanched, but responded again, less convincingly. "Absolutely not."

"I object to these absurd questions." Senator Mitsunaga shouted. Senator Bankhead leaned over to him, covered his microphone, and urged him to keep quiet.

"What are you talking about, Tom? You can't be serious." Mitsunaga whispered. "This is Parker and his goons. You've got to stop this."

"Ken, I'm telling you again, let the chairman continue."

"But Tom."

"Ken, he's got it on tape." Bankhead's voice cracked on the last word, and he looked over at his friend with moisture lingering in the corner of his eyes. "Ken, I'm sorry. This all came out last night, and they have us. If I told you in advance, and Rebecca had disappeared, they would've crucified the whole party. I couldn't let that happen."

"Tom, what are you saying? You can't be serious." Senator Mitsunaga's voice wavered just once. "I've known you for thirty years. Are you saying I'm taking money from the Chinese?"

"Ms. DeLaurio," the chairman continued, "I will hold you in

contempt of Congress if you fail to answer this question truthfully. But before I ask you again, I'm going to request that the clerk replay a conversation which I believe you had with a Mr. John Wan of Los Angeles on August fifth of this year."

Missie played the tape to a stunned audience, no one more stunned than Ms. Rebecca DeLaurio. She broke down. Senator Mitsunaga watched, shocked, as she tearfully admitted she had, in fact, received funding from John Wan and was fully aware the PLA was involved.

It was Senator Parker who asked point-blank if Senator Mitsunaga was aware of the source of the funds. Rebecca hesitated then denied the accusation. She testified the money was deposited directly into the senator's campaign fund and that his staff hadn't been aware.

Parker continued. "Ms. DeLaurio, do you really expect this committee is going to believe the senator from Hawaii had no idea these funds were coming from the PLA? What kind of fools do you think we are?"

Rebecca opened her mouth to speak, but Senator Parker continued with a glare. "Ms. DeLaurio, isn't it true that when you worked for Senator Mitsunaga, you traveled alone with him on seventy-one occasions? Isn't it true you were his closest advisor and—" he paused to hold up his fingers to make quotation mark signs "—'confidant'? Isn't it true that Senator Mitsunaga introduced you to the Asian-American PAC and its donors? And, as you have already testified, the staff was unaware of the scheme. But the staff doesn't include the senator. Isn't that right?"

Rebecca's face had turned ashen, and the trembling in her hands was visible to Senator Mitsunaga as he leaned forward in horror.

"Again, Ms. DeLaurio," said Senator Parker. "I remind you that you are under oath. Why won't you admit the truth? Senator Mitsunaga is a crook, and you're no better."

Senator Mitsunaga leaped from his seat; he could stand this no longer. His voice rose to a near scream. "Untrue! Falsehoods! Lies! Senator Parker, we've had our disagreements in the past, but you go too far, sir! I'll have no further part in these idiotic proceedings." He stormed out of the room with a dumbfounded Harry trailing him.

After the hearing, Senator Parker rushed to the Senate floor to speak on the subject, declaring Senator Mitsunaga should be impeached. He argued that if Mitsunaga had been caught, there were probably other senators involved as well. Parker demanded a full investigation into the fundraising activities of the Asian-American PAC, and he threatened to hold up all appropriations matters until the leadership would capitulate to his demands.

CHAPTER XXX

US Capitol

Reporter Harris Ward wandered back to the press gallery in a state of disbelief. He'd watched hundreds of senators up close. He'd seen them rise and fall. Watched some who went from quiet, respectful freshmen to bombastic, callous experts-on-everything in a few short years. A couple were crooked when they got to the institution. A few were corrupted by the power and opportunities available. But never would he have expected Ken Mitsunaga to be among the crooks.

Mitsunaga was a Vietnam War hero, but that was just a small part of his impeccable credentials. He'd gained a reputation as a guardian against corruption when, as a junior congressman, he uncovered the attempts of organized crime to turn Hawaii into the western version of Cuba in the late 1970s. His efforts reportedly put six mid-level Mafioso behind bars, which convinced the Nevada mob that the aloha atmosphere wasn't all that welcoming. They'd have to look for another tropical location to replace pre-Castro's Havana.

Mitsunaga had surfed the Watergate wave to election to the House on a foundation built on his ties to the military and the unions. That election and the Mafia scandal paved his way to the Senate to finish the term of Senator Richardson, whose plane was lost over the Pacific. He wasn't seriously challenged in that first bid for the Senate. His five subsequent races were more coronations than campaigns.

In the Senate, he held a reputation for fairness and a willingness to cross party lines. But he remained a fiercely loyal Democrat when his party called on him. Serving on Indian Affairs, Energy, and Appropriations, he advocated justice for the downtrodden, pushed renewable energy efforts, and above all, jealously defended the rights of small states, particularly Hawaii.

Harris had watched him through the years. Sure, there were stories of dalliances with female staff, but that wasn't unusual in the Senate. Harris had lived through the Packwood and Adams scandals and knew of countless others, all the way back to Wayne Hays. Rumors of affairs circulated about most senators. Many were accurate, but just as many were the work of political opponents eager to expose potential vulnerabilities.

When the earmarking scandal broke that brought down Nottingham, some reporters tried to tie Mitsunaga to it, but with no success. Mitsunaga's efforts to guide funds to his constituents and the causes he championed, while legendary, never appeared to be for personal gain.

What gnawed at Harris was why would a distinguished veteran and apparently clean politician with a 75 percent approval rating in his state think he needed to take funding from the Chinese military?

Before writing his story on the hearing, Harris searched the internet to refresh his memory and uncover clues from Mitsunaga's background. He wanted something that might provide some rationale for his treason. Instead, all he found were tributes.

The first article he pulled up was a piece highlighting his

military and early political career that had run in the *Hawaii Tribune* three weeks earlier. In part it read:

> Ken Mitsunaga enlisted in the army after graduating from high school in 1963 at the age of eighteen. He was inspired by President Kennedy's visit to Fort Bragg in 1961 where the youthful president and World War II veteran highlighted the heroism and unique mission of the Army's Special Forces, dubbed the Green Berets. Ken made up his mind right then and there to join the army and wear the green beret. He applied to Special Forces and was accepted for airborne training. In September 1964, Private First Class Mitsunaga was sent to Vietnam to serve with the Army's Special Forces.
>
> The Special Forces units in Vietnam fought fiercely, often behind enemy lines. They were among the most decorated units in US military history. In May of 1965, Corporal Mitsunaga became part of that legacy. Ken's platoon found itself nearly surrounded by Viet Cong guerillas on the Cambodian border. The unit fought the enemy for nearly three hours, taking heavy casualties. Reinforcements were on their way, but it was feared they'd arrive too late. In a last-ditch effort, the navy deployed two A-4C light attack aircraft to blow open a corridor for the trapped Green

Berets and root out the Viet Cong. Within minutes, the Navy A-4 Skyhawks, loaded with napalm bombs, came screaming onto the scene, diving low and releasing their bombs.

The attack cleared a path to the trapped unit, but one bomb was released a few seconds too late and exploded adjacent to the trapped Green Berets. Three soldiers died immediately, and several others were seriously injured. Corporal Mitsunaga was hit below the waist by the burning jelly. It tore through his uniform and into the flesh. He rolled on the ground to put out the fire. Using his rain poncho, he wiped the remaining jelly from his body to minimize the burns, but the damage was done. The pain was excruciating. He could stand up using his M-16 as a crutch, but his left leg was nearly useless. Second Lieutenant Tom McNeil, the platoon leader, had burns across his torso and face. He'd lost consciousness but was still alive.

With his right arm, Ken grabbed McNeil by the back of his t-shirt and dragged him forward; his left arm held his makeshift M-16 crutch. Together they began the slow journey through the napalm-burned vegetation back to the US forces.

Ken was awarded the Silver Star for his heroism. The damage to his lower body was described by the army doctors in Japan as "some of the worst they'd ever seen." He spent eight months in hospitals in Tokyo and Honolulu and had fifteen operations. Ken saved Lieutenant McNeil's life that day, although both of their military careers were over.

After he got out of the army, Ken studied political science at the University of Hawaii, determined to warn others about the horror of war. His love of the military hadn't waned, but his support for the war in Vietnam had. Upon graduation, he worked briefly for the city of Honolulu in the office of records, but soon grew bored of the tedium. By 1970, he knew his true calling was politics. He ran successfully for the Hawaii House of Representatives, followed by a run for Congress in 1972. His whirlwind campaign focused on three principles: ending the war in Vietnam, cleaning up corruption in politics, and fighting for the common man. Despite being heavily outspent by his opponent, he sailed to victory and flew to Washington, DC. He served two terms in the House and won election to the Senate in 1976. He was granted a seat on the Appropriations Committee and its defense subcommittee in 1980. There he gained seniority and stature in the Senate.

"Brave fellow. Nothing damning in that," Harris muttered,

shaking his head.

Continuing his search, Harris found another Hawaiian newspaper article from February 1975. It touted the young congressman for his efforts to root out corruption in the Hawaiian islands. As a junior member, Mitsunaga had convinced the House Judiciary Committee's chairman to hold a hearing of the Organized Crime subcommittee in Honolulu. Harris laughed. It probably hadn't been too tough to convince Chairman Dixon of North Dakota to hold a hearing in Honolulu in February. As the newspaper reported,

> Using his "local boy" connections, Ken Mitsunaga coerced leaders of the local chapter of the Longshoremen's Union to testify that members of Las Vegas's Gambona crime family were attempting to bring the Mafia to Hawaii through legalized gambling, drug trafficking, and prostitution. The testimony from union leaders before the subcommittee was instrumental in leading the state legislature to reject efforts to legalize casino gambling in the state, despite heavy lobbying from mainland interests. Ken Mitsunaga is credited with the conviction of several Mafioso officials who attempted to bribe members of the state legislature.

Harris also found several local newspaper editorials recommending Ken Mitsunaga first for the House of Representatives as a respected war hero and later, in his bid for the Senate, adding his efforts to clean up corruption. In article after article, Harris found nothing that hinted at impropriety or corruption.

The only conclusion he could draw was that pillow talk trumped good sense. He wouldn't have believed it if he hadn't heard the tape and seen DeLaurio break down. She'd admitted that she knew what she was doing. And she hadn't been at all convincing in her avowals that Mitsunaga wasn't aware of the scheme. Harris pulled out his work-worn laptop and began to compose.

> Today the Senate once again relearned that power corrupts, that our heroes are mortals. They are not immune to temptation. We in the media share the blame. We find ourselves drawn to the exemplary individual. We lavish praise on the good ones, those who demonstrate a keen intellect or unbridled decency. We build them up, place them on pedestals, and curry their favor. We laugh too heartily at their jokes and marvel at their everyday accomplishments.
>
> We treat them like demi-gods, like a modern-day Hercules who can do no wrong. As if they truly were the sons and daughters of Zeus descending from Mount Olympus. But, in fact, they are no different from ourselves. As we hear the details of another fallen politician and watch yet another tower crumble, we can't help but agonize over our own sense of loss. Add another layer to our scar tissue of skepticism.

The facts that he included were no different from a dozen other stories. Unnamed senators spoke with apparent certainty of the longtime affair between DeLaurio and Mitsunaga. None defended him. No one questioned his guilt. The Parker supporters sought to tie the scandal to the Democratic Senate campaign and the Democratic National Committee, with little success, but with religious fervor. He concluded the story noting that his repeated attempts to contact both Mitsunaga and Rebecca had been unsuccessful.

It was the best he could do.

CHAPTER XXXI

The Senate majority and minority leaders held a series of meetings over the next two days on how to proceed. The minority leader was adamant: they wouldn't be steamrolled into impeaching their colleague. This was a matter for the Ethics Committee to examine over the next several months. Nothing could be done before the election.

The majority leader understood. But with Parker and others up in arms, he had little choice but to call for an immediate Ethics Committee investigation. He recommended that it be wrapped up in four weeks—leaving enough time to take action before adjournment.

Senator Parker was exuberant. He called for campaign finance reform. He excoriated Senator Mitsunaga in daily diatribes on the floor. He questioned other donations the senator had received and linked programs supported by the Senator to tainted campaign contributions. Senator Parker offered a series of amendments to appropriations bills eliminating any funding identified by his staff as sponsored by Senator Mitsunaga or linked to Hawaii.

Senator Jackson tried to stop Parker from stripping out the funding, but he didn't have much support. He even tried to convince his Republican colleagues that this money would support a new Republican member if Mitsunaga lost the election. Nothing worked. It angered him to see his old friend vilified, but he couldn't see any way to help.

Senator Mitsunaga was too busy responding to inquiries from the FBI and the Ethics Committee to counterattack. He said he was determined to fight the charges. But as each day passed, and after each nearly unanimous vote went against him, he seemed to shrink a little more into himself.

On September fourteenth, eight days after the DeLaurio hearing, the body of Mitsunaga's chief of staff, Harry Alaka'i Quinn, was found floating in the Potomac River. At his home, the police found a hand-written note, in which he condemned himself as a failure. He'd failed to protect Senator Ken from corrupt influences. He'd failed to keep sufficient oversight of the campaign books. He'd failed even in any attempt to take the fall for the senator, doomed by Rebecca's testimony. In essence, he'd failed in the only task he had: protecting the man who meant everything to him.

CHAPTER XXXII

Thursday, October 19th

Paula fought hard to pick up the pieces after the hearing. There were still appropriation conferences to track for Senator Mitsunaga—even if he showed little interest in them. She received word from the campaign staff that Keahole had caught up to Mitsunaga in the polls and was cresting in popularity.

The senator went to Hawaii every other weekend and continued to deny all the charges. She still believed in him and wanted to believe that this was all some big misunderstanding. He blamed the Republicans and racism, and for a few days, it looked like he might be able to turn things around. But on every nightly newscast, excerpts from the hearing were replayed. Comments from Senator Parker were highlighted. Parker, the media-depicted dedicated reformer, was doing more to damage Senator Mitsunaga's popularity than his actual opponent.

Paula decided to visit Hawaii. She wanted to gauge the mood of the electorate and assuage those who depended on federal funds protected by the senator. Neither he nor she had forgotten them. They would continue to work to keep their programs alive. She made the arrangements with John Silease, who seemed happy to do anything he could for her, repeatedly expressing his sorrow that her boss, a man for whom he had great respect, was in such trouble.

First stop: Oahu, and dinner with her friend and soon-to-be private citizen, General Al Gianini. They met at Jack's Fish Market near her hotel on Waikiki. Dinner was subdued. Neither wanted to talk about what was really on their minds—the senator's predicament.

At last, the general broke what had grown to be a rather uncomfortable silence. "Paula, you know, I hesitate to tell you this. Last summer we saw a classified fax from the folks at NSA. Looks like it was part of this Chinese campaign funding mess the senator's involved in."

"What are you talking about?"

"We intercepted a message asking the Chinese to send more money to someone, perhaps that agent in Los Angeles. It kind of sounded like a college kid asking for money. But it was encrypted and went to a PLA regional headquarters. So we were suspicious. Now, unfortunately, it looks very much like it was the real thing."

Paula tried to suppress her crestfallen expression. There went her last hope that this was all just a big misunderstanding. The NSA had classified communication verifying PLA involvement? It was the smoking gun Parker needed. She couldn't help but still support Mitsunaga, but his contention that it was all a racist obsession was fallacious. As hard as it was to believe, Senator Parker was right. The Chinese were involved in US elections.

The following morning, Paula flew to Maui. The situation there was looking desperate. Senator Parker had stripped out funding for research at the Maui Space Surveillance Site. The telescope would still be maintained for at least a year, but any new scientific research would be put on life support. Senator Parker had also successfully terminated three programs that were on-going at the Maui supercomputer: support for the marine warfighting lab at Quantico, enhancing CINCPAC's information technology, and new sensor netting software development for the navy. At least most of the supercomputer's funding was in the president's request, so it would survive another year.

At the Pacific Disaster Center, a worried Johnny Taylor greeted her with a frown. "Paula, what are we going to do? The Senate stripped out all our money."

"I know." Paula shook her head. "I'm truly sorry, but there's nothing I can do. Aren't you still sitting on $8 million from this year? Won't that cover you for next year?"

"Yes, but we were going to use that money to expand our capabilities to track and evaluate tsunamis and earthquakes on the Northwest coast. Isn't there any way you can get us funds for that?" Johnny's expression had moved from worried to stricken.

"Not this year. If the senator survives this crisis, I'm sure he'll get you funding next year. If not, Johnny, I'm not sure what I can tell you. I'll talk to Jackson's people about getting money for your northwest initiative next year. But I don't even know how we'll get support for your basic budget without the senator."

Johnny opened his mouth to speak, but Paula plunged ahead. "Look at it this way, if the senator survives, you're going to be OK. If he doesn't, you've got one year to find a sponsor, maybe someone else in the delegation, or maybe CINCPAC. At least you have a year. A lot of other people in the state don't even have that."

"I guess you're right," Johnny said. "But it just kills me. We're making so much progress, and the Koreans and Japanese are interested in buying our products. We're only a couple years away from making this a self-financing activity. Without your support, we won't get over that hurdle."

Paula's sigh came out almost like a groan. "I know. I'm so sorry." She searched for something more to say, something the senator could do.

At each stop, someone new expressed these same fears. The jobs of hundreds of college-educated, Hawaii-bred engineers, who were doing great research for DoD, were hanging by a thread. Programs for native Hawaiian education and health care and alternative energy were dead. Everything that the senator had done to move Hawaii beyond its plantation and hotel service economy was in jeopardy.

No wonder that those who depended on the senator's influence for their survival felt betrayed. *How could he have done this? How could he have jeopardized all that we've worked on together?*

Yet, no one came to Mitsunaga's defense. Harry was gone. No one else rushed to his side. Paula tried to put up a brave front, but her face told the real story. She no longer believed him either.

CHAPTER XXXIII

The election went as predicted, though it took until 1 a.m. to get the results in Washington because of the time difference. For weeks the outcome had been preordained. The Republicans plowed money into Keahole's campaign up to the last day. They ran ads showing DeLaurio's testimony. A recording of Senator Mitsunaga shaking the hand of John Wan, now identified as Xian Huan Nod and suspected of being a Chinese agent, plastered TV screens.

Mitsunaga had gone home to campaign for the entire month of October after the Senate adjourned. But his heart wasn't in it. Perhaps it was the betrayal by DeLaurio. Perhaps it was the loss of Harry, his best friend and most trusted staffer. Paula wasn't sure. All she knew for sure was the senator had stopped calling, and she hadn't made much effort to reach out to him.

Through the end of October, the scandal played out in the press. The *Washington Herald* filed a freedom of information request for the records of Mitsunaga's contact with Ms. DeLaurio during her tenure on the Indian Affairs Committee. The seven-part series recounted the trips they'd taken together, the private meetings they'd held. Unnamed sources in the Senate whispered about the senator's relationship with Rebecca. The *Honolulu Tribune* ran the story word for word. By Election Day, it had become an accepted fact that the two shared an intimate relationship. Still, Mitsunaga refused to answer questions about his personal relationship with Rebecca. He insisted, as a matter of principle, he wouldn't allow anyone to delve into his private life.

On the question of Chinese money laundering, however, the senator continued to vehemently protest his innocence, claiming he wasn't aware of the PLA donations. He defied all those who accused him to prove any complicity on his part.

Some of his most ardent supporters wanted him to implicate Harry. They urged him to speculate that Harry killed himself because he was responsible—that Harry kept the truth from him. In a final demonstration of honor, Senator Mitsunaga refused to besmirch the memory of his friend. The voters of Hawaii felt betrayed. They could accept a scandal from their elected leaders. They were sophisticated enough to understand all people are mortal. All heroes have flaws. The "Indian affair," as it was labeled by the Washington media, received a lot of attention in the state. That alone probably wouldn't have cost him the election. What the voters couldn't accept was that the "Chinese laundry" had reinforced an unfair misconception. Asians and Pacific Islanders couldn't be trusted. It didn't matter whether Japanese, Chinese, Filipino, or Hawaiian, the exit polls in Hawaii showed clearly the overwhelming sentiment on Election Day was the bitterness of his betrayal.

The Justice Department indicted Rebecca DeLaurio for illegal campaign activities, fraud, and espionage. Her lawyers, however, were able to get the charges dropped. They convinced the

Justice Department there was no case. The taped recording was inadmissible. Her testimony was given under duress, clearly the result of badgering. The charges would never stand up in court.

Before the scandal, Rebecca had contracts with three tribes and two Native American related companies. Together they paid her almost five hundred thousand dollars per year. Within a week, the three tribes severed relations. They claimed her felonious behavior, even if unproven in court, was a breach of contract. The two companies chose not to extend her contracts.

Rebecca knew she was done in Washington. Her fundraising gambit had ended in disaster. Her reputation was ruined. Torn between feeling betrayal and regret, Rebecca knew one thing for sure—her schemes had nearly cost her freedom. Time to escape before anyone started asking more questions.

The Justice Department examined the campaign records from the senator's office. With Harry's death, the records were in shambles, and they couldn't find concrete evidence of Chinese contributions. The Justice Department considered charging Mitsunaga, but decided to await the election results. They agreed to not press charges if he was defeated. The evidence was deemed insufficient to attain a conviction.

The Senate seemed a bit more somber leading up to the election. Senator Mitsunaga had always enjoyed one of the finest reputations in the body. This most august club knew only too well the damage that scandal can bring to an institution, and through it to its members. No one in politics is without some scar. For some, it was overstating a résumé on their first run for office, or an illicit affair. For others, it was dirty tricks against campaign opponents or the shady dealings of campaign contributors, who never broke the law, but skirted the edge.

Politics is not an innocent game—the higher the office, the greater the stakes and the dirtier the game. There are no virgins in the Capitol. Most politicians justify the questionable actions of rough-and-tumble politics as a necessary means to an end of serving their constituents. The other guy is going to play dirty, and they'll be outmaneuvered if they don't do the same. In politics, nice guys finish second.

Ken Mitsunaga, war hero, anti-corruption crusader, and friend of the common man, suffered a crushing defeat. Anton Keahole received 69 percent of the vote.

At 2:05 a.m. Washington time, Senator Mitsunaga appeared on all the major networks to concede the election. "My friends here tonight, thank you for your continued trust and belief in me. I am deeply indebted to you, and I shall never forget you. To all my fellow citizens of Hawaii, particularly those who voted against me tonight, I want to say, 'I'm sorry.' I apologize to you—not for any wrongdoing on my part, but for the mistakes, the situations I was unaware of, which caused you to lose faith in me. Senator-elect Keahole, I congratulate you, sir. I wish you much success in representing our state and its great people.

"Over the next several months, I'll continue defending my reputation. I'm not a young man. My day in politics has come to an end. But, mark my words. I will regain my good name. I will uncover this plot and its originator whose motives are still unknown. This is vigilante politics, my friends, and I will not rest until I have found those responsible for this travesty. They've stolen my good name. Eventually, that I will recover. What none of us can ever recover—and I can never forgive—is that they caused my dearest friend and most loyal aide, the mighty Harry Alaka'i Quinn, to end his life. It's for Harry's spirit that I'll fight on. My fellow Hawaiians, I shall never forget the trust you placed in me for more than forty years. For now, let me just say, 'mahalo and aloha.'"

Tears and applause greeted the senator's speech. The news anchors in New York and Washington, and pundits across the country, expressed surprise at the vehemence and passion of his words. Yet an unstated sadness permeated the mood as the country watched their former hero reach such an ignominious end to his political life.

CHAPTER XXXIV

Wednesday, November 8th

Georgetown

Paula was rudely awakened by the phone on Wednesday morning after less than five hours of fitful sleep.

The night before, she'd just had to wait up for the returns from Hawaii, hoping somehow he'd pull it out. She knew she should just go to bed—it would take a miracle for him to win. Finally, she cried herself to sleep wondering what would happen to her now.

At the sound of the phone, a groggy Paula was immediately alert.

"Paula, it's Chauncey. I just had to call and tell you how sorry we all are. Are you awake?"

"Chauncey, it's two in the morning in Hawaii. What are you doing up?"

"I couldn't sleep. I know you might think I'm a creep, and I apologize for not calling you before. Tonight, as I lay awake, I knew I could never forgive myself if I didn't call and find out how you were."

"Oh Chauncey, that's sweet. I'm fine. I'm sad, and yes, I guess a little heartbroken at what happened, but I'll be OK. Did you see the senator's speech? He sounds like he's still in denial."

"Maybe it's his pretrial strategy."

"I dunno. He sounded pretty sincere."

"Paula, what are you going to do now? Will you be fired?"

"I'm not sure, Chauncey. Technically, I work for Senator Lackland. He's the one who hires and fires the Democratic staff. But Patterson will take over the subcommittee, and he's got his own guy, so I expect I'll be dismissed. It's not really 'fired.' In the Senate they abolish your job if your boss loses. It's kind of like being laid off. I don't know what I'll do. I know I can find a job, but I won't be a lobbyist. After this mess, the thought sickens me."

"Will you go back home? Will your family help you out?"

"Washington's my home now. I grew up in southwest Virginia with my dad, but he died sixteen years ago, right before I started college. I don't have any other family. In fact, that's how I got to the Appropriations Committee. I had a scholarship to Georgetown, but when he died, I didn't have money for room and board. So I had to get a job to stay in school. I blanketed the Hill with résumés. It was just dumb luck that I landed on the committee as a staff assistant, a receptionist really. But that's how it happened. The boss took me under his wing and taught me about budgets and politics. He promoted me to professional staff, and when he retired, Senator Mitsunaga chose me to take over. The committee's been my family for fifteen years. Now that's over, and I have to figure out what's next."

"Have you thought about coming to Hawaii? We'd all love to have you here."

Paula's mouth fell open. She hadn't considered relocating to Hawaii. She hadn't considered any alternatives really. Now, after a mostly sleepless night, out of the blue comes a call from a nice guy that she slept with once, asking her to move to Hawaii.

"Chauncey," her voice had taken on a quizzical tone, "why're you doing this? You feeling guilty or something? Because if you are, you don't have to. I'm fine. I'm a big girl. I'll be OK. Chauncey, what's going on?"

After a brief silence, Chauncey stammered, "Oh . . . I uh . . . I don't know. I just, well, I don't know. We're all just worried about you."

"Chauncey," she said, softening as she sensed his vulnerability, "that's really sweet of you." She sighed. "I don't know what I'm going to do. I don't think I should be making any decisions right now, but I'm touched by your call. Now get some sleep. I don't want you so tired you end up screwing up the adaptive optics package testing tomorrow, or today I guess. Hey, and Chauncey, really, thanks."

"OK, Paula, but I meant what I said about coming to Maui."

"Thanks, Chauncey. But you know, with the senator gone, I don't know how much longer the air force will be operating the telescope. You might be needing a job more than I do."

"C'mon Paula, you know AEOS is the newest and biggest and best telescope in the air force. They'd never shut it down."

"I hope you're right, but you know Mitsunaga's been providing about 75 percent of the funds to keep it going. And, if it doesn't fly like an F-35 or even a C-17, you know it's not a priority for your service. Anyway, like I said, get some sleep, Chauncey. Good night." Paula hung up the phone.

Oh, Chauncey. My heavens. She thought back to that night on Maui, remembering his touch. She rolled over and decided to go back to sleep. *No one's going to need me at work this morning, that's for sure.*

Chauncey couldn't follow Paula's advice. He tossed and turned, wondering whether he'd done the right thing by calling her. It wasn't that he was surprised by her reaction, though he'd hoped for something more positive. As he replayed the conversation in his mind, he wished he'd been less obvious. He wondered if she thought him a fool—better that than a jerk, but still not good.

His only solace was the warmth in her voice as she told him how sweet he was and when she said "good night." There was something there, something different. As he lay there awake, his mind kept wandering from the present back to that night some three months ago. He longed for her again.

CHAPTER XXXV

Honolulu, Oahu

Ken Mitsunaga awakened early but didn't get out of bed. His wife, Rosie, got up around seven and made coffee. At eight she peeked in on him, but he lay motionless, pretending to be asleep. At nine she came in again and gently touched his shoulder. "Ken, are you OK? It's nine o'clock."

He nodded but didn't speak.

"You know, honey, lying in bed isn't going to make you feel better. It's a beautiful morning. The coffee's ready." She paused for a second, looking at him. "You need to get up. Ken?"

He sighed heavily and nodded again. "I know. It's just . . . I'm not ready yet."

The phone rang, and Rosie answered. "Ken, it's Sam Jackson."

He sat up, cleared his throat, and took the phone. "Hello."

"Ken? Sam. I wanted to tell you how sorry I am. But you know, you're lucky to be getting out. This place has gone to hell. It's not like when we started. Our old friends would hardly recognize it. At least you won't have to beg for money ever again. Hell, I'm not sure I wouldn't trade places with you now that I think about it."

"It's good of you to call. You didn't have to do that."

"Well, of course I did. You're my friend, and you always will be. Listen if there's anything I can do for you, just say the word. You OK? I mean, uh . . . financially."

"Oh, we're OK. Rosie's saved a lot over the years. We'll be fine. It'll take a little time to get used to, but we were pretty sure it was going to turn out this way, so it isn't a shock."

"Well, I meant what I said. You need anything, just ask."

"Thanks. Maybe you could do me one favor and take care of my successor. Teach him the ropes. He's not a bad fellow, and he's a Republican like you. Hawaii needs him to be successful. Parker's killed a lot of good programs for my state. Keahole will have a tough time getting much done without your help."

"I hear you, my friend. I'll do what I can, but it's going to be tough for all of us. Parker's got a majority of my colleagues supporting a ban on earmarks. We're all going to be losing valuable projects."

"Oh, that's a shame. He can't actually think Washington bureaucrats know more than we do about what our constituents need."

"Who says he thinks? You know that jackass only cares about one thing, and that thing's James Parker. It's been that way ever since he got here. Now it's all about how James Parker can be the next president."

"Heaven help us. There's one more thing if you don't mind. I'm worried about my staff. A lot of them have families, and you know we don't pay most of them much. Keahole won't be hiring them because they're mostly Democrats. They can't get by on just unemployment. Could you ask your staff to keep an open mind about recommending some of them if they hear of any openings?"

"Well, I'm not sure how much help I can be, but I'll do what I can. So what's next for you?"

"For me? I don't know. I guess I'll tend to my garden, catch up on my reading. Be a better husband. Stay out of the limelight. My people are angry. They think I betrayed them. For now, the garden is the best place for me."

"Ken, no matter what they say, you were always a great husband. I'm sure Rosie feels that way. Take care of her, and take care of yourself. And, I mean it. If I can do anything else for you, let me know. Well, I got a plane to catch. Those damn fools want us back in DC tomorrow. Jesus Christ, what a mess. We'll talk soon."

Ken hung up the phone, his eyes alight with fresh hope. Rosie gave him a questioning look. Ken smiled up at her. "Sam Jackson's a good friend; he doesn't put party ahead of friendship. Who else would do that? Calling and offering to help a member of the other party."

Rosie clasped his hand for a moment, then left to pour a cup of coffee for him. Ken watched her fondly. *Maybe I'm ready to get out of bed. It's going to be OK. Different, but like he said, I don't have to beg anymore.*

CHAPTER XXXVI

Friday, December 1st

White House

Larry Smith threw the folder down on his desk. "Damn it, Jack. I said bury this."

"Sir, I know, but it's not that easy now. Senator Parker is making a federal case out of this, literally. If it appears you're trying to hide this, he'll come down on you with a Senate investigation. You know better than anyone that you're into the AAPAC guys to the tune of five hundred thousand dollars. You've got to be real careful about this."

"Jack, there's nothing that says we took a nickel from the Chinese. Did we take contributions from this Johnny Wan character? No. Not a nickel from him. All our money came from American citizens."

"Sir, all your money came from AAPAC. In the minds of many American voters, rightly or wrongly, that means you took money from the Chinese. Larry, all I am saying is you have to be careful. Time will lessen the impact of this thing. This was the midterm election's scandal. The Republicans might be able to ride this up to the presidential nomination. But it won't decide the election unless you look like you're covering something up. That'd kill us."

"Maybe you're right, Jack, but who would've thought he could kill off Mitsunaga. That guy was a legend."

"Yeah, well, the legend got his hand and pecker caught in the cookie jar, and that was one appendage too many. He might've talked his way out of the Indian Affair, as they say, or the Chinese laundry, but not both. That'd be too much for even Christ to overcome."

"OK, Jack, we'll play this your way. But we'll need something big if this thing doesn't die down. What else you got?"

CHAPTER XXXVII

Honolulu, Oahu

Right in the heart of Waikiki stands the army's Fort DeRussy—the only open, green space on Hawaii's most famous shoreline. At one time, large cannons sat atop this small outpost to guard the American colony against dangers all around in the middle of the Pacific. Now, the old fort has become a museum. Next to the museum stands the twin towers of the Hale Koa Hotel. They look like all the other high-rise hotels that line the coast along Waikiki Beach. But the Hale Koa is a military facility. It is both a wonderful spot for military families to visit and a great money-maker for the army's Morale, Welfare and Recreation fund. Its profits support recreation activities throughout the army.

As might be expected, some local businesses have resented the army owning such prime real estate on Hawaii's gold coast. But most now recognized the army was the only reason why 75 percent of the property remains open space. The locals enjoy picnicking on the lawns and relaxing on the white beaches adjacent to Fort DeRussy almost as much as the lucky military members who happen to vacation there.

Away from the beach, partially hidden behind a large parking garage, a small two-story building houses the Asia Pacific Center for Security Studies—a small training school run by DoD.

It was established to teach foreign military and political leaders about democracy and civil military relationships. The goal was three-fold. First, bring upcoming leaders to the United States and expose them to the viewpoints of other Asian leaders in an academic environment, free of the daily pressures and frequently hostile views of their own governments. Second, teach the next generation of Asian leaders how the US military supports democracy, instilling in them the concept of civilian control over the military in hopes it might lead to self-restraint by these future leaders. And finally, establish personal relationships and generate goodwill so that one day US leaders might call upon former students for assistance and be welcomed by leaders with fond memories of their experience in the States.

These objectives could be achieved in no better location than Hawaii, with its friendly people and aloha spirit. And the natural choice to lead the center? Retired Lieutenant General Al Gianini, a leader whose military rank guaranteed respect and whose knowledge of the region gave him insight into the students and their cultures.

The APCSS director reported directly to the CINC. Al could keep his same boss in a job that didn't require the hours or the headaches of his last assignment. His office didn't have the same view, but who could complain about Waikiki Beach? Midge wasn't thrilled they weren't moving back to the mainland. But she knew this was a much easier career transition for him. She knew, as well, the grandchildren would be happy to visit Hawaii anytime.

Al began his day with a video teleconference staff meeting with Camp Smith. Then he'd visit several seminars. Sometimes he'd comment about the subject matter. Just as often, he'd simply listen to the exchange among the students. He shared lunch in the dining commons with the students, and he hosted guest lectures in the afternoon. It was quite a change of pace, but he soon fell into the routine. He took particular pride in bringing cultures, religions, and political philosophies together—the Indians with the Pakistanis, Cambodians with Vietnamese, and even a couple of times mainland Chinese with Taiwanese.

None of the sponsoring governments would have welcomed the discovery that enemy nations were establishing such relationships. That part of the school curriculum was generally not reported back to the capitals.

It was a good spot for Al. He was still serving the public and still had his hands in international relations. He could speak proudly of the military service he loved and yet relax in a way that had been impossible for many years. The greatest stress he faced was making sure the student discussions didn't end with fistfights. With Al Gianini at the helm, there was no dispute which couldn't be settled amicably.

CHAPTER XXXVIII

Tuesday, January 2nd

Washington, DC

Winter hit the capital hard. For nearly two months, frigid temperatures kept Washington in a state of semi-hibernation. The election results actually brought pretty good news for the Democrats. Senator Mitsunaga lost, but he was the exception. The Republicans had been unable to turn the two scandals into widespread upheaval. The only winner in the process seemed to be James Parker. Already the darling of the media, he now portrayed himself as the hero who saved America from the Chinese.

The first day back to work after the Christmas and New Year's holidays, Paula was called to the office of Pat Sistrunk, the committee's Democratic staff director. It came as no surprise. Pat said it all very kindly. He informed her Senator Lackland was going to make a change. He'd done everything he could, but Senator Patterson had his own guy. The chairman, Senator Jackson, would be abolishing her position. She'd need to be moving on. Pat promised to help any way he could. Paula appreciated the gesture but knew her contacts as a defense expert were a lot better than his. With the Senate restarting in earnest on January twentieth, she'd have to leave by the fifteenth but could stay on the payroll until March first.

Paula thanked him for his support and courtesy over the years. Pat expressed his condolences over Senator Mitsunaga's defeat. Like everyone else, he expressed how shocked he had been to discover the senator was taking bribes from the Chinese. Paula bit her tongue. She didn't defend the senator, but he hadn't been tried or convicted except by Parker, the media, and those who really matter to politicians, his constituents.

She kept her composure through the meeting but burst into tears as she walked out of the office. It was 15 degrees outside. She had no coat but walked outside from the Capitol back to her Dirksen office to ensure no one saw her cry.

A phone message from John Silease immediately greeted her return. *Jeez, this news spread fast. Senator Lackland hasn't even signed the letter requesting the chairman to fire me yet.*

As tempted as she was not to call right away, she knew she had to. It wasn't a good time to not return anybody's phone call, particularly not one from the committee staff director.

"John, this is Paula, what's up?" She could predict the coming obligatory apologies and offers of assistance. Maybe there'd be condolences over the boss's demise.

She was completely unprepared for what he said instead.

CHAPTER XXXIX

White House

"Jack, it's Larry. I need to see you ASAP."

Jack Ralston grabbed his coat and headed for the vice president's cubbyhole office in the West Wing.

"Madeline, he called. Says it's urgent," Jack called out as he hustled into the boss's office. He knocked on the door and entered without waiting. "Hey, boss, what's up?"

"Jack, we've got to do something. I just got the latest polling data. Parker's numbers are unbelievable. Right now, 81 percent of the American public has a favorable opinion of him—81 percent! I'm at 49! His numbers are the highest ever recorded since they started asking this question back in the '70s. We've got to do something to stop this, or he'll coast to the presidency next year."

"Sir, he hasn't even declared his candidacy. We can't be sure he's going to run."

"Oh, he's running, Jack. He's running hard. This whole Mitsunaga thing wasn't an accident. I heard from Charley Johnson it was Parker who got the goods on him. I don't know who he's working with, FBI, CIA or what, but this is clearly a springboard."

The vice president's face was flushed, and Jack spoke slowly, attempting to assuage his concern. "I don't know, sir. As you might have guessed, I've been paying a lot of attention to this. I've talked to both the FBI and DHS. It's hard for them to admit, but they were completely unaware of this mess until right before the hearing. The director told me Parker sent him a copy of the tape the day of the hearing. That was the first he heard about it."

"Well, what about that NSA report we saw? Surely they saw the same thing."

"Sir, I'm sure they saw it, but I think it went under the category of uncorroborated evidence. In the intel business, almost nothing gets into finished reports unless it can be verified by more than one source. Sure, that limits the possibility of catching every clue. But it's the best way to make sure a crazy, unsubstantiated report doesn't trigger a dangerous response. We got this because I have a contact at Fort Meade who thought I might want to see it. I'm sure the FBI had it, but I think it's unlikely anyone passed it up the chain."

"Well, damn it, Jack, you've got to get this under control now. I don't want that little prick picking me off for raising money. I follow the law. Just because he doesn't like it, he has no business insinuating we're doing something wrong."

"Yes, sir, I'll do what I can." Jack missed the connection between Mitsunaga's corruption and Larry's fundraising. But it didn't take a genius to see that Parker was planning his campaign on finance reform, tainted elections, and corrupt politicians. Larry wasn't actually tainted, but he sure was aggressive in his fundraising. *He's right. This might be a problem.*

CHAPTER XL

Washington, DC

John had asked Paula to stop by his Capitol office after the rest of the staff and, more importantly, the chairman had gone home. Over the years he'd learned that the most productive time of the day was usually after hours. It was when you finally had a chance to think or write without the phone interrupting. It was also when you had a chance to relax with your colleagues and brainstorm about the issues of the day. Paula and John had spent many evenings together. Frequently those included a couple of beers, a bottle of wine, or glass of scotch.

Paula arrived at 7 p.m. Only Melissa, the junior staff assistant, was still around. Paula walked past her, waving hello, and proceeded back to John's office. She'd already rehearsed her speech. Before John could even say hello, she started. "John, you didn't have to do this. I met with Pat. Senator Patterson has somebody in mind for the defense job, and it isn't me. But you and your boss have always been very fair to me. You and Janie are my friends. I'll be OK. You don't need to worry. There are plenty of

opportunities out there for me. I've had a dozen offers already."
Her voice cracked a couple of times, but she was pulling it off
without tears.

"Listen, John, I'll clean out my desk tomorrow, so you can
begin the office musical chairs—"

John raised a hand of protest. "Well, Paula, I'm not sure we
can accommodate that just yet."

"What?"

"Paula, Chairman Jackson wants you to stay on the committee." Her jaw dropped, and John chuckled. "It's true. The
Democrats don't have a spot for you, but the chairman directed
me to keep you around. Yes, you'll have to move. Your office be-
longs to the minority, and you'll have to move here to the Capitol
instead. We have room in that office," he pointed to his left, "but
it'll take us a couple of weeks to get it arranged. Unless, of course,
you don't want to work for him."

"What are you talking about?" Paula's mind whirred, and her
words tripped over each other. "What would I do? John, you're
Jackson's guy. What does he need me for? You have a great staff
handling defense for you, and you know it all anyway. John, it's
very sweet, but you don't have to do this. I'll be fine."

"So you want me to tell him you don't want to work for him?"
John chuckled.

"Well, no, but John, what would I do?"

"Well, I've been giving it some thought ever since the chairman directed me to hire you this afternoon when I told him
you'd be leaving. First, like all of us, you'd do whatever Senator
Jackson wanted you to do, but seriously, you've got a lot to offer. You've learned the appropriations process well. You know
defense, and the chairman cares deeply about defense. But, just

as importantly, you have a great work ethic. You're very smart and a pleasure to have around. Paula, let me be frank. I wouldn't have thought of hiring you in a million years, but he did. And now that he has, I think it's a fine idea. I don't want you to decide tonight. I want you to think about it for a week. Hell, you can have to January twentieth if you want, but I'm serious. The boss wants you to stay, and I'd love to have you on our team. You know being in the majority isn't all that bad, and on this committee, it's pretty hard to tell which party you work for anyway. Money doesn't know party lines."

Paula and John both chuckled at that.

"So, go home, relax, take a couple days off, and let me know when you've worked through it. Only the three of us know about this, and I'm going to keep it that way."

"But . . . "

"Paula, I know you almost as well as you know yourself. Don't say anything right now. Go home, take a bath, curl up on the couch with Bo and *Aviation Week* or something, and we'll talk later." He flapped his hands toward the door. "Now, go."

Paula was speechless. She turned around and walked out of the office, breaking into tears for the second time that day. At least she had her coat this time as the temperature was dipping into the single digits.

CHAPTER XLI

Shanghai, China

Agent Xian Huan Nod stepped off the plane and breathed a sigh of relief. He'd made it back to China. It had been a circuitous four-month route from LA, quickly across the border to Mexico, and slowly from there to Colombia, Australia, Indonesia, Vietnam, Hong Kong, and now Shanghai. He steered clear of Beijing and the meddling bureaucrats from the Central Committee. Shanghai was almost a western city. Party officials shouldn't be looking for him here. Outside the airport, he hailed a limousine taxi—another sign Shanghai was different from the rest of the People's Republic. He stepped into the cab. The driver looked vaguely familiar, but Xian didn't recognize him until it was too late. He'd reached his final destination.

Yong-Li parked the limo taxi next to the magnetic levitation train station near the airport. He wiped it down, tossed the chauffeur's cap on the front seat, and headed home. *That'll teach anyone else who thinks they can fail the People's Liberation Army. And, it'll keep the Beijing dogs at bay.* From his hotel,

Yong-Li called to confirm his mission was complete. Li Pen was still not amused.

"You think that solves our problem? Beijing is sending auditors here to examine our records. They've put two and two together and don't like the result. I need you back here now to fix this."

Yong-Li urged the general not to worry. He already had a plan, and it couldn't fail. "I can't talk about it on the phone, but I'm sure it will please you. I'll be back at headquarters by tomorrow afternoon and explain it to you then. For now, you must hold off the auditors. General, you have my assurances this will work."

"That's what you said about Agent Xian, Yong-Li. I'll hold them off, but get back here now."

CHAPTER XLII

Thursday, January 18th

Hart Senate Office Building

Missie Walsh sat at her desk reviewing the list of detailees requested by senators' offices for the coming year, normally a perfunctory task. The Rules Committee was charged with approving all temporary work arrangements. The Hill had long depended on free labor from the executive branch to augment its paid staff. Agencies begrudgingly went along with requests to provide civil servants to the standing committees and even to the occasional senior member whom they did not want to risk antagonizing.

On occasion, the practice had led to minor scandals. A few detailees had acted either to benefit or hinder their home agencies. Cries to reform the process followed. After a few months, the outcry would subside, and Congress would go back to relying on free labor. In recent years, Congress had found a way to tap into new manpower sources—its own Government Accountability Office. The GAO was created by Congress to act as the legislative branch's independent audit service. Although it was hardly independent. The same members who opposed executive branch detailees often wanted a GAO mid-grade employee for their staff in some pseudo-investigative role. While the executive branch balked at sending detailees to Congress, GAO knew better. After all, they served Congress. So what if the assignment violated any concept of independence expected of any professional audit organization? GAO knew all too well its budget and, in fact, entire existence was dependent on keeping Congress placated. So at the beginning of each year, a handful or more of GAO employees reported to offices on the Hill instead of their agency.

At the top of Missie's list, Justin Armor's name jumped out at her. "No fucking way," she said. "Melanie, take this guy off the list."

Her deputy staff director was looking over her shoulder. "Missie, are you sure? That's the guy Parker used for your Mitsunaga hearing. You don't want to challenge Parker, do you?"

"Melanie, this guy's a prick. He was rude to me on every occasion I had to deal with him. His dress is sloppy. His personal hygiene is atrocious. Seriously, this asshole is an embarrassment to the Senate. I won't have him assigned to this institution for another day, let alone another year."

"You're the boss, Missie, but do you really think you can tell Parker no?"

"Watch me. Chairman Wilson was none too happy with the way Parker commandeered the committee for his own political purposes. If Parker screams, I'll take it to the chairman. But once the chairman knows who this guy is and how he treated us, Justin's history. So get him off the list."

She scanned the remaining names on the list and said, "Go ahead with the rest, and let me know if you get any pushback from Parker."

Within an hour, Steve Simpson, Parker's chief of staff, called to protest her decision. She listened to his outrage with growing annoyance.

What makes these Parker people think they can dictate to the rest of the Senate? Sure, Parker's a media darling and the frontrunner for the election in twenty-two months. Doesn't mean squat to the rest of the Senate. He's going to need a couple of successful primaries under his belt before we start to worship at the Parker altar.

"Listen, Steve, this isn't about your boss. The Rules Committee doesn't like to approve detailees for longer than a year. Our records show that Justin Armor has already been with your office for nearly two. We can't do that to people. He has a career to think about back at GAO. Chairman Wilson promised the comptroller general we won't extend detailees for more than a year except in unique situations. I don't see any reason why the committee should make an exception for Justin Armor."

"You listen, Missie, Senator Parker isn't going to take this lying down. He trusts Justin Armor. If you don't fix it, I'll have Senator Parker call Wilson and fix it."

"OK, Steve, I'll tell the chairman to expect a call. In the meantime, Justin Armor is not to have a Senate email account, desktop computer, or BlackBerry after 6 p.m. today. If he does, I'll have the sergeant at arms send someone down to collect them. Thanks. I hope you had a good recess. It should be an interesting session."

Missie hung up the phone, punched the air, and clapped. "Take that, you contemptible blowhard. There's no way that little asshole is staying up here. It's back to the bowels of GAO for him."

To Missie's surprise, Senator Parker didn't reach out to the chairman. Justin Armor was sent packing back to GAO. She wondered if the senator had decided he'd already got what he needed from Armor. Maybe Justin wasn't important enough for Parker to waste a bullet on. She was a little chagrined to have let the asshole get to her and a little embarrassed to have made such a big deal of this. But, mostly she was proud she'd fought back against Parker and prevailed. Justin Armor had his fifteen minutes on the stage. Now he faced a career in the windowless offices of the GAO.

There was one more thing Missie felt she had to do. She picked up her phone.

Paula was sitting at her desk in the ornate Appropriations Committee office looking out the window at the National Mall when the phone rang.

"Paula, this is Missie Walsh. First, I wanted to say, 'welcome aboard.' I heard the news from John Silease that you signed on with Senator Jackson's staff. I wanted you to know how pleased I am to hear that."

Paula began to stammer a surprised "thank you," but Missie continued in a lowered voice. "Between you and me, I found the whole situation with Senator Mitsunaga very disappointing. When Senator Parker came to the chairman with the evidence, well frankly, I could hardly believe it. We had no choice but to let him engage in his show trial, but I can assure you Chairman Wilson was none too pleased with the way Parker handled it. Anyway, I wanted to call and let you know we're glad you landed on your feet."

Paula spoke more calmly this time. "Thanks. I appreciate that."

"Oh, and one more thing." Missie's voice sounded triumphant now. "The investigator who Parker had working on that mess was Justin Armor, a detailee from GAO. Chairman Wilson has decided the Senate doesn't need him around any longer, so we sent him back. I thought you might want to know."

Paula stared dumbfounded out the window. Why was Missie telling her this? All she could think of to say was, "Thanks again, Missie. It was very kind of Chairman Jackson to keep me on, and so nice of you to call. I hope the session proves to be productive for both our committees. Thanks again."

Paula turned away from the window and back to her computer screen. She still didn't know exactly why Chairman Jackson had kept her on, nor was she convinced it would last. Sam Jackson was a good senator, but he was far more conservative than she. Paula doubted she could support Jackson's agenda over the long term. Plus, here, she was just another staffer, monitoring activity on the Senate floor. Writing talking points. It pained her that this job wouldn't be like being a defense clerk. It would never be that good again.

She shook herself and repeated her internal mantra. *Just be grateful you still have a job.* She glanced back out the window as the sun dipped below the horizon, bathing the Washington Monument in an orange glow beneath a violet sky. *And try to enjoy the opulent surroundings of your new life in the Capitol.*

CHAPTER XLIII

Chinese-North Korean border

A large military truck crawled up to the border crossing and stopped. Major Yong-Li got out and walked up to the border. With a wave of his hand and display of credentials, he dismissed the guards and entered the customs station. He paid his respects to the three North Korean officials seated in the room. Tea was offered and accepted.

The North Korean vice minister of internal security, Kim Jong Pak, flanked by two senior North Korean military officials, eyed the major warily. "So, Major Yong-Li, why has the People's Liberation Army requested this meeting under such surreptitious circumstances? We always welcome a visit from our Manchurian cousin. We are curious, however, as to the unusual request and choice of location. Can you please explain your . . ." He turned to his colleagues with a wry smile. "What do they call it in the imperialist movies, your cloak-and-dagger approach?"

All three North Koreans laughed together. Yong-Li was not amused but smiled politely at the attempted humor. "Most honorable minister, your wit is well-known throughout Asia, as is your uncanny ability to recognize the value of an opportunity."

The North Koreans grew quiet instantly as Yong-Li continued. "Minister, my government was most pleasantly surprised by your recent, how shall I say it, satellite launch. My superiors want to congratulate you on your tremendous achievement. We recognize the small part we played in this matter, an appropriate role for cousins who have been partners for so long. But we note the satellite which you launched, and I say this with all due respect, had very limited capability. We believe your current capabilities could be upgraded by the infusion of a . . . technology transfer."

Yong-Li used the Western term describing the exchange of sophisticated new hardware. Material that North Korea was banned from receiving. He hoped to trigger the senior minister's interest. "Let's say we'd like to make a contribution to your efforts. Give you a better bang for your buck."

The North Korean military men leaned forward in their seats as Minister Kim, the head of North Korean intelligence, leaned back.

"So, Major, that would be a very enticing offer. Can you tell me why the People's Republic is suddenly interested in seeing us join the club? Is it because you know we'll be there soon, and you think this will win our trust and confidence?"

"Minister Kim, I cannot divulge the reasons why my superiors want to advance your cause. But, for a small handling fee, we could achieve your goal this very evening.

"If you'd be so kind as to look outside, you will see an inconspicuous truck parked on our side of the border. I could provide you that truck tonight, in the spirit of goodwill, for a minor cash sum. I know of your importance. I am sure this could be arranged as we share dinner here this evening. I have taken the liberty of bringing some of my nation's delicacies for us to enjoy while we await your courier. Please, may I offer this gesture in congratulations for your recent success and wise leadership?"

CHAPTER LXIV

Friday, January 19th

Wahiawa, Oahu

"Sandy, it's Amy from the Hawaii RSOC."

"Amy? Oh no. Not you again. Last time you called me we ended up with a national scandal. A decorated war hero got hammered, and I nearly got canned for not following regs—someone at the top of the food chain in the White House got all bunched up over that one. Please don't tell me you have found more Chinese laundry."

"Oh come on, Sandy, you know you love it. All you computer geeks at Fort Meade spend every day staring at bits and bytes. I'm probably the only red-blooded American woman who actually speaks to you in English."

"Alright, Amy, enough of that; whaddya got?"

"Three things. First, we got message traffic from that same fax machine at PLA headquarters. It suggests the Chinese agent from LA bit the dust. Second, it looks like something funny happened on the Korean peninsula yesterday. We picked up some encrypted Chinese military signals from just over the border in North Korea. We can't crack it. But nothing in our intel database says there should be Chinese comms at that location. Maybe our GPS signal is off and the message is from eastern China, but that's not what the computer is telling us."

Sandy made a sort of strangled sound, but Amy charged cheerfully on. "Finally, there is a lot of encrypted chatter going on in the North Korean rocket forces. Can't understand any of it, but there's clearly lots of talk. The last time we saw that level of comms was when they launched their Sputnik."

"What the hell, Amy. Why are you telling me this? Christ on a crutch. Look. I am going to forget this conversation ever happened, and I'd suggest you do the same. But this is what I think you should do. First, report the fax message to your supervisor and prepare a report for your boss. Second, send the captured signals info through regular channels to us. Third, keep your speculation about the level of chatter in North Korea to yourself. Or put it in your daily report, if your supervisor will let you. But I don't want to know about any of it."

"Jeez Louise, Sandy. What's your problem? Where's your spirit of adventure?"

Sandy's voice had reached a subdued but distinctly higher pitch. "Amy, my idea of adventure is to kayak down the western Potomac. Talking to you is likely to put me up shit stream without a paddle. You should report this stuff through routine channels. Please, please, please forget you talked to me."

"Nice talking to you too, Sandy, goodbye." Amy shook her head in disgust. *So much for trying to do a good deed. Maybe I should grab my board and head out to Sunset Beach. Beats some silly kayak on the Potomac any day.*

CHAPTER XLV

Wednesday, April 5th

Maui

Chauncey hadn't heard a word from Paula in the months since the election. Rumors of contractor layoffs and defense project cancellations spread across the island. AEOS was still safe—at least for now. But 75 percent of its annual funding was usually added by Mitsunaga. He knew it wouldn't be long before they, too, would face layoffs, if not a complete shutdown. And his rookie head was likely one of the first on the chopping block. For hours, he tossed and turned thinking about Paula, the telescope, and his dreams in paradise going up in smoke. He was finally drifting off to sleep when the chime of his phone startled him awake. *Paula?* He picked up the receiver.

"Chauncey, this is Manny Kunio from the telescope. The major says you need to get up here as soon as possible."

"Manny, what time is it? What's going on?"

"It's 4:15, man. We're in terminator, and the boss saw something. He wants you up here to take the captured image and smooth it with the AO. Come on, guy; get your ass moving. This is big. We need you."

"OK, but hey, it takes two hours to get there. What good is that going to do?"

"I don't know. All I know is the boss wants you here, so get moving."

"OK, I'm up. I'm on the road in five."

The more Chauncey thought about it, the more convinced he became that he was wasting his time. The telescope would capture images, and the on-site technician could use the adaptive optics to get a clearer image. Once the data was captured, there wasn't much for him to do. Jeanine's supercomputer experiments did some neat stuff with post-processing techniques, but it wasn't groundbreaking. And besides, he wasn't involved with that.

Had the telescope caught a Russian satellite launch? Nah, we know their launch schedule. In fact, he recalled the main event scheduled for this morning's watch was a routine star track. The only reason the boss was up for the early morning view was because he was acquainted with the National Science Foundation researcher who was recording the precise activity of the star. And the boss hoped to hit him up for more cash. The task had something to do with the number of times the star appeared to pulsate every five minutes. Why ever that mattered.

He wished he'd told Manny to call Captain White and get her cranked up down at MHPCC. He'd call her himself, but cell phone coverage on the island was spotty in general and virtually non-existent as one traveled the winding road up the mountain. So he sped up the mountain, fighting fatigue and a growing sense of unease.

CHAPTER XLVI

Saturday, August 19th

Maui supercomputer

Jeanine White jumped out of her chair, let out a huge war whoop, and hugged a startled Freddy Watanabe. "We did it! Look at that!"

Freddy touched his cursor on three separate images and clicked the mouse. Immediately, up came a picture of a fuzzy, but discernible missile. It rose from out of the shadow as a dark blob. As soon as it was illuminated by the daylight that was still some several hours away on the ground but visible in low Earth orbit, there it was. Boom. The sophisticated smoothing of the data by advanced algorithms and a powerful supercomputer changed a fuzzball into a missile.

"OK, do the other one, the one they got in April."

The second image was even clearer as it crossed the screen.

"Freddy, you're a genius. I mean you are a certifiable totally cool Albert Einstein for the new millennium."

"It wasn't me, Jeanine, it was our newest upgrade, which has more than doubled the processing power of last year's model. It's a good thing we got that funded before Mitsunaga lost." Freddy turned to her with a broad grin. "But, you know, it wasn't even really the upgrade. It was linking the intel on what all the bad-guy missiles look like. When we plugged that into the computer, we taught Adonis to recognize missiles as well as satellites. That was the key. Jeanine, your algorithms worked all along. I just needed to expand the database."

Jeanine dropped back into her chair, pride and adrenaline coursing through her veins. "It might have taken us half a year to figure it out, but we're quite a team. When the NORAD guys see this, it's gonna knock their socks off. Our sugar daddy may be gone, but there's no way they're going to shut us down—not now. I think we just saved the day. We got to tell the boss. And we got to get the space weenies, especially Major Lane, to come down the mountain and see this."

VIGILANTE POLITICS

PART TWO

A Turbulent Pacific

CHAPTER XLVII

Captain Jeanine White had been correct. It had taken several more months to work out all the bugs, but the video images she and Freddy sent to the Air Force Space Command put Maui on the map. Their data proved North Korea had launched two- and three-stage ballistic missiles. This feat came much earlier than predicted by the intelligence community. While the first one had exploded, the second landed in the Pacific Ocean. The attempts by the spooks at Bolling and Langley to challenge the data had fallen on deaf ears. One, or in this case, two pictures were indeed worth a thousand words. There could be no doubt the North Koreans were well ahead of the Intelligence Community's predictions. The question of what rode atop that missile kept the Washington, DC analysts busy speculating and rehashing arguments for months.

The State Department argued, what good is a ballistic missile, albeit one clearly capable of reaching the United States? The Koreans' outdated chemical warheads exploding on American soil could trigger panic, but the actual damage would be minor. Furthermore, the retaliatory strike would annihilate North Korea. Even a regime as unstable as North Korea's posed no serious threat with this rudimentary capability.

The Defense Department countered that a first-strike capability, even limited, threatened stability. If we hadn't expected the missile, perhaps we'd underestimated the nuclear program as well. They argued vehemently that ballistic missile defense efforts had to be bolstered immediately. It was time for a new Manhattan Project. No expense should be spared.

The Central Intelligence Agency questioned whether the video was accurate, but in the end, they proposed increasing resources for intelligence collection to ensure that this type of surprise couldn't happen again. In short, the DC bureaucracy reacted as would be expected.

CHAPTER XLVIII

Wednesday, January 24th

White House

Vice President Smith tapped his fingers on the desk as he waited with his phone to his ear.

His assistant clicked back online. "As requested, Mr. Vice President, I have Jack Ralston on the line."

The assistant clicked back off, and Smith squeezed his phone tighter and stood. "Jack, what the hell's going on? The North Koreans launched an ICBM. How the hell is that possible? We were told they were years away. How sure are we that this happened?"

Jack's voice was calmingly assured, as always. "Sir, the evidence is pretty conclusive. One of DoD's newest telescopes picked up the launch. Using sophisticated computational analysis, it showed, with near 100 percent probability, that the North Koreans launched a multi-stage missile. The missile boys estimate it could reach Kansas if the North Koreans were so inclined."

"Let me get this straight." Smith dropped back down into his chair. "We're basing this on a telescope. What about all our assets that are designed to track these things? Did any of our early warning assets verify this?"

"Actually no, sir, but that shouldn't come as too much of a surprise. Do you remember a few years ago when the intelligence committees zeroed funding for our early warning sensor because it had both defense and intelligence missions? They thought DoD should pay for it, but DoD didn't. That little gambit backfired when our current sensor failed last year. We've been scrambling ever since. As you would expect, our limited assets are focused on Russia and China—not Korea. So, sir, we're just lucky the folks in Hawaii happened to pick it up."

The vice president ran a distracted hand through his hair. "So we get caught with our pants down again. OK, Jack, but wait a second. The intelligence committees don't fund us. That's the appropriators' jobs, right? They haven't been exactly shy in overturning what the other committees recommend. Plus, they've always been strong supporters of intel. How'd they let this happen?"

"Actually, sir, it's one of those weird quirks of Congress. In this case, Chairman Jackson didn't have a choice." Smith knew it wasn't his fault, but Jack's voice sounded apologetic all the same. "If the intel committee kills a program, by law, the intelligence community can't spend any money on it—even if Jackson funds it. It's the only part of national security in which the so-called authorizing committees have real authority to call the shots on funding."

Jack sighed. "So, when the intel committee boys and girls get their undies in a bunch over something and can actually get a bill passed, we're stuck unless the president is willing to use the veto pen. The guys at Langley, Bolling, Fort Meade, and various other unnamed spots all unanimously recommended that pissing off the intel committees wasn't worth it. Well, that little mistake is now coming back to bite us in the ass, big time."

"Jesus Christ, when are we going to get one right? What's the agency saying? What's the president saying? What are our options?" Vice President Smith struck his desk with a hand. "We certainly can't just take this lying down!"

"Yes, sir." Jack paused. "Well, at first the agency tried to downplay the incident, but the video is conclusive. As for the president, what's he supposed to do? We knew the North Koreans were working on this; we just didn't expect them to get there this fast. At this point, short of taking out the missile launch pad or a couple of research facilities, what can we do?"

"I guess you're right, but Parker is going to be all over this. We'll be going through another damage control exercise to cover our butts. Jack, we've got to figure out a way of getting in front of this."

CHAPTER XLIX

Friday, February 23rd

Kihei, Maui

At the Pacific Disaster Center, Johnny Taylor, the DC program rep, watched the staff pack boxes. PDC was out of money. They had survived more than a year by cutting back research on the effect of wind patterns on the dispersal of chemical agents. The center was only funding tsunami and typhoon warning and disaster mitigation efforts in the Western Pacific. Plans to expand the capability to Alaska and the Northwest had been eliminated. He was unable to convince the budget weenies in DoD to even provide bridge funding to keep the center open for the rest of the year. His eleventh-hour effort to get information to Senator Jackson on the center's potential benefits to Washington State had failed. Johnny had briefed the chairman two or three times in the past. But without Mitsunaga, he was unable to get past the gatekeepers. The wires went dead right after the election, and now, more than a year later, all was still radio silence.

With nowhere else to turn, Johnny sought out former Senator Mitsunaga.

Mitsunaga leaned forward in his armchair at his Manoa Valley home and plucked the ringing phone off the receiver.

"Senator Mitsunaga, my name is Johnny Taylor; I represent the Pacific Disaster Center. You probably don't remember me, but I met you several times when you visited our facility on Maui. I apologize for calling you out of the blue, but sir, I have nowhere else to go. Senator, the PDC's out of money, and we'll have to shut down at the end of the month unless we get some financial assistance. For years we relied on your help to keep funding for the program. Since your departure, we haven't been able to find another champion. I know you're no longer in the Senate, but sir, is there anything you can do to help us? Sir, we're desperate, or I wouldn't be asking."

"I remember you, Johnny. You say you're out of funds?"

"I'm afraid so, sir. We were able to cut back some projects to save money, but that only bought us a few months. Congress didn't appropriate any money for the PDC this year. And, we haven't been able to convince the Defense Department leadership to transfer other funds to keep us going. Can you help us?"

Ken Mitsunaga shook his head in disbelief. It was a crying shame, but what could he do? No one in DoD was going to listen to him. And, like Jackson predicted more than a year ago, Congress was no longer doing earmarks. It would have been tough to figure out how to keep the PDC funded even if he'd been reelected. Now there wasn't anything he could do. "Johnny, I wish I could help you, I really do, but there's nothing I can do. You'd be better off talking to Senator Keahole than talking to me. I'm not sure why you called."

"Sir, I knew it was a long shot, but we saw you work so many miracles for Hawaii for so long; I just had to try."

"I'm sorry Johnny, but those days are over. Like I said, you'd be better off asking Keahole."

"Yes, sir. It's just Senator Keahole doesn't have your clout. He's just a freshman. He tried to help, but he wasn't able to. So, I'm sorry to bother you, but like I said, I'll try anything at this point. Thank you for taking my call."

Senator Mitsunaga hung up the phone and sighed. Another important state project was falling apart. So many of his initiatives were dying. So many of his former constituents were losing jobs. So many worthy ideas were withering. And he was powerless to do anything. He sat back in his chair and picked up his book.

CHAPTER L

Monday, March 5

Monday, March 5th

Waikiki, Oahu

Throughout the state of Hawaii, similar scenes continued to play out. Education programs at the University of Hawaii shut down. Start-up firms looking to break into the defense business scrambled for dollars. DoD program managers had been very pleased with most of the work Mitsunaga had sponsored, but they were unprepared for the funding cut-off. Many had no choice but to cancel projects. A few of the more established Hawaii firms succeeded in acquiring small business innovative research funds. Several had progressed far enough that they were part of a program of record and had their funding included in the Pentagon's budget request. But those companies were few.

Even after all the big defense company cost overruns and delays, even with the procurement scandals implicating defense and business officials, most DoD program managers were still extremely risk adverse. They'd rather contract with a big, established company with a long, bad track record than with a new, small business with a good track record. Program managers weren't blamed if the well-known firm they hired failed to perform. But program managers could be fired if their small, unknown company performed poorly. So why take the chance? The hungry little guy was usually left out in the cold while the big fat guy got the work. And, on those rare occasions when a little guy beat the system and won a contract, the big guys swooped in and bought the company.

The Asia Pacific Center was the exception to the rule. Mitsunaga got it started, but the previous deputy secretary of defense gave it a permanent role in DoD. He recognized the value in establishing links to up-and-coming government leaders in the Pacific. Seven former APCSS students were now chiefs of staff of their respective military services. Four ambassadors were among their ranks, as was the defense minister from Singapore. All still had access to Asia Pacific Center networks, which had been set up to maintain connections among alumni.

Paula Means walked into Al Gianini's office. "Sir, you wanted to see me?"

"Paula, what is the 'sir' crap? First of all, I'm no longer the D-CINC. Second, I have known you too long for you to call me sir. Third, it makes me feel ancient. It's Al. And if it isn't Al, I'm going to fire your ass."

"OK, got it, sir. I mean, Al. What's up?"

"Paula, I'm concerned about the growing passion over the North Korean rocket launches. The media have started to pick up on it. The Fox News guys sound like William Randolph Hearst and 'Remember the Maine.' What do you think?"

"Sir—I'm sorry, Al, what do you mean? What has this got to

do with me? I thought you hired me to teach a course on congressional oversight, not to dabble in world politics."

"Jesus Christ, Paula, what's the matter with you? You're one of the brightest, most astute observers of national security and politics that I've ever known. Did something happen to you when you finally ventured outside the beltway? You've been here—what—less than a year? Has your brain turned to mush in that period?"

Paula rankled at the criticism. She'd made a conscious effort to not think about politics during the past year. She suppressed her liberal/moderate leanings. For the first time, she wasn't working for the Senate.

Her few months with Senator Jackson had been very unsatisfying. Despite the chairman's support and John Silease's sincere efforts to provide her with meaningful work, it wasn't enough. She was just another staffer with none of the responsibility of her previous job. And boy, did she miss national security.

When Al had called her in March and suggested that she join him at the Asia Pacific Center, teaching how congressional oversight protected the Constitution, she'd been stunned. John and the chairman both agreed it was the right thing for her to do.

She pulled up stakes and, with Bo by her side, headed to Hawaii. For three months, she researched and planned her classes. For another three months, she practiced her lectures and teaching style. By October, when the new batch of students arrived in Waikiki, she was ready. And, as Al expected, now nearing the end of the school year, the results had been very positive. In fact, outstanding.

Al leaned over his desk to hand her a crumpled newspaper. "Did you see the paper today? The vice president is talking about the North Korean threat again. This is the fourth time in the past two weeks; it sure sounds like he's trying to make a case for a preemptive attack."

"I agree. And it's been well received. I hear he's narrowed the gap between himself and Parker. At this point, the war drumbeat is trumping the reform mantra. I know that's mixing metaphors, but it's true."

"Paula, I don't see the intel. I'm not part of war planning anymore. But judging from the late nights I keep hearing about up at Camp Smith and Hickam, I think these guys are preparing to strike North Korea."

Paula let the paper drop down onto the desk and stared at Al. "You've got to be kidding me. I thought preemptive strikes fell out of favor after the Iraq debacle. I can't believe the president has the stomach to attack."

"Well, this is a little different, Paula. In this case, I bet we'd send a few B-2s to take out the missile sites and maybe the nuclear research facilities. I don't think we're talking regime change."

"But, wait a minute, Al. I haven't seen anything recently, but I thought all their hot stuff was underground. How do we think we're going to get that? We gonna fire some tactical nukes at them and make the place glow for a while? I don't think the UN is gonna see the humor of that, not to mention the Chinese."

"I'm guessing our guys have a new way to go after deeply buried targets. I sure hope it's not nukes. That would be a real mess."

Paula pressed her lips together as she stared down at the paper again. "Do you ever miss being in the game, Al? I mean with all this going on it would be fascinating to be watching up close."

"I guess, but I was never big on war, Paula. I've seen too many kids maimed or killed; I've had to write too many widows and mothers. Maybe we need to stop the Koreans from building ballistic missiles. But I sure as hell would be worried about what happens after we take out their stuff. In war, you never really know what'll happen. I mean, will the Chinese respond? Or even the Russians? And what will the world reaction be if we look like a Wild West cowboy again? The war in Iraq set our foreign policy goals back a generation. We still have years to go before we fully recover. But this one is tough. If the Koreans are building a missile strike capability that can potentially reach the American heartland, well, they're just crazy enough to use it." Al shook his gray head. "No, I don't miss running the world's most powerful military right now."

Paula nodded in agreement, but in reality, she missed the challenge. She longed for the days when her ideas and actions made a difference.

CHAPTER LI

Charleston, South Carolina

Super Tuesday was twenty-four hours away. Senator Parker charged down the jetway. It was his sixth stop in thirty-six hours. He'd hit all twelve states. The race, what race there was, was for all practical purposes over. Governor Fernandez of Florida had never gotten on track. He was big on immigration with his Hispanic background and record of turning back the Cuban boat people. He appealed to the jingoism that existed in much of America, but that wasn't enough. When the press found out he'd employed an illegal Cuban alien as a housekeeper, the show was over.

The senator from Texas never had a chance. He tried to be the anti-Parker. He played it calm and cool, with reasoned positions on not rushing into constitutional amendments on campaign reform. He might've been the darling of Wall Street, but that didn't count much this time.

It was Parker's race all the way. Neither of his primary opponents could poll over 20 percent outside of their own states. Parker held a clear 30-point lead. By Wednesday morning, he'd be the Republican nominee.

His strategy was already changing. Over the past twenty-four hours, he was focusing less on reform and more on the administration's softness on defense. Greeting the thousands of well-wishers in Charleston, he continued down that road.

"It's great to be back with you here in the Palmetto State. I want to thank Governor Klingle and Congressman Baker and all of you for such a warm welcome. I think South Carolina is becoming my second home. And tomorrow, with your help, South Carolina is going to put me over the top as your nominee. My friends, we've come far, but we still have a long way to go. Together we can clean up Washington. Enough is enough. We're sick of corruption. We're sick of special interests running the government. We've had it with the sale of the Lincoln bedroom. And, we're going to stop the erosion of our national security strength—where tin horn dictators can threaten this blessed nation, and we do nothing about it.

"With your help tomorrow in November, we're going to clean up government and restore our security. But I need your help. Over the coming months, talk to your neighbors; make sure they get to the polls. Together we can turn this around, and we will. God bless you all, and God bless America."

The governor beamed. The congressman gave Parker a bear hug and wouldn't let go until he was certain every camera got a good shot. Hopefully one that would make the national news. Certainly one that'd be seen again and again on the stations here in his district. His campaign team captured the event on video, too, with the plan to turn it into a thirty-second spot. Parker's raucous reception here mirrored those in the Midwest, the East, and throughout the South. He was approaching rock star status.

Back on the plane, Parker called his senior staff into his private cabin. "OK, gang, the race for the nomination is over. Steve, what's the assessment of our delegate total?"

"Sir, we expect you to capture all twelve states tomorrow. Our polling shows you over the top."

"C'mon, Steve, all the states? Florida, too? The Cuban Solution isn't even going to win his own state?" Parker knew the answer, but he wanted to bask in the glory, hear it again from his staff.

"Sir, it's the panicked Hispanic. He's toast, morte. Tomorrow you are the Republican nominee, and, in eight months, you'll be the president-elect. Nothing can stop you now."

CHAPTER LII

Guangzhou, China

Major Yong-Li was pleased, very pleased. The Central Committee auditors spent six months examining General Li Pen's books. They'd found nothing. Agent Xian's body had been discovered by the local Shanghai police and written off as a murder-robbery. The Central Committee recognized how convenient that all was but couldn't find a connection.

General Li wasn't pleased, but he was relieved. No longer was he threatening to transfer the major to Tibet. He still griped about the wasted money to buy a Senate seat and the little matter of the two "lost" nuclear warheads. But, luckily, they hadn't been discovered. And as time passed, General Li Pen got back into the business of managing his offshore companies and stopped worrying about Beijing.

Yong-Li still assured him the attempt to buy a Senate seat hadn't been wasted. They understood now it was much more complicated. Staff loyalty wasn't as absolute in the US as in China. The notion of subservient staff prospering without the politician was unbelievable. In China, no female staffer would still have her head if she publicly betrayed her superior.

General Li dismissed any further thought of meddling in US politics. He felt fortunate he'd survived with his head. His only very minimal insurance was Major Yong-Li. So the major would be staying very close even if his advice would no longer be sought.

The last suggestion he'd approved was the transfer of two nuclear warheads. So far it had worked. The major was right that their disappearance wouldn't be noticed. The general had worried whether providing nuclear weapons to North Korea would unleash a serious conflagration, but he dismissed the possibility. Even the North Koreans weren't crazy enough to launch a nuclear weapon. Besides, what choice did he have? The Beijing auditors were on his trail, and he'd had to replace the funding provided to Agent Xian. Major Yong-Li's connections to the North Koreans had served him well in this instance.

He'd weathered the storm, the audit, and the prying eyes of the Central Committee. No, the major wouldn't be reassigned to the border. Perhaps in time, his connections would come in handy again. In the meantime, General Li wasn't going to be dragged into any more crazy schemes.

CHAPTER LIII

South Pacific

The island of Tetiaroa sits thirty miles from Tahiti. With its pristine beaches and swaying palms, it once served as a vacation community for the ancient nobility of Tahiti. It's said that Captain Bligh was the first European to land on the atoll in search of his mutinous *Bounty* sailors. He didn't find them. The island was left for another *Bounty* sailor, Marlon Brando, to discover 175 years later. Brando purchased the island in the 1960s. It became his personal refuge for more than a decade.

In the 1980s, his family began to rent out the island's rustic thatched-roof cottages. A few years ago, the Brando trust built an eco-resort with a fifty-room luxury hotel and several individual cottages for semi-permanent residents. The small cottages contained a single bedroom, kitchen, bathroom, and living space. The developer maintained the old thatched-roof motif but upgraded the houses with modern conveniences. The new cottages acquired running water, ceiling fans, and a small pool adorned with a few fresh flowers each morning by the hotel staff.

Tetiaroa's contact with the outside world comes from small planes landing twice a week on a crushed-coral World War II landing strip. Power is supplied by solar arrays atop the hotel and backed up by three diesel generators. Together these are adequate to maintain the fifty-room hotel and eight cottages.

There's no television, no internet, and no phone service in the guest cottages or hotel rooms. Emergency communications are provided by short-wave radio. Here most guests found the end of the earth that they sought.

Rebecca DeLaurio liked it that way. She was the third person to lease a million-dollar unit, paying in cash, and live there in seclusion. Her naturally black hair and darkly tanned skin gave her the appearance of Tahitian ancestry. She reveled in playing the role. No one there knew her past, and no one in her past knew where she was.

She lived serenely, enjoying the gentle sea breezes, the crystal-clear shallow ocean waters, and the brilliant starry canopy of the evenings. Occasionally she'd visit the hotel restaurant and bar, but mostly she kept to herself, a castaway, alone in her island paradise.

Rebecca had left Washington as soon as she was cleared by the Justice Department. She sold the BMW and the house and bought a one-way ticket to Auckland, New Zealand. A few weeks later, she paid cash to sail on a freighter to Tahiti. She applied for a driver's license under the name of Rachel Hoani and gave her place of birth as the island of Mo'orea. From there it was a short flight to Tetiaroa. It wasn't Hawaii, but it was as close as she could come and maintain her anonymity. Most days she smiled a lot.

CHAPTER LIV

Sunday, May 27th

Honolulu, Oahu

Paula smiled and arched her back, stretching like a cat as she kicked off the blankets. She cradled the cordless phone between her shoulder and ear. From her bed, she glimpsed the Pacific's brilliant blue water between the palm trees, with hardly a white cap beneath a royal blue sky. Just another summer day in Hawaii. She laughed a little and spoke into the phone, "Chauncey, you always make me laugh. I love that."

With her free arm, she reached over to her bedmate, ran her fingers through his short blond hair, and stroked his shoulder. He rolled over, turned around, and looked deep into her eyes. After a moment, he licked her hand and thumped his tail noisily on the bed.

Her cell phone buzzed the arrival of a text, and she reached over to the end table to check it. Bo jumped off the bed, thinking it must be time to get up. As she scrolled through the message, she sat up and spoke, interrupting Chauncey. "Hey Chaunce, sorry, but Al just zapped me and asked me to call ASAP. Strange to get a message like that on a Sunday morning but looks like I got to run. Let me know if you are planning to come to Oahu, and maybe we can get together for lunch or something. It was sweet of you to call, but I gotta go. Take care and keep that telescope running. I'll see ya, bye." She hung up the phone and dialed Al Gianini.

"Hi, Midge. It's Paula. I'm not sure why I'm bothering you on a beautiful Sunday morning, but Al asked me to call. Is he around?" She waited a moment for Al to pick up.

"Hey, Al, it's Paula. What's up?"

"Paula, sorry to bother you on Sunday, but I just got a call from the CINC, and he wants us to meet him at Hickam. Can I pick you up in thirty minutes?"

Oh shit, she thought, *thirty minutes means no breakfast, very quick shower, get Bo outside to pee, and me out the door.* But she said, "Sure thing Al, what's this about?"

"Well, I have my suspicions, Paula, but I truly don't know. I'll fill you in when I see you. Are you still in that apartment across from Ala Moana Shopping Center?"

"Still here. I'll meet you out front in thirty." She was already stepping out of her pajamas in the bathroom. She turned on the shower and jumped in. *What the heck can this be? The admiral wants to meet with us at Hickam, which must mean PACAF HQ. Why not Camp Smith? On Sunday. What the . . . What sense does any of this make, and why me?*

Paula rushed through her shower. She applied the minimal makeup necessary for being seen in public. It wasn't up to the standards of most air force wives, all of whom seemed sure their looks could make or break their husbands' careers. They didn't take any chances when it came to looking their best. Paula threw on a pale-blue spring dress. She grabbed a white cardigan, recalling that the temperature in air force briefing rooms was usually set to arctic. Poor Bo had just enough time to water the palm tree outside. Paula devoured an apple and drained a glass of orange juice before running out the door.

In precisely thirty minutes, Al's Prius pulled up, and she jumped in. "OK, Al, what the heck's going on? Doesn't this all seem a bit strange? Hickam, on Sunday, with the CINC? What do you think it is?"

She noticed Al was wearing a sports coat and dress shirt, which amounted to formal wear in the islands. She wondered if she was supposed to have worn something more dressy. Before Al could respond to Paula's first question, she blurted out, "Oh crap, Al, was I supposed to dress up? You didn't say this was formal."

"Relax, Paula. You look fine. In fact, you probably look too good for the sake of the poor air force captain who'll be briefing us and the attention span of most of the officers in the room. Now don't tell Midge I noticed." He smiled. "In answer to your first question, I don't know what this is about, but I have my suspicions. Let me tell you what I do know.

"About an hour ago, when we got home from mass, Stu called. He said he wanted to read me in to something and get my, and I quote, 'political advice.' I said, 'Since when does the navy seek political advice from a GI?' He laughed and told me I'd understand once I had the briefing. I said, 'If it's political advice, I should bring Paula. She's the closest thing we have to a politician.' He laughed again but agreed that might not be a bad idea. So here we are."

"Wait a second. That's it? That's all you know?"

"That's all I know, but it's not all I think. It's got something to do with all the late nights at PACAF, and I'm worried that means North Korea."

Their short trip brought them through downtown, around the piers, past the airport, and onto Hickam Air Force Base. The security officer at the gate saluted the car with the three-star sticker on its bumper after glancing in at both passengers. They wound around Hickam and approached a second security gate at the Pacific Air Forces, PACAF, headquarters building. Paula noticed the bullet holes in the building. They had remained untouched since December 7, 1941. She bet more than one PACAF commander wanted them repaired. But the Hawaii Historical Society wasn't about to let that happen. Only in recent years had the air force decided to embrace the flaws and proudly point out to visitors that it wasn't just the navy which had been attacked on that Sunday morning.

The security guard asked Al his business. Seeing the three-star sticker on the car, his question was more perfunctory than probing. He waved them through. As they drove up to headquarters, Paula saw an air force colonel and major waiting outside—a clear sign they had arrived before the admiral.

They parked in one of the designated flag officer spots and followed the major to the second floor of the building. Paula remembered walking into this building many times in her previous life. On most of those occasions, the four-star PACAF commander would be waiting for her at the top of the stairs. The commander would raise his budget concerns. They always highlighted their need for military construction funds even though that was the one part of the Pentagon's budget that she didn't oversee. Occasionally they'd solicit her support for new equipment like C-17s and F-22s. With Paula, they were all business. Lay out the issues, and ask her advice. She'd candidly tell the commander what she thought. Once a year Senator Mitsunaga would join her. For those visits, the commander usually just said "thank you" and offered pleasantries over coffee.

General Donnelly, the new, tall, and bald PACAF commander, greeted them at the top of the stairs. He was dressed in a pilot's flight suit, complete with PACAF's blue, gold, and white flowered flight scarf. He told them the CINC was about three minutes out. Al introduced Paula. The general asked if she'd like to be escorted to a room where she could wait while the meeting was taking place.

Al chuckled a little. "Sorry, General, I don't think you understand; Stu invited her to the briefing."

"Oh, he didn't tell us that. Perhaps he misunderstood. We're going to discuss classified matters here, extremely sensitive stuff. We can't have a civilian in these meetings. The SecDef would never approve that. I'd have my ass handed to me, pardon me, ma'am."

Paula bristled and blasted. "With all due respect, sir," the venom rose a little in her voice, "I still hold all the tickets for the most sensitive classified programs in national security. I have access to all DoD top secret and special access programs. And I mean all. I have access to CIA covert action, NSA eavesdropping activities, and quite a few programs that I can't even tell you about, sir."

General Donnelly stared blankly at her, clearly stunned, but not quite convinced.

"Attention!" came the cry from the guards at the door as Admiral Lockwood arrived. The admiral, dressed in his summer whites, bounded up the stairs, two at a time. His height equaled that of Generals Gianini and Donnelly, but he was far thinner than either of them. And he had a full head of gray hair, which was a perfect complement to his light blue eyes. He greeted them with a wide smile and shook Al's hand. "Paula," he said, looking down. "How are you? It's good to see you. You look well. You don't have that Washington pallor anymore. Hawaii must agree with you. I assume Al's taking good care of you?"

Paula calmed down a little and returned the smile. "I'm fine, sir. How are you, and how's Marge?"

"Oh, we're fine. Thank you for tagging along. I want to get your take—both of yours—on the matter General Donnelly's going to brief us on."

General Donnelly cocked his head to the side and looked at the CINC. "Sir, I don't think it would be appropriate to include Miss—Means, is it?—in this briefing. This is extremely sensitive. The SecDef's limiting access on this, and I don't have the authority to read in a civilian. I'm sure you understand."

Al grabbed Paula's arm before she could react.

Admiral Lockwood chuckled. "Jasper, I'm sorry. I guess you haven't had the pleasure of meeting Ms. Means before. Before coming to the Asia Pacific Center, Paula Means worked for Senator Mitsunaga as the staff director for the Senate's Defense Appropriations Committee. For several years, she was in charge of the defense budget for the Senate."

The admiral flashed a broad smile at the general. "She handled your funding, my funding, and the funding of every other US defense entity on the planet. Now, I imagine you never met the good senator, and obviously not Paula. Senator Mitsunaga was the biggest supporter of the Defense Department in Congress. Setting aside the ethical lapses that cost him his career, there wasn't a better public servant and steward of the taxpayer's money in government. And, for many years, it was Paula who was providing the advice that helped him be so wise. Heck, those C-17s and F-22s on the ramp outside wouldn't be here if it weren't for Paula. So, Jasper, let me assure you there's nothing in this briefing Paula hasn't heard before. She's kept our nation's secrets and advised our leaders for longer than you and I have worn stars on our shoulders. She's here today at General Gianini's suggestion because of her background and expertise in these matters. A suggestion that I believe is totally appropriate. Now, I'm sure you understand."

General Donnelly's personal assistant, May Lou Hayakawa, a fixture in the PACAF commander's office for the past twenty years, watched this showdown. She stepped forward, gently touched the general on his arm and said, "Sir, the briefers are ready for you." She continued in a calm and friendly tone. "Hello Paula, it's good to see you again. I didn't know you were in Hawaii."

Paula smiled back at Mary Lou. General Donnelly looked at his assistant, who smiled, bowed a little, and withdrew to the back of the gathering.

General Donnelly released a deep breath and turned to Admiral Lockwood. "Sir, if you're ready, the staff's prepared to brief you now."

"We're ready, aren't we, Paula? Al?"

"Yes, sir," Paula replied, "I'm all ears."

Paula was still muttering under her breath as they walked down the hallway. Al glanced at her, arching his eyebrows. She looked at him and in a not-too-soft whisper said, "This wouldn't have happened if I was born with a Y chromosome."

CHAPTER LV

Pacific Air Force Headquarters, Oahu

General Donnelly leaned forward. "OK, Major Leonard. Instead of picking up where we were at 0800, please give us a little background for the CINC and his guests. And for all in the room, many of you may remember Lieutenant General Gianini from his time at Camp Smith. With him today is Ms. Paula Means, a civilian instructor at the Asia Pacific Center."

Several senior civilian staff in the back of the room stifled a little laugh at the commander's description of the former staff director, but none spoke.

"Go ahead, Major."

"Yes, sir, thank you. General Donnelly," he hesitated, shifting weight from foot to foot uncomfortably, "I'm not quite sure exactly how to proceed. This briefing is above top secret. While I'm informed that General Gianini was read in last year, Ms. Means isn't cleared. I can dance around the issue, but . . ."

Admiral Lockwood interrupted. "Major, I can vouch for Ms. Means. Just go ahead with your regular brief."

"Yes, sir, but the SecDef has limited access to this program. I'm not authorized to brief civilians."

"Listen, son," Admiral Lockwood spoke sharply. "These four stars on my shoulder are all the authorization you need. Now proceed."

"Yes, sir, sorry, sir. Admiral Lockwood, General Gianini, Ms. Means, this briefing is top secret code word. General, I believe you were read into this program last year before you retired. Ms. Means, we'll need you to sign the requisite forms after the briefing. If that's OK with you, Admiral?"

"Whatever's required. Just get on with it, and try to minimize the acronyms. RAM means one thing to the air force and something entirely different to the navy. And something else altogether to the rest of the world."

"Yes, sir. Gentlemen, ma'am, today we're discussing a classified special access program, Senor Thumbprint. It's under the rubric of Sensor Have. Please put up the first slide. This is a QF-117 Zulu, an unmanned version of the F-117 Nighthawk which we retired in 2008. It's been upgraded with more powerful and more fuel-efficient F-412 engines. These engines were originally manufactured for the navy's canceled A-12 program. The bomb bay has been enlarged and redesigned. A new sliding bomb bay door maintains the stealth characteristics of the aircraft even when open. The changes allow this pilotless vehicle to fly one thousand and five hundred nautical miles carrying a fifteen-thousand-pound bomb, the mini-MOP. That is the Massive Ordnance Penetrator, designated the GBU-57M. It's shown here. The vehicle is also now air-to-air refuellable, allowing it to fly longer distances.

"Today there are four of these UAVs, these unmanned aerial vehicles, in the inventory. They're located at Plant 42 in Palmdale, California and currently housed in an old NASA facility. They can be transported by C-5B air lifters to any air force facility on the globe and take off within twenty-four hours. They're remotely piloted by air force personnel at Nellis Air Force Base.

"Under direction from Secretary of Defense Worthy, PACAF has been tasked to plan a mission to destroy the underground ballistic missile and nuclear facilities in North Korea using the 117s. The secretary has designated this Operation Restore Balance.

"The UAVs will be deployed to Misawa Air Base in northern Japan. The UAV operators will be brought here to Hickam for operational command and control.

"Once the order's been issued, the UAVs will fly west from Misawa over the Sea of Japan and enter North Korean airspace. Intel tells us there are two known underground facilities located near Chik-Tong and at Yongbyon. CIA suspects that there are two additional nuclear facilities. One is in the Chagang province— that's the green icon on the map. The other is in Tongchang-ri, the red icon. To guarantee total destruction of North Korea's nuclear capability, all four sites will be targeted. The mini-MOP can destroy any hardened underground facility that the North Koreans might have.

"The most difficult target to neutralize is the one at Chagang. A QF-117 will have to fly more than three hundred miles across North Korea, release its weapon, and return undetected through North Korean airspace.

"The attack will be synchronized so that all four targets will be hit within ninety seconds of each other. Upon releasing their weapons, the aircraft will retrace their path out of North Korea. If any of the birds are detected before releasing their weapons, the mission will be aborted. In the event of mechanical failure, we'll land the UAVs at Osan Air Base in South Korea. In addition, the aircraft have a self-destruct mechanism. Any vehicle lost or shot down over enemy territory will be automatically destroyed. The entire mission should take less than five hours from takeoff to recovery.

"We'll deploy KC-135 tankers with F-22 Raptor escorts over the Sea of Japan for the flight back to Misawa. A squadron of EA-6Bs will also be available in the event a decision is made to jam North Korean air defense. However, intel insists the 117s won't be detected.

"Our analysis predicts an 85 percent probability of mission success, defined as taking out all four targets. The vehicles are in mint condition. They've flown one hundred and fifty hours in this new configuration with no mechanical failures. The mini-MOP has a 95 percent probability of success. It can penetrate one thousand feet of concrete, and its aim is very precise. Based on past experience and intelligence on North Korean air defenses, we have near-complete confidence that the vehicles won't be detected."

"Sir, that concludes my briefing, and I am ready to answer any questions."

"Thank you, Major." Admiral Lockwood turned to General Gianini. "Al, do you have any questions?"

Al leaned back and sighed loudly. "Admiral, I have many questions, but I don't believe the major or even General Donnelly are the right people to ask. As to the details of the plan, I have one. First, why Misawa? Why not fly out of Osan? The transit time would be cut by what, 80 percent?"

"Actually, Al, I'll take that one," Admiral Lockwood said. "We looked at every conceivable launch point from Guam to all the other bases in Japan and, yes, even South Korea. First Guam. Anderson would require too much air-to-air refueling to make it viable. Second, Japan. Kadena works, but the flight distances are quite long. The marine base at Iwakuni is an option, but it would require us to fly the 117s over quite a bit of Japanese real estate. The White House thinks that would make the Japanese prime minister very nervous. Third, Korea. Osan makes sense, but the White House wants to keep the Koreans out of this if at all possible. Moreover, maintaining operational security would be very tough. The North Koreans are all over that place.

"The upgraded QF-117 has the range to fly from Misawa and back without refueling. That allows us to avoid flying over South Korean airspace. The White House politicos believe we could get permission to use South Korean airspace if we had to, but they'd prefer not to ask. We don't want to jeopardize the security of the operation by talking to the Koreans."

"Paula, anything you want to add to this discussion?" Admiral Lockwood asked.

"Sir, this might be a little off base, but Major, how long has this 117 drone conversion program been underway? I ask because to be at this stage, I am guessing this program is at least three years old. Less than two years ago, I was responsible for programs like this, and I never heard of this one."

"Ma'am, I'm not sure I can answer that one, but many of these programs are briefed on a need-to-know basis and . . ."

"Major, I represented the United States Senate. There is no program in the Defense Department that I didn't have the 'need-to-know.'"

Admiral Lockwood turned to Paula and said, "Actually Paula, I might be able to explain that. This wasn't an air force program until about a year ago. I imagine you were briefed on the original MOP, the GBU-57. This mod was put together by the Boeing guys in response to my QRC—quick reaction request—for a slightly smaller version. It probably just didn't bubble up to your level. There was nothing classified about that.

"As far as the 117, this is a Rich Kelly baby. His Lockheed

Skunk Works guys started working on this right after they were retired. We gave him the A-12 engines, and Lockheed corporate kept it going on their own nickel. It was only last year that DoD agreed to buy the four birds. And you know those Skunk Works guys; once we turned them on, it only took six months to complete the modification."

Paula slunk back a little in her seat and spoke softly. "OK, sir, thank you for that explanation. Is it OK if I ask another question?"

"By all means, Paula. That's why I invited you."

"Major, your intel analysts believe this mission has an 85 percent probability of success. Is that right?

"Yes, ma'am."

"So the Intel community is convinced these are the only four sites in North Korea. But, isn't it a fact that we have very limited actual knowledge of what the North Koreans are up to? Has this command gone back to the intel community to confirm their assessment of the North Korean capability?"

"Ma'am, we're confident that the QF-117 can fool North Korean air defenses. We're confident if there is a mechanical failure, we can destroy the UAV before the North Koreans get to it. We are confident the GBU-57s can take out the underground targets. But in answer to your question about the number of nuclear sites, ma'am, all I can tell you is that's the community assessment."

"And, despite the fact that we've been wrong twice about what they're up to, that's good enough for you."

"I am sorry, ma'am, but that's above my pay grade."

"Yes, of course it is. Excuse me." Paula swallowed hard but continued in a gentle but firm tone. "But Admiral, who's making the judgment that we should rely on an intelligence assessment based on what I can reasonably guess is very limited information about the most heavily guarded program from the most secretive regime on the planet?"

The admiral grimaced. "Paula, I think you know the answer to that question. The president directs us to plan a mission, and we give him our best military advice on the way to succeed. It's up to the White House to determine if this is the right policy."

"Of course, sir." Paula's voice tightened as she continued. "It's just hard to stand by and watch what could be a monumental disaster. Even if the QF-117Z is a complete success, which I would argue is at best a fifty-fifty proposition given the 117 shot down over Serbia and losses of other sensitive UAVs in recent years, the notion that we know enough about the North Koreans' air defenses and nuclear forces to risk a counterattack is baffling to me."

Al leaned over in his chair and whispered, "Stu, I think we get the gist of this. I don't think discussing it further here makes much sense. I think it'd be better if you, Paula, and I met privately—along with General Donnelly if you're so inclined."

"I agree. Why don't the three of us meet in my office in thirty minutes? No reason to put Jasper in a box on this. He might have to run this show."

Admiral Lockwood thanked the briefer and concluded the meeting.

CHAPTER LVI

Pacific Air Force Headquarters, Oahu

Paula and Al headed to the Prius for the short drive to Camp Smith.

"Holy cripes, Al, is this even worse than what you were imagining?"

"It's not great, but we better watch what we say, even in my car. In this day and age, who knows who, or what, could be listening."

They exited Hickam and headed up the hill to Camp Smith. As they rounded the last turn and entered the camp, CINCPAC headquarters came into view. Paula remembered how Senator Mitsunaga fought to get the building built. The old headquarters was a dump. But it was still there serving as the headquarters for MARFORPAC, the Pacific-based marines. The old wooden World War II hospital was held together by baling wire, duct tape, and termites. As such, it was perfect for marines. It was a visual reminder that marines could serve anywhere and thrive in the castoffs of the other services. The marines were proud to serve anywhere, but privately, they envied the new building. Ever so quietly, they had sought Paula's support to replace the hospital.

The new state-of-the-art, beautifully decorated CINCPAC headquarters building stood nine stories high, overlooking all of Oahu. It was equipped with the latest Wi-Fi technology and continuously tracked military action from Vladivostok to San Diego and from the Seychelles to Anchorage. Senator Mitsunaga had pushed the previous administration to build it. He saw it as a signal to Asia that CINCPAC was a man of stature, not one to be taken lightly. The bureaucrats in the Pentagon had objected. The oversight committees in Congress had balked. Mitsunaga had prevailed by convincing the defense secretary that Asian military leaders needed to see the power that PACOM possessed with their own eyes. After a decade he finally got his way, and CINCPAC got a castle.

Instead of proceeding to the CINC's palatial digs on the top floor, they were led to a ground-floor, windowless conference room. Admiral Lockwood was waiting for them. Coffee was served by orderlies who then departed. The CINC asked his exec to wait outside as well. This meeting would have as few ears as possible, and no notes.

"OK, you two. Let me hear it. What's your assessment of the plan, in particular the politics of this approach? Al?"

"First of all, I can't really say I'm surprised. It was pretty clear something was up. The chatter in military circles on the island is that everyone at Hickam is burning the midnight oil. The rhetoric on the campaign trail has heated up. Parker's criticizing the White House for creating a North Korean missile gap. It wasn't hard to put two and two together and figure out PACAF had been tasked with planning a mission.

"But actually, Stu, on a couple of levels, what they're planning is better than I expected. By that I mean we won't be putting boots on the ground or risking pilots. From the sound of it, they have a pretty strong plan of attack. There should be minimal collateral damage and little risk to US forces.

"Second, keeping the ROK in the dark will make it tougher for the North Koreans to justify attacking them. Not to mention that any attack would be met with an equal, if not superior, response. That would devastate the North."

"Paula, what's your take?"

"Well, sir." Paula rested both arms on the table and clasped her hands, looking first at Al and then at the admiral. "I agree with everything Al said, but from a geostrategic perspective, it's a pretty thin reed. Attacking a sovereign nation based on a perceived increase in nuclear threat is the same thing we've been telling the Israelis not to do in Iran. Second, by going after known or suspected nuclear sites, we could potentially miss one or more locations. Or we could blow up a civilian site, with grave repercussions. Imagine the international frenzy if the North Koreans prove that one or more of the sites we attacked was not part of their nuclear program.

"We might all agree that no sane political leader would risk a counterattack. But are we willing to bet the North Korean leader is sane? We have to assume the North Koreans will respond, but how, and in what way? And the Chinese? Do we really think the Chinese are going to watch us take out Pyongyang's military capability and just yawn? Surely the NSC considered what the response from the PRC would be. And Russia? Do we think that no one is going to react?"

Paula knew her voice was getting heated, but she couldn't seem to slow herself down. "Furthermore, what will our allies think? I'd bet the Europeans cheer in private but fume in public. And consider this. If we can take out these hardened sites with impunity and stop countries from joining the world's most exclusive club, who's next? The Paks? The Indians? Heck, maybe even the Israelis. Have we already forgotten the furor in Pakistan when we went in and took out the most despised terrorist on the planet? International public opinion will be overwhelmingly negative. The non-aligned nations might even try to get us kicked off the UN Security Council. China and Russia could lead a UN effort to enforce trade sanctions against us.

"Only the Japanese, who have no love for Koreans of any stripe, will probably defend us. But then they might harbor notions that their attacks in 1939 or 1941 were no worse than what we just did. Is that the reputation we want?"

Paula hesitated a moment before continuing, but Al and the admiral just stared intently at her. She grimaced. "You know this all sounds like a political gambit to jump-start the campaign of an incumbent president with declining poll numbers. But he's not running. If Hollywood were making this film, we'd all say it was too far-fetched to be realistic.

"So I'm hard pressed to believe President Andrews is actually serious about this. The benefits of delaying the North Korean nuclear program by maybe a decade would be offset by the negative reaction around the world. And that, Admiral, is if it works." She raised a hand and began ticking off possibilities. "If a bird strikes an F-117 engine while flying over Pyongyang, the mission has to be scrubbed. If one of the sites remains up and running, we now face a very angry Kim Jong Un with perhaps some form of retaliatory capability."

Paula frowned and gave the admiral a questioning glance. "Thinking of that possibility, what would cause the president to take this step? I can only imagine what the State Department thinks of this idea—if they know about it—and Congress. In most instances when missions like this are planned, the Hill isn't told anything until the birds are already in the air. It was that way under Reagan, Bush, Clinton, hell, it was probably the same in Washington's time. Sam Jackson told Mitsunaga he was invited to the White House to learn about the so-called rescue mission in the Falklands after it was underway. Sure, if it's successful the vast majority of Americans might cheer. But what if it doesn't work? What if the intel community is wrong? What if the North Koreans have more underground facilities that we haven't found yet? What then?"

The admiral exchanged glances with Al and then looked back at Paula.

"I agree with both of you. Before I have a back channel with the Chairman of the Joint Chiefs, I wanted to get a sanity check from you. I appreciate it, and especially on a Sunday. I imagine we'd all be happier sitting on the beach at Fort DeRussy than cooped up in this SCIF. But, Paula, one positive note. Even if there are additional undetected nuclear sites at this point, the one piece of intelligence we and all our allies agree upon is that the Koreans haven't figured out how to manufacture a nuclear warhead for their ballistic missiles. So other than sailing a ship into a US port carrying a rudimentary nuclear weapon, there's little they can threaten us with."

"I hope to God you're right about that, Admiral," Paula said.

He nodded. "Me too. It's been good to see you guys. Al, please apologize to Midge on my behalf for stealing you, and thanks again to both of you."

CHAPTER LVII

Tuesday, July 3rd

White House

Vice President Larry Smith entered the Oval Office speaking rapidly. "Mr. President, I've just returned from a Pentagon meeting with the Air Force Chief of Staff General O'Reilly. He briefed me on their plan to take out the North Korean nuclear infrastructure. It's foolproof. They're locked and loaded. All they need is the thumbs-up from you."

Smith rested both palms on the desk and leaned forward. "Sir, it's past time to act. The North Koreans have surprised us twice now. They're much farther along than anyone anticipated with their no dong and tie po dong rockets. Hell, for all we know, they've got a ding dong that's going to ring the White House doorbell and deliver a candy gram on top of the Oval Office."

He rose back to his full height and began pacing. "We can't work with them. We can't trust them to dismantle their weapons, even if we hit them with trade sanctions, even if the UN demands it. They're the least responsible, most untrustworthy regime on the planet. They're also the most dangerous. Mr. President, you need to act now before we find out it's too late."

The president leaned back in his chair. "Larry, it sounds like your campaign manager is trying to run US foreign policy. We can't attack North Korea without provocation. What would the UN say? And, of greater concern, what would Beijing do? Now, you know I share your concern, as do the secretaries of state and defense. But, frankly, even though our intelligence estimates were wrong about their missile capability, they still don't pose a credible threat."

The vice president frowned and opened his mouth to object, but the president held up a hand and continued. "Look at the record. They've had five missile launches in the past five years. Three were complete failures. Their two-stage missile launch was successful after years of failure. Yes, they surprised us by successfully launching a satellite. Sure, that's a sign their three-stage missile is a lot further along than we believed. But the fact that they have a missile doesn't mean the United States is at risk. Our batteries of Ground Based Interceptors are on alert at Fort Greeley in the event of a bolt out of the blue."

The president shook his head and threw up both hands. "But, Larry, c'mon, these guys aren't the old Soviet Rocket Forces. They might have a missile capable of reaching Alaska or Hawaii. At best, their missile might reach the Midwest, but so what? They don't have nuclear warheads. And if they launched an ICBM with a chemical warhead on it, we'd shoot it down before it reached the Aleutians. Our missile defenses are ready. And don't forget we have Aegis ships with missile defenses. We have THAAD batteries in Hawaii and Anchorage in the highly unlikely event that their missile got that far. Hell, we even have one on Guam if they shoot to the south. So I appreciate your concern, but no, Larry, there's no justifiable reason to strike North Korea."

"Mr. President, listen to you." Larry stiffened, and his face wrinkled into a deep frown. "Our intel guys haven't got it right yet.

You know as well as I do that the GBIs have failed at least half their tests. You can't seriously be willing to risk the lives of millions of Americans from that madman with his finger on the button."

"Larry, calm down. Don't you think the North Koreans will lash out if we attack? The contingency plans that I directed DoD to prepare are designed to take out their nuclear capability. We're ready to attack if the Koreans act provocatively, or if they deploy missiles with nuclear warheads and decoys that could spoof our defenses. No one believes the North Koreans have a nuclear warhead for their missiles let alone the capability to spoof our missile defense systems."

The president leaned forward, and his face softened. "Larry, I hate to say it, but the polls are making you think this way. I know you're ten points behind Parker, and he's blasting the hell out of us for not standing up to North Korea. Sure, he says, if he were president, he'd knock out their weapons. That's easy for a candidate to say. It's not easy for a sitting president to do.

"It would be irresponsible to attack North Korea without provocation. Unthinkable. What would President Rhee say if I told him we're going to attack North Korea? He'd scream 'no' at the top of his lungs. Seoul is in the range of ten thousand North Korean artillery pieces. If we strike the North, Kim Jong Un will most certainly retaliate against our ally. And, if that isn't bad enough, remember we still have twenty-nine thousand US troops stationed in South Korea. How could I put those men and women at risk unnecessarily? What do I say to their families when their coffins show up at Travis? We wanted to teach the North Koreans a lesson?"

The president shuddered and shook his head. "Larry, I directed the air force to deploy its unit to Japan to be ready if the

North Koreans do something. But if they don't, no, I won't order an attack. It's irresponsible. It's too risky. It's simply wrong."

Larry took a step back from the desk. "Hal, you're jeopardizing the Democratic Party with that position, and you know it."

"Larry, you want this job. I get that. But in this job, Larry, we don't put the country at risk for the good of our party. When you're sitting in this office, you understand that."

Vice President Smith left the office shaking his head and cursing under his breath. President Andrews slumped into his chair and rubbed his temples. His headaches were worse than ever, and the tingling in his left hand was back.

CHAPTER LVIII

Friday, July 13th

Palmdale, California

At midnight a giant C-5B transport plane landed at Air Force Plant 42 and rolled to a stop near the facilities of Boeing, Lockheed Martin, and Northrop Grumman. At the far end of the site was an old aircraft hangar now used by NASA. The C-5 taxied across the runway toward the NASA hangar.

Outside the hangar, off to one side, sat a U-2 reconnaissance plane painted in NASA's red, white, and blue color scheme. On the other was a larger, DC-3-sized plane with a strange bulbous nose, a humped back, and a distended belly with the same red, white, and blue color scheme.

Air force ground equipment towed the C-5B toward the hangar. The wings were too wide to get through the hangar doors, but the first third fit inside. The hangar doors were closed as much as possible, and the C-5 nose swung open up to the ceiling. The ceiling of the building was just high enough to accommodate the massive aircraft with the opened nose. Immediately, workers began the task of loading the four QF-117Z unmanned aerial vehicles into the belly of the plane.

Rich Kelly frowned as he watched. He'd wanted to fly the

215

birds across the Pacific, but that was too risky. The possibility of an equipment malfunction or discovery eliminated that option. Operational security required that no one knew the drones even existed much less that they were deployed to Misawa. But the bird's wings had to be removed to fit inside the C-5. And Kelly knew the task of reattaching the wings and restoring the birds' radar cross sections was hard enough to do at the Skunk Works factory. Doing it in the field would be very tricky. He was sending ten of his top technicians on the C-5 with all the equipment they'd need to reassemble the vehicles. They were told to wear casual civilian clothes with no visible Lockheed or Skunk Works logos.

Rich called his guys together in the hangar. "OK everybody, listen up. First of all, I want to thank you for volunteering. It's never easy to pick up and travel overseas, leaving your families behind. Especially when you don't know if it'll be a week or a month before you return. So, sincerely, I appreciate your willingness to be part of this operation. Second, I want to reiterate how important you are to its success. Your work in putting the birds back together is essential. Without your skilled craftsmanship, this mission could not succeed.

"Third, as you know, secrecy must be maintained wherever you are. If you're in a restaurant in town or at the All Hands Club on base and some air force tech or even a general asks why you're on their base, the answer is always the same. You're providing contractor support for an Air Mobility Command training mission that can't be discussed further.

"Finally, I want you all to realize the historic nature of what you're doing for Lockheed Martin and the nation. When you walked in here, you saw the U-2 parked outside. Across the hangar you can see the SR-71 that NASA still flies. We just loaded these birds onto the C-5, another Lockheed classic. These aircraft represent our company's legacy, the Skunk Works legacy. Your work reconfiguring the Nighthawk into these drones will stand shoulder-to-shoulder in aviation history with these other legacy aircraft. I'm so proud of you. Taking this idea and turning it into reality for Skunk Works and the air force will help protect the American people. From the bottom of my heart, I thank you all and wish you Godspeed."

By 3 a.m. the C-5 was fully loaded and lifted off toward the northwest heading over the pole to northern Japan.

CHAPTER LIX

Wednesday, July 25th

White House

President Andrews quietly changed into his pajamas so as not to awaken his wife, Barbara. He tried to slip into bed but was jolted by a sharp pain on his left side. He fell backward, hitting his head on the nightstand and collapsing on the floor.

A crash jolted Barbara awake.

"Hal? Hal?" She rubbed at her sleep-filled eyes. "Hal, everything OK?"

At first there was no answer, then she heard a terrible gurgling, gasping sound. She fumbled for the lamp and blinked in its bright illumination. Then she froze. The president lay on the floor beside their bed. His eyes were open, and blood trickled down the side of his face. With an inarticulate scream, she leaped out of bed and to his side. Within three seconds, two Secret Service agents were administering first aid. Within ninety seconds, an ambulance was wailing toward the White House. Admiral Paul Casey, the White House physician, was at the president's side.

The president had suffered a seizure and concussion. The preliminary diagnosis was a heart attack, but a stroke couldn't be ruled out. Admiral Casey accompanied the president to the emergency room at George Washington University Hospital. Within ten minutes, the president was in the operating room at the hospital. It appeared he had suffered a stroke. He remained unconscious. It was too soon to tell what impact it would have on his brain.

CHAPTER LX

Thursday, July 26th

White House

Larry Smith leaned back in the chair and surveyed the Oval Office. He'd been awakened by the Secret Service and shuttled to the White House in the middle of the night. A groggy chief justice administered the oath of office at 4:30 a.m. That was two hours after the president slipped into a coma following surgery, and the doctors determined that his recovery was questionable. The swearing-in was captured on film by the White House photographer but not on video. While the Twenty-Fifth Amendment makes an oath unnecessary, Smith and the president's advisors agreed the photo of the vice president swearing to uphold the Constitution would be reassuring to the public. Two photos were released to the media as evidence to America and the world that the country was not rudderless.

At noon the acting president addressed the nation asking all Americans to pray for President Andrews. He assured viewers he would continue his predecessor's policies. He also announced he would suspend his campaign to tackle this job and spend most of his time in the White House.

The Washington Post immediately labeled his suspension as

Rose Garden Redux. It noted this campaign strategy, used most recently by George H.W. Bush, had been unsuccessful. *The New York Times* banner headline read "Mr. Smith Stays in Washington." The talking heads on MSNBC praised the vice president for his selfless sense of duty during this difficult period. Those on Fox criticized him for trying to shift the focus away from his lackluster campaign where he trailed Parker by nearly ten points. But Larry Smith wasn't paying attention to the media. He was focused on turning this tragedy into a personal victory.

"Madeline," the president spoke into his intercom, "ask Jack Ralston to come to the office, please."

"Yes, sir, Mr. President."

Mr. President. He liked that. President Smith. Jack Ralston walked into the Oval Office and smiled widely as he saw Larry Smith seated at the president's desk. "Mr. President, let me be among the first to congratulate you. You fit right in. It looks like you've been here your whole life."

"Thanks, Jack, but under the circumstances—oh hell, I'm not going to lie; it feels great. Now we've got to take full advantage of this opportunity. It doesn't look like Hal will be getting better. This is my job now. I need to show the public that I'm up to the task. I need to be decisive, presidential. And I think I know just what to do to restore this office to its past power. Show everyone that Larry Smith is the new leader of the free world."

"Are you thinking North Korea?"

"That's exactly what I'm thinking. You said it yourself. The air force is ready to go. O'Reilly told me their plan is foolproof. And, it was President Andrews who ordered the Air Force to put together the strike package. Anyone who accuses me of ordering a strike will be told I am putting into effect the plan that Hal Andrews prepared."

"It's a big step Larry, uh, Mr. President, but I agree it's the right one. Parker and the Republicans in Congress have been all over this administration, decrying its weakness. The Koreans are thumbing their noses at us, calling us a "paper tiger" like the Chinese did a half-century ago. If you act, the Republicans have to cheer. If they don't, we'll work with the press to remind everyone that in foreign policy crises, politics stops at the border. Even Democratic congressional candidates will be cheering as their reelection chances soar. Mr. President, this is exactly what you need to turn this campaign around, change the subject. Most of all, it's the right thing to do. The last thing this nation needs is a North Korea with the capability to strike us."

"OK, Jack. I want you to talk to O'Reilly and get him working on finalizing plans. We have to act soon. We're getting too close to the conventions as it is. Hell, I just wish I could have convinced Hal to act weeks ago when the plan was drawn up."

"Yes sir, Mr. President. I'll get right on it." Jack Ralston flashed another broad smile, turned, and walked out of the Oval Office.

CHAPTER LXI

Friday, July 27th

Misawa Air Base, Japan

Big Willie Lanier was the head tech sent by Rich Kelly to Misawa to run the operation. Willie had worked for Lockheed's Advanced Development Program, the Skunk Works, for more than thirty years. He was just a youngster from Compton when his uncle got him a job right out of high school working at the old plant located at the Burbank airport. He helped manufacture the original F-117 prototype. He had seen the birds go from the cradle to the grave and now, like the phoenix, rise from the dead in a new role.

Relocating to Palmdale hadn't been easy for him. It certainly wasn't LA. But he and his wife had made it work. Enough of the old guys had made the move along with him that it wasn't too big a culture shock after all.

His task this time was to put the birds back together, making sure they maintained their stealth characteristics. His team knew the job. They'd built and rebuilt the 117s so many times it was old hat. Except this time they wouldn't be doing it in their factory. They'd be on the road and quite a bit out of their comfort zone.

Rich had estimated it would take about two days to reassemble the birds. A good estimate, but the stealth checks and tweaks had actually taken an extra forty-eight hours. Now, all was in order, and the team spent the rest of its time waiting. Willie contemplated sending half the guys home after the first week but didn't want to mess with the synergy of the team. So, they all sat around, played cards, watched the Armed Forces Network on TV, and generally tried to lay low. Willie was worried. The longer they waited, the greater the likelihood someone would blow their cover. But he didn't control the clock. So they waited.

CHAPTER LXII

Friday, August 3rd

Camp Smith, Oahu

"Admiral, General Gianini is on the phone. Are you available to take the call?"

"Certainly, Sam, put him through." The admiral leaned back in his chair with a smile.

"Good morning, CINC, another beautiful day in paradise, but I was hoping I wouldn't find you in."

"Right, Al. What'd you expect? I mean, all things considered."

Al laughed. "I guess it makes sense, but I thought you were wheels up today?"

"Well, Marge is leaving in an hour or so, but I'm staying behind. I'm sure you understand."

"Well, I guess. Where were you heading again? Seattle?"

"Marge is flying to Seattle to visit our son, his wife and, of course, the grandkids. But she's not staying there. We rented a beach cottage at the navy recreation facility at Pacific Beach. It's about 150 miles from Seattle. The plan was for us to grab the grandkids and take them to the beach for a week. Their folks would join us for the weekend."

"Stu, I think you might want to look out your window. You're at the beach." Al chuckled at his own joke, but Stu didn't join in. "Why aren't they coming here? We've got the most beautiful beaches in the world. And if you want a military cottage, the air force has some at Bellows, the marines have theirs at Kaneohe. Heck, you navy guys have some over at Barbers. And, if you're looking to really get away, you've got the ones at Barking Sands, Kauai. People dream about coming to Hawaii for vacation. You must be the only guy in America who wants to go to the mainland for the beach."

"Al, it's not the beach that's driving this. It's the kids. Marge is hell-bent on spending time with the grandkids, and Tom can't get away. So Marge cooked up this deal. To be honest, I was looking forward to getting away from here and being a little less recognizable."

"You're hilarious. You think you won't be recognized at a navy base?"

"Well, it's got to be better than here. My face is on the wall in every military building for every soldier, sailor, marine, and airman to see every working day."

Al snorted. "I guess so. So now what? You sending Marge on her own?"

"I'm not sending her. I told her we might have to cancel because of the situation here. She said she wasn't canceling her family plans, regardless of what I did." Stu caught himself slumping forward and straightened his back, even though no one could see him. It made sense after all. Marge had every reason to go.

"That sounds about right. I'm sure Midge would do the same thing. We drag them around the world for thirty-five years, moving every two or three years. The kids grow up, and settle somewhere else, and start popping out little ones. Only so much a grandma can take of being away from babies. I suppose she can manage without you. Lord knows she's probably had a lot of experience with that."

Stu winced. "That's true enough. I'm not sure what good I'd be anyway. I could probably handle Tommy—he's nine now—and take Sally for ice cream or something. But Henry's not even three. I'm not much good with toddlers. I can bounce him on my knee for five minutes, but that's about it. It's always been Marge's department. Anyway, I'm sure she'll be fine. But, damn it, I wish I could have gone."

"Yeah, that's too bad, Stu. So, you think something is about to happen?"

"You on a secure line?"

"Yeah, I can go secure. Hang on a second; I'll link us." Five seconds later the display on the phone lit up indicating the phones were securely linked for discussing top secret codeword information.

"You there, Stu?"

"Yeah, I'm here, Al. Not sure where we stand. The president is still in a coma, and Vice President Smith is running the show. His campaign rhetoric has been full of tough talk. I can't believe President Andrews would have acted without provocation. Frankly, I'm not at all sure about Smith."

"You can't be serious. You think the vice president would order an attack? Is that what General Gallagher thinks? And, where's Secretary Worthy? Surely they're not recommending an attack?"

"Al, this has to stay between us, OK? But Sonny Gallagher says he thinks the VP wants to launch, and soon. Maybe as early as this weekend. Secretary Worthy is staying silent. Sonny is playing this by the book. He advised President Andrews that we are ready to execute. But when asked, he offered his opinion that it was a risky proposition.

"Truth is, he's not really worried about the North Koreans. There probably isn't much they can do to us. The betting money is President Rhee will be furious if we attack. Not because of the act, but because we kept him in the dark. Our guys expect Rhee to publicly criticize the US for acting and let everyone know he had nothing to do with it. The North Koreans will be royally pissed off. But the NSC expects China to stop them from attacking the South."

Al let out a low grumble of uncertainty, but just said, "And?"

"Well, Sonny told POTUS that unilateral action will undo all the work we've done to restore our international reputation since we attacked Iraq. He said a far more effective approach would be stepping up our missile defense capability—in particular, our ability to counter decoys. Our guys figure that once the North Koreans can miniaturize their nuke and get the bugs worked out of their missile accuracy and reliability, they'll turn to building decoys. Gallagher's confident the interceptors at Fort Greeley can shoot down any missile headed toward CONUS. What keeps him up at night is the fear that someday one of these rogue actors will perfect decoys. Those, we still can't stop. Sonny feels if the president focused on that, he could get the upper hand with the American public and preserve international support."

"That makes sense to me. Did Andrews buy it?"

"Sonny thinks Andrews agreed there was no way in hell we could attack without provocation. But, Andrews told him we can't afford to pump up the defense budget. He challenged DoD to come back with a means to pay for it. All Sonny could come up with was closing bases, which doesn't have a snowball's chance during an election year."

"So with Smith acting for Andrews, does that change the equation?"

"Sonny's starting to think so."

Al's voice raised in pitch. "Jesus Christ, Stu, I can't believe the VP would attack when he must know the president doesn't support it."

"He's desperate." Stu let out a long sigh. "Parker's killing him, and without something like this, there doesn't seem to be anything he can do to reverse the tide."

"Heaven help us." Al's voice thickened. "Is there anything I can do to help?"

"I don't think so. I've racked my brain trying to come up with something that could allow cooler heads to prevail, but I got nothing." Stu hunched forward. "One thing's for sure, though; if we do this, we're going to need a hell of a lot of help in restoring our good name. We'll be counting on you and your folks at the Asia Pacific Center to get us back on the right path with our friends in the Pacific, including the PRC."

CHAPTER LXIII

Misawa Air Base, Japan

At 2330 hours, four QF-117s rolled out of the AMC hangar where they'd been sequestered for more than a week. A command and control console was set up in the hangar to track the vehicles, but flight ops were going to be conducted out of Hickam. The Skunk Works techs at Misawa were given the task of getting the birds in the air and then back on the ground after the mission. Once airborne, they'd be turned over to PACAF ops. They were all aware the Serbs had located, tracked, and shot down an F-117 with a mix of good luck and some innovative radar cueing after it opened its bomb bay doors. Rich Kelly and his guys had solved that weakness. The new doors slid open sideways, underneath the plane instead of swinging down. Range tests proved that the only way you could find the F-117 now was if you knew exactly where to look for it. They were counting on the fact the North Koreans weren't looking at all. And, if they were, they'd never think to be looking for F-117s.

Within five minutes, all four birds took off in a nearly simultaneous launch. This minimized the number of curious eyes watching operations at the base. UAV 1 would fly at top speed with no escort straight for the site in the far western part of North Korea. The speed of the other three was calculated so they'd arrive at their targets at precisely the same time to minimize total time spent in North Korean airspace. At 0200, the birds would drop their payloads. Laser rangefinders would guide them to their targets.

The ground control guys at Misawa watched them depart the base and tracked them until they were clear of Japanese airspace.

At 0130, two KC-135 tankers lifted off from Osan Air Base in South Korea and proceeded east over the Sea of Japan. The crew hoped they wouldn't be needed. In-flight refueling any aircraft was tough. Tanking a drone with one guy piloting thousands of miles away increased the pucker factor way beyond comfort levels.

Four F-22 Raptors departed Okinawa from Kadena at nearly the same time. They screamed toward the KC-135 orbit zone. The aircraft carrier USS *Abraham Lincoln* sailed ninety miles northwest of Misawa. A squadron of EA-6B prowlers on deck were ready to launch if PACAF asked for help.

General Donnelly sat on a raised platform at the back of the PACAF Command Center. At the center of the wall, directly in front of him, a big screen displayed exactly what the drone pilots saw. On the right was a map of the Sea of Japan. The USS *Abraham Lincoln* was on station. The USS *McCain*, a guided missile destroyer equipped with ballistic missile defense capability, accompanied her. To the left, a map of East Asia showed all air traffic in the region. Flights were minimal at this hour. The location of the four UAVs was simulated and displayed on the center screen. The tankers were on station flying figure-eight holding patterns.

The first bird was approaching its strike location. ETA was fifteen minutes. The second and third birds were a little behind schedule. General Donnelly instructed the pilots to increase their speed to catch up to the first bird. The fourth bird was still outside of Korean airspace near the coastline. So far the mission was a complete success. There was no sign the North Koreans had picked up any sign of the vehicles. If the North Koreans were aware and talking, the NSA would know even if they couldn't decipher what they were saying in real time. Right now, there was no chatter.

At 0200 the first bird reached its target in the western part of North Korea, near Chagang. Within two minutes, all four vehicles were on target. General Donnelly gave the weapons release order. The bomb bay doors slid open, and the GBUs dropped. The laser range finders in the nose of the drones guided the missiles to their targets. Each hit within three feet of their target and within twenty seconds of each other. Low-light thermal imaging video from each bird showed the flash. The command center monitors lit up with the flash and then were obscured by smoke. With each explosion, the command center erupted in shouts, war whoops, and applause.

After the fourth weapon exploded, General Donnelly leaned back in his chair and grinned. He muttered, "Take that, you bastards." To the room, he announced, "OK, let's get the hell out of there."

The four pilots turned the UAVs around and made a beeline for the coast. NSA comms lit up with chatter from the North Koreans. It sounded like everyone in North Korea was awake.

The UAV pilots flew at top speed toward the east. It would be forty-five minutes until the last bird cleared North Korean airspace, and two hours before they all returned to Misawa, God willing. SIGINT monitors showed dozens of North Korean radars lighting up. They seemed uncertain of where to search. Most pointed toward the south or east. The ROK was eerily quiet.

The screen in the center now displayed a replay of the attack as captured by an overhead asset. All four sites had exploded within thirty seconds' time. Secondary explosions occurred at the sites in Chiha-ri and near Yongbyon. The explosion near Yongbyon had been particularly large. Explosive experts in the room feared it might have been nuclear. They hoped that most of the blast had been contained underground.

Within sixty minutes, all four 117s had cleared North Korean airspace. The tankers and raptor escorts waited more than 150 miles off the coast in case any of the birds were threatened or thirsty. None needed gas. The tankers topped off the Raptors, and together they headed south to Kadena. No one wanted to tempt fate flying over Korea. Japanese air defense was alerted. Four US Air Force planes would be flying over the Sea of Japan and into Japanese airspace. Once inside Japanese airspace, flaps on the 117s were opened to allow Japanese air defense and US radars to pick them up. The UAV pilots at Misawa also picked them up and guided them back to the base. By 0500, forty-five minutes before sunrise in the DPRK, all four UAVs had been recovered. The Skunk Works team returned the four birds to the AMC hangar and locked the door. There were smiles and congratulatory hugs all around. The boss told his crew, "Let's go get some shut-eye, and tomorrow we can get these birds and us on an AMC flight home."

CHAPTER XLIV

Saturday, August 4th

Camp Smith, Oahu

Stu Lockwood rose from his chair in his basement command center. His view of the battlefield mirrored General Donnelly's. He was also linked with General Scott's USFK headquarters at Yongsan Garrison in Seoul, General O'Toole's USFJ headquarters at Yokota Air Base on the outskirts of Tokyo, and, of course, with JCS Chairman Sonny Gallagher at the Pentagon. Admiral Lockwood had decided to watch the battle from Camp Smith to stay out of General Donnelly's show.

Except for the national intelligence assets monitoring the action and the two navy ships patrolling the Sea of Japan, this was an air force mission. There was no need for the admiral to throw his weight around, or to get in the way. If things went wrong, the admiral's staff was on alert. It was ready to respond with all available assets in the Pacific. As it turned out, the mission had come off without a hitch. Preliminary damage assessments at the North Korean sites were very positive. All four weapons had performed as expected. The ground above the underground shelters appeared to have collapsed, consistent with destruction of the facilities.

The NSA outfit at Wahiawa was tracking a huge amount of military signal traffic in North Korea. Misawa had launched two U-2 reconnaissance planes to watch from outside of Korean airspace. It was dawn in North Korea. Admiral Lockwood called General Pak, the head of the South Korean Army, thirty minutes after the attack on the North. He followed that up with a call to the Japanese self-defense force commander, General Yamashita.

General Pak was shocked the US had attacked and furious his government had no advance notice. Admiral Lockwood explained he was acting on the president's orders. This was a unilateral action by the United States. No one was informed in advance. He stated that the president would address the nation shortly, and he'd make it crystal clear no Asian allies were involved. Admiral Lockwood stressed that keeping the ROK out of the loop was necessary to try and avoid the North retaliating against his country. He also noted that US forces in South Korea were being placed on alert as a precaution.

General Yamashita's reaction was more restrained. He asked whether the US had placed the Patriot and THAAD missile defense batteries in Japan on alert. Were the missile defense ships prepared to defend Japan if the North Koreans fired medium-range missiles in retaliation? Admiral Lockwood assured the Japanese commander all US forces were on alert. All national assets were targeting the Korean peninsula in case the Democratic People's Republic of Korea retaliated. He noted that three additional DDG-51 BMD-equipped destroyers in the region were also on alert.

The next call was more daunting; he picked up the phone to call Admiral Chiang Shendu, the commander of the Chinese People's Liberation Army-Navy. He'd met Admiral Chiang ten years ago when he first visited China. They weren't friends, or even particularly friendly, but they'd developed a mutual respect.

Admiral Lockwood expressed assurance that the Chinese shouldn't view this as a threat or in any way as a challenge to the PRC. The United States merely sought to deny the unreliable government in North Korea access to weapons of mass destruction. He reminded Admiral Chiang that the North had promised on several occasions not to build nuclear weapons. He raised the failure of the six party talks to rein in the North Koreans' nuclear program. And he was frank. His government had determined the North Koreans could not be trusted. Their political leaders had behaved erratically for more than three decades. Moreover, the North Koreans had surprised everyone, including the PRC, with the pace of their development efforts.

Therefore, the president had decided that he must act to defend his nation. Admiral Lockwood emphasized the US military was maintaining a defensive posture in Korea and throughout Asia in case of a North Korean response. The US abhorred any hostile engagement with China or any other actor in the region. He urged Admiral Chiang to counsel restraint to his government and to the North Koreans. He thanked him for his many courtesies over the years and for allowing him to speak so frankly on a matter of such international importance.

At 11 a.m., Admiral Lockwood called Al Gianini. "Good morning, Al, have you turned on the news?"

"Who needs the news when my phone's been ringing off the hook all morning? But, yes, I've been watching the news. So, he finally did it. God help us, and South Korea. Any sense of what North Korea is planning?"

"Not yet, but I can't say much without going secure. Actually, though, I was calling for another reason. I want you to activate your network. Get ahold of as many Asian military and political leaders as you can from your alumni group. You mentioned once that you maintained email connection with most of them. I spoke with Admiral Chiang this morning. The ambassador reached out to the political leadership in Beijing. President Smith called President Wu, but we need to do more. I want you to reach out to your previous students from the PRC. Tell them the United States holds no animus to China. Ask them to urge their leaders to do whatever they can to restrain the North.

"We know we'll prevail if the Koreans lash out against the South, but the loss of life on both sides would be horrendous. We need China to assume the role of peacemaker. I know your program. One of the benefits of bringing up-and-coming leaders to Hawaii is to show them that Americans don't have horns. We're kind and warm. The Hawaiian people are a perfect example of the goodness of America. Al, I need your help."

Stu sucked in a quick breath. "You and I know this was ill-advised. But we owe it to the American people and those of Korea and Japan, and maybe even China, to make sure we stop this here and now. I'm counting on you. Perhaps you and Paula can join me here tomorrow morning for brunch after services to brainstorm. Would 10 a.m. work for you?"

"Good speech, Stu. Sure, 10 a.m. is fine with me, and I'll bring Paula. You know we'll do what we can, but I've got to think most of our students are going to be plenty p.o.'d over the attack. Frankly, it goes against almost everything we teach and all the subliminal messages we try and send these guys home with. Sure, we know the North Koreans aren't responsible actors. The vast majority of the students who came to the Asia Pacific

Center agree on that. But, I think most of them will also believe that the US action was as bad if not worse than what they might have expected out of North Korea.

"Like I said, it's going to be a tough sell. Still, I agree with you. Consider it done. We teach them that our military carries out the orders of our elected civilian leadership. We can point out that leaders owe it to their citizens to act responsibly even when others aren't. It'll be tricky, but I'll try. We'll reach out through email to some of our more successful students and gauge their reaction. Then we'll telephone Chinese alumni. We have one or two senior PLA officers and one member of the Central Committee who might be able to influence the process."

"Thanks, Al, whatever you can do to help would be appreciated. We need to make sure it stops here."

"Well, I agree with that. I'll use that theme in my discussions."

CHAPTER LXV

Las Vegas, Nevada

Campaign manager Steve Simpson broke the news to Senator Parker. "Turn on your TV, sir. I understand Acting President Smith is about to address the nation. Sir, Fox and CNN are reporting that the US attacked North Korea early this morning to take out its nuclear research and ballistic missile operations."

"Holy shit, Steve, are you kidding me? That son of a bitch; I can't believe he'd go after them."

"Well, sir, you and the defense leadership in Congress have been hammering him for weeks on the need to do this sort of thing. Every Republican with a role in defense policy has criticized the administration for—"

"Not Jackson. That son of a bitch won't play ball."

"That's true, sir. You had everyone except Sam Jackson criticize them for letting the Koreans build a first-strike capability."

"Yeah I know, but we knew Andrews didn't have the balls to do anything. We just didn't plan on him having a stroke and our getting stuck with Larry Smith. Don't kid yourself, Steve—this is all about politics. That son of a bitch can't catch me without some type of October surprise, even if it's August in this case. What do we do?"

Steve's brow furrowed in deep concentration. He spoke slowly at first, speeding up as he warmed to his subject. "Well, sir, there's not much you can do. Luckily the convention is still over a week out. He can bask in this for a week, and then the country will turn back to you and your anti-corruption campaign. I guess we go quiet on the Korean rhetoric at this point. When the press asks, you can say that the Andrews administration never should've let the Koreans get this far. You can remind them how over the last eight years, Andrews and Smith let the Koreans develop new missiles and continue nuclear research."

"That sounds good." Parker's tense frame relaxed back into his armchair. "Where are we in convention planning?"

"We're in good shape. Denver is ready for us. With a ten-point lead in all the polls, we expect to have our delegates in great spirits and primed for a party. It should be a great week."

"What's the media saying about the VP selection?"

"Well, there's a lot of talk. Most are expecting you'll tap Governor Klingle of South Carolina or Lieutenant Governor Sara Martinez of Florida. I haven't heard anyone even speculate that you'd pick Mayor Sam Sanchez."

"That's great. Sam's a great choice. He's young and attractive. He's from LA, so he keeps California in play."

"Yes, sir, and being Hispanic doesn't hurt."

"Well, that's for sure."

"His program to round up the illegals in LA and send them packing appeals to those who oppose amnesty and the strong law-abiding types. He can get away with it without being labeled a racist because he's Hispanic. He's the perfect pick, sir."

"OK, Steve, let's let Smith continue to stew in his own juices.

We'll give him his moment of glory. Then we'll change the subject back to the economy and corruption when we get the mic back next week. We aren't missing anything are we?"

"No, sir, you're in perfect shape. He'll get a blip for this, but that's all it'll be. And like you said, after you take back the floor, you'll coast to victory. There's nothing he can do to regain enough momentum."

"So, one last thing." President Smith's nostrils flared. "What can we do about Jackson? The press has noticed that bastard's absence. He's the God damned chairman of the defense subcommittee. He represents a Pacific Coast state, but he won't say a damn thing about the Koreans and the weak administration."

"Sir, I'd say let it go. When you're president, you can think about how to pay him back. You know he still resents your crushing Mitsunaga. They were awfully close."

"That's bullshit. Mitsunaga was a crook. He got what was coming to him. But believe me, I'll get the son of a bitch when we take over. Jackson's people of Washington State are going to wish they never elected him when I'm done with him."

CHAPTER LXVI

Sunday, August 5th

Honolulu, Oahu

Captain Dawson at the NSA facility in Wahiawa dialed the CINCPAC watch officer. "Commander Baker, this is Captain Dawson at the RSOC. We're picking up a lot of comm activity in North Korea. It's encrypted, so we can't yet tell you what they're up to, but something's up. Wanted to make sure you knew. I'm about to call it into Fort Meade as well."

"Roger that, Captain. Appreciate the heads-up. I'll alert the Intel Center and the boss."

"Admiral, sir, this is Commander Baker at the watch office. RSOC tells us they're getting a lot of North Korean chatter. It's all encrypted, but they say the level of activity is very unusual in the middle of the night."

"Thanks, Commander, let the Intel Center know. Message the Pentagon right away, and tell the component watch offices we got a hot one."

"Yes, sir, will do."

Admiral Lockwood put down the phone. *Son of a bitch. This doesn't sound good.* He picked up the phone and dialed Washington. "Sonny, it's Stu Lockwood. My guys are picking up a lot of Korean SIGINT. Something's up. I don't know what overheads you've got in range, but you better start looking. They say most of the activity is coming from the East coast. And Sonny, I'm not sure what that means, but it sure doesn't sound like they're heading south. That's the good news, I guess. That would've been real ugly. But we all ought to be a little nervous if they've got something we didn't know about in the northeast."

"Oh dear God, this sounds bad. Thanks, Stu. We'll take it from here. And Stu, heaven help us all."

"I know, Sonny. I hope a lot of people are in church praying right now."

Stu put the phone down, then picked it back up to call Marge, but she didn't answer. *That's strange. It's got to be noon in Seattle. I didn't think Pacific Beach was that remote.*

He stood up and walked to the window. From Diamond Head to the Coast Guard Station at Kalaeloa not a cloud touched the sky. Sailboats bobbed off of Waikiki, and a cruise ship was tied up at Aloha Tower. A carrier floated in port at Pearl, and it looked like a couple of Aegis destroyers were there as well. He couldn't see any subs from his vantage point.

Yet something was missing. *Ah, the floating golf ball is gone. The SBX must be at sea, maybe a sea trial.* The SBX was a barge with an X-band radar housed in a ten-story spherical structure. Its radar could track missiles or anything larger than a baseball for thousands of miles. This Missile Defense Agency platform for missile warning was designed to operate in the waters around western Alaska. But it had never been able to withstand the tough weather conditions and high seas in that area. So, it spent most of its time sitting in Pearl Harbor. It wasn't a white elephant. The radar worked. The barge was, more or less, seaworthy. It could accomplish its mission.

It's a beautiful morning out there. I hope people can continue to enjoy it.

CHAPTER LXVII

Northeastern North Korea

Fifty miles northeast of Chongjin, North Korea, Colonel Pak Re Sing climbed out of his jeep and surveyed the landscape. The mountain to his right rose straight up two thousand feet. On the ground, dark evergreen brush rose about three feet high. He scraped his foot back and forth along the ground, uncovering railroad tracks. He signaled for his men to clean the area. It was 0500, and dawn was in about fifty minutes. He wanted everything ready to go before the sun rose.

The tracks ran 150 meters from the side of the mountain to a large concrete pad suitable for launching missiles. The pad was covered in camouflage, which the soldiers removed. The rail line split into two lines on the concrete pad. After clearing away the brush, the workers cleaned the rail line of any remaining debris. Colonel Pak examined the area. He nodded approval and signaled to his radio operator. The operator bowed and spoke into his radio.

At that moment, a seventy-foot high section of the side of the mountain opened up, sliding aside like a giant pocket door. In the doorway stood an assembled missile on a flatbed rail car. Behind the missile waited a small locomotive. On the colonel's command, the rail car rolled slowly to the concrete pad. Within five minutes the missile and rail car were locked into place on one end of the concrete pad, and the locomotive returned to the mountain. Ten minutes later, the locomotive delivered a second missile to the other side of the pad. The locomotive returned inside the mountain, and the doors slid closed behind it, remaining open enough for a person to squeeze through. Cables were unreeled from the opening in the doorway and connected to each missile assembly. By 0530 the missiles were ready for launch.

The sun was not yet visible, but the clouds to the east were turning from dark purple to violet. Colonel Pak knew it would be light in ten minutes. They would be visible to anyone watching from overhead. Heat from the missiles would already show up on any thermal imaging system if anyone knew where to look. He hoped they didn't.

He admired his unit's work and commended them. His brow furrowed as he stared at the two Unha-3 rockets rising before him into the early morning sky. He agreed that the US sneak attack could not go unanswered. Still, he feared that attacking the US using his country's only nuclear-tipped missiles would lead to a massive retaliatory strike. One that would wipe his country off the map. But, it wasn't his call. He'd done his job; the site was ready. All he needed was the order to launch. He would carry out the order if it came.

He spoke into the radio. "This is Colonel Pak at site twenty-three. We're a go on your order."

There was silence. His hands started to shake as he waited. A voice on the other end finally spoke. "Colonel Pak, in memory of the Dear Leader and our ancestors, launch the missiles and restore the honor of the Democratic People's Republic."

Colonel Pak nodded and replied, "Yes, sir."

At 5:38 a.m., the first Unha-3 missile was launched. Seven minutes later the second missile followed it. The men cheered as each missile rose into the sky on an eastward trajectory. Colonel Pak stood at attention, holding back tears. He thought about his wife and sons in Pyongyang and wondered if any of them would survive the day. As he watched, the missiles disappeared from view just as the first golden rays of the sun started to peak over the horizon. A new dawn had arrived.

CHAPTER LXVIII

Off the coast of Kauai

Seventy-five miles out to sea the SBX-1 barge picked up the track of the first Unha-3 missile at 10:41 a.m. Hawaii Standard Time. Captain Paul McCoy was alerted by his watch officer and rushed to the control room.

"Tommy, what's going on?"

"Sir, we picked up a North Korean launch with target coordinates of 61 North by 150 West."

"English, Tommy."

"Sir, yes sir. The missile is headed for Anchorage Alaska. It's targeted to hit at 10:53 a.m., sir HST."

"Jesus Christ. Any word from Schriever or Buckley or Fort Greeley?"

"Sir, we hit the alert to all three, sir, but it looks like we picked it up first."

"What about the early warning sensors? They don't have it?"

"Don't know, sir, but you know the new one, SBIRS, has still got some comm glitches. But it's clear we have about nine minutes until—check that, we have eight minutes now." Tommy's hand trembled over the screen. "Holy shit! Sorry, sir. Sir, we have a second missile launch at 10:45 a.m. HST. Sir, it looks like this one is headed straight at us—to be precise, at Honolulu."

"Oh my god." McCoy's jaw dropped, but he shook himself. "Get Admiral Lockwood on the phone. Now!"

"Sir, this is Captain McCoy on the SBX. We are tracking two North Korean missiles headed toward the US. The first is aimed at Anchorage with an impact in seven minutes. Two Greeley GBI interceptors have locked onto it and will be firing in ten and fifteen seconds. The second Korean missile is headed here, sir, right at Honolulu. It was launched approximately four minutes after the first missile. Impact's in nine minutes. Greeley has two missiles locking on to it now, but the cueing angle isn't great."

Lockwood's voice came out in a hoarse, gravelly tone. "Oh mother of God. Thanks, Captain. Stay on the line. I'll be right back." He turned a pale face toward the pair at the table with him. "Al, the North Koreans have launched two ICBM's: one at Alaska, the other here. Greeley's locked on to the first, but they aren't sure they can hit the one coming here."

"Sir," Paula blurted out. She continued in rapid sentences. "Alert the Aegis ships. If the standard missile can take out a satellite, you've got a chance it can hit the incoming missile. Light up all the assets in Hawaii—the daylight imager telescope, the Aegis ashore test bed. Tie that into the SBX data, and you might be able to enhance the missile track. Run all the sensors through the Maui supercomputer, and send the target cueing to the ship."

"Solid, Paula. But it's Sunday. How do we get the supercomputer up and running?"

"Let me check."

Paula dialed Chauncey's cell. "Chauncey, where are you; it's Paula."

"Paula!" Chauncey's bright tone jarred Paula's tense nerves. "Right now I'm carrying my bike into the supercomputer. I'm gonna use the $50 million supercomputer to jazz up my résumé. You know, in case the telescope shuts down. It's great to hear from you."

"Chaunce." Paula fought to keep her voice clear and firm. "We got about five minutes before a Korean missile hits Honolulu. We need Captain White to fuse sensor data from all the island sensors and send the targeting info to the fleet. Is she there?"

"Holy shit!" Chauncey sucked in a deep breath and continued in a rapid tone. "I don't see her name on the list, but Freddy Watanabe, the UH grad student, is here. He knows the machine upside down."

"OK, get Freddy set to receive the data ASAP!"

"Got it, Paula. Freddy is here and getting set up. He says thirty seconds, and he can start to synthesize the data."

"Thanks, Chaunce. Don't hang up." She turned her head. "Sir, the supercomputer is all set."

Admiral Lockwood raised his phone back to his ear and shouted out the door to his aide-de-camp. "Colonel Jones, I want every asset in the state to try to lock onto the incoming missile. The Aegis ashore test facility on Kauai, the telescope on Maui. I want every Aegis ship in Pearl Harbor to light up their radars and give us the best possible track. Send all that data to the Maui supercomputer. And get Commander Johnson on the *Lake Erie* to prepare his SM-3 missiles. We've got to be ready to hit this thing."

"Yes, sir."

"Captain McCoy, you still there? What's the status?"

"Sir, the first two GBIs are away. It looks good. The second two should launch in ninety seconds."

Sudden shouting broke out in the background, and the admiral tensed. "What's going on, Captain?"

"Sir. The first target just changed course. Sir. It's impossible, but, oh shit. Sir, both GBIs missed the target. The incoming missile looks like it's out of control, sir. It's no longer headed to Alaska. Our computer says it'll hit in the ocean off the coast of Washington."

"What about the second missile, Captain?"

"Sir, I'm sorry, sir, but it's still on course for Hawaii, impact in three minutes. Sir, the GBIs are away headed toward the second missile, but sir, in all candor, it's a tough ask."

"Captain, stand by. Colonel, is the *Lake Erie* ready to fire? Where are we?"

"Admiral, the *Lake Erie* is at her battle stations and ready to go. Her Aegis fire control system is linked to the supercomputer. They know the missile's precise location."

"Colonel, tell the *Lake Erie* to fire on my command."

"Captain, where are the GBIs?"

"Sir, the GBIs are on track to impact the missile in five and fifteen seconds."

The phone line went quiet. "Sir, the first GBI has missed the target, and it looks like the second GBI has lost its tracking. I'm sorry, sir, but it doesn't look good."

"Colonel, put Commander Johnson on my line."

"Yes, sir."

"Commander, this is Stu Lockwood. The GBIs have missed. We have about two minutes before this missile strikes us. What's your status? Are you ready to fire?"

"Aye aye, sir. We got a great track from the Maui guys. It's synced to Aegis, and we're locked on the target. It's headed straight at us. We're ready to launch."

"Commander, hit it with everything you got. Fire when ready, and may God be with you."

"Aye aye, sir."

Admiral Lockwood put the commander on speakerphone and grabbed his head with both hands. *How did we let this happen? Intel was so sure we'd neutralized their launch capability. What went wrong?*

"Sir." Commander Johnson's voice jolted the admiral to full attention. "Three missiles away. They're tracking the incoming target and locked on. Impact in five, four, three, two, one." A sudden deep intake of breath and then whoops from the background. "We got it, sir! It's a direct hit with the first SM-3."

Admiral Lockwood gave a thumbs-up to Al and Paula and fell back in his chair. "Commander Johnson. Thank you. You and your crew have saved the lives of many people here in Hawaii. Who knows what kind of warhead it carried, but your heroic efforts have saved us. Can you put me on the ship's PA system?"

Paula spoke into her phone, her voice high and rapid, "Chauncey, you and Freddy are superheroes. We knocked it out of the sky! Tell Freddy he just earned his PhD. Thanks so much. I gotta go. I'll talk to ya soon."

The speakerphone crackled back to life. "Admiral, I've got you on the ship's PA. Go ahead."

The admiral threw back his shoulders and straightened in his chair. "Officers and sailors, men and women of *Lake Erie*. This is Admiral Lockwood at CINCPAC headquarters. Your bravery under fire and your impressive technological skill saved the lives of countless Americans today. For all of us whose lives you've saved, I want to offer you my deepest appreciation and thanks. And I want you to know how proud I am to be your commander in chief and a member of the same navy as you." His voice choked, and he swallowed hard. "May God bless the captain and crew of the USS *Lake Erie*, and may God continue to bless the United States of America."

The crew erupted with cheers. Commander Johnson spoke into the phone, "Is there anything else, Admiral?"

"No sir, Commander. You've done us proud." The phone clicked off, and the admiral frowned as he spoke again.

"Captain McCoy, are you still on the line? What's the latest?"

"Sir, the first missile landed in the North Pacific Ocean about 150 miles southwest of Seattle. It looks like that's the last one. HQ is telling us they have visuals from the North Korean launch site. There's no further activity. They've spotted what looks like two abandoned, scorched flatbed rail cars. The analysts say that the railroad tracks from the launch site dead end at the side of a mountain. They're speculating it's an entrance to a cave but can't confirm that from the images they have."

"Did the missile's warhead detonate?"

"Don't know yet, sir."

"OK, Captain, thanks. And good work today. Without your fine work, we might've lost Anchorage and Honolulu. That'll be all. Keep me informed if anything else pops up."

"Yes, sir. Goodbye, sir."

The admiral shook his head as if to clear it of the dark cloud that had so nearly engulfed them. Then, he put down his phone. "Colonel, what do we know about the first missile?"

"Sir, not much yet."

"Are we hearing anything from the Disaster Center on Maui about an explosion or tsunami?"

Paula spoke up. "Sir, the center was closed last year. Once Mitsunaga stopped providing funding for it, they had no choice. NOAA couldn't afford it, and the DoD wouldn't continue to foot the bill."

Major Molly Atkins knocked and entered the CINC's office. "Sir, CNN is reporting from its Seattle affiliate that people on the coast of Washington heard an explosion out to sea. They don't know precisely where, but it sounds like it was southwest of Seattle. And one plane in the area reported seeing a mushroom cloud off the coast."

"Oh my god, nukes. Thank God it was out to sea."

As the words left his mouth, the admiral jerked straight up in his chair and then slumped back. The blood drained from his face. "Marge," he whispered.

In a choked voice the admiral gasped. "Colonel, check in with our folks at Bangor, Everett, and Puget Sound to see what they know. And, Colonel, can you try and see if you can get through to the navy facility at Pacific Beach. Marge is there."

Admiral Lockwood leaned back in his chair and moaned. "Please God, anything but that."

Al whispered to Paula, "Marge and the grandkids are at a navy beach cottage on the coast of Washington."

"Oh my god."

CHAPTER LXIX

Seattle, Washington

Tom met Marge at the airport early Friday evening and waited for her outside the rental car agency. She picked up her minivan and followed him back to their home in Tacoma. Hard to say who was more excited: the grandkids expecting and receiving presents, Marge, or Susie, who was anticipating a week to herself.

Marge checked in with Stu, who was relieved she'd made it OK. He was a little jealous he couldn't be there but mostly stressed over the unfolding events. Marge knew something was stopping him from joining her but had no idea what it might be. It wasn't the first time he'd missed a family vacation.

Tom and Susie made sure she was very comfortable. The guest room was spotless. The children's toys were put away for the most part. Susie made a light dinner, and they all retired early. It was particularly early for Marge, whose body clock was still on Hawaii time. She was eager to go to sleep, though, to speed the arrival of the next day's adventures.

At 7:30 a.m., Marge woke to whispers and giggles. She opened one eye and saw six peering back at her from her doorway. The door was cracked open, and there they were, waiting outside it for her to wake up. Susie always warned them not to wake Grandma, but they were too excited to pay much attention today. Marge beckoned the children with one finger. They ran to her bed and jumped on, squealing at the top of their lungs. Her eyes glistened with happy tears, and she grabbed each one and gave them a hug and a kiss. Susie popped her head in the room and shooed them out. She apologized to Marge for the surprise attack, but Marge couldn't have been happier. The family spent Saturday sightseeing in Seattle and getting reacquainted.

On Sunday morning, Tom loaded suitcases and backpacks into Marge's car as the children washed their faces and brushed their teeth. They piled into the car, and Susie and Tom waved goodbye as the kids laughed and waved. Even Henry, who might normally have cried for his mother, was caught up in the excitement. Susie fought off tears as they drove away. *It's only five days—five glorious days at that. We'll see them Friday.*

Marge loved the cottage at first sight. It sat on a bluff overlooking the Pacific about twenty-five feet above the ocean. There were three bedrooms: one for her, one for Tom and Susie, and one for the children. Although, she was prepared to have any or all of them sleep with her if they got scared.

A fence surrounded the house so the children could play in the yard. She wouldn't have to worry about them stumbling over the bluff. A gate led to stairs down to the beach. They looked a little steep, but she was sure they could make it. Tommy could help Henry if need be.

The sky was clear blue. The waves rippled on the water. It wasn't as warm as Hawaii, but there were no clouds, not a hint of rain—unusual on the Northwest coast even in August.

The children carried their suitcases and backpacks into the house and got settled in.

Henry and Sally lay down for naps, and Tommy played a video game on his iPad while the little ones slept. Marge had arranged for groceries to be delivered from town, and she stocked the shelves and refrigerator.

It was going to be a lot of work keeping them entertained, but she loved it. She pulled out her cell phone to check the time and realized the battery was dead. Shoot, where had she put the charger?

It was about time to wake the kids. Marge sat outside on the porch, enjoying the gentle sea breeze. Off to the west, there was a bright flash like a lightning strike at sea. *That's odd. Lightning without a cloud in the sky.* A few seconds later, she heard a loud thunder clap. She looked out to sea as a wall of water appeared.

Marge jumped up and turned for the door. Before she could open it, she was smashed from behind by the tidal wave. It ripped the door off its hinges and lifted the house off its foundation. Marge and the kids never had a chance.

The wave was seventy feet high and five miles long. It hit the coast with such force it decimated the town of Pacific Beach. Wooden structures were totally destroyed. Only a few brick buildings a quarter mile on shore remained standing, or partially standing.

Three hundred people lived in the Pacific Beach area. Another five hundred were in town or in the cottages and hotels nearby that Sunday enjoying the rare August sunshine. The water rushed a mile on shore and retreated carrying bodies, furniture, cars, and even whole houses with it. It was all over in five minutes. Nothing within a half a mile of the coast survived. The energy from the wave dissipated rapidly. Fifteen miles to the south in Ocean Sands, a ten-foot wave struck the coast, but damage was minor.

CHAPTER LXX

Tuesday, August 7th

Oak Harbor, Washington

Admiral Lockwood exited the C-40, saluted the base commander at NAS Whidbey Island, and headed straight for the MH-60S helicopter awaiting his arrival. Al Gianini and Paula Means followed. Petty Officer Maxwell saluted CINCPAC. He tried to hand the three of them navy-issued helicopter helmets and life vests, the kind which are provided to passengers on Navy helos. The admiral waved him off with a stern expression and hopped onto the helo, motioning Al and Paula to do the same. He didn't need a safety briefing or to be encumbered with any ill-fitting vest or helmet. He gave a thumbs-up to the pilot, and the helicopter lifted off the tarmac and headed south.

It had only been forty-eight hours since the North Koreans' counterattack. Acting President Smith had addressed the nation, vowing to "avenge the deaths of our navy servicemen and American civilians." He informed the nation that US forces were at DEFCON two in a heightened state of readiness. B-2 bombers were on their way to bases on Okinawa and mainland Japan. Trident submarines were steaming to their launch zones in preparation for an all-out missile strike on North Korea. Navy

Aegis ballistic missile defense destroyers—the heroes of Pearl Harbor II—were positioned off of Hawaii and Japan in case of a second strike. The SBX was positioned about 150 miles northwest of Hawaii. F-22 fighters were on alert at Anderson Air Force Base in Guam. F-22s from Hickam and Elmendorf air force bases in Hawaii and Alaska were in transit to Misawa.

As Khrushchev had warned Mao fifty years earlier, the US "paper tiger" was baring its nuclear teeth. President Wu of China called for a meeting of the UN Security Council to protest the mobilization. He cautioned Acting President Smith that no further attack on North Korea would be tolerated.

The first press reaction had been an outpouring of emotion and patriotic fervor like that following the attack of 9-11. As the reality of a possible nuclear attack set in, millions of Americans flocked to churches and synagogues. CNN ran old World War II footage of the devastation from Hiroshima and Nagasaki. Even Fox was circumspect about whether a call-to-arms was warranted.

Admiral Lockwood stared pensively out the window as the helicopter flew south over Whidbey Island and the Olympic Peninsula. His first reaction to the strike had been a determination to make the Koreans pay. As he reflected on it, though, he, like millions of other Americans, worried about the potential for miscalculation, escalation, and the loss of countless more lives.

He thought back to his conversation with Al Gianini on the flight to Whidbey from Hickam. As had been the case since the attack, Stu Lockwood couldn't sleep. He'd exited his private cabin and found General Gianini reclining in a business-class-like seat equipped with a foot rest. It wasn't quite as comfortable as the CINC's cabin, but it sure beat coach on commercial flights.

Stu looked at Al—eyes closed, breathing quietly. He turned to head back to his cabin. Al opened one eye and whispered, "What's up?"

Admiral Lockwood shook his head from side to side and scrunched his shoulders. He motioned for him to go back to sleep. He didn't speak, not wanting to awaken Midge and Paula, who were sleeping in the seats across from General Gianini.

Al pulled his seat upright and tilted his head, motioning to the rear of the plane. Stu nodded, and the two of them headed back to the admiral's cabin.

"Can't sleep?" Al asked once inside the cabin.

"I don't know how anyone can right now. Jesus Christ, what a mess. Remind me who Vice Chairman Sheng is and what he said."

Al grimaced. "Sheng is the head of the Chinese People's Congress and a close ally of President Wu. He said Wu is furious with the North Koreans, but equally upset with President Smith. The majority on the Standing Committee wanted to strike Kadena in retaliation. President Wu and the moderates fought them off.

"The North Korean retaliation was not a complete surprise to them. They expected a missile launch which, they were sure, would land somewhere in the Pacific Ocean. Such is the state of the North Korean missile program. But the fact that they possessed nuclear weapons was a horrifying wake-up call. Like us, no one in the Chinese leadership suspected the Koreans had nukes. Wu reached out to Kim Jong Un, protesting the use of nuclear weapons. He was told, 'What did you expect us to do?' He was surprised by the inscrutable response.

"Sheng warned me that Wu won't even try to fight the hardliners if we attack again. From China's perspective, the US was totally wrong for attacking North Korea. Privately, Sheng says Chinese leaders are grateful the North Korean missile program has been disrupted. But they oppose the attack. They view the North Korean nuclear response as foolish and destabilizing. But they also believe it was justified.

"Wu counseled the Koreans not to attack south or toward Japan. That left attacking the US as the only logical option. Again, Sheng insists Wu believed the response was appropriate. He assumed it would fail. If you ask me, I think the Chinese wanted to get a chance to see our BMD systems tested in real time.

"But Smith's move to DEFCON 2 has the Chinese president furious. His ambassador in Washington tried to get a meeting with Smith but was rebuffed. Secretary of State Archer tried to assuage the Chinese, but it hasn't worked. Wu is livid. He thinks he has no choice but to respond in kind if North Korea is attacked again. Sheng wouldn't say what the target was, but I believe Guam would be a logical choice. It's US territory and thereby doesn't get the Japanese or South Koreans involved. The Chinese would welcome the destruction of Anderson Air Force Base. Furthermore, I'm sure they know it would be almost impossible for our NMD missiles to defeat a missile strike on Guam.

"If Wu's forced to attack, he'd want to be sure it succeeded. Wu's message to the Chinese people yesterday was clear. The Chinese would consider any military action by the US to be very grave. Sheng insists this is not posturing. Wu is dead serious. If Smith acts, he will too."

"So much for helping my insomnia. What are our Asian partners thinking?"

Al stopped to ponder for a moment. "We've reached out to our former students in Singapore, Malaysia, Vietnam, and, of course, Seoul and Tokyo. The South Koreans are scared to death. They're still furious the US acted unilaterally but are coming around to the notion that being left in the dark was actually in their interest. The Japanese are pleased about the attack but upset the US launched the attack without notifying them. They're very worried they might be targeted by the North Koreans or Chinese. Our former students in Singapore and throughout Asia have universally condemned the attack. Many have likened it to the Japanese attack on Pearl Harbor. They're outraged that our so-called democratic government would act so irrationally. Any additional US action is likely to drive them—except Taiwan—into the Chinese camp, even the Japanese."

"So you're saying we've set our Asian partnerships back a generation."

Al sighed. "That's about the gist of it."

"When we get back to Honolulu, I want you to continue to talk to them. I'll pass on your comments to the chairman and recommend restraint. Now you should try and get some sleep. We'll be on the ground in less than three hours. And, Al, thanks for coming along on this trip. No one likes to go to funerals. There wasn't any reason for you to come."

"Stu, you couldn't have kept Midge and me away, even if we had to fly coach on a red-eye. We both thought the world of Marge. We can't imagine not being there to celebrate her life and those of your grandchildren, not to mention all the navy families who lost their lives. We're just glad you invited us to join you on this plane. It beats flying steerage on the airlines. And that goes for Paula too. She had a particular fondness for Marge."

Admiral Lockwood smiled a little and clapped Al on the shoulder as he left his cabin. He lay down on the bed, still unable to sleep. After a while, he recognized the telltale smell of coffee and the sounds of stewards walking up and down the aisle signaling dawn.

The whining of the helicopter engines and *wop wop wop* of the rotor kept a constant beat. Admiral Lockwood jerked back to the present when the pilot announced they were coming up on Pacific Beach. The admiral looked at the scene below. The remains of an uprooted village were displayed below in a topsy-turvy kaleidoscope. Overturned cars, fiberglass insulation, and torn-up building materials, a stainless steel sink, shingles, overturned suitcases, broken chairs and tables, couch cushions—all littered the landscape. Evergreens lay on their sides or upside down. A Navy Seabee work party with heavy equipment was clearing the rubble. Little remained standing along the coast except a few pieces of cinderblock foundations from the beach cottages that once sat on the bluff overlooking the ocean.

He choked up at the thought of Marge and the kids being swept away by the tidal wave. He hoped the terror and agony had not lasted more than a few seconds. From the location of their cottage on the bluff he was pretty sure the surge would've hit them with its full fury and minimized their suffering. He thought about his son and Susie. They were young and could probably have more children. But nothing prepared a parent for losing a child. Losing all three, and a beloved mother, in an instant would be a pain which they might never overcome.

He knew his anger and grief were shared by thousands of

others who lost family members in the destruction. Mostly he was angry at the arrogance of those who'd boasted that the North Koreans had no nuclear weapons and preached confidently that their infrastructure could be obliterated in one move. *How often have we let our hubris delude us into assuming victory?* In his lifetime he'd witnessed the catastrophe of Vietnam, the indifference to Al Qaeda until it was too late, and the intelligence failure that led to the attack on Iraq. Now this fiasco had cost thousands of innocents their lives.

He signaled the pilot to return to base, closed his eyes, and leaned back in his seat. It was 10 a.m. in Washington, DC. The Joint Chiefs of Staff were on their way to the White House to meet with President Smith. They simply had to convince the president not to attack. Could Smith actually believe that Armageddon would help his presidential aspirations? He must know the risk of escalation was far too grave.

With the rhythmic pounding of the rotary wings in his ears, Admiral Lockwood finally gave in to sleep, even if it was only for the thirty-minute flight back to Whidbey.

CHAPTER LXXI

Walter Reed National Military Medical Center, Maryland

Admiral Casey, the White House physician, paced up and down the corridor outside the president's room. It had been nearly two weeks since the president's collapse. Andrews had not regained consciousness following surgery. He remained in a comatose-like state, perhaps a result of the concussion. An MRI revealed little clear damage to his brain. His vital signs were generally good. There was no way of knowing his mental acuity and physical wellbeing unless he regained consciousness. The admiral was troubled about the nation's state of affairs. Losing 472 navy family members, officers and sailors, husbands, wives, and children, including the wife of the CINCPAC and his grandchildren, was tragic. Add to that the civilian losses that were still being calculated. All because of a miscalculation. It was unthinkable.

And Acting President Smith was contemplating another attack. Even if hostilities ended after an all-out assault on North Korea, he feared that fallout from the nuclear attack would spread to South Korea and even Japan. Millions of innocents would be threatened with radiation poisoning. And what if just one of the nation's aging ICBMs veered off course. Seoul, the capital of South Korea, sat only thirty-five miles south of the border with North Korea. Nearly 10 million people inhabited the capital and its surrounding communities.

Admiral Casey had prayed that the president would regain consciousness. But to what end? The president might be left with little mental capacity and no chance of resuming the office of the presidency.

After twenty more minutes of pacing, the admiral had decided. He had no choice but to act. He had been poring over recent medical literature on strokes. He discovered that a few patients had awakened from comas after receiving amantadine, a drug originally manufactured for influenza. It might not work, but Admiral Casey knew he had to take that chance. The nation desperately needed its president back. He found Mrs. Andrews in the private waiting room. He asked the others to leave them alone and sat down next to the first lady.

"Mrs. Andrews, the president has been unconscious for two weeks. The MRI didn't show permanent damage to his brain, but we can't be sure. Because we got him to GW hospital so quickly, we've been guardedly optimistic. For two weeks we've been hoping he'd regain consciousness. But, as you know, patients can remain in comas for weeks, months, even years. Some wake up eventually, but many never do.

"In my review of the recent literature on comas, I've found several instances in which patients have regained consciousness after being treated with different drugs. Ambien sleeping pills and another drug, amantadine, which was used first to treat patients with the flu but now is frequently prescribed to patients suffering from Parkinson's disease, have had some limited success. We don't know why they've worked on a few comatose patients, but they have. Normally I wouldn't even suggest this step. The prudent treatment is to wait. But, Mrs. Andrews, these aren't normal circumstances."

He swallowed hard and looked into her tear-filled eyes. "Your husband is the leader of the greatest power in the world. This great power and the entire world are in danger. Please forgive me for being so frank, but I fear that the acting president is leading us down a path toward global destruction. I know your husband would stop it if he were conscious."

She wiped her eyes with the back of a hand, but her lips were tightening into a grim line, almost a smile.

"It's up to you," Admiral Casey said. "But I'd like you to allow us to try amantadine on the president and see if he regains consciousness. I have to warn you, though, it might not work. It's entirely possible the president has suffered devastating brain damage from the stroke. He might remain in a vegetative state even if he regains consciousness. It's your choice. I apologize for burdening you with this. But I'd be racked with guilt if I failed to raise the possibility and more lives were lost."

Barbara Andrews looked up at Admiral Casey's tense, compassionate face. His hands were shaking. She had been slumped over when he first started talking, but now she sat up straight and stared deeply into the admiral's eyes. Her face was heavy with fatigue, but her gray eyes had a piercing, steely quality to them that took the admiral by surprise. She sighed and looked away for a moment. When she turned back, her eyes were moist with tears. She spoke softly but firmly.

"Admiral Casey, I want to thank you for everything you've done for Hal. I'll never forget your efforts to save his life and to care for him. I thank you also for caring so much about our country and her people that you could suggest this. I agree with you; Hal would never risk nuclear war. He wouldn't have made the same decisions as Vice President Smith.

"It'd be far easier for me and my family if we were to let him lie in peace, see where God takes us. But, like you, I couldn't forgive myself if we didn't try to revive him and see if he regained his mental acuity. So please, give him the medicine, and may God have mercy on us."

"Yes, ma'am." Admiral Casey rubbed away an unexpected drop of moisture on his own cheek. "And thank you so much. I know this isn't easy for you."

Under Admiral Casey's watchful eye, navy nurse Eva Claril administered the amantadine to the president. Mrs. Andrews asked the admiral to join her in prayer, and together they knelt at the foot of the president's bed. The admiral reminded her it could take many hours or even a few days before the drug worked—if it was going to work at all. He suggested she head back to the White House to sleep, but she declined. Instead, she pulled up a chair, sat down, and grabbed the president's hand. "This is where I belong now, Admiral. I know he can hear me, and I want to be here when he wakes up."

She smiled and blinked back a few tears. The admiral nodded to her with an approving smile. "The couch might be more comfortable," he added, before turning to leave the hospital room.

CHAPTER LXXII

Guangzhou, China

The North Korean nuclear weapon launch did not sit well with General Li Pen. "I knew it, Yong-Li. I knew it was a bad idea to trust the Koreans. What were you thinking?"

"It is too bad that the Koreans used the weapons. But it is also most helpful to our forces to see the strengths and weaknesses of the American capabilities."

"How can you think about that now? Don't you realize the danger this creates for us?"

"Sir, I recognize the Koreans' actions were most unfortunate, but I don't believe it should matter to us."

"Not matter!" Li Pen boomed. "Are you crazy? Of course it matters."

"Sir, our leaders will believe the Koreans are further along with their weapons design than we believed. The Koreans won't say anything. They want everyone to think they have nuclear warheads. They can use that leverage against the imperialists. There's nothing to trace the weapons to China or to you."

"'To me,' you say? You mean 'to us.' This was your crazy idea, Yong-Li. I only went along with it because of the debacle you created with Agent Xian. I never should have listened to you in the first place about trying to buy a congressman. What did it get us? I'll tell you what it got us. The loss of a million dollars, the loss of one of our finest agents, the watchful eyes of Beijing on our necks, and now this."

"Don't worry, sir. This will pass. I'm certain the Americans won't respond, and soon this will all blow over."

"I don't like it one bit, Yong-Li. I never should've listened to you. But you better be right this time, or you'll regret it."

"Please, sir, don't worry. It'll be alright. There's no way anyone will ever know what we've done. The social democrats in Beijing have no way to tie this back to you. They already cleared you of any wrongdoing in the Xian Huan Nod incident. There is nothing to lead them here. Your glass is more than half-full, sir."

"Half-full, my ass. Now get out of here. I don't want to hear any more about this."

Major Yong-Li bowed and left the general's office. He smiled a little as he shut the office door and shook his head. *Can this guy get any more paranoid?*

General Li Pen picked up the phone and called his assistant for personnel matters. "Major Yong-Li is to be reassigned today. I want him shipped off to the border with Nepal, away from the party functionaries of Beijing, and away from me. You understand? I want him out of headquarters today. Put him on a truck and send him to the border. I've had enough of his foolish ideas."

He slammed down the phone and paced across the floor. *He better be right, but I need to prepare as if I'm sure he's wrong.*

CHAPTER LXXIII

Wednesday, August 8th

Walter Reed National Military Medical Center, Maryland

At 5:30 a.m., nurse Roxanne Fowler checked in on the patient. She found Mrs. Andrews asleep on the couch. Someone from the previous shift had given her a blanket and pillow. Roxanne was careful not to wake her. She checked the president's blood pressure. It was low, but stable. She lifted his arm to make sure all his monitors were still connected. As she did, she thought she felt him flinch and saw his eyes flutter a little. She hit the assistance call button. Still trying not to wake up the first lady, she whispered, "Mr. President, can you hear me?"

The president stirred a little, and then parted his lips and mumbled, "Coffee."

Roxanne Fowler screeched and held her hands up to her face. Mrs. Andrews jolted awake and rushed to the president's bed.

"I'm so sorry, ma'am, but I swear he said 'coffee.'"

At that moment, Admiral Casey barreled through the door. "Nurse Fowler, what is going on in here?" Like Mrs. Andrews, Admiral Casey had decided his place was here with the president, and he'd been resting in the hospital room next door when he heard the commotion.

"Admiral, sir, when I reached over and spoke to the president, I think he said, 'coffee.'"

"Oh my lord. Nurse Fowler, I suggest you get the president a cup of coffee."

The president opened his eyes halfway and smiled. "Heavy cream, please. I've had navy coffee before."

The First Lady burst into tears of joy and bent over to hug her husband. Her tears fell onto his cheeks and lips.

"Salty," he said, licking his lips. Barbara Andrews wiped her eyes and laughed even as she apologized and wiped the fallen tears off of his face with her sleeve.

Two navy doctors, four nurses and two Secret Service agents all looked through the door at the president. A broadly grinning Admiral Casey instructed them on the next steps, checking his vital signs and making sure he was comfortable.

Nurse Fowler stepped into the room accompanied by the smell of strong coffee. The president beckoned her over to the bed and motioned for the bed to be raised so he could drink. She offered him a sip, gripping the cup and leaning in toward him. But he reached for it and took it from her hands. The doctors and nurses gaped at the miracle cure occurring before their eyes. Admiral Casey instructed the Secret Service to call the national security advisor and chief of staff. "Tell them the president is awake and appears to be lucid."

CHAPTER LXXIV

White House

Jack Ralston awakened Vice President Smith with the news a little after 6 a.m.

"Mr. Vice President, it's Jack. President Andrews has regained consciousness. He is described by the White House physician as lucid. If this is true, I imagine he'll be retaking the office of the president later today. His COS Hank Wallace is on his way to Bethesda to brief the president on North Korea and Pacific Beach. My bet is he'll call the Joint Chiefs to the hospital later this morning for their assessment. And Mr. Vice President, Larry, I'm sorry. We always knew this was a possibility, but it sure didn't seem likely."

"Oh my Lod, Jack, how's this possible? He had a massive stroke, and he's been in a coma for two weeks. How can he be lucid?"

"I don't know, Mr. Vice President. All I know is what the doctors are saying. The president is awake and cracking a few jokes with his wife and staff. He isn't aware of what has happened in the world, but that's only a matter of time. We both know he won't be pleased."

"Holy shit, Jack, I better talk to him. Do you think I should go to the hospital?"

"I don't think so. You should wait for his call and be ready to explain your actions. You need be clear that what the country needs right now is to see strength and resolve. And then you need to plead with him not to repudiate your actions on the basis of party loyalty and unity. And, most of all, you need to get his assurances he won't go public with any policy disagreements between the two of you."

"Fuck, Jack, just when we started to gain on Parker this has to happen."

CHAPTER LXXV

Walter Reed National Military Medical Center, Maryland

As Jack had predicted, the president called the Joint Chiefs of Staff to the hospital. By noon, the president was briefed on the situation with North Korea and the Chinese. And he'd learned their collective view—Vice President Smith was carrying out the president's orders by attacking North Korea. At 2 p.m., he summoned the vice president to Bethesda. Despite warnings from his doctors that he should not get overly agitated, he reamed him out. The president agreed it would not be good for him to denounce the attack on North Korea, but he was seething.

"What the hell's wrong with you? Surely you wouldn't put your election prospects ahead of the national interest. You can't seriously believe attacking North Korea was in the best interests of this nation. I'm outraged. You knew I opposed attacking North Korea without provocation. And yet, you went forward. Doesn't the Constitution mean a damn thing to you?

"The people of America didn't elect you president. They elected me. It was my policies you were supposed to carry out when you took over. Instead, you did exactly the opposite of what I told you I'd do. If the Hill knew this, the articles of impeachment would be drawn up in minutes. I wouldn't be at all surprised if you became the first vice president convicted and thrown out of office. How can I support you as my replacement if this is an example of your judgment?"

Larry bristled. "Mr. President, I know you and I disagree on this, but I did what I thought was best for the country. As the North Koreans demonstrated, they're further along with their nuclear program than our intel suggested. The fact they could launch two nuclear weapons is inescapable evidence that we had been underestimating them. Mr. President, with all due respect, we simply cannot allow a nuclear nutcase in North Korea. We should act to take him out and make him pay for the lives lost at Pacific Beach."

"And to what end, Larry? So the Chinese can launch a retaliatory strike against us? And even if they don't respond. What about the millions of North Koreans trapped in a totalitarian police state who'll die? Do you want their deaths on your conscience? Well, I don't."

President Andrews fixed the vice president with an icy stare. "At 3 p.m., in less than thirty minutes, you're going to go before the press and announce that, thank God, I've fully recovered and resumed my office. You'll inform them that I'm still going through testing at the hospital, but the doctors are planning to release me this evening.

"Furthermore, you'll tell them you and I have agreed we're lowering our readiness to DEFCON 4. Tell them that I've reached out to President Wu to discuss the crisis. Express your regret for the loss of more than one thousand American lives. Apologize to their loved ones, but explain nothing's to be gained by retaliating against the people of North Korea who are trapped in a police state. Say that instead of attacking, we'll take this to the

United Nations, deploring North Korea's use of nuclear weapons and demand sanctions against the regime."

Larry's face had grown increasingly red throughout the president's speech, but now he exploded. "Apologize? You expect me to apologize?"

If his tone before was icy, now it was glacial. "Mr. Vice President, I'm ordering you to apologize for the loss of American lives, including hundreds of our servicemen and women. If you don't, I'll have the senate majority leader and the speaker summoned to this hospital. I'll demand they begin impeachment proceedings. Is that clear enough? Now get the hell out of here, and prepare your apology."

"Yes, sir, Mr. President."

Larry Smith turned abruptly and left the hospital room.

Rage burned across Larry's face. Jack could tell the meeting hadn't gone well. The vice president barked at the staff to take him to a room where he could compose a statement. He motioned for Jack to join him.

"That motherfucker wants me to apologize. Apologize! Doesn't he know what that'll do to my campaign? Ten days before the convention, and he wants me to apologize?"

"Yes, sir. Now what exactly did he say? Are you to apologize for attacking North Korea?"

"No. I'm supposed to apologize to the families who lost loved ones. He wants me to say that, instead of retaliating, we're going to run to the UN like some little girl with a skinned knee running to mama."

"Is he going to stand by your decision to launch the first strike on North Korea?"

"Yes, he agreed it wouldn't be good for the nation to repudiate the attack. He agreed not to go public with his opposition. But, Jack, he fucking threatened to have me impeached if I didn't apologize. I can't apologize. I'll look like a fool. Parker will have a field day with this."

"Mr. Vice President, you don't have a choice. If you don't do what the president directed, number one, you'll be viewed as insubordinate by the voters. Number two, I'm sure he's seriously threatening you with impeachment. And, number three, now that he's back in command, there won't be a second strike on North Korea. With all due respect, sir, an apology is not only what you have to do, it might actually work in our favor."

"What the hell are you saying? An apology might help us? You're crazier than he is."

Jack held up both hands in supplication. "Sir, I know you're upset, but listen to me for a moment. First, what's most important? That he doesn't disavow the strike. Second, you aren't apologizing for the attack, you're apologizing for the loss of American lives. You already did that for all practical purposes with your speech to the nation last week. Third, in some ways the president awakening lets you off the hook. You had little choice but to retaliate. But all indicators suggest the Chinese weren't going to let this go unanswered.

"While the American public rallied around you when you attacked North Korea, the polls are showing they're not at all that keen on a second strike. They're worried about an all-out nuclear war. You know as well as I do that if the Chinese launched a serious attack, we couldn't stop all their missiles. The resulting devastation on both sides would set the global economy back a generation, if not more. No one knows what the impact would be from a nuclear conflagration between two superpowers. But, everyone agrees it would be devastating.

"So, Mr. Vice President, on one level the president has done you a favor. Most Americans now see you as a strong leader who stood up to the Koreans. You can campaign on that. You'll stand up to the Koreans, the Chinese, anybody. That's a good thing for any Democratic nominee. And now you don't have to risk the chance of it getting out of control. Sir, the military knows you are a strong leader. We can back channel to your friends on the Hill and in the press that you wouldn't have backed down. The fact that we were at DEFCON 2 this morning is proof you're one tough stud. Parker can claim we're running to the UN like a weak schoolgirl, but the public will know it wasn't your idea. You come out looking strong and decisive. We've shifted the focus away from Parker and his charisma and toward you as a hard-nosed leader.

"So, sir, let me draft a short statement for you in the next ten minutes. It will apologize for the loss of lives and express your gratitude to God for reviving President Andrews. At the same time, I'll explain that the president is working with the Chinese. He has directed that we take our forces off alert and go to the UN. It'll be clear this is his idea. You can look compassionate and maintain your resolve in the eyes of the American public. As long as the president stands by your decision for the first strike, you can come out the winner. Sir, I know this wasn't the outcome you were hoping for, but I think we can make the best out of it. With the right spin, we can actually work it to your advantage."

"Jesus Christ, Jack, I'm not sure about this. I sure hope you're right. But seeing as I don't have any choice, just get me the fucking statement."

CHAPTER LXXVI

Thursday, August 9th

Pearl Harbor, Oahu

Commander Chuck Syracuse set the USS *Bremerton*'s course to-ward the northwest in search of any remnants of the ICBM shot down by the *Lake Erie*. On Sunday morning, all Hawaii-based radar and imaging assets had been focused on one trajectory— that of the incoming North Korean missile. On Monday morn-ing at the Maui supercomputer, Freddy Watanabe and Captain White had taken the data and, using image processing, identi-fied a large fragment that had fallen intact from the destroyed missile. They took radar imagery from the SBX, matched it up with the imaging from the MSSS telescope, and projected a path that the debris would have traveled down into the Pacific Ocean.

Now it was Chuck Syracuse's job to find it and retrieve it. His Los Angeles class submarine was nearly thirty years old, but sitting in its forward torpedo tube was the navy's newest un-manned underwater vehicle. This UUV was designed to search for artifacts on the ocean floor. It was equipped with a low-light imaging camera, a side-scan sonar able to map the ocean floor, and an articulating arm that could grab items off the bottom and carry them to the surface. A surface ship, in this case the

USS *Paul Hamilton*, could retrieve the UUV and its treasure.

The Maui supercomputer identified a search area approximately one hundred miles northwest of Kauai. At ninety-five miles out, Commander Syracuse gave the order to deploy the UUV. Less than two hours later, the UUV spotted a three-foot-long item on the ocean floor. It looked like the one Maui had identified. The UUV's camera took a close-up of the item. It appeared to be the front end of a reentry vehicle from a ballistic missile.

The commander gulped in a swallow of air. This so-called remnant might include an active warhead. Hard as it was to believe a warhead could still be intact after the blast and descent through the atmosphere, that was certainly what it looked like. Commander Syracuse radioed the Pacific Command's submarine headquarters, SUBPAC, at Pearl Harbor.

Admiral Henry "Huck" Finn was standing by, awaiting word on the *Bremerton*'s progress.

"Sir, this is Commander Syracuse on the *Bremerton*. We've located a missile remnant which appears to be the front end of a reentry vehicle. We can't be positive, but the image from the UUV is pretty clear."

Admiral Finn leaned forward, his eyes widening as he continued to listen.

"Sir, I'm not a missile expert, but it sure looks like the area where the warhead was housed is intact. We can't tell if there is interior damage. From what it looks like, the interceptor sliced the RV in half or blew up the back end and left the front intact. Sir, requesting instructions on how to proceed. The UUV technicians believe they can pick it up and take it to the surface. But sir, if this is a nuke is that what you want us to do?"

Huck Finn was sitting in his office on top of the old dive tower at the sub base. From this position, he had a great view of the Pearl Harbor naval base and the vast expanse of Pacific Ocean beyond. He shook his head slowly, trying to process what he'd just heard.

"Commander Syracuse, could you repeat that? I thought you said you think you spotted the North Korean warhead. Did I hear you right?"

"That's affirmative, sir. The UUV has found an item which matches the description from the imagery explosion. It's about one meter in length and looks like it could be the front end of an RV. I'd have a hard time believing it myself, sir, but I'm staring at it. The image from the vehicle is pretty clear."

"Wow."

"Yes, sir. But, sir, how should we proceed?"

Huck Finn had no idea how to respond to his sub commander. He had no idea if the warhead was still intact. He had no idea whether it was still capable of exploding. The one thing he did know was that he couldn't leave it in the middle of the ocean.

"Commander, sit tight for now. Don't touch the weapon. But at the same time don't let it out of your sight. And send me a copy of the images. I'm going to have to talk to the ordnance experts about what we should do next."

"Roger that, sir. We're standing by and will maintain positive visual contact."

CHAPTER LXXVII

Off the coast of Oahu

"Admiral Finn, this is Commander Syracuse on the *Bremerton* again. Sir, I've been talking to the captain of the *Paul Hamilton*, Commander Chip Cooley. Sir, he has an explosive ordnance detachment on board that he believes could safely acquire and control this thing—even if it's a nuke. I have him on the radio and can patch him through to you if that's alright."

"Very well, Commander, put him on."

"Commander Cooley, you're on the line with SUBPAC. Why don't you tell him what your guys think we should do?"

"Yes, sir. Admiral Finn, I'm Lieutenant Commander Chip Cooley, the captain of the USS *Paul Hamilton*. We're sitting about twenty miles from the *Bremerton*. We were supposed to take possession of the missile fragment once it was raised it to the surface."

"Go ahead, Commander. I'm aware of your mission."

"Yes, sir. Sir, I deployed this morning with an EOD team as a precaution since we were dealing with a missile. They're part of this new unit that combined the harbor clearance unit with the mobile EOD detachment at Pearl. Sir, these guys are in charge of all explosive ordnance disposal, including radiological material. Sir, they've seen the image from the UUV. They recommend you have the drone bring the fragment to the surface. They'll sail to the site on a small watercraft and take control of the fragment from the UUV at that time. Once the *Bremerton* has recaptured the UUV and deployed away from the area, they'll inspect it. They've got the expertise and equipment to monitor and contain any radiological or chemical leaks.

"If they're sure it's inert, we'll bring it back to the *Paul Hamilton*. If it looks active, we'll tow their vessel back toward Pearl where we can offload it on a barge that handles nuclear weapons. And, sir, the EOD team says, while it is very unlikely the weapon is still active, they can't rule it out. There are a couple of cases where nuclear weapons lost over the ocean have had their warheads remain armed. In most cases the RVs are destroyed at impact; the interceptors burn up re-entering the atmosphere. But since this appears to be intact, there's a small chance it could still be extremely dangerous."

"And are they prepared to neutralize the warhead if it's still active?"

"Sir, they believe they might be able to, but it depends on the amount of damage."

"OK, Commander, that does seem to make the most sense. We can't leave it where it is. We have to either bring it in or destroy it, and without knowing if it's armed, we can't take a chance and destroy it on-site. I hope your guys are up to the task."

"Sir, I've seen these guys in action. They're amazing. If anyone can deal with this, it's them. They can be ready to go in about thirty minutes. We'll be standing by when the fragment gets to the surface."

"Alright, Commander. Chuck, how long will it take you to grab it and get it to the surface?"

"Sir, we've been studying the fragment and believe we know

how to grab it. If we're right, it shouldn't take more than thirty minutes."

"OK, gentlemen, proceed on that basis. Commander Syracuse, please keep the *Paul Hamilton* and me apprised of your progress. And, gentlemen, Godspeed."

"Yes, sir."

Commander Syracuse rang off and turned to Petty Officer John Stilwell, who sat at the controls of the UUV. "Petty Officer Stilwell, she's all yours."

"Aye aye, Captain. We'll lower her right over the RV and deploy the arm to the back end. We should be able to clamp the jagged edge there and lift her off the bottom. Once we get moving, as long as we keep ahold of it, we shouldn't have a problem raising it to the surface."

"Have at it, John."

Petty Officer Stilwell lowered the UUV into position. He swung the UUV's arm down and clamped it onto the rear of the fragment. He increased the pressure of the clamp until he was sure it had a very firm grip. Taking a deep breath, he inched the UUV off the ocean floor. The RV rippled free from the sandy bottom and began a slow journey to the surface. Commander Syracuse shared a hug with his executive officer. He barely resisted the temptation to slap Petty Officer Stilwell on the back.

As predicted, the fragment reached the surface in thirty minutes. Commander Syracuse informed HQ and the *Paul Hamilton* that all was ready for the EOD experts.

Within five minutes after deploying from the *Paul Hamilton*, the EOD vessel reached the UUV. Divers began a visual inspection of the fragment. They confirmed that the item was, in fact, the housing for a warhead. They placed an inflatable raft underneath the fragment and radioed back for the UUV to release its hold. Once the UUV released control, they moved the fragment away. The divers waited while the *Bremerton* took control of the UUV and left the blast area.

Once *Bremerton* was away, the EOD technicians began their check for radiation or signs of any chemical leak. To their great relief, there was no active radiation. But it was clear they were staring at what was left of a nuclear device. They radioed the *Paul Hamilton*. The fragment was the remains of a damaged nuclear warhead but shouldn't pose a significant threat. They recommended the *Paul Hamilton* tow them and the fragment back to shore instead of offloading the item onto the destroyer.

Admiral Finn agreed with their assessment, and the *Paul Hamilton* began a very slow crawl back toward Pearl Harbor. The ordnance personnel at West Loch were informed that the *Paul Hamilton* was towing a damaged nuclear warhead in for safe storage at the magazine.

Commanders Syracuse and Cooley arranged to meet at Schooners, the Pearl Harbor base club, at 1930 to share a cold one and toast their good fortune.

CHAPTER LXXVIII

Pearl Harbor, Oahu

Captain Hicks, the commander of Naval Magazine Pearl Harbor, was dockside at West Loch when the *Paul Hamilton* arrived. After a brief examination, NAVMAG technicians carefully lifted it from the water. They packed it in an airtight container. Radiation monitors showed only traces of radioactive material remaining on the fragment. But no one was taking any chances. Once Captain Hicks's crew confirmed that the fragment was inert, it was transported to the weapons laboratory at West Loch for closer inspection. Navy weapons experts at the lab examined the fragment for evidence of its origin. Dr. Fran Ho led the navy examination. Chinese characters were identified on the inside of the fragment. Traces of nuclear material on the inside were identified as coming from the Chinese nuclear program.

Dr. Ho informed Captain Hicks. He relayed the information to Camp Smith.

Admiral Lockwood was on his way back from Seattle when he received the call from his deputy, Lieutenant General Schofield.

"Good afternoon, Hugh. How is everything in Hawaii?"

"Good afternoon, Admiral. Sir, I understand you received a message from staff earlier today that the USS *Bremerton* found a fragment of the North Korean ICBM. We sent the fragment to the navy ordnance labs at West Loch where the NAVMAG experts took a look at it. Sir, the reason for this call is West Loch has identified the origin of the ICBM." He paused for dramatic effect. "Sir, it's Chinese."

"Chinese!" Stu leaped to his feet. "Good god, Hugh, that can't be right. We tracked that missile launch from North Korea. This wasn't a Chinese attack. It was North Korean. We're sure of that. There must be some mistake."

"Sir, the EOD experts are positive it's Chinese. They even called in language experts from UH to certify that the markings were, without a doubt, Chinese. We've also verified that the traces of plutonium are Chinese."

"So, the Chinese must have supplied North Korea with nuclear weapons? Oh my god, why in the hell would they do that? Hugh, report this to the Pentagon immediately and keep me posted. We'll touch down at Hickam in about three hours."

"Yes, sir. Safe flight."

Admiral Lockwood signaled for Al and Paula to join him in his cabin. "You aren't going to believe this."

"What's up, sir?" Al asked as Paula followed him into the admiral's quarters.

"Hugh Schofield called. The EOD experts at West Loch have confirmed that the RV contained a Chinese nuclear warhead." Stu held up a hand as two jaws dropped, and two pairs of eyes widened in shock. "Yes, I know. The Chinese must have given nuclear warheads to North Korea. On the one hand, that should calm the fears of the intel community and the Pentagon. The North Koreans haven't developed a nuclear warhead.

"On the other, it'll raise eyebrows in the White House when they realize what the Chinese did. It's crazy. The Chinese have believed the Kim regimes, from Kim Il Sung to the present, were all too nuts to have nukes. We've discussed this at all levels of leadership. Every Chinese political and military leader has agreed—the North Koreans shouldn't get their hands on nuclear weapons. This makes no sense, but they tell me the evidence is irrefutable. The North Koreans fired an ICBM equipped with a Chinese nuclear weapon. There's no doubt."

Al's dropped jaw had risen back to place, but his brows had leaped to his hairline, and he scrubbed at his chin with one hand. "Stu this doesn't make sense. We've worked with the Chinese for years on this issue. While they haven't actively stopped North Korea from developing nukes, it's been clear they didn't want that regime to have them. Nothing in our intel suggests the Chinese transferred warheads to the Koreans. What do you think, Paula?"

Paula frowned in fierce concentration. "Admiral, I agree with Al. Everything we know about the Chinese confirms that they don't want the Koreans, either North or South, to get nuclear weapons. They don't trust the North Koreans. For them to provide full-up warheads doesn't meet the test of reasonableness. Could the North have stolen them?" She held up a hand to fend off the immediate protests. "I mean, I understand Chinese security is pretty tight on its nuclear stockpile, but so is ours. That didn't stop an air force plane from carrying nukes to Taiwan by mistake. It didn't stop the B-52 from flying nuclear bombs to Barksdale that no one knew about. To me, as farfetched as it sounds, theft's more reasonable than the Chinese giving warheads to the Koreans."

Stu nodded slowly. "I agree with both of you. Something isn't right. But if the Chinese provided warheads to the Koreans and they launched them at the US, we have a new ball game. The White House can't accept this. They will have to react. We could be back threatening nuclear retaliation again." He turned toward Al. "You better check in with Beijing on a back channel and see what you can learn. The White House will go nuts when they hear that the Chinese are supplying the North Koreans with nukes. Andrews had just defused this crisis, and now I fear it isn't close to being over."

"I'll reach out to Sheng as soon as we land. If it hasn't gone public yet, I'll need to be a little cryptic, but I'll find out what he has to say about it."

"Al, the White House knows. We don't land for three hours. There's no way this stays quiet that long."

"Yeah, you're right. I'll keep an eye on CNN while we're flying and text him as soon as we land. Let me know if you hear any more."

"Tell Midge I'm sorry. We're going to have to shut off the movie and link to CNN to see what the rest of the world knows."

CHAPTER LXXIX

White House

"Mr. Vice President, Jack Ralston is on the line. Do you want to take the call?"

"Yes, Madeline, put him through."

"Mr. Vice President, it's Jack. You aren't going to believe this."

"What's up, Jack?"

"Sir, the nuke experts in Hawaii confirmed that the warhead which nearly blew them up was made by the Chinese."

"The Chinese? What, Jack? Are you sure? That doesn't make sense." Larry rubbed both palms across his face, then took a gulp from his coffee cup. "We know the North Koreans launched that attack—not the Chinese. What are you saying? The Chinese attacked? That can't be right."

"Listen, sir. The warhead was Chinese even though the attack was by the North Koreans. The Chinese must have provided the Koreans with nukes. This answers the million-dollar question: how did the North Koreans build a nuclear warhead without our intel being aware of it? They didn't. The Chinese gave it to them."

"Those dirty bastards. They gave the Koreans nukes so they could launch a counterattack." Smith smashed his fist into the desk. "This is outrageous."

"Well, sir, we don't know if the Chinese gave the Koreans nukes

CJ Houy

in response to our attack or if they did it earlier. Considering the timing of the counterattack, I'd say it's more likely the Chinese had already provided the Koreans with the weapons. Either way, it's unbelievable."

"That's even worse. Beijing is playing us for a fool. They talk a good game of trying to rein in the Koreans. They sat in the six party talks and counseled restraint to the Koreans while supplying them with weapons behind our backs. Even Andrews can't wish this one away. He's going to have to do something. I'm going to talk to him."

"You should. But let him tell you what's going on. I don't want him to know I clued you in on this. There are already rumors in the media about something like this, so you can refer to that."

"OK, Jack, thanks for the tip."

"Madeline, tell Betty Lou I'm on my way down to the Oval Office."

294

CHAPTER LXXX

White House

"Mr. President." Larry stood rather formally before the desk in the Oval Office. "The press is reporting something to the effect that it was the Chinese who attacked us last week, not the Koreans. What the hell's going on?"

"Larry, I was going to call you. The press, as usual, is not exactly right. The navy found a remnant from the missile fired at Hawaii. Our experts in Hawaii examined it and are sure the warhead was Chinese. Now, we're certain the Koreans fired it. That means it somehow made it from the Chinese to the Koreans before launch. It raises a lot of ugly questions about what the Chinese are up to. I just got off the phone with Ambassador Keating. He's headed to the Chinese foreign ministry to protest this outrage. He'll tell them in the strongest possible terms that the United States will not tolerate this criminal action."

"That's it? The Chinese attack, and you're ordering a demarche? Have you raised our DEFCON status? Have you ordered a counterattack on the Chinese? Mobilized our fleet in the Pacific? The Chinese gave the Koreans weapons to attack us, and your answer is to issue a diplomatic protest? Mr. President, with all due respect, that's outrageous." Larry's face flushed as he struggled to keep his voice under control. "That's like wagging a finger in a bully's face after he's pummeled your little sister. You're only encouraging them. You've got to respond, Mr. President. When this gets out, America will be the laughingstock of the world. Jesus Christ, Hal, grow a pair."

Andrews rose slowly to his feet and pointed a shaking finger at the vice president. "Get the hell out of my office. This is your fault. None of this would've happened if you had followed my direction. The blood of thousands of Americans is on your hands, Larry. You did this. You ordered the attack." He lowered both hands to his desk and leaned forward, face grim. "I'll confront the Chinese with the evidence, demand an apology and an explanation. And I'll go to the UN. But I'm not going to have this escalate into World War III. Now get out!"

"Yes, sir, Mr. President, I'll get out." Larry's mouth twisted into a snarl. "But, you listen to me. The American people won't stand for this. Once they know, they'll rise up in protest to your weak-kneed response. Your legacy will be worse than Chamberlain's. Appeaser, that's what they'll call you, the Great Appeaser."

Vice President Smith turned on his heels and stormed out of the office.

CHAPTER LXXXI

White House

Larry Smith shouted at his assistant Madeline, "Get Jack in my office now."

He slammed his door and proceeded to circle around the room, unable to calm himself. Within minutes Madeline informed him Jack Ralston was coming in.

"Mr. Vice President, you wanted to see me? How did it go with President Andrews?" Jack's normally calming voice had no effect on Larry this time.

"I'll tell you how it went. The Great Appeaser is issuing a demarche to the Chinese and threatening to take the case to the UN. Jesus Christ, it makes me sick. The Chinese attack our homeland, thousands of Americans die, and he wants to go to the UN like a silly schoolgirl. Jack, I can't stand it. The public won't stand for it. They'll be outraged by this chickenshit reaction. I have to go public on this, Jack. Our convention is a little more than a week out. The Parker coronation begins on Monday. If Andrews comes out with this weak shit, the GOP will crucify us. We won't have a chance of turning this thing around. I have to protest. The Chinese have to pay. We can't take this lying down. This country doesn't shrink from a fight!"

Jack jumped in as Larry paused to suck in a few lungfuls of air. "Well sir, you're right the GOP will decry the weak response, but I'm not sure what you can do. President Andrews holds the cards. Don't forget—he's threatened to have you impeached."

"He can't do that. The American people will be outraged when they learn about the Chinese deception. They'll agree that we did the right thing in trying to take out the North Korean infrastructure. Jesus Christ, Jack, we know now the North Koreans have access to any number of nukes. Who the hell knows how many more the Chinese gave them. Those bastards have already shown they're crazy enough to use them. The Chinese must be made to back down and pay for this outrage."

"Sir, you might be right about the public sentiment, but I'd be careful about challenging Andrews. He still has a lot of friends on the Hill, and you need his support."

"Jack, in two weeks he'll be old news. This'll be my party. I've got the nomination. The convention is a formality. The party functionaries and the congressional leadership will all rally around me. They need me to do well to protect their asses. But if I am going to have a chance in November, I have to let the American people know that I wouldn't take this lying down. People rally around a strong leader when faced with adversity. Andrews is a proven weak leader. I have to let them know I won't follow his lead."

"OK, Mr. Vice President, I see your point. But, I still don't think you can challenge him outright." Jack bit his lip as he paused in thought. "Tell you what. Why don't you let me confirm the news about the Chinese warhead—off the record. CNN is already tapping around about it. They know something is up. I can let them know on background that you're outraged. You want to put our forces on alert, go to DEFCON 2. If we get this out there before the president goes public, which I'm confident we can do, you might be able to force his hand. And, even if you don't, the press will be playing up the fact that you are demanding a strong response. That'll remind the American people you're the candidate of strength."

Jack warmed to his subject, a smile back on his face. "Once we get past the convention, and it is, in fact, your party, you can campaign on forcing the Chinese to pay for their transgressions. Parker won't have any counter to that other than to say 'me, too.' You can show that this election is about standing up to foreign aggressors, not cleaning up Washington."

"That's right, Jack. We'll hit him hard on my national security credentials. We'll take that away from the GOP. OK, you go with the leak. I'll talk about this at the convention and all the way to the presidency."

CHAPTER LXXXII

Honolulu, Oahu

When they arrived back at Hickam, Al drove Midge home and headed over to his office in Waikiki. She tried to convince him to stay home for a rest, knowing he hadn't had much sleep over the past couple of days. He told her there were a few things he needed to do to help out the admiral.

She smiled up at him. "Just don't work too long." She rested a palm against his cheek. "I'm proud of you, Al. You've been a great assistance to the admiral in this dangerous time."

They parted with a kiss.

When he arrived at the Asia Pacific Center, he was surprised to see he had an email from Vice Chairman Sheng asking him to call. He checked his watch, calculated that it was morning in Beijing, and placed the call.

"Mr. Vice Chairman, it's Al Gianini. How are you this morning?"

"General Gianini, thank you for calling me. I'm very concerned. We have received news from your CNN television. Your president is saying the nuclear weapon launched by the Koreans was a Chinese device. I can assure you, that is not the case. We have never provided the DPRK, North Korea, with nuclear weapons, nor would we. General, you must understand this information is wrong. Either your military is mistaken, or your politicians, again, are risking catastrophe. We heard Vice President Smith saying this could not stand. We can only assume he is speaking for President Andrews. We understand the president is still recovering from his illness." Sheng's normally cool voice grew heated. "Is he threatening to attack China? Is he a madman? Does he not know this would mean destruction for the United States? Don't kid yourself into thinking your missile defenses would stop our weapons. This is outrageous and foolish.

"President Wu has called a meeting of the Central Committee. I am sure it is to gain their approval for readying an attack on the United States. General, some of us were counseling restraint, but what's the use? You have shown you are willing to attack those who have not attacked you. You have defended your actions as a response to the Korean lies. Now it is you who are lying when you say the weapon is Chinese. You are threatening to attack our nation, which has long sought peaceful coexistence. How can you do this?" His voice turned bitter. "You teach democracy and preach peace, but you are a nation of warmongers. You have to understand how grave this situation is. I fear we are on the path of global destruction. I don't see how we stop it. And, General, if that is the case, the fault will be entirely on the Americans."

"Mr. Vice Chairman," Al kept his voice calm, but it didn't stop his hand from shaking with frustration and a twinge of fear. "I didn't hear the vice president's comments. I was on a plane returning from the funeral for the thousands of Americans who lost their lives because North Korea attacked the United States with a nuclear weapon. We were lucky the weapon missed its mark. Even so, we lost hundreds of navy sailors and their families who were enjoying a well-deserved vacation. All the residents of a small beach community in our state of Washington were murdered.

"But, Mr. Vice Chairman, our naval forces recovered the Korean reentry vehicle. Our nuclear experts know the warhead came from China. So, either your military is not telling you the truth, or the Koreans stole your weapons. But we have 100-percent-clear proof the warhead was yours.

"Mr. Vice Chairman . . . Sheng, please believe me. I'm certain our president doesn't want war. But China has to explain how the North Koreans had Chinese nuclear weapons. I cannot comment on what the vice president said. But, I can assure you, if you mobilize your forces, the United States will be forced to do the same. Neither you nor I want us to go down that path. I urge you to assure your president that we know the weapon was Chinese. If you didn't provide it to the Koreans, you need to find out how it made its way to Pyongyang."

"General Gianini, I am sure you think the weapon was Chinese, but I am confident you are mistaken. You must convince your leaders to stop the calls for war, or we will all regret it."

"Mr. Vice Chairman, I'll get you proof it was a Chinese warhead. Then, please convince President Wu to stop his mobilization plans. I'll send you the information as soon as I can. Please don't let anyone do anything foolish in the meantime. I'll call you back shortly."

Al Gianini hung up the phone and dialed Stu Lockwood. "Admiral, it's Al. Sir, we have a real problem. I spoke with Vice Chairman Sheng. President Wu is calling a meeting of the Central Committee to mobilize the Chinese military. He is preparing a strike against the US. He was unclear if the strike would be a response to a US attack or if the Chinese would initiate.

As you know, there are many Chinese military experts who believe the Chinese could only defeat the US by striking first. And they're probably right, given the superiority of our nuclear forces and missile defense capability.

"Admiral, we're facing a very grave threat. They don't believe that the warhead was Chinese. They believe this is just another excuse to attack them—like we attacked North Korea. I can't express this with sufficient gravity; we are in mortal danger, sir. I told Sheng I'd get him proof the warhead was from China. I don't know if that'll solve the problem, but at least it might stop this from immediately spiraling out of control. Stu, please, you have to get me a copy of a video or at least stills that show the evidence that the warhead is from China. That may be our only chance."

There was silence on the other end for an uncomfortable moment. Al frowned. "Stu, are you there?"

"I'm here, Al. As you can imagine, the photographic evidence is highly classified. It's being examined in DC now. I'm not authorized to release it."

"Jesus Christ, Stu, you know how serious this is. The Chinese are getting ready to attack. They could strike first. We have to do something."

"Al, never in my professional life have I leaked classified information. I've never violated my oath to protect and defend the Constitution. I'll talk to Sonny and see if he'll declassify the photos, but I can't do it on my own. We have to find another way."

"Stu, I understand the dilemma. I admire your integrity, but in this case, respectfully, you're wrong. The situation is too grave. We can't allow a bureaucratic regulation that overclassifies information to stop us from preventing a nuclear holocaust. We've got to give the Chinese this information to save us all."

"Al, I'll do what I can, but it's not for me to decide what's classified and what can be shared with a foreign government. We are a nation of laws, and that's the law. It's my duty to uphold the law even when I don't agree with it."

"OK, Stu, but do your best to get this declassified. I'm not sure how much time we have, but I'm sure it's not a lot."

Paula Means was standing in the doorway and had heard most of the conversation.

"That doesn't sound good, Al. Where are we?"

"Paula, Vice Chairman Sheng says the Chinese think we're lying about the warhead. They think we're using it as an excuse to attack. From what I understand, the vice president's comments haven't discouraged that notion. I tried to get Stu to give me pictures of the warhead to pass back to Sheng, but he won't do it since they're classified. He's going to ask General Gallagher to authorize the release. In the meantime, the Chinese are readying an attack. We're powerless to do anything."

Paula's tired eyes had gone wide with shock. "Oh my god, Al, that's unbelievable. What can we do?"

"Paula, I think it's out of our hands. About the only thing we can do is pray."

"Wait a second, Al." Paula's eyes snapped with inspiration. "Who do we know that can declassify this? The president, right?"

"Yes, the president can declassify anything."

"Who else?"

"Technically, I suppose the person who classified it could if he or she was persuaded it was classified in error. Short of that, we're stuck."

"OK, so we just convince the guy or gal who classified the pictures to change their mind. The info came from the *Bremerton* right?"

"Yes, they took the video and the first photos of the RV."

"OK, so talk to Huck Finn and get him to declassify it."

Al slammed a hand on the table. "Paula, you're brilliant. It's worth a shot."

Admiral Finn picked up on the second ring.

"Admiral, it's General Al Gianini from the Asia Pacific Center. Sir, we have a real problem and need your help. I understand your crew took a video and pictures of the ICBM that verifies the warhead was Chinese. Is that right?"

"That's right, General. What gives?"

"Sir, the Chinese think we're lying about the weapon. We'd like to show them the pictures or video, but it's classified. Admiral Lockwood is going back to DC to see if they will declassify it, but that's going to take too long. Sir, I'll be frank. The Chinese are getting ready to mobilize their forces for attack. They're afraid we plan to strike them, and they're likely to consider striking first. We have precious little time to convince them that we, in fact, have proof the warhead was theirs. What would it take to get you to declassify the images and allow us to send them to the Chinese?"

"General, it's not so simple. I can't declassify something just because I want to. You know that's not how the system works."

"Admiral, sir, of course I know that, but sometimes we classify things because it's the easy way out as a CYA exercise. I'm not accusing anyone of that, but we need to make sure the reason for classification is legitimate."

"OK, General, hold on. Let me pull up the images and see if I can figure out why they're classified." A tense pause followed. "Alright, I can see the image. Well, I'll be damned. I know why they're classified. The code name of the UUV that took the pictures is on the photo. Let me get that removed, and I think I can send you the images. Give me two minutes. If I'm wrong, and it's something else, I'll get back to you. You should expect to get an email from me with pictures that don't identify the vehicle in a couple of minutes."

"Admiral, thank you so much. Please hurry. I appreciate it."

"Sure thing, General."

General Gianini dialed again. "Stu, it's Al. Paula and I decided to talk to Admiral Finn over at SUBPAC. As it turns out, his guys classified the photos because they include the code name of their new UUV. He's checking but is pretty sure if he takes the code name off the photos, they'll be unclassified. I should have them in two minutes, and I'll pass them on to Sheng. I wanted to call to update you and—" Al swallowed and bit his lower lip. "And to apologize for asking you to release them on your own. You were right. It's not for us to decide when something should be classified. In the heat of the moment, I lost track of that. I'm proud you didn't and wanted to tell you so."

"Thanks, Al, you're a great friend. Let's hope Huck can get them declassified and you can get them to Sheng. Let me know what you hear."

"OK, Stu. I'll call you. Oh, wait a second. Here's the email from SUBPAC. I've got it, sir! I have the sanitized images to send to the Chinese. Wish me luck."

"For the sake of the world, good luck, my friend."

Sheng stared blankly at the images from Al—the Chinese markings on the inside of the RV were undeniable. The North Koreans had fired a Chinese nuclear warhead at the United States—just like the Americans were claiming. He made a beeline for the president's office with the photos.

CHAPTER LXXXIII

Beijing, China

President Wu viewed the images from Vice Chairman Sheng with skepticism. Yes, the Chinese markings were clear, but who was to say the photos were genuine? He was very aware of the ability of smart computer technicians to change images. He suspected the United States military had manipulated the data. In his view, the United States had been acting erratically. The attack on North Korea was unprovoked and completely uncalled for. Then, following the tragedy of the North Korean attack, the United States had again readied its forces for a second attack. Sure, President Andrews put a stop to that, but now the vice president was threatening another attack, only this time on China.

"Why should I believe these photos are real? You say you received them from a retired American general. Why should I trust him?"

"Mr. President, I can't say more than I trust General Gianini. I do not believe he would lie about this. He is very worried that events are spinning out of control. Please, sir, call President Andrews."

"I am reluctant to do so. The president is very ill, but he is not beyond playing political games."

"Again, Mr. President." Sheng's voice was soft but increasingly urgent. "We need to do whatever we can to avoid war if at all possible."

"Alright. I will call him, but you shouldn't get your hopes up. The Americans are acting more erratically every day."

Sheng stood by while President Wu made the call.

"Mr. President." Wu spoke formally, with as little of an accent as possible. "I hope you are feeling better. We have received word of your miraculous recovery and wish you good health."

"Thank you, Mr. President. I'm doing well, all things considered. I wish you and I were speaking at a time of less tension."

"Yes, Mr. President." Wu's voice tightened. "I am concerned your country's behavior is becoming erratic and destabilizing. We don't know who or what to believe. You say the Koreans used Chinese nuclear weapons to respond to your unprovoked attack. I know for a fact China did not provide them any nuclear weapons. We have worked with you for years to prevent the Koreans from developing them. What possible reason would we have to give them warheads?"

Andrews spoke warmly and reassuringly. "President Wu, I agree with you. It makes no sense to give that madman nuclear weapons. But the evidence is irrefutable. The remnants we recovered show, beyond a shadow of a doubt, the warhead was made in China. Mr. President, we have even checked the residue of radiological material from the fragment. Our scientists have confirmed it comes from one of your nuclear plants. We can share the evidence with your scientists, but that will take time. In the meantime, I'm told you're beginning to mobilize your forces to launch an attack. Mr. President, if that's accurate, it would be a very serious mistake. Now, I'm willing to send this matter to the United Nations if you're willing to apologize for providing nuclear weapons to the North Koreans. But you must also assure me the North Koreans do not have more Chinese warheads."

"President Andrews, why would I apologize?" Wu's tone grew more distant. "We did not give the North Koreans nuclear weapons. Why would I stand down China's forces when your vice president has threatened to attack us?"

"Mr. President, first, I can assure you we're not planning to strike China. Directly after my recovery, I ordered our forces to resume a military readiness level consistent with peacetime operations. Certainly your intelligence shows that. But if you insist on mobilizing your forces, I'll be forced to increase our readiness posture. You'll be leaving me no choice. Furthermore, Mr. President, it was your weapon that was responsible for the deaths of thousands of Americans. How do I explain to my people that you won't apologize for the loss of American lives when your weapon took those lives? Without your warhead, the North Korean attack would have been a complete failure. Mr. President, I repeat, I can assure you I will not order a first strike on China. In return, you have to assure me you will not strike. Second, you must apologize for your role in the loss of American lives."

"Mr. President, I will delay the mobilization of our forces. You must make clear in a public statement you have no intention of attacking China." Wu's lips tightened into a thin line. "And your vice president, who started this madness, must receive a public rebuke."

"President Wu, I'll make a public statement that the United States is taking this matter to the UN Security Council, not planning an attack. You must apologize for the loss of lives from your weapon. If you doubt my word the weapon was Chinese, send your scientists to Hawaii tonight. They can be there by morning and verify the weapon is Chinese. If you won't do that, Mr. President, you leave me little choice but to exact revenge for the loss of American lives." President Andrews's voice softened. "I'm sure you'd do the same thing if an American weapon had taken the lives of thousands of Chinese. We don't have a lot of time to stop this from escalating out of our control."

"Mr. President, I will take you up on the offer to send our experts to examine the weapon. We never provided the DPRK with weapons. However, if my experts agree the weapon was manufactured in China, I will apologize for the loss of lives. But you must apologize for the unprovoked attack on North Korea."

"Mr. President, I await the review of your experts. I'll prepare remarks to reassure the world. The United States will stop preparations to strike China if you stand down your forces. But, Mr. President, we will not apologize for taking out the illegal weapons production facilities in North Korea. You and the rest of the world should be thanking us for that instead of demanding an apology. A North Korean regime with nuclear weapons is a threat to every peaceful nation, not just the United States."

"President Andrews, let me hear from our scientists. Then we can better know how to proceed. I will give the order to stand down our forces, but if there is any change in your defense posture, I can assure you, you will regret it. Good night, Mr. President."

"Good day to you, President Wu. I look forward to continuing this dialogue when you've received the assurances from your experts."

President Wu hung up the phone and sat quietly for a moment, then turned to General Hun. "President Andrews is emphatic that the warhead is Chinese. I have known him for more than six years. While I would not say that I trust him, I am confident he believes the weapon was ours.

"Tonight, I will dispatch a team of our nuclear experts to fly to Hawaii and examine the weapon in question. The president assured me they can conduct an examination without interference. While I know that we did not provide the DPRK with nuclear weapons, one can never know for sure if they acquired them illegally. Therefore, General Hun, I am ordering you to conduct a review to ensure that 100 percent of our warheads are safe and secure. I expect this review to be completed within twenty-four hours. Please inform your forces immediately."

"Yes, sir, Mr. President." General Hun saluted and hurried from the room.

"Now, Vice Chairman Sheng, thank you for interceding in this matter. We do not know the truth yet. But the president has assured me the United States military will not attack China. Therefore, we will take no further steps to mobilize. If we receive a report back from Hawaii confirming that the weapon was ours and hear the president's public statement, we will stand our forces down."

Sheng bowed to President Wu. "Thank you, Mr. President, once again you have proven to be very wise. I trust you will sleep well knowing that the United States is not planning to attack. I know I will."

CHAPTER LXXXIV

White House

It was midnight when President Andrews put down the phone and collapsed into his chair. While he had regained consciousness and was mentally alert, he was exhausted and weak. He tried to make sense of the phone call. Could President Wu really believe the weapon wasn't Chinese? Was he toying with him? Sending his experts to verify the origins of the warhead could be a ploy. He could claim the information was falsified. *But, surely, he knows we'll call in the IAEA to confirm the origin of the weapon if the Chinese deny responsibility.*

President Andrews knew Wu well enough to realize he was not one to make idle threats. Wu was smart enough to know that mobilizing his forces was a serious step which would draw a strong reaction from the United States. *The only way this makes sense is if Wu actually believes we're lying about the weapon, using it as an excuse to attack.* And that only made sense if we thought our missile defenses could defeat the entire Chinese arsenal and were hell-bent on wiping out their regime and most of their people.

Why would he believe that?

He looked up and narrowed his eyes. Turning to his intercom, he yelled, "Betty Lou, have the vice president come see me now."

Vice President Smith was still angry over the way the president had treated him. He was furious about his plan to kowtow to Beijing. When he received Mary Lou's message, he welcomed a chance to share his views on why Hal Andrews was so backasswardly wrong.

♦ ♦ ♦

President Andrews sat stiffly at his desk, hands clenched in front of him.

"Mr. Vice President, you've got to be the stupidest man on the planet. Do you realize your comments to the press almost resulted in a first strike by China? Is that your idea of constructive policy engagement with a hostile nuclear power? Is that how you plan to conduct yourself as president?" He struck the desk with one hand.

"Well, I guess we already know the answer to that question. Yes, that's exactly how you'd carry out your responsibilities. You demonstrated it with your bone-headed decision to attack North Korea. Gee, that turned out well, right? We only lost a few thousand innocent Americans from that move. How does that compare in significance to poll numbers? Do you really think you have what it takes to be president because I sure have my doubts. Now, you jackass, you're going to shut up, especially to the press.

"President Wu has agreed to send his experts to Hawaii to verify that the weapon is, in fact, Chinese. He thinks we're lying,

314

but he's agreed not to mobilize his forces until they examine the weapon. I told him we'll take this matter to the United Nations if he'll apologize for the loss of American lives. And do you know what his counter was? He wants us to apologize for attacking North Korea—"

"—That's outrageous, you can't apologize for that. How could you be so stupid?"

"Me? Stupid?" President Andrews allowed himself an uncharacteristically unprofessional eye roll. "You've got a monopoly on stupidity, Larry. And, no, I didn't agree to apologize. But in my statement I'll make it clear this administration is not contemplating an attack on China. Too many Americans have died already. I will not risk the deaths of millions more to improve your election chances."

The vice president's face was bright red, and his eyes flashed fire. "God damn it, Mr. President, that's ridiculous. The Chinese provided North Korea with nukes, and they attacked us, and this is your response? Your approval ratings will hit zero with that move. But do you know what?" Larry leaned forward with a leer. "It doesn't matter, because you only have one more week. Sure, you'll be president for another five months, but no one is going to pay any attention to you.

"In ten days, I'll be the face of the Democratic Party, and you'll be a has-been, a lame duck. My face will be on the evening news. My views will be touted by the Democratic pundits. You'll pad around the White House waiting until we kick you out. The Democratic leadership across the country will be following my lead, not yours. And you know what, Mr. President? There isn't a damn thing you can do about it. So, enjoy your last week, Hal, because that's all you're going to get."

President Andrews leaped to his feet. "You arrogant, stupid son of a bitch. You can't talk to me like that. I'm the president of the United States. You might not like me or agree with me, but we're talking about the office of the presidency that you're trampling on. Now get the hell out of this office."

Larry Smith looked at the president and smiled like a man who knew he held all the cards. "Yes, sir, Mr. President. Thank you, Mr. President." He bowed, still grinning, and backed out of the Oval Office.

President Andrews hardly noticed the slight. He was feeling lightheaded as his blood pressure spiked. He lowered into his chair and dropped his head into his hands. *You've got to calm down. There is no frigging way you can die now and turn the country over to this idiot.* He took a few deep breaths and felt better. But he knew he had to be careful. He couldn't risk another stroke.

CHAPTER LXXXV

Friday, August 10th

Honolulu, Hawaii

At 4 p.m., the Chinese examiners had completed their review. Dr. Chiang Sun Lu was charged with placing the call to the president's office. Never before had he ever even seen the president, and now he was supposed to call him directly on the phone? Dr. Chiang was very concerned that his report would cost him his job at the Institute for Peaceful Nuclear Research and Policy. His hands shook as he read the phone number he had been instructed to dial. He took two deep breaths and punched in the last digit.

"This is President Wu's office. How may I help you?"

"This is Dr. Chiang Sun Lu in Hawaii. I was instructed to call this number once our work was completed."

"Just one moment, sir. The president is expecting your call."

"Yes, ma'am."

"This is President Wu. Is this Dr. Chiang?"

"Yes sir, Mr. President, this is Dr. Chiang." He gulped. "Sir, let me say it is a distinct honor to speak with you. I'm not worthy to be talking to Your Excellency."

"Dr. Chiang, what can you tell me about the weapon the Americans have?"

"Sir, we've reviewed the fragment that the American navy has." Dr. Chiang's face paled. "Mr. President, we can confirm it is indeed a warhead manufactured at the facility in Hei Fei. There are traces of plutonium on the weapon that we can also trace to our facility near Guangzhou." He bit his lip and continued. "Mr. President, I'm sorry that I have to inform you of this, but the evidence is clear."

"And you are certain it is a Chinese weapon? Is there any doubt?"

"Mr. President, I am so sorry to have to tell you this, but no, sir, there is no doubt. It is a Chinese warhead."

President Wu took a deep breath. Dr. Chiang's hands started to shake as he waited. "OK then, Dr. Chiang. Thank you very much. Oh, one more thing."

Uh-oh, here it comes. Dr. Chiang scanned the room, wondering if he could seek asylum in Hawaii. *I'm a coward to think of leaving my family behind, but maybe the government won't hold it against them. After all, they are not at fault.*

"Dr. Chiang?"

"Yes, Mr. President?" His voice started to quiver, and tears welled in his eyes.

"Dr. Chiang, is there any way to tell from which army unit this warhead came?"

Dr. Chiang was stunned by the question but gathered his composure.

"Mr. President, no sir, not really. We can identify where it was manufactured by the specific markings. We can't say which unit had the warhead. I'm sorry to disappoint you, sir."

"Oh Dr. Chiang, yes, I am disappointed, but not with you. I

thank you for your service to your country. Have a safe trip back to China."

"Oh thank you, Mr. President. Thank you, sir. Yes, sir, we are scheduled to leave within the hour. Sir, I can't wait to get back to Beijing. Thank you, sir."

The line went dead, and Dr. Chiang collapsed. His younger colleagues had crowded around him, hoping to hear the president's voice. They caught him before he fell to the floor, and he regained his footing.

"Colleagues, the president is a wise and gracious leader. He thanks us for our service and has assured me he is not upset with us for our findings. Come, let us gather our equipment and prepare to leave for the airport. We have escaped with our heads, and I don't want to spend another minute away from our beloved homeland."

The others clapped him on the back, then scurried around packing their instruments.

President Wu turned to look at Vice Chairman Sheng. "You were right, my good friend. Your American general was telling the truth. Somehow the Koreans were able to get their hands on at least two of our nuclear warheads. Thankfully, their missiles are of such poor quality that the damage was relatively minor." He turned toward the silent figure standing near the door. "And now, General Hun, you need to find out how these weapons found their way to the North Koreans. How close are you to completing your inventory?"

"Mr. President, we have examined our facilities in the north and east and have found nothing out of the ordinary, no missing weapons. Our inspectors are now reviewing our stockpiles in the south. We expect a report from them within the next four hours."

"Well, General, they need to hurry. President Andrews will speak to the American people within the next two hours. I must follow shortly thereafter with an apology for the loss of American lives. I cannot go apologizing on television until I know how we let the Koreans steal our weapons."

"Yes, sir, Mr. President, I can assure you our inspectors are working as fast as they can. It has only been eighteen hours since we began the search."

"That well may be, General, but we are nearly out of time. You must tell them to hurry."

"Yes, sir, Mr. President." General Hun saluted and hurried from the room.

"He's a good man, Sheng, but the army can be so damned slow. They will never understand politics."

"Yes, Mr. President, but you know, we don't really want the army to understand politics. That would make them very dangerous."

President Wu chuckled. "Well said, Sheng, very well said."

CHAPTER LXXXVI

Sunday, August 12th

Zhangmu, China

Major Yong-Li sat in a tavern in a small town on the Friendship Highway near the border with Nepal. A small black-and-white TV was broadcasting the news. President Wu had just finished speaking to the nation. He'd informed the Chinese people that General Li Pen would be hanged for treason. Acting on a tip, they'd discovered two nuclear warheads were missing from his supply. Army inspectors had long suspected General Li of corruption and insubordination. Now they knew he was also a traitor. A video of General Li being led away in handcuffs was shown in the background.

The president assured the Chinese people of the security of its nuclear stockpile. He cautioned the world that no nation can protect its weapons if traitors at the highest levels of government betray them.

He reminded his people that tonight they were a nation at peace. He welcomed the statement by the American president that the United States would not threaten the People's Republic. He also decried the recent belligerent statements from other leaders in the United States. He reminded the world that none of this would have happened had the United States not authorized an unwarranted and unprovoked attack.

President Wu apologized to the American people for the loss of lives. He noted that North Korea joined the United States as the only two countries to ever use nuclear weapons. He concluded, thanking the people of China for their love of peace and prosperity, and vowed to continue to serve them.

Major Yong-Li ordered another beer and a shot of Maotai, the white lightning liquor of presidential toasts in China. He raised the glass of Maotai, toasted the president and drank it in one gulp, slamming the shot glass down on the bar. The white liquid burned on the way down, and he chased it with a big swig of beer. He took another couple gulps of beer, draining his glass, and stood up. He paid the barkeep and headed back to his quarters on base. On his way back, he sang an old Chinese folk song about how the fox had made off with the chickens, and the farmer had cut off its head. He repeated the line about the farmer cutting off its head over and over, growing louder each time as he staggered along.

VIGILANTE POLITICS

PART THREE

Unconventional Outcomes

CHAPTER LXXXVII

Tuesday, August 14th

Hart Senate Office Building

Missie Walsh, the Rules Committee staff director, walked into her office, switched on the lights, and started up her computer. She sat down at her desk with a heavy sigh. She had seventy-five new email messages. Her phone was blinking that the voicemail on her private line was full of twenty new messages.

Welcome back, Missie. That's what you get for disappearing for the first couple weeks of August. She decided to get a cup of coffee before digging in and stood up, grabbing her cup. She bumped a five-inch-tall stack of mail on her desk as she turned to leave in search of coffee.

"Oh shit," she muttered as the stack spilled onto the floor. She put down her cup to collect the magazines, trade newspapers, and dozens of large envelopes. She grabbed a large envelope that was bulky, different from the rest. She opened it out of curiosity. It contained a videotape cassette and nothing else. *That's odd. I wonder what this is. Nobody uses these anymore.*

Curious, she shoved it into her TV. Lucky for her she still had that old-fashioned television with a built-in VCR, an ancient perk once reserved for senators and staff directors. She searched around for her remote control. When she didn't see it, she grabbed her cup and headed off for coffee.

Walking back in, she spotted the remote on her desk, half-buried beneath last month's projects. Dropping into her chair, she switched on the video. The black-and-white image was that of a hallway. Resolution was snowy but recognizable. She couldn't quite determine the location, but it looked vaguely familiar. After a few seconds, a doorway on the left side of the hallway opened. A man came out and walked away with his back to the camera. She was mystified. *What the heck is this? Who was that guy?* Thinning gray hair, probably six feet tall, medium build, dressed in a business suit. That was all she could tell. Still, something about him seemed familiar.

The video played on showing nothing more than an empty hallway. She reached over to punch the fast-forward button when the door opened again. A woman emerged from the same room. She was average height, thin, wearing a dress and carrying a medium-sized purse. She was wearing a hat that obscured her face. She peered down the hallway in the direction the man had departed and turned facing the camera. Missie had a hard time not spitting out her coffee.

What the hell? What is this? Where is this? Wait a second. It's the Capitol. It's a corridor off the rotunda by the Office of the Sergeant at Arms. What is Rebecca DeLaurio doing there? I haven't seen her since she testified before the committee almost two years ago. I heard she disappeared.

Missie rewound the video a couple seconds. Which office was that? Not the sergeant at arms'. It must be a hideaway. *Why would someone send me a video of Rebecca? What is she doing back in DC?* The image froze with the top of Rebecca's hat and an empty hallway, and the screen went blank. Rebecca turned off the VCR, and C-SPAN's gavel-to-gavel coverage of the Republican convention filled the screen.

Missie had returned to Washington this week because the Republican convention was underway. Everybody else was likely on vacation except her assistant, Maria, who had volunteered to come in and answer the phones. Missie expected to have plenty of free time to catch up on her mail and messages. The chairman was in Denver at the convention, as were most of the Republican political and leadership staff and lobbyists. Yet, she sat in her chair staring at the TV but paying little attention. Jake English, the congressman from Utah, was addressing a nearly empty convention hall on the sanctity of marriage. On this Tuesday, most delegates had something better to do than sit in the convention hall.

Where did that tape come from? Why send it to me?

Missie dove into her pile of mail, throwing out advertisements, old newspapers, and magazines. She skimmed a few GAO reports, tossed a few, and threw the rest in her outbox for Maria to pass on to the staff. Within an hour she had completed the stack of mail. She scanned her email and deleted nearly half the messages. She read about a dozen and forwarded or responded to them.

With a sigh, she picked up her phone and started through voicemail messages. The first four or five were from lobbyists—former colleagues wanting to get together during the recess. On the seventh message, a distorted voice said, "Pretty interesting video," and hung up. Missie had been only half paying attention, but she jolted back to alertness. She played it again and confirmed that was really what she'd heard. She didn't recognize the voice. She checked the number, but caller ID was blocked. She checked the time, 10 a.m. Tuesday, a week ago today. Obviously, whoever sent the video wanted to make sure she saw it.

She saved the message and continued with her voicemail. Nothing special. Several were from the Capitol Police, warning staff of suspicious packages around the Capitol complex. Those came all too frequently—whenever a tourist forgot their back-pack or shopping bag somewhere in the Capitol. Her fifteenth message was dated last Thursday morning. Again, a distorted voice spoke, this time with a little anger. "Watch the video, and do your duty."

Again, the number was blocked.

She completed the remaining messages with no more sur-prises. The last message was from Friday afternoon—another notification from the police about a suspicious package in the Hart office building. No all-clear message followed because her voicemail had filled up. Having walked through the Hart build-ing, Missie was pretty sure it had been another false alarm.

The anonymous messages were more troubling. What did he mean, "do your duty"? Why would anyone care if Rebecca was back in DC? There weren't any charges pending against her. Why was it Missie's responsibility to alert officials about Rebecca's whereabouts? She picked up the plain manila envelope—no re-turn address and no postmark. It must have been dropped off in the office or left in the Rules Committee mailbox right outside the door.

Missie called the information security office of the Capitol Police. One benefit of being staff director of the Rules Committee was that the Senate bureaucracy was sensitive to your needs. Everyone knew Rules controlled office space and parking. The committees knew Rules also controlled their budgets. Rules could screw around with any department or office. When the staff director called, the response was prompt. Sergeant Wallace, a twenty-year veteran of the Capitol Police, took her call. "This is Sergeant Wallace, ma'am. What can we do for you?"

"Sergeant Wallace, this is Missie Walsh from Rules. I received an anonymous voicemail, and I was wondering—do you have technology that can identify callers even when the number is blocked by caller ID?"

"What sort of phone call was it, ma'am? Was it threatening or offensive?"

"No sir, but it'd help me if we could identify the caller. The call involves a former staffer who was investigated a while back. Under confidentiality rules, I'm not allowed to disclose any more details." Missie's answer was not very forthcoming although it was technically truthful. She couldn't discuss private personnel matters.

"OK. Well, we don't have the capability. I could check with Verizon. They handle the local phone lines, but I doubt they track them."

"Gee, sir, I thought Verizon captured all the data for the NSA."

"Well, Ms. Walsh, you might be right. Of course, you'd need a court order to get that data. Unless we were talking about a terrorist threat or a federal crime, that'd be pretty unlikely. But I tell you what. Let me call Verizon and see what they can tell us. Anything else I can do for you?" Sergeant Wallace was clearly trying to be as helpful as possible.

Missie thought about the video but decided to keep that to herself for now. No reason to alert the police to the sighting of Rebecca DeLaurio in the Capitol. "Thanks, Sergeant, let me know what you hear from Verizon. You have my number?"

He laughed. "Of course I have it, Ms. Walsh—it's showing up on my phone right now. Your caller ID isn't blocked."

She chuckled a little, thanked him, and ended the call. *I guess there's nothing more to do except wait for Verizon.*

CHAPTER LXXXVIII

Wednesday, August 15th

Hart Senate Office Building

Missie arrived at the office around 10:30 a.m., about average for workers during the August recess—especially during the conventions. She grabbed her coffee cup and noticed her voicemail light flashing. *Sergeant Wallace?* She dialed voicemail and was surprised and a little irritated to hear the same anonymous caller.

"I warned you about sitting on this. You should have listened to me. This is the fourth time I've called in the past two weeks. Your time is up. The world's going to know you tried to squash this. That's what I get for trusting a Radcliff bitch. Your chairman won't be looking too good after this gets out."

The line went dead again. Missie sat stone-faced. She was unable to make any sense from the message, but it sure sounded like something was about to blow up in her face.

Maria buzzed her on the intercom, "Missie? Mr. Harris Ward, the *Roll Call* reporter, is on the phone. Do you want to take it?"

Harris Ward is the last thing I need right now. She paused before responding.

"He said it's important, if that matters, but I think he always says that when he calls."

She had no idea what was going on with Rebecca and no idea why the caller was threatening her. As much as she wanted to tell Ward that she was out of the office, her instinct told her she'd better hear what he wanted. She already had one problem on her hands; she didn't need another by blowing off Ward. "Tell him to hold for a second Maria, thanks."

She took a deep breath trying to calm her nerves, not sure why she was even nervous. Still, it wasn't every day she had an anonymous caller threaten her and her chairman. She picked up the phone. "This is Missie Walsh."

"Missie, Harris Ward. I received an anonymous tip that suggested I needed to talk to you. The caller said it related to Rebecca DeLaurio. Anything you can tell me?"

"Hello, Harris. Rebecca? What about Rebecca?"

"Well I don't know, but the message said you have new information about Rebecca. Do you know anything new about Rebecca?"

"I haven't seen Rebecca in two years. But you know, I did hear she was seen in the Capitol recently."

"Rebecca is back? When was she in the Capitol? Who saw her? I heard she left town. I wanted to talk to her after Mitsunaga's defeat, but she wouldn't return my calls. Any idea why she's back? Can you tell me who saw her?"

Missie wanted to tell him that his anonymous caller saw her, but she knew not to let on. Instead, she responded, "Harris, I'm not sure where I heard it, but I don't know any more than that anyway."

She racked her brain trying to figure out how Rebecca's return could be used against her and her chairman. She knew better than to lie outright to a reporter. But the more she said, the more questions Harris would have. He would keep asking her the same question in different ways until he was sure he got as much as he was going to get. She had to stay a step in front of him, or she'd fall into a trap. She wasn't ready to tell him what little she knew, and from the tenor of his questions, this was only a fishing expedition. He had nothing.

"Harris, I need to run, but if I hear any more, I'll let you know."

Harris knew he was being brushed off, but he wasn't sure what to ask. What did it matter if Rebecca was back in town? There must be more to the story, but Missie wasn't saying, and he wasn't all that sure she knew much more than she was letting on. "Well, thanks for taking my call. I'm at the convention. If anything comes up, please give me a ring." He left his hotel and cell numbers with her just in case.

Harris looked over at the TV and clicked on the volume. Governor Klingle of South Carolina was trying to rev up the faithful. He charged organized labor with wanting to get rid of secret ballots and pressuring free-thinking workers to unionize. Harris muted the sound to call Andy Davidson the Senate's deputy sergeant at arms. Davidson was a blond-haired, blue-eyed, six-foot-five thirty-something guy from somewhere in the South, who only weighed 160 pounds, and, best of all, always had something to say.

"Andy, it's Harris Ward. How are you? Quiet in the Capitol? I figured Howard would be on vacation and you'd be stuck monitoring the doors and tourists. Got it about right?"

"Harris, why are you calling? Yeah, sure is quiet here. Howard's taking in the Mayan ruins on the leader's Senate trip.

He called yesterday—seems there've been a few problems with local security. The leader didn't want to take his own security detail since foreign countries won't let them carry weapons. And, without weapons, they don't provide any security." Andy chuckled to himself, and Harris joined in.

"So, the embassy hired a local company it uses, but their laid-back attitude hasn't pleased the sergeant at arms. He has me putting together a backup plan to send our security detail down south and meet up with the group when they get to Rio. But I don't know why. They'd still be unarmed and unable to stop an attack on the leader. Still, you know Howard. He wants things run by the book. Off the record, I think complaining about security helps to justify his presence on the trip. But you didn't hear me say that."

Harris's mind was working overtime. He'd called Andy to talk about Rebecca, but he could smell a new story in the making.

"Did Senator Jacobs complain about security? Did he ask Howard to get him his own detail?"

If the leader was complaining about security and demanding that taxpayers pay to send a half-dozen Capitol Police officers to Brazil to act as nursemaids, that was news indeed. *Forget Rebecca's return. We have waste, fraud, and abuse brought to you by the majority leader and all during his party's convention.*

Andy tried to backtrack. "No, no, no, the leader had nothing to do with this. C'mon Harris. There's nothing here. This is all Howard being anal. I'm sure the leader has no idea any of this is going on. In fact, Howard never said the leader was even aware of his backup plan. You can't run this, Harris."

Had this been any other reporter, Andy would probably be joining the ranks of the unemployed tomorrow. But Harris wasn't really interested in a story criticizing the leader for traveling overseas during the convention or chastising the sergeant at arms for visiting the Mayan ruins. Questioning security was a tricky thing these days.

Now he could write a story suggesting Washington, DC security details were out of control. Most senior government officials had security details these days, despite there being a scant hint of a threat. His article might succeed in trimming security details. But what if it did? Some crazy guy from Detroit might read the piece, decide to get even with the SBA administrator because he didn't qualify for a small business loan, and drive to DC with a couple of handguns. Well, now you had a mess on your hands.

No, not worth it.

Harris reassured Andy he was just asking about the leader from curiosity, then returned to his original intent. "So, I got a tip that Rebecca DeLaurio has been seen in the Capitol. You hear anything like that?"

"Haven't heard that, Harris." Andy's voice flushed with relief.

"Uh-huh. With today's restrictions, she'd have to sign in with your office unless she was escorted into the building. Isn't that right?"

"That's right; again that's Howard being Howard. All visitors must have a member's office sponsor them or be on a pre-approved list to get into the Capitol."

"And you keep that list?"

"That's right."

"What if she came in with a senator?"

"Well if she comes with a member, she walks right in. Even Howard can't control what the senators do."

"So unless she had come in with a member, you'd know?"

"Well, the office would have a record of her visit."

"Isn't Lilian Anderson still signing visitors into the Capitol?"

"Yes, she's still the one. She's been working the reception desk for more than twenty years."

"Now, Andrew, if Lilian saw Rebecca DeLaurio in the Capitol, I'd say the chance that you weren't aware of that was less than zero."

Andy laughed. "You got me there, Harris. If she signed in, I'd know it."

"So unless she came in with a senator, my source was wrong. She wasn't in the Capitol."

"Yeah, I guess that's probably right."

"OK, thanks. Anything else going on besides the leader's security detail requirements?" Harris returned to the irritant, hoping to catch Andy off guard once again.

"No that's about it. I'm still looking at how our security system got hacked last month, but that's becoming a regular activity."

"Somebody broke into the Office of Senate Security? Isn't that where you keep all the classified files?"

"No, no, no, not that security system." Andy's conversational tone switched immediately back to a chagrined urgency. "It's just that last month someone broke into the video archives for our security cameras. This has nothing to do with Senate security. All our classified material is safe.

"Look, Harris, we get targeted at least once a week by someone trying to hack our system. We're no different than any other government entity. We fend them off. We get a lot of help from NSA and occasionally the FBI, but we stop virtually all of them with our firewalls."

"Uh-huh, but somebody got through last month?" Harris smirked, picturing Andy's frantic face as he tried to do damage control.

"Well, not exactly. We stopped them. They got into our video files, but we found them before they could damage anything."

Throw him a softball, Harris. Loosen him up. "Your video files—do you mean the video of Senate proceedings? I thought C-SPAN controlled that?"

"Well, yes and no, we control the recordings with C-SPAN, but that's not what I meant. We have security cameras recording activity in the Capitol complex. But there's no story here, Harris. Like I said, we stopped the guy. He was unable to screw anything up. We brought in IT experts from the FBI last week to check the whole thing out for us. They verified that, while someone had gained access to the database, we didn't lose any data. They didn't insert any malware or damage the system. We plugged the hole in the firewall, and the FBI assured us we're now protected again. Nothing for the public to worry about, seriously."

"So, any idea what they're up to?"

"Probably some Russian or Chinese hacker or college student trying to hone their skills. But, it's only a matter of time, Harris. These hackers are always a step away from being able to break into our system and those of everybody else in this town. In this case, at least, there isn't anything in that database to interest anyone. I mean, who cares who's walking through the halls of Congress anyway?"

"I see. How long do you keep the data for?"

"Once again, that's Howard. He insists we keep the files for two years before we delete them. None of us can figure out why we should keep them longer than a week or two tops. That's the industry standard. But that's Howard. Like I said, he's anal."

"Uh-huh. Well thanks, Andy. If you hear anything about Rebecca being in town, could you let me know?"

Andy breathed a sigh of relief, but Harris smirked as the loquacious deputy still couldn't just say goodbye, even after dodging two near-story disasters. "So Harris, why do you care if Rebecca is back in town anyway? Where's the story in this?"

Harris didn't know why—not yet. But with anonymous tips, he knew enough to ask questions until he found out why. "I don't know, Andy, but like I said, I got an anonymous tip, and that alone drives me to see what's up. Thanks for taking my call. Let me know if you hear any more about the leader's security requirements."

"Sure thing, Harris. If I find Rebecca roaming the halls, I'll be sure to let you know. Talk to you later."

Harris hung up the phone and turned back to the TV. Governor Klingle was still speaking. "And there will be no amnesty for illegal aliens. Do you hear me, Mr. Vice President? I said no amnesty." The half-empty convention hall responded with polite applause. C-SPAN cut to a couple of delegates on their feet wearing tri-corner hats, red, white, and blue Uncle Sam suits with fake white beards and waving American flags. Harris hit mute again.

Andy put down the phone, laid his head on his desk, and moaned.

Shit, shit, shit. That was close. I think I convinced him not to go with a story on Jacobs. The security breach isn't really a story anyway. I've got to be more careful when I talk to him. He always gets me to say more than I should. I guess that's why he's so damn good at his job.

CHAPTER LXXXIX

Thursday, August 16th

Denver, Colorado

Harris woke early. It was 4 a.m. Too early to get up, but he couldn't sleep. Something was nagging at him. He thought about his call to Missie yesterday. He had a hunch she knew more than she was letting on, but what? The Rebecca sighting didn't seem to pan out. Andy had no record of her being in the Capitol.

The only other way she could have entered the Capitol was if she had come in with a senator. What senator in his or her right mind would be seen in the Capitol with Rebecca DeLaurio? And if they had, Lilian would have been the first to know. The guards at the door wouldn't keep that secret.

No, Missie's story couldn't be accurate, but why give him bad information? She seemed very sure of the rumor, but she was nervous. Harris knew he could make staff nervous, especially when they had something to hide. He'd known Missie for more than ten years. He'd never known her to hide anything or be nervous. Frankly, she probably never knew anything worth hiding. What did he care if Senator Jacobs was changing hideaways? That was a story for some other reporter. He thought back to her demeanor around the time of the Mitsunaga hearing. She was definitely stressed out then. She seemed like that yesterday. But Rebecca couldn't have been in the Capitol. How could she get that wrong? And Andy, he was sure Rebecca wasn't in the Capitol. And what was with the video hack? Why would someone want to hack into the Capitol security camera system? And when they did, why didn't they try to mess with the system? It didn't add up unless—could Missie have it wrong? Harris looked at his watch. It's only six in DC. *I can't call yet.*

CHAPTER XC

Denver, Colorado

Andy was in a very good mood. His anxious scan of *Roll Call* first thing that morning broke the good news. No stories on the leader's trip, and no stories on security breaches. It was going to be a good day.

Harris had posted a story on the lack of attendance and attentiveness at the Republican convention. Yes, he'd mentioned that Jacobs wasn't there, but he noted that most Republican senators were absent. His story focused more on what anyone could've seen on TV. The convention hall was barely half-full. Most of the delegates weren't paying much attention to the speeches. The up-and-coming Lieutenant Governor Sara Martinez from Florida had delivered a spell-binding speech on how Parker would call on all citizens to revive the American dream. Even that hardly got the delegates on their feet. Andy was sure the article wasn't going to be well received by his Republican colleagues, but he was thrilled.

The phone's chime interrupted his cheerful thoughts.

◆ ◆ ◆

"Andy, it's Ward again."

"Harris Ward, as I live and breathe." Andy laughed. "I don't think today's story gets you invited back to the Republican convention, Harris."

Harris was a little surprised and hurt by the slam. He'd tried to be fair in the story. Parker had locked up the nomination months ago; everyone knew the convention was merely a formality. Harris had reminded the readers of the similar scene four years ago at the Democratic convention when President Andrews was re-nominated. Sure, he made fun of the delegates with the silly costumes. He called out those who appeared to be sleeping as the evening wore on, but Harris wrote what he saw. Presidential conventions had become more like insurance industry conventions than political events. They were still opportunities to rally the troops to the cause. But mostly they were a chance to get together with colleagues and share some good times. He wasn't going after Republicans, and he was hurt that Andy thought it would be seen as an attack. Accepting criticism had never been his forte, and his instinct was to defend his story. But he stopped himself. He had a different agenda today. "Well, I hope all Republicans don't see it that way, but that's not why I called. Yesterday, we were discussing the security breach."

Andy's muttered "hell" was barely, but satisfactorily, audible over the line. Harris grinned.

"And one thing I was curious about. Did you tell your leadership and the committees about the breach?"

"Like I said yesterday. We get pinged at least once a week by a hacker; it's no big deal. Since they didn't damage anything, we treated it as pretty routine."

"So you didn't brief anyone outside of the Sergeant at Arms Office?"

"Well, let me continue. We informed both leaders' staff. We talked to the FBI and NSA. We let the House know we'd been attacked to warn them. But that's about it."

"So, no one on Rules or in Senate Security?"

"No, no reason to. Why do you ask?"

Harris was afraid of that. Andy was going to ask him for details that would tie this to Missie. He had to be forthcoming if he expected his cooperation in the future. So, he chose his words carefully. "Well, it's mostly a hunch. The anonymous tip suggested the Rules Committee might know about Rebecca's visit. I was wondering if they or anyone else might also know about the attack." The last thing Harris wanted was for Andy to call Missie Walsh. "Well thanks for your help, Andrew. I hope you're wrong about the reaction to my article."

Harris hung up, dialed Missie Walsh, but got voicemail. He left a message asking Missie to give him a quick call this morning and once again left his number. He was pretty sure Andy would call Missie at some point, but hoped he'd get to her first.

Harris was right. Andy called Missie seconds before Harris tried her. Lucky for her, Andy connected.

Missie's intercom buzzed. "Missie, Andrew Davidson, the deputy sergeant at arms, is on the phone for you. Do you want to take the call?"

Why's Andy calling? Especially in the middle of August? She took the call. "Andy, it's Missie. What's up? Are you in Denver?"

"Hi Missie, no I'm the stuckee in DC. I could ask you the same thing. Why aren't you in Denver?" Harris' article was triggering many conversations between senior Republicans who'd opted out of the convention.

"Well, Andy, I figured they could nominate Parker without me, and I could get caught up on a few things here. What's up?"

"This is just FYI, but I've had a couple of phone calls from Harris Ward in the past two days."

Missie's eyes widened, and she sat up straight in her chair.

"I don't think there's anything here. But, he seemed intent on trying to find out if Rebecca DeLaurio, I'm sure you remember her, had been seen in the Capitol."

Oh shit. I should have known Harris would try and track that down.

Andy drawled on. "I know. It's pretty crazy; I mean why would Rebecca be in the Capitol? Anyhow, he didn't mention you in relation to Rebecca. But we got off on another subject, and he asked whether the Rules Committee was aware of it."

"Oh yeah, what was that?"

"Well, last month our security camera system was hacked. Nothing bad happened. It was routine, but someone got into the system. Harris wanted to know if your committee knew about it. That's all there is really, but I wanted you to be aware Harris Ward is tapping around on Rebecca and this security breach. I don't know how you'd be involved, but since it was Harris Ward asking, I wanted to make sure you were in the loop."

Missie was nearly speechless but was able to thank Andy for the heads-up before hanging up. She grabbed the video with trembling hands, pushed it into the TV, and hit rewind.

Missie watched the tape again. Yes, she must be seeing footage from the Senate security camera. Someone had hacked into the system and stolen this footage. The caller wanted her to have it. He'd gone to a lot of trouble to hack into the Senate and steal it, but why? She watched it again for clues. Man comes out and walks away. Rebecca comes out. Tape goes blank. What was she missing? She started it again. At the bottom corner of the screen, she saw a video counter running the time of the tape. The image was fuzzy. She froze the screen. She looked at the numbers in the corner and at the back of the man's head. She jumped out of her chair when she realized the number at the bottom wasn't a video counter. It was a date and time stamp, and that man was . . .

"Oh shit. It can't be. Oh shit. Oh no. I gotta talk to the chairman."

She yelled out the door, "Maria, I need you to find the chairman! Now!"

CHAPTER XCI

Honolulu, Oahu

Paula Means checked her mailbox before heading home. It was only 1 p.m., but her only class that day was already over. August was slow at the Asia Pacific Center but not as slow as Congress that time of year. Only one group of students was in town. It was the right time to work a few half-days. She was going to meet Chauncey for a late lunch that she owed him for saving the day.

She grabbed a manila envelope out of her box, noted the DC postmark, and felt the contents. Not heavy enough for a book, but something rectangular in shape. *Wonder what it could be?* She hopped in her car and took off for the airport to pick up Chauncey.

"Hey, Chauncey, Pacific superhero, how are you?"

"I'm great, Paula; it's good to see you. You look relaxed and so tan, not the same person I knew in DC."

"Hard not to be tan here, Chaunce." She reached behind her seat and tossed him the envelope. "Would you open this for me? I grabbed it as I ran out of the office and have been wondering what it is ever since."

Chauncey ripped open the envelope and looked inside. "Now here's something you don't see every day." He pulled out a video-tape and showed Paula. "This is ancient. What's on it?"

"I have no idea. There wasn't a return address. Is there anything else in the envelope?"

Chauncey looked inside, shook his head, and turned it upside down. "Nada."

"That's weird. What am I going to do with that? Nobody has VCRs anymore."

"Well, they've got tape drives at the supercomputer. They don't use them much, but they're still there. I can run by this evening and take a look if you're really curious. Unless maybe there's something on there you don't want me to see." He winked at her and smiled.

"Well I doubt that, but how would I know?" She scrunched up her face. "I am really curious. Yeah, you know, it'd be great if you'd check it out for me when you have time."

"Hell, why not? My return flight gets in at 4:30, so I'll swing by the center and check it out before heading home. Add it to the list of favors you owe me. Now where are you taking me for lunch?"

CHAPTER XCII

Denver, Colorado

Harris Ward paced around his hotel room. He hadn't heard from Missie. The convention was gearing up for the big finish. Soon the delegates would vote to nominate Parker and the Republican mayor of Los Angeles, Sam Sanchez, as his vice president. The only surprise would be how long it'd take. Would the acceptance speech be at 9:30 as scheduled or would it slide over until 10 or even 11? If they waited until 11 Rocky Mountain time, no one on the East coast would even be awake to see it. Harris wanted to visit the convention hall and ask a few members about the process. After today's story, he guessed some politicos would have corrections to offer. Others would privately tell him he had it exactly right. To do that he'd need to stop by. Yet, the desire to check out his story with Missie Walsh had him delaying as long as possible.

At 5:30 p.m., Harris gave up on a callback from Missie and grabbed a cab to the convention. The hall was a lot more crowded. His press pass gave him access to the convention hall floor, but he did most of his work in the lobby and outside of the meeting rooms. There, he could catch members of Congress walking in and out of the hall. As would be expected for a party that was ten points up in the polls, the mood was gleeful. He caught a minute with the house majority whip, Steve Castle, who poked him about his article. He wanted to be sure Harris knew he wasn't off on some junket. Senator James from Arkansas buttonholed him for a second. She, too, wanted to make sure Harris knew she was there. Harris was a little relieved. Andy had it wrong. Maybe the members who weren't in attendance were pissed at him, but the ones here weren't mad. He asked the standard questions about what they thought of the VP choice and the mood of the delegates. All was good at party central. *Happy days are here again.* The Republicans had stolen the Democrats' theme.

Harris saw Senator Wilson across the lobby huddling with Senator Lee, the assistant majority leader of the Senate. Wilson looked both ashen and animated in the discussion. Harris fought his way through the packed lobby hoping to catch up to him and ask about the security breach. As he approached the group, Wilson made a quick exit onto the elevator. He pretended not to notice Harris trying to get his attention. Harris stared at the closed elevator door. *That's odd. Everyone here is floating on air, and he looks like a guy who found out his wife's cheating on him.*

At 7 p.m., Harris entered the rear of the convention hall. The nomination process had begun. By Michigan, it was all over. Parker was the Republican nominee. He lost Iowa and Alaska, but that was it. The first was the caucus result; the second the lunatic fringe in the forty-ninth state. Harris looked around and realized no Republican senators were in the convention hall. Stranger still, the head of the Republican National Committee was also absent. He looked over at the Texas delegation. Congressman Castle wasn't there. Speaker Thompson wasn't sitting with the Illinois delegation.

The convention floor was bedlam. The Parker supporters were cheering and chanting "USA" and "No more years"—the new Republican slogan against Andrews and Smith. Parker and Sanchez were on stage, arms lifted in a victory salute. Their wives and families stood by their sides, waving and smiling.

By 9 p.m. it was all over. Perfect timing for the 11 p.m. news on the East coast. Harris waited in the lobby, hoping to catch a member of the leadership to get a comment for his story. None showed up. At ten he gave up and returned to his hotel. No message from Missie or anyone else. He posted a perfunctory story about the success of the convention and the outlook for Parker. All was positive.

His gut told him all wasn't fine, but he had nothing to base it on. Instinct didn't write a story.

CHAPTER XCIII

Maui Supercomputer

"Hey Freddy, I got an unmarked video from Paula Means. You as curious as I am to see what's on it?"

"What, you think it's porn or something?"

"Knowing Paula, it's probably a promo for a new fighter jet or destroyer, but I thought that'd get your filthy mind working. Here, I pulled an old tape drive out of storage; hook it up so we can see this thing together."

Freddy made the connection and ran the tape. "What the hell do you make of that? It's a frigging hallway and two people coming out of a room. I've seen more interesting film on signed-off TV channels."

"Beats me, Watanabe. Can you save it digitally and send me a copy? I need to show Paula."

"Still trying to work that, Hayes? You got better luck with a local Wahine than with that blonde bombshell. Don't you know she's outta your league, dude?"

"Persistence, Freddy. Patience, kindness, and consideration. Watch and learn."

"I've been watching, dude, and you ain't learned nothing." Freddy shook his head. "OK, it's all yours. And good luck. I'm sure this riveting video is gonna be the key to unlock her heart."

"Thanks, bud."

"Hey Paula, it was great seeing you today." Chauncey glanced over at Freddy and smiled as wide as the Cheshire cat. "So we took a look at the tape and copied it. Not much on it—a woman and man coming out of an office. We can watch it together. I forwarded you the file."

"Thanks, Chauncey. Let me pull it up. Hold one second. OK, here it is. So a hallway. Funny, that looks like the Capitol to me. What are those numbers at the bottom?"

"It's a time and date stamp. It shows this video was recorded in August two years ago."

"Pretty thrilling, ain't it?"

Chauncey laughed. "Well, the girl and guy action is about to start. See, this old guy walks out of the office—"

"Oh, wait, I see him. Too bad you can't see his face. You said there's a woman too? Oh, there she is. Holy cow, that's Rebecca DeLaurio. She's the woman who testified against Senator Mitsunaga. That's the Capitol; I'm sure of it. Who was the guy?" She paused, and Chancey could hear her muttering to herself, followed by a sharp intake of breath. "Wait. This is August two years ago. Let's go back and take another look at him."

"What difference does it make, Paula? So, she and some guy were in an office together in the Capitol, big deal."

"OK, there he is. Holy shit. I don't believe it. So, this is before the hearing, and she's meeting with him. Oh shit, Chauncey, this is huge. Do you realize what this means? Cripes, where did this come from? Somebody knew what was going on. I got to figure out what to do with this. Chaunce. If I wanted to send this out without anyone tracing it to me, do you know how I could do that?"

"I don't, but I'm sure Freddy Watanabe does. I'll put him on the phone, but don't hang up until you let me know what's going on."

CHAPTER XCIV

Friday, August 17th

Washington, DC

Harris caught the 7 a.m. flight back to National Airport and headed home for the weekend. He checked his cell in the taxi and was surprised to find a new email message from an anonymous source. He clicked on it. There was no text, but a file was attached. He decided he'd check it from his PC when he got home.

Harris dropped his backpack on the couch and went to change into shorts and a t-shirt. It was hotter than hell. The AC hadn't been on all week, and it was 90 degrees outside with 90 percent humidity, a typical August day in DC. It was only 2 p.m., but, hell, it was Friday; he grabbed a beer. He flipped on his PC and clicked on the mysterious email attachment. He took his backpack into the laundry room to dump his dirty clothes. Walking back into the living room, he spotted the image of Rebecca DeLaurio on the screen. He froze the shot. That was Rebecca alright.

He reversed the video frame by frame, watching her emerge from the doorway. He recognized the Capitol. It looked like the hallway of the Capitol rotunda, prime real estate, but he wasn't positive. He rewound it frame by frame. An empty hall in poor black-and-white video quality. He studied the numbers scrolling backward at the bottom of the screen and stopped the video when it hit him.

This was Rebecca DeLaurio leaving a Senate Capitol office at the beginning of August two years ago. This must be from the Senate security camera. It was too much of a coincidence. This had to be what the thieves were looking for when they hacked into the Senate video library. But so what? Rebecca was all over the Capitol two years ago. She was a lobbyist with close ties to lots of members, particularly Mitsunaga. But that wasn't Mitsunaga's office. Mitsunaga had the office next to Jackson on the west front of the Capitol, the one with the view of the mall. If he was right, this was a side hallway. He continued to reverse the video at normal speed until the gray-haired man left the same room. Harris nearly dropped his beer. Even from behind he recognized him immediately. "Well I'll be damned, James Fillmore Parker!"

Harris tried to reach Missie Walsh, but she wasn't in—already gone for the weekend, her assistant told him. He had no idea what she knew, but he knew she had heard something. After all, she was the one who said Rebecca had been spotted in the Capitol. Yes, she got the date wrong, but the video showed Rebecca in the building. He placed a call to Andy Davidson's cell phone, a number he'd copied down the last time Andy called him. After two rings, Andy picked up. "This is Andy."

"Andy, Harris Ward."

"Harris, good to hear from you again so soon. What's up now?"

"So Andy, what more can you tell me about the breach of security? Do you know what they were after?"

"C'mon Harris, there's nothing here. I don't know what they

were after. The FBI forensic specialists and the NSA spooks both said it looked like a prank. They didn't screw with anything. They just had a look around."

"Uh-huh. Any idea what they were looking at?"

"No. The experts don't know. They didn't erase anything or add anything or tamper with anything. They assume it was someone fooling around. It could've been some 400-pound high school dropout in Colorado, sitting on his bed, smoking pot, and seeing what government site he could hack his way into. We're an easy target. No one saw much reason to protect the video database. None of us, except Howard, thought we even needed to keep it for more than a couple of weeks."

"Uh-huh. How long did you say you kept it for?"

"Two years."

"So, you have video from two years ago this August?"

"That's right, but since the incident was at the end of July, we have video back until then. We haven't deleted the older files. Technically, we're still looking into this intrusion. But, Harris, seriously man, there isn't anything here. Nothing was lost or stolen, deleted, or messed with."

"What about copied? Could something have been copied?"

"Yeah, I suppose, but so what? The Capitol is a public building. Who cares if someone copied a view of people getting on and off the subway? Or walking in the entrance? There's no story."

"Uh-huh. You may be right. So you have cameras at the entrances and by the subway. Anywhere else?"

"That's pretty much it. We have them at all the doors to the Capitol. We have one in the basement hallway that connects the House and Senate."

"Is that all?"

"Oh, and Howard has one by our office."

"Huh, why does he have one there?"

"Between you and me, off the record, I think it's hilarious. Howard figures if terrorists or a deranged citizen get into the building, our office represents the last line of defense. He had a camera installed in our hallway so he could track any intruder headed his way."

"Seriously?"

"Yeah. Now don't get me in trouble with this. It's just Howard being Howard."

"No, don't worry about that. Can he watch the hallway from his office?"

"Yeah, he has a link to the Senate recording studio on his computer."

"Do you think he sits there and watches for terrorists?" Harris coughed and stifled a laugh.

"C'mon, Harris. Be serious. Howard's a good dude. He's a bit anal, and he's serious about security, but he's not a weirdo watching the hallway."

"No, you're right. I've got nothing against Howard. He's always been fair to me. Well, thanks for clearing this up. Any more Rebecca sightings?"

"Harris, nobody has seen Rebecca for two years. I don't know where you got that idea from."

"OK, thanks, Andy. Just checking." Harris hung up the phone. Bingo. Somebody saw Rebecca leaving a Capitol office before she testified against Mitsunaga. Because he couldn't get Missie on the phone, he sent her a text.

Harris: *Missie, I need to speak with you about Rebecca and what you know about seeing her in the Capitol. It's very important that I talk to you before I run a story on the issue. Please call me. Thanks.*

If Missie knew something, she wouldn't want him to run a story that might implicate her or Senator Wilson without having a chance to get her say in. She'd need to find out what he knew. He didn't like being disingenuous. But it was true he was going to run a story—even if it might have nothing to do with her and Senator Wilson. Maybe she could help him clarify a few things. He sat on the couch, watched the video again, and sipped his beer.

CHAPTER XCV

Bethesda, Maryland

It was hotter than hell sitting on the deck, even in the shade, but it was quiet and serene. Missie needed any serenity she could find. She sipped a glass of white wine and propped her feet up against the railing. The events of the past seventy-two hours had been unbelievable. Memories of two blissful weeks at the Cape were long gone. Now she twisted under the burden of what she knew, what her role in it had been, and what her boss wanted her to do.

She wasn't happy, but she was loyal. The chairman was a good man. He treated her, and nearly everyone else, well. And, he was right. This could all be a setup. The film could be fake. In this day and age, almost anyone could doctor a video image. But boy, it looked bad. She felt set up. She hadn't wanted to hold a hearing on money laundering. She liked Senator Mitsunaga and couldn't believe it when she heard he was crooked. And what did he possibly have to gain by taking money from the Chinese? He had been well ahead in the polls. Hawaii public polls were frequently wrong. But, this time everyone had agreed with them. The internal Republican polls and the Mitsunaga campaign shared the same belief. The incumbent was far ahead. Keahole didn't have a chance until the two scandals broke. The questions nagged at her. *Was he set up? Who set up whom?*

Like most senior Senate staff, her BlackBerry was attached to her hip. It buzzed; she picked it up and read the message from Harris.

Missie set down her wine glass and shook her head, trying to collect her thoughts. Harris knew something about Rebecca. He had a story. She didn't know what he knew about her role in the story, but he could easily be thinking of this as a cover-up. Senator Wilson wanted her to stay out of it. She was to lock up the tape until he told her otherwise.

The leaders of the Republican Party had met on Thursday evening while Parker was being nominated. Even Senator Jacobs took part by telephone from Rio. None of them had seen the video, but they all knew that if it was anything like what was described, it looked bad. Most of them believed it was probably a fake, planted by the Smith campaign. Smith's numbers had gone from terrible to disastrous. The aftermath of the attack on Korea was not turning out well for the vice president. Next week he'd be his party's nominee, and once he was anointed, they'd spend six weeks crushing him. By the beginning of October, they figured the election would be all but over, even before the debates. The video seemed like the last gasp from a desperate campaign.

They agreed to confront Parker in the morning over coffee. Speaker Thompson, the chairman of the RNC Smithfield, Congressman Castle, Senator Wilson, and Senator Lee arrived at Parker's suite at 9:30 a.m. Parker waited until they were all assembled before emerging from his bedroom. He was smiling and laughing. He expected they were all there to kiss his ring and his ass. The election was his. The presidency was his. Nothing could stop him now.

Instead, he faced a grim room. The speaker asked Senator Wilson to fill in the candidate. Before Wilson even finished his pitch, Parker denied everything. He blew his stack, turned beet-red, and protested the outrage. He accused the leaders of trying to sabotage his campaign. He called them tools of the Northeastern establishment. He demanded that Wilson destroy the video. He threatened each of them with retribution from the White House if this story leaked out. After twenty minutes of discussion, they all agreed—the video was almost certainly a fake (or "certainly a fake" in Parker's words). Next week they'd get some trusted IT experts to take a look at it and determine if they could prove it was a fake. If they couldn't prove it was fake, they'd destroy it.

The message from Harris turned Missie's day from bad to worse. He had a story. If she ignored him and he accused Wilson of covering up the story, it'd be her fault. If she called him back, she was acting against her boss's direction to bury this. She tried to call Senator Wilson, but he was on a plane from Denver to British Columbia. Her chances of getting through to him that afternoon were next to nil. For the chairman's sake, she couldn't take the chance that Harris knew their role in the story. She'd have to talk to him—and choose her words carefully. She needed to find out what he knew without telling him what she suspected.

Missie finished her glass of wine and headed inside. She was determined not to be distracted by the heat or nature. She closed the door to her den and placed a call to Harris.

When Harris saw the caller ID, he smiled a little and said, "I knew it." The fact she was calling meant she knew something she hadn't told him before. Could it be she'd also seen the video or heard about it? He figured Andy didn't know anything, or he wouldn't have been able to keep it secret. Missie, though, was much shrewder than Andy. If she called, she knew something.

"Hello," Harris said innocently enough, not letting on he knew it was her.

"Harris, this is Missie Walsh. I got your text and wanted to know what was up about Rebecca."

"Ahh, Missie, thank you for calling. I got to thinking about what you told me about Rebecca being seen in the Capitol and asked around a little. Did you get a sense of when it was she was seen or who she was with?"

She took a deep breath. "OK, Harris, where are you going with this? Why is this a story you are interested in? What are you really after?"

"Missie, I'll be honest with you. I suspect what you told me about Rebecca being in the Capitol wasn't something that happened recently. I think it happened about two years ago. Right before your hearing on Chinese bribes. Now do you want to talk to me about what you know, or should I publish what I've seen on video? I can speculate about the rest, including what Chairman Wilson must have known when he investigated Senator Mitsunaga?"

"Harris, I'd be very careful about this. Let me say two things. Number one, I'd be very suspicious if I was looking at a video that implied wrongdoing by my chairman. Second, if you think you know something, I'd suggest you talk to the guilty party."

"Can I get a quote from Chairman Wilson denying any knowledge about any potential wrongdoing?"

"Harris, Chairman Wilson is on a plane leaving the country. You can't get anything from him today. If you want to talk to me again tomorrow, I'll try and get a statement for you then, but I'm not promising. The chairman is on a well-deserved week of R-and-R, and I don't want to disturb him if I don't have to."

"Missie, this story isn't going to wait until tomorrow. When I tell my editor what I know and what I suspect, this is going to blow a hole in the Capitol dome. You can expect to see the story and the video on *Roll Call* online by tomorrow morning."

"Harris, all I am going to say is before you print anything, you better be damn well sure you have your facts straight. You don't want to get duped by someone trying to trick you. I've said all I am going to say on the story. I suggest you do some soul-searching and a little more research before you run wild with something."

"Thanks for the call, Missie. I wish you'd have been a bit more forthcoming."

"Harris, I've said all I am going to say on the subject. Goodbye."

Harris hung up the phone. He thought about what Missie said. What did he know about the origin of the video? Could this be a fake planted by the Smith campaign? Heaven knows they were desperate enough. He figured he'd better dig to the source and connect the dots before his next step.

CHAPTER XCVI

Denver, Colorado

Steve Simpson, Parker's campaign manager, sat back in his chair by the Hilton pool. This might be the last quiet moment he'd have for the next four years. Hell, if all went well, maybe the next eight. It was 80 degrees with a clear blue sky. He sipped a vodka tonic and smiled. The self-destruction of the Smith campaign was more than anyone could have hoped for. New York and Massachusetts were tied. His guy was up in almost every other state. Polling in all the West Coast states showed Parker ahead by five, six, or even seven points. The Democratic convention would start on Monday. So Parker was taking the traditional break from politicking. Steve was kicking back as well. This two hours in the sun in Denver was his moment of relaxation.

And Steve needed a break. He'd been going full speed for eighteen months straight—from the first day he moved from being Senator Parker's chief of staff to campaign manager. Parker caught fire after the Mitsunaga investigation and hadn't cooled off since. He'd hinted it wasn't just Mitsunaga who was on the take since so many Democrats had taken money from AAPAC. Those charges hadn't stuck, though. The best moment was when the vice president agreed to return half a million dollars in AAPAC contributions. Smith's action, more than anything else, encouraged doubt to creep into many voters' minds. Instead of clearing the air, Smith had muddied the waters. Smith was running on competence in government, a theme from the successful Andrews campaigns. The intelligence failure in Korea had eroded confidence in Smith's competence. The ensuing disaster in Washington State left his campaign in disarray. By the end of the coming week when both candidates were anointed, Parker would be coasting to victory.

Well, Parker might be coasting. Steve Simpson was going to be working his ass off over the next nine weeks up to and including Election Day. For now, he had two hours to himself, and he was going to relax and enjoy them. He wanted to be tanned, rested, and ready for the onslaught to come.

Steve's cell phone rang with a US Senate number that he didn't recognize. He thought about not answering it, but figured it was probably a former colleague calling to congratulate him and ingratiate himself—or herself. He hoped it was the latter.

"Hello, this is Steve Simpson."

"Steve, this is Harris Ward, from *Roll Call*, I'm not sure if you'll remember me. Do you have a minute?"

"Of course I remember you, Harris. I followed your articles when I worked on the Hill. What can I do for you?"

"Steve, I'm working on a story about Rebecca DeLaurio, the woman who testified against Senator Mitsunaga. I imagine you remember her."

"Sure," Steve drawled. "I remember all about Rebecca and the 'Indian Affair' as you press guys labeled it. What about her?"

"Well, I'm not sure exactly how to tell you this. I have a video that shows her meeting with Senator Parker in his hideaway before she testified against Senator Mitsunaga. Doesn't that seem a little strange? I mean, what would she be doing in his hideaway? Why would she be meeting with him before the hearing? I was at that hearing. He made it sound like he didn't know her. And she must be a great actress. She sure made it sound like he was able to squeeze the damning testimony out of her. You were Parker's chief of staff at the time. What do you know about this? What was Parker meeting with her about?"

Steve was standing upright by now, his hand clenching the phone in a fierce grip. But his well-trained voice remained cool and collected. "Harris, I don't know what you're talking about. I'm sure Parker didn't know Rebecca. I mean, she'd been a staffer on the Indian Affairs Committee. He'd have known who she was, but I can tell you categorically he didn't know her personally."

"Can I quote you on that? I mean she met with him alone in his hideaway. Doesn't that seem odd to you if she didn't know him?"

"Harris, I'm sure there's a mistake here. I can assure you Senator Parker didn't meet with Rebecca in his hideaway."

"But, Steve, I have the video. I've seen it with my own eyes."

Steve took a step backward and narrowly missed tripping over the lounge chair he'd been reclining on. *What the fuck? How can—Wilson's staff director has the only copy. No way she'd have given it to Harris Ward. No way. She'd be dead in DC if she did that. Forget her; Wilson's dead.* He stared blankly at the rippling water of the pool. *No, Ward must be bullshitting me, but somebody's leaked some shit. Parker's going to be ripping someone a new asshole. I don't care who it is, even the speaker.*

Steve's voice was icy. "Harris, I'm not sure what you're talking about, but I'd be very careful about what you're accusing Senator Parker of doing."

"I'm not accusing him of doing anything. I just want to know why he was meeting with Rebecca before the hearing that crushed Mitsunaga. I'm sure you remember that hearing. It's the one that catapulted him into frontrunner status for the Republican nomination."

"And I'm telling you any video you have is a fake. Look at it reasonably, Harris. The Smith campaign's desperate. They'll do anything—and I mean anything—to try and stop the Parker momentum. I find it outrageous they'd stoop this low, but I can't say I'm surprised. They'll sink to any depths to try and stop Parker. But, I'm telling you it won't work.

"If you go forward with this, we'll prove it's a fake, and you, Harris Ward, will be fucked. Your career will be over. You won't be able to even write a blog. You won't be able to tweet. No one will touch you, Ward; you're finished in DC. You're finished in politics. I'm warning you, Harris. For your own good, do not publish this story."

"Steve, what would you say if I told you the video's not a fake? What would you say if I told you the FBI has a copy and verified that it's legitimate?"

"I'd say you're a lying sack of shit. That's what I'd say. And if you publish it, you're a fucking dead man. Is that good enough for you?"

"Can I quote you on that?"

"Fuck you, Ward. Fuck you. You're dead. RIP motherfucker."

Steve barely restrained himself from tossing his phone in the water. The people sitting around the pool were all staring at him. Some frowning, a few laughing, but most with astonished looks on their faces. He gulped down his drink, grabbed his towel, and stomped into the hotel.

Harris Ward sat on his couch, reflecting on the discussion. Max Welsh at the bureau had in fact already validated that the tape was genuine. Max had seen the same thing on the files they examined for the sergeant at arms. He hadn't made the connection between Rebecca and Parker. The bureau and the NSA both had verified that the video hadn't been tampered with.

Harris had asked Max, "Could it have been copied?

"It certainly might have been," Max had said. "We wouldn't know. We know the hacker watched it. We know he hadn't changed it."

Before hanging up, Harris asked him one more favor. "Can you tell me how long the man and woman were in the office together? Did anyone else either enter or exit the office that afternoon?"

Max paused a minute, muttering as he tapped away at his computer. "Sure, Harris. The gentleman arrived at 6:00 p.m., and Rebecca entered at 6:15. He left at 6:30, and she followed about two minutes later. No one else went into the office that day."

"Thanks, Max. Just a tip, but the FBI might want to make sure to keep a copy of this film." They exchanged parting pleasantries and hung up.

CHAPTER XCVII

Saturday, August 18th

The story was posted at 11:30 a.m. Saturday morning. By noon it was the subject of special reports on CNN and MSNBC. Fox covered the story as well; though in its version, the Smith campaign had photoshopped a video and was presenting it as evidence that Parker had colluded with Mitsunaga's girlfriend, Rebecca DeLaurio.

Harris had been very careful in his story. He wrote how he'd received an anonymous video file showing Rebecca DeLaurio leaving Senator Parker's private office in the Capitol. This had occurred before she testified before the Rules Committee, implicating Senator Mitsunaga in a Chinese money laundering scheme. Ward reported that someone hacked into the Senate security system four weeks earlier. The FBI verified that the hacker watched the video of Rebecca. The experts confirmed the Senate recording had not been altered. Rebecca was, in fact, in Senator Parker's office that day with a man who looked a lot like Parker from behind.

Harris wrote that no one knew what Parker and Rebecca had been discussing. The fact they were meeting in private before Rebecca broke down under brutal questioning from Parker was curious. He quoted Parker's campaign manager, Steve Simpson, denying the meeting ever took place. Harris concluded the story with an introspective passage on Mitsunaga.

This reporter has covered the Capitol for more than twenty years. Rumors of improper liaisons and illegal contributions are not new in politics. History is filled with examples of talented men and women who have fallen prey to corruption. The temptations are great. Most politicians resist, but some fall victim to its clutches. Before the DeLaurio testimony, this reporter would never have believed Ken Mitsunaga would betray his country. Ken Mitsunaga was a war hero and steady rudder in the Senate. His quiet demeanor harkened back to an earlier era, an era of greater statesmanship and less partisan bickering. Like the Senate, he'd changed with the times, tweeting and blogging. But at his core, he'd never wavered from serving the people of Hawaii. He used his position on the Appropriations Committee to protect his state. He was successful in shepherding hundreds of billions of dollars to the fiftieth state.

Watching Mitsunaga become corruption's latest victim pained the entire country. This proud man was humiliated by the accusation and apparent proof that he had, in fact, sold out to the Chinese. While he never admitted guilt, in the eyes of Hawaii's voters and the American public it was clear he'd been found guilty by a jury of his peers.

And, now, what do we really know about this crime? Only this: someone let his desire to attain or maintain power skew his moral compass. Politics can be a beguiling and bewitching mistress.

CHAPTER XCVIII

White House

Larry Smith was ready to pop champagne. "I tell you, Jack. Yesterday I couldn't see how we could win; now I don't see how we can lose. Since the news hit this morning, the bottom has fallen out of Parker's campaign. His numbers are dropping like a rock. Even Fox News is starting to come around to the idea that maybe Parker staged the whole Mitsunaga attack.

"MSNBC had a branch chief from the IT division of the FBI confirm what *Roll Call* said. The video's not a fake. Rebecca DeLaurio was, in fact, in Parker's hideaway with him, alone, before the hearing. *The New York Daily News* is calling it a third sneak attack on Hawaii. The Parker camp hasn't come up with a credible alibi. The idea that your campaign planned it was disproven by the FBI. He's got nothing, Jack, nothing. The candidate hasn't been seen or heard from. We think he's on his ranch in Nevada, but we don't know."

Larry paced enthusiastically, his mouth spread in an exultant grin. "It's incredible, Jack. The Asian-American community is furious. The clean-cut Washington caucus is mortified. His Republican colleagues are backing away from him at lightning speed. Five Republican candidates for state office announced schedule changes today. They aren't going to join the nominee on his bus tour through their states. It's only the beginning, Jack. He's done."

Jack lounged back on the office couch, smiling along with the vice president's excitement. "Congratulations, Mr. Vice President. I don't see how Parker can recover from this. What'll be his excuse? He called her to his private office to feel her out on the scandal without letting on what he planned?"

"Yeah, more likely he was feeling her up."

"Well, that's certainly possible. But that wouldn't help him out either. He ran his campaign on cleaning up corruption based on a scandal that he manufactured. He destroyed one of the most revered members of the Senate to achieve his goal. Now this champion of reform has been caught in an even bigger scandal."

"Sir, I'm sure you already know this, but all you need is a glitch-free convention, and you coast to victory. It's there for the taking, sir. It's all yours."

CHAPTER XCIX

Honolulu, Oahu

Rosie Mitsunaga called out the window to her husband. As usual these days, he was puttering in the yard. He used his cane to push pebbles off the walkway and back into the garden areas where they belonged. He picked up a dead leaf and put it into a plastic bag held by the same hand which grasped his cane. He plucked a couple of dying blooms from a small plumeria tree.

"Ken, Paula Means is on the phone."

"Paula? What does she want?"

"I don't know, but she says it's important. She said you should be watching the news."

"The last thing I want to do is watch the news. With the convention coming to town next week, that's all reporters are talking about. I don't want to hear about it."

"Well she didn't say why, but she said it was important. You should come in and talk to her. It's not polite to refuse."

"OK, I'm on my way. It takes me a little longer these days, you know."

"I'll tell her you're coming."

Ken picked off another dying bloom, kicked a couple more pebbles, and walked up the path to the back door. Leaving the bag on the back stoop, he entered the kitchen and took the phone from the counter. "Hello Paula, it's Ken. How are you? What's up?"

"Senator, turn on CNN."

"Paula, unless the North Koreans are attacking again, why would I want to turn on the news?"

"Senator, it's Parker. He met privately with Rebecca DeLaurio before she testified against you."

"What? What are you talking about?"

"Senator, sir, turn on CNN. They have film of Parker and Rebecca coming out of the same door in the Capitol."

"So what, they came through the same door. Big deal."

"No, Senator." She sighed. "I'm not saying this right. Turn on the TV. You'll see what I mean."

"OK, just a second." The last thing he wanted was to be reminded of Parker and Rebecca. It was nearly two years since he'd been blindsided and betrayed. He wasn't sure why Paula thought it so all-fired important to be reminded of the past, but he switched on CNN.

The news anchor was so excited he was nearly shouting. Ken recognized the Senate corridor immediately. He saw a man walk out of an office away from the camera. It sure looked a lot like Parker from behind. In the voice-over, the anchorman was asking someone off camera to explain what they were seeing.

"So you see Parker comes out of the door and walks away. You can also see at the bottom of the screen a series of numbers counting the time. If you look closely, you can see that the date was August third. That's weeks before the famous hearing in which Senator Parker accused Rebecca DeLaurio of taking money from the Chinese military for Senator Mitsunaga's campaign. Now you see a woman exiting the same office. As she turns toward the camera, we can clearly identify her. It's Rebecca DeLaurio, the former Mitsunaga staffer who testified against her boss."

"What office is that?" the anchor asked.

"It's a private office in the Capitol, a so-called 'hideaway.' Most long-serving senators have an extra office in the Capitol where they can rest or hold private meetings. Two years ago, that office was Parker's."

"So who else would've been in the office?"

"That's just it. From what we've heard, only Senator Parker and Rebecca DeLaurio were seen going in and out of the office that day."

"So Senator Parker, the Republican candidate for president, met privately with Rebecca DeLaurio before she testified against Mitsunaga in a bombshell hearing that cost Mitsunaga the election?" The anchor's voice peaked at a frenzy.

"That's right."

"But we have no idea what went on behind closed doors."

"True, but you can bet she wasn't selling Girl Scout cookies."

The image on the screen switched to an outraged Parker slamming down a handful of papers and glaring down from the dais. It cut to Rebecca sitting at the witness table with her head down, apparently crying.

"Let's get Zack Trap on this from the Capitol. Zack, what's the Parker camp saying about this?"

A picture of Zack Trap appeared in the bottom corner of the screen with the video still playing.

"Well, they claim it's a setup. Steve Simpson, Parker's campaign manager, issued a statement claiming the video is a fake. They're saying Vice President Smith is so far behind, he's desperate. That this is an amateurish attempt to denigrate their candidate."

"And what about Parker? What's the candidate saying?"

"Well, Parker's taking a week off from campaigning, as candidates traditionally do following their convention. So far, he hasn't said anything. Candidates tend to ignore these scandalous bombshells unless the heat gets too great. Bush did that with his National Guard service. Clinton did with Gennifer Flowers. That's their approach so far, but he'll have to deal with it eventually."

Ken Mitsunaga sat at his kitchen table, stunned. *I can't believe it. Rebecca and Parker meeting together. Rebecca responsible for this whole mess? Why would she do that?*

A glance at his hand still holding the phone reminded him Paula was still on the line. "Well." His voice was a bit unsteady. "Isn't this interesting."

"Senator, it's great. It proves you were framed. No one's going to believe the video's a fake. Everyone's going to know Parker was working with Rebecca on this. Your good name is back!"

"We shall see. If the Parker supporters continue to claim it's a fake, that story will take hold in some quarters. I bet Fox is already playing that angle, but they're going to need some proof to show the film was doctored. I'm curious; where did the video come from?"

"Sir, it's a video from the security system in the Capitol. The sergeant at arms had it installed in case of a terrorist attack or another security breach."

Mitsunaga drew in a deep breath. "Well I'll be darned. Then we've got a good chance of proving it's the real deal. Of all the luck. Too bad this didn't turn up two years ago, before the election."

"Yes sir, it sure is. Well congratulations, Senator. I wanted to make sure you knew."

"Paula, thank you. I couldn't be happier. I hope everything's OK with you. What are you doing now?"

"Senator, I'm working at the Asia Pacific Center with General Gianini. It's not quite the Senate, but they pay me well enough, and I like the mission of the center. How are you?"

"I'm fine. Working in the garden and reading. I guess now I'll be watching the news again. What a crazy year, with Andrews' stroke, Smith's war on Korea, and now this. I don't think politics has ever been wilder. Thanks again for calling, and I'm glad you're doing well. I think I'm going to sit for a while and let this sink in. Thanks, Paula. Goodbye."

"OK, sir. Thank you, sir."

CHAPTER C

Honolulu, Oahu

Ken retreated to his office, turned on Vivaldi, and sat back in his recliner. What the hell. He reached over to his desk and pulled an old newspaper article from the stack. It was a piece highlighting his career that ran in the *Tribune* before the scandal hit:

> Ken Mitsunaga enlisted in the army after graduating from high school in 1963 at the age of eighteen. He was inspired by President Kennedy's visit to Fort Bragg in 1961 where the youthful president and World War II veteran highlighted the heroism and unique mission of the Army's Special Forces, dubbed the Green Berets.

Ken stopped reading and put down the article. *So what? Nothing's left.* The loss of dignity and respect cut him deeply. Some of that might be regained. But they couldn't undo the election and the tragedy of Harry's suicide. To think it was all caused by the betrayal of one of his closest staff members—

Rosie knocked gently on the door in case he'd fallen asleep and spoke softly, "Ken, are you awake?"

"Yes dear, please come in." Rosie walked in, bowing slightly as she entered, an old habit from her Japanese upbringing.

"Are you alright? What does all this mean?"

"Well, it means I may die a little happier if the news media has it right and Rebecca was working with Parker all along. Though it still doesn't make any sense to me. All the years she worked for me, she was a hard-working member of my team. She was as loyal as any of my staff. I never would have thought she'd betray me like this, but it looks like she did."

"Ken, you know I never doubted your honesty for a minute. Still, I must say I'm a little relieved to know that your 'Indian Affair' was a fantasy of the media."

"Oh, Rosie, you of all people knew that wasn't true."

"Yes, Ken, I did, but you can't blame me for allowing a little doubt to creep in at times. It was pounded into me every hour of every day on the news."

"Rosie, you were my sweetheart from the first day I met you at Tripler. That never changed. You nursed me back to health and gave me the will to live. It was you who convinced me to go to college and enter politics. If it hadn't been for you and Harry, I'd still be in the Office of Records. Your faith in me kept me going. You've been the love of my life and my only love; I hope you know that."

"Yes, Ken, I do." She smiled down at his sweet, earnest face. "Still, it's good to see the truth about that woman coming out. But what does this mean for you? Do you go back into politics?"

"Oh, Rosie, I'm too old to start over. Besides, politics is different today. The days of going door-to-door and asking for votes are over. Today it's all about raising money and running TV ads attacking your opponent. It's fifteen-second sound bites and tweets. I'd go back into politics if it were a little bit civilized, but that's not the case."

"Well, Ken, that's fine with me. I like having you around, and I love being back home in Hawaii."

"Well, Rosie, I don't think you've anything to worry about. It'd take a miracle to get me back into politics."

CHAPTER CI

Arlington, Virginia

Justin Armor sat on his couch watching TV. The table was covered with empty Coke cans and bags of tortilla chips, Cheetos, and pork rinds. A pile of dirty laundry sat on the chair next to the TV, and a sports coat hung on its back.

Over the couch was a poster of dogs playing poker. One corner was ripped, and another curled up at the edges. The couch was covered in orange and gray stains from repeated hand wiping. The carpet was a hideous shade of gray from years of dirt.

Justin's disheveled shirt was unbuttoned near the waist, and his belly popped through. His khaki pants were wrinkled. The front pocket openings were frayed and gray after years of stuffing his dirty hands in. His scuffed brown loafers completed the ensemble.

He sipped his Coke and ate chips out of the nearest bag. For the ten-thousandth time CNN was running the clip of Rebecca coming out of Parker's office. "Serves him right," Justin said to his empty apartment. "Never should've sent me back to GAO. I could've protected him, but he was too stupid. Oh well, that's how it goes. It's going to be a long nine weeks for him now." He let out his high-pitched Woody Woodpecker cackle and stuffed another handful of chips in his mouth.

CHAPTER CII

White House

The news of Parker's downfall troubled President Andrews greatly. He was convinced that Larry Smith had no business replacing him. But Parker's clear superiority in the polls had alleviated his concern. With Parker's new vulnerability, the president was soul-searching. That evening in the private residence he shared his thoughts with his most trusted advisor, his wife Barbara.

"Barbara, for one of the first times in my life, I don't know what to do. When I was incapacitated, the vice president almost unleashed a holocaust on the world. It would have made 9-11 look like child's play. I'm disgusted he attacked North Korea to boost his campaign but horrified he was on course to attack China. And even now, after the disaster he caused, he still insists attacking China is the right action. We came terrifyingly close to backing China into a corner and forcing them to attack the United States."

Hal ran a hand through his rumpled hair and looked at Barbara in appeal. "Our missile defenses are barely adequate against a petty dictator like Kim Jong Un. Given the size and sophistication of China's nuclear force, had they attacked, the United States would no longer exist as it is today. They could've easily taken out this city, New York, Chicago, St. Louis, and on and on. The consequences on our economy, our psyche, and our optimism would've been devastating. It would've taken generations to get back anywhere near to where we are today. I didn't criticize Smith at first because Parker had an insurmountable lead. But now, Parker's popularity is collapsing. The media loves a reformer, but anyone who plays the media for a fool will incur its wrath and that of the American people. I don't think he can recover.

"So what do I do? If I stay silent, Larry Smith could be the next president, but if I turn on him, I'm turning against my party and all my friends. Barbara, I think Parker would be a terrible president, but Smith would be worse. I can tell myself Smith's actions were all based on election-year politics. That, once elected, he'll be more rational. But the fact's inescapable. He risked our nation for the sake of an election. That's a gamble no president can take."

Barbara shifted closer on the couch so she could clasp his pale hand in her own. Hal returned a grateful squeeze and turned his anguished face to his wife. "I'm at a loss, Barbara. I'm not sure I could forgive myself if my silence allows Larry Smith to win. But if I speak, I'll feel like a traitor, and I'm sure millions of good, loyal Democrats will agree. I just don't know what to do."

"Hal, my darling." Barbara lifted his hand and kissed it. "You've always displayed the best judgment and taken the right steps in each crisis you've faced. I'm confident you'll do so again now."

"Barbara, I appreciate your confidence, but tonight I'd really like to hear your thoughts."

"Hal, if you're having trouble deciding, you should pray for an answer and sleep on it. I'm sure you'll come to the right decision in the morning. That's what I think."

"But don't you have an opinion?"

"You know, when you were unconscious . . ." Barbara's eyes

filled with unexpected tears that she brushed fiercely away. "I didn't know what I was going to do. What would happen to me? I suppose I would've gone home to Butte, but you know, we've come a long way since we lived there. I don't know if I'd fit in anymore. And who'd want to have anything to do with me? Our children are grown, with lives of their own. Oh, I'm sure they'd visit for holidays or for summer vacation, but mostly I'd be alone. I suppose it was selfish of me to think about my problems while you were lying there, unconscious, but that's what I did. All I could do was hang on to the hope that you'd return to me. And through the grace of God, you have. You are all that matters to me now. I know that whatever you decide, it will be the right answer.

"But—" She paused and frowned as she returned her husband's earnest gaze. "The night before you woke up, Admiral Casey talked to me. I have to tell you, Hal—he was very, very concerned. He was afraid Larry was leading us on a path of destruction. He truly feared the vice president was going to attack China. He was certain you would've never allowed that. I knew he was right."

Barbara squeezed his hand gently and smiled. "So, my dear, I have complete confidence in your judgment. If you are unsure what to do, I really think you should pray. The answer will come. Kneel with me. You can ask God for wisdom. I'll thank him for returning you to me, and we can go to sleep knowing God will answer your prayer. He's already answered mine."

CHAPTER CIII

Sunday, August 19th

White House

Early on Sunday morning, President Andrews called his press secretary, Jeff Sallinger, to the Oval Office. "Jeff, I want to do a one-on-one TV interview today before the convention starts. I want to show the American public I'm fine. And, frankly, it's my last chance to speak as the standard bearer for the Democratic Party."

"Mr. President, I must say I'm a little surprised, but, in many ways, it makes sense. Your popularity has been sky-high since the stroke, despite the concerns with North Korea and China, and the right-wing talk of appeasement. You seem to be healthy, although still a little weak. You can reassure the public about your health. Your public announcement on the Chinese stolen warheads was scripted. Americans are smart enough to know we could prop you up in front of a teleprompter. You could fake it, even if you weren't fully recovered. But if you sat down with one of the national news correspondents, you couldn't answer their questions coherently if you were still ill. This way the public would see you are fine. I'm sure every newscaster would welcome the opportunity to interview you. I'd suggest a female correspondent. A woman might be a little more empathetic."

They agreed on Janie Trudeau at CNN. Before leaving, Jeff said he'd have talking points prepared for the president on the topics of the day. The president brushed him off. He said he didn't need any. He was ready to go, comfortable he was up to speed on anything that might come up.

CHAPTER CIV

Pearl Harbor, HI

Admiral Lockwood and Al Gianini stood in the CINC's dining room looking out the window. It had been quite a couple of weeks. Stu had invited Al to come over early on Sunday morning for breakfast to thank him for everything.

"You know, Al, if you hadn't talked to Sheng, I'm not sure we could have stopped Wu from launching an attack. From what I can tell, they were positive we were lying just to justify an attack on the PRC. I don't think anyone realizes how close we came to doomsday."

"You're right, Stu. You know in many ways we have Mitsunaga to thank for this."

"For this? Do you mean this house?" Stu swiveled to take in the spacious surroundings. "Yeah, I'm aware he led the charge to build the headquarters building, but this house goes back to Nimitz I believe."

"No sir, I mean for the Asia Pacific Center. Mitsunaga had the vision to create the Asia Pacific Center, to establish lines of communication with military and political leaders throughout Asia. It's true that DoD now considers the center its own, but this was Mitsunaga's brainchild. Without the center, I couldn't have talked frankly with Sheng. We wouldn't have had a back channel to get to Wu."

"Well, we can thank the good senator for his vision, but you deserve most of the credit. You nurture the relationships with these students even after they go home. Without that, none of this would've been possible. Don't sell yourself short, Al. You're the one who convinced the Chinese to delay mobilization. You're the one who figured out how to get the evidence to the Chinese that allowed cooler heads to prevail."

Al chuckled. "Actually, that was Paula. She's the one who suggested we go to Huck Finn and have him declassify the images."

Stu grinned and shook his head. "Well, thanks to Paula, too. I'm sure she's doing a good job for you. I enjoy having her political expertise to rely on as well."

"She's doing a great job, sir."

There was a knock on the door. "Excuse me for interrupting, Admiral, but the White House is on the phone."

"The White House? Who could that be? I'll pick it up, Sam, thanks." Picking up the phone he said, "This is Admiral Lockwood." He nearly dropped the phone at the voice he heard in response.

"Admiral, this is President Andrews. I wanted to thank you for your hard work and to express my condolences for the loss of your wife and grandchildren. That's a terrible tragedy to have to live with, especially given the events of the past couple of weeks."

"Thank you, Mr. President." Stu fought to sound collected, but he felt dangerously close to tearing up. "Thank you for calling and for the kind words."

"Admiral, it's I who should be thanking you. Your ships shot down the missile that would've struck Hawaii. And I'm told your back channel to the Chinese convinced President Wu the bomb was Chinese."

"Sir, it was a team effort. The officers and sailors of the *Lake Erie* get the credit for knocking out the missile. They were assisted by the crew on the SBX and by the staff at the air force telescope on Maui, as well as by the crews on the Port Royal and even the Aegis ashore project on Kauai. And sir, it was actually Lieutenant General Al Gianini, the director of the Asia Pacific Center, who got through to the Chinese. Without his contacts with former students at the Asia Pacific Center, there's no way we would have been able to get to the PRC. So, Mr. President, I want to thank you for the compliment, but actually my role was minor."

"Well, Admiral, that's not what Sonny Gallagher tells me. I think you're being modest. Please, thank General Gianini for me as well."

"Mr. President, there's one favor I'd like to ask. It's not every day the President of the United States calls. General Gianini is here in my home. Would you thank him yourself?"

Al Gianini was shaking his head and waving his arms in protest.

"I'd be happy to thank him, Admiral. Put him on the phone."

"Mr. President, this is retired Lieutenant General Gianini. It's a great honor to speak to you."

"General, from what the Admiral told me, it is I who should be honored. So, you were the one who got through to the Chinese?"

"Yes, Mr. President, I guess I was. I reached out to a former student, Vice Chairman Sheng, who now serves on the Central Committee. I shared pictures of the Chinese warhead with him. He convinced President Wu to call you before mobilizing his forces."

"In that case, General, I'm very grateful to you and to Vice Chairman Sheng. President Wu's call defused this crisis. So, General, you and the admiral have my deepest appreciation for all your efforts. The nation is in your debt. Please express my appreciation once again to the admiral. Goodbye."

"Yes sir, Mr. President. Goodbye." He hung up the phone and smiled at the admiral. "Well, that was something. They say he's not a big supporter of national defense. Still, you have to like a guy who reaches out and thanks folks for their efforts."

"You know, Al, our DC colleagues sometimes think if you're not for increasing our budget, you're against us. That's not always true. President Andrews is a straight shooter whose heart is in the right place."

"Thanks for doing that, Stu. It was an honor to talk to him."

"I'll tell you, Al. After all we've gone through, you know, it actually makes a difference that he took the time to call and thank us. Even when you wear stars on your shoulders, it's still nice to know you're appreciated."

"Well, we certainly appreciate you, Stu."

"Thanks, Al. And I certainly appreciate all that you and Paula do as well. Give my best to Midge, and enjoy the rest of the weekend."

CHAPTER CV

White House

The noon interview was a complete success from the president's viewpoint. As Sallinger suggested, Janie Trudeau from CNN proved to be a very empathetic inquisitor. She focused first on the president's health. She asked him if there were any restrictions on his activities. He said he wasn't likely to take up skydiving. Other than insisting he get a bit more rest, he added, the doctors had given him a clean bill of health. He'd resumed his duties and was not suffering from any effects of the stroke. He thanked the office of the White House physician, singling out Admiral Casey. He praised the outstanding care he received from the surgeons at George Washington University hospital and the nurses at Walter Reed. He even thanked his wife who, he told Janie, had stayed by his side for days and nights while he lay unconscious.

Janie turned to foreign policy. The president told her he grieved for those Americans, especially the sailors and their families, who lost their lives at Pacific Beach. He wished it had never come to that.

Janie continued, "Mr. President, the vice president says you ordered the military attack on North Korea. Isn't that correct?"

The president responded, "Well Janie, the military plans for a lot of contingencies. We need to be ready to respond to any act of aggression. I had the military draw up the plan to attack North Korea in case we were provoked."

"But, Mr. President, what was the provocation that led to the attack?"

"Well, the vice president felt the North Korean nuclear program was destabilizing enough to warrant the attack."

"Do you agree with that assessment?"

"Well actually, no, Janie, I didn't agree with that assessment."

Janie's eyes had gone wide as she fought to maintain her calm, professional manner. "Are you saying you wouldn't have attacked North Korea?"

"Janie, hindsight is always twenty-twenty. I can't speak for the motivation of the vice president. Knowing what I knew before my stroke, I can assure you I hadn't planned to attack."

Janie asked one more question. "Mr. President, was the vice president aware you weren't planning to attack?"

"Janie, Vice President Smith knew my views. But, as I said, he believed the North Korean program was too unstable not to attack."

"But Mr. President, the attack led to the counterattack, and the loss of thousands of American lives."

"And I pray every day for those lost souls."

"Mr. President, are you saying the vice president gave the order to attack even though you opposed it?" Janie was losing the fight for composure as her face flushed, and her thoughts turned to those lost in the tsunami. "You were still president, despite the fact you were incapacitated. Do you think the vice president acted appropriately?"

President Andrews's voice was gentle and calm as ever. "Janie, as I said, I won't speak for the motivation of the vice president.

I had been unconscious for more than a week at the time of the attack. The doctors had no idea if I'd ever regain consciousness and, if I did, they didn't know if I'd be able to resume the presidency. The vice president had every reason to believe he was going to be filling out the rest of my term when he acted."

"So you don't fault him for the attack?"

"Janie, I wouldn't have attacked, but, as I said before, I won't question his motivation."

Janie's intense frown shifted to wide-eyed suspicion. "Are you suggesting his motivation might have been something else?"

"Janie, reasonable men can disagree on the proper course of action. I can only tell you once again that I wouldn't have launched the attack."

"Mr. President, we've come to the end of our time." Janie swallowed hard and reached an earnest hand out to President Andrews. "I want to thank you for appearing on our show today. I also want to wish you the best of health in the months and years to come."

"Thank you, Janie."

Jack Ralston stared dumbly at his TV screen. *Oh shit! How could he do that? Parker is going down. We're walking on air. Now he's blaming Larry for the attack on Korea and the loss of American lives. This could kill us.*

CHAPTER CVI

Honolulu, Oahu

At 9 a.m., the minority whip of the Senate, Tom Bankhead, placed a call to Ken Mitsunaga. Ken was sitting at his kitchen table when the phone rang.

"Ken, this is Tom Bankhead. It's good to hear your voice. You know we're having a little get-together downtown, starting tomorrow afternoon. The fellas were wondering if you were going to stop by."

"Tom, are you hitting the bourbon already? It might be 3 p.m. in Louisville, but it's only 9 a.m. here in the fiftieth state. What the hell are you talking about?"

"C'mon Ken, you know me better than that. I'm as sober as a judge, and I'm serious. Can we convince you to come down to the convention? After all, we're in your hometown."

"Tom, you can't be serious. Why would you want me to come to the convention? I was tossed out, kicked aside, branded a traitor and a philanderer. You were on the jury. You let them attack me without a chance to defend myself."

"Ken, you're right. I was the one who let them attack you, but their evidence looked airtight. What were we to do? If we'd defended you, we'd have been killed in the midterm election. Andrews could've been facing a Senate with sixty Republican

votes. We didn't have time to think or analyze. They jumped us."
Tom sighed. "It's no defense. I was wrong, Ken. I know that now.
I never could believe you'd betray your country, but damn, their
case was strong.

"Seriously, who would've believed Parker was working with
Rebecca? We all saw her performance that day. She looked like
Parker set her up. We know there's a lot more to come out about
this, but the party wants to rally around you.

"Look, we've got a mess on our hands. Between you and me,
Andrews has withdrawn his support from Smith. And if you
saw that interview on CNN, you know he's now gone public. The
party leaders are talking about a revolt. I don't know what we're
going to do. We're ten points behind with Smith as our candidate, and the DNC leadership is about to walk away from him.
There's even a movement to draft Charley Johnson. Charley'd do
it, but he doesn't generate a lot of enthusiasm with the money
people—or anybody else for that matter.

"But Ken, the one thing we know we must do is to draw attention away from our problems and pile on to Parker's. You're
the best way to do that."

"Tom, I ought to hang up right now. You all tarred and feath-
ered me and ran me out of town on a rail. You forced me to walk
the plank. You lynched me. You fragged me." Mitsunaga's voice
cracked. "What other metaphors do I need to come up with? You
fucked me, Tom. Don't you remember?"

"Ken, I know what we did and why. But you need to forgive us.
You of all people should realize we can't turn this country over
to Parker. Ken, I wouldn't be asking you if we weren't desperate.
The party needs you. We need you to come to the convention
and speak about your lynching at the hands of the Republican

candidate. We want you to speak tomorrow night in prime time. We're willing to bump anybody to get you on that stage."

"Tom, what would I say? 'See? I told you so?'" Ken shook his head. "I've retired from politics. It sickens my stomach to think of showing up tomorrow."

"Ken, I understand, and it pains me to think about what happened to you. But, Ken, this is your chance and, believe me, the American public will listen. You have the opportunity every innocent man wants; the chance to set the record straight. I wouldn't be asking if we didn't think it was not only the right thing to do, but the responsible thing. We need you to speak out against that megalomaniac."

"Tom, I'm not sure the party wants to hear what I'd say. I've done a lot of thinking in the past two years. My views are a lot harsher than when I was one of the get-along-go-along guys for you and Charley. My thinking involves a lot more than just attacking Parker. Politicians today of both parties have gotten off track. We spend far too much time worrying about winning and far too little running the country. Parker's a symptom of the disease. He's not the disease. Us politicians fell into the trap of wanting to ensure our reelections. I doubt that's a speech you want me to deliver."

"Ken, I told you. We're desperate. Our candidate almost started World War III, and why? To improve the polls. Everyone in America knows it. By the end of the week, he might not be our candidate any longer. It's crass, but the only chance we have is to shift the focus to their candidate. There's no better way to do that than to put you on that stage. You could read "Mary Had a Little Lamb"; the media would still focus on Parker's dishonesty and the shoddy treatment we gave you. The media needs to make up for deifying Parker, and they know it. I can't say it any better than this, Ken: your party needs you, and so does the country."

Ken sighed. "Tom, let me think about it. But one thing's for sure, no one gets a chance to censor my speech—is that clear?"

"Ken, for what it's worth, you have my word. You agree to speak, and we'll give you fifteen minutes to say anything you want. We just want you on that stage."

"What time?"

"Name it, but we want you in prime time on the East Coast, what's that, around 3 p.m. here?"

"Yeah, 4 p.m. would be better. That's 7 in LA and 10 in New York."

"Ken, you agree to do this, and I'll have you on that stage at 4 p.m. tomorrow afternoon."

Ken drew in a deep breath and nodded slowly.

"OK, Tom, I'll do it. It's not a lot of time to prepare, but I'll do my best."

"Ken, thank you. I'm not sure you understand how important this is. Please give my best to Rosie. We miss you in DC. The Senate hasn't been the same since you left. Thank you, my friend, we're in your debt."

"OK, Tom, I better get to work. I'll see you tomorrow afternoon."

CHAPTER CVII

Monday, August 20th

US Capitol

Sam Jackson stripped off his clothes, wrapped a towel around his waist, and headed to the senators' steam room. That was where he could be found most afternoons around 4 p.m. It was almost an unwritten rule in the Senate. There wouldn't be any votes between 4 and 4:30. Jackson, Bankhead, Wilson, Corrigan, and a half-dozen old bulls from both parties took in the steam and the stress relief then. They were free from staff, BlackBerrys, and phones for thirty minutes. With the Democratic convention starting that evening and Congress on recess, Jackson had the steam pretty much to himself. John Brinkman, the stalwart old timer from Nebraska and chairman of the Armed Services Committee, was there. So was Jesse Taft, the senator from Ohio and great-grandson of former Senator Robert Taft.

Brinkman came over and sat down next to Jackson on the bench. "Unbelievable about Parker."

"I don't find it unbelievable at all, John. Parker's always been an asshole, ever since he got here. He's been a thorn in your side for years, trying to get you to step out of the way so he could take over your committee. And he's done his level best to ruin the appropriations process, albeit with little, if any, success. From his very first day in the Senate, only one thing mattered to that son of a bitch, and that was James Fillmore Parker."

"But can you believe he was getting it on with Rebecca DeLaurio? She was Mitsunaga's girl."

"John, she wasn't Mitsunaga's girl. Ken's devoted to Rosie. Mitsunaga wasn't the type to chase skirts."

"Oh c'mon, Sam, you can't be that naïve. All those trips they took together. We read the same papers. You know what the press reported."

"John, you should know not to believe what you read. The press is jealous that there are dozens of beautiful young women who work on the Hill. They've convinced themselves we're screwing all of them."

"Well, some of us are, Sam."

"Yeah, some of you talk a good game. In today's world, if you get caught with your pants down, you're done. You drop 10 percent of the women's vote overnight. If you're stupid enough to take the risk, it's going to bite you in the ass—and it won't be some twenty-year-old hottie's teeth marks. It'll be that fifty-five-year-old bag of a reporter. She'll take a big bite out of your butt, spit it out, and watch you writhe around in agony while the press has a field day. In this environment, pal, you better be like Ken Mitsunaga and find a woman you love. Leave the interns to the other interns."

John stared at him in wonderment. "You are that naïve. You seriously think Mitsunaga wasn't getting it on with Rebecca."

"God damn it, John, I know for a fact Mitsunaga wasn't getting it on with Rebecca or anyone else."

"Sam, I know Ken was your friend, but c'mon."

"OK, John, I shouldn't tell you this, but it doesn't make a hell of a lot of difference at this point anyway. Did you ever see Mitsunaga in the steam room?"

"No. I guess he wasn't the type."

"Oh yeah? Well, he has a sauna in his home basement, so that wasn't it."

"OK, Sam, what's the point? Not everyone comes to the steam room to brag about who they're boning."

"John, the reason Mitsunaga never came to the steam room is because he didn't want anyone to see what the war did to him."

"What do you mean?"

"Ken Mitsunaga was a war hero, right?"

"Yeah, he dragged his CO to safety. What does that have to do with anything?"

"Listen to me. Ken didn't want the fellas to see his scars. It was bad, John. One time when we were visiting the troops in Afghanistan, he and I were both showering. I saw him naked when his shower curtain blew open. John, he was one scar from his waist to his knees. He still had his pecker, but he didn't have any balls. I told him that day I'd keep that secret, and I have for the past ten years. But when they said he was having an affair, I knew it was bullshit."

"Why didn't you defend him?"

"Seriously? And what do you think the Parker goons would've done? I'll tell you what they'd have done; they'd have stripped me of my chairmanship. I couldn't do that to my constituents. Besides, it was the corruption scandal that cost Ken his seat. If I had told the world about his scars, he would never have forgiven me. I would've sacrificed my seniority and my friendship, and it still wouldn't have made one wit's bit of difference. So to find out that the son of a bitch manufactured this whole Chinese thing with Rebecca rips my heart out.

"Ken Mitsunaga was one of the finest public servants—hell, one of the finest people—I've ever met. To think that that blowhard bastard caused his downfall just kills me. His outrageous actions might allow a prick like Larry Smith to be president. I don't know about you, John, but I'd sooner vote for Mickey Mouse than either one of those two jackasses—and I probably will."

"Jesus Christ, Sam, is that why you didn't support Parker's calls to go after the North Koreans?"

"That's just one reason, John. You served in the marines. You know what it's like to face the enemy. None of us should ever take the risk of war lightly. Get this straight. I'm not defending Smith, but Parker kept hounding him to act, and he finally did. So what's the result? Thousands of my constituents were killed."

Sam's face tightened, and his voice choked. "John, they were my people. And Stu Lockwood's wife—I had brunch at her home in Honolulu. She was the sweetest woman. You know, I held town halls in Pacific Beach every year or two. They were good people, and they were sacrificed for political gain. It sickens me, John. It sickens me.

"Enough is enough. I don't know where this country is going. I tell you right now, I wish we could just ask Andrews to stay on. I don't agree with most of his policies, but at least he isn't corrupt like these bastards. We need a different option. John, I truly fear for the republic. We're a strong nation with a vibrant population of good people. We'll get past this in time, but God damn it, at this point, don't ask me how."

"Jesus Christ, Sam, that's unbelievable. I agree we need another option, but that's not in the cards. Well, I think my core temperature has shot up about 10 degrees. I'm going to get out of here. You better do the same, my friend."

"I'm right behind you, John. And, John?" Sam grimaced. "I shouldn't have told you about Mitsunaga. I hope you can keep that to yourself."

"Not to worry, Sam; I'm not saying a thing."

CHAPTER CVIII

Honolulu, Oahu

Mitsunaga stood on center stage, facing an audience waiting with bated breath for him speak. He bowed, cleared his throat, and began.

"My fellow Americans, today I stand before you no longer a politician, but a victim of politics in a country too quick to judge. Two years ago, I stood for reelection to represent the people of Hawaii. My opponent was an honorable man who represented a different political philosophy than mine. He was the champion of the well-to-do, who he believes are the engines which spur the economy and provide for a strong safety net through their job creation and charitable giving. I championed the little people: the shopkeeper who hires veterans and single moms, the day laborer who works two jobs to support his family, the suburban wife who must balance her career, her children, and her checkbook.

"The polls showed I had a fifteen-point lead, but then a scandal erupted of which I was the center. The campaign no longer centered on which of us would better represent the people of Hawaii. It was about presumed corruption. My reputation was dragged through the mud by a self-serving politician hell-bent on building himself up by trashing my good name. My friends, this is no way to run an election. More important, this would be no way, no way, to run this great country.

"The attack on me was vigilante politics at its worst. I was accused, tried, and convicted in the court of public opinion without regard to due process. The fourth estate, the watchdog over corrupt politicians and defender of liberty, became the lapdog of one conniving man.

"Where was the impartial investigation of the evidence by the media? Who sought the truth—not the headline, but the truth? The answer, sadly, is no one.

"My friends, we're all guilty of being too quick to judge, too quick to condemn. There are those in the media who are too eager to build up politicians, athletes, Hollywood stars. They sing their praises from the hilltops as if they've found the next son of God. Then they relish tearing them down when they make mistakes, and we discover they're only human after all. As I learned only too well. Heaven help the public figure who finds him or herself accused of misdeeds, regardless of guilt.

"With our zeal for instant news, we've become a nation of conclusion-jumpers. We are led down that path by a ravenous media more intent on tweeting first than reporting facts.

"Campaigns today are composed of two parts: raising money and attacking our opponents. The media chastises us for raising millions. But it reports each attack on our opponents with zeal—the more sensational, the better.

"And what about those of us who serve? We've watched as the Senate bogs down into partisan squabbling on nearly every issue. On one side, the minority is determined to stop the majority from legislating. On the other, the majority denies the minority the right to offer amendments. As such, it takes days or weeks of procedural shenanigans to pass a bill in the Senate. This process ultimately rewards those who refuse to compromise. It penalizes those who seek to improve bills. It takes more time to pass a non-controversial measure today than it took to pass complex legislation twenty years ago. This, my friends, is no way for the greatest deliberative body to function.

"And, it's not just the media or Congress. My fellow Americans, I never thought I'd live to see a day when the nation was brought to the brink of a nuclear war by a White House politician worried about his poll numbers.

"That catastrophic decision cost thousands of Americans their lives. It put millions more at risk. You should all be asking yourselves, how did we get to this point? You should be demanding that your elected leaders stop the bickering, stop the attacking, stop the politics of stonewalling and delay. Remember, they were elected to serve you, to improve the country, to address our problems, to safeguard this unique and wonderful republic.

"I've come to the stage tonight, not to seek your vote or ask you to support a particular candidate. I've come instead to plead with you to punish unscrupulous politicians of both parties. Demand that your elected officials return to the business of governing. The country faces too many problems for public servants to dither about. Our children and grandchildren deserve better. You deserve better. I urge you. Find a candidate who can honestly say, and has genuinely demonstrated, that he or she will put your interests first. He or she must be willing to work with both parties to improve this country. It's up to you. Demand that your nominee act to better this nation. Reject the politics of blame and name-calling.

"My friends, the choice is yours. Will you choose to continue the politics of hate and stalemate? Or will you embrace the poli-

tics of cooperation and compromise? Will you nominate someone who promises four more years of the same? Or will you select a candidate who vows to work across party lines to move the
nation forward? Will you allow vigilante politics to run rough-
shod over our electoral process? Or will you demand honest debate about the issues and accountability? My fellow Americans,
I can see only one path forward, and I hope you agree. It's up to
you. You must choose wisely. Our future depends on it. May God
guide your judgment, and may he continue to bless the United
States of America. Thank you."

The Honolulu Convention Center erupted with a roar. The
delegates were on their feet cheering wildly. Mitsunaga saluted
them with a wave and walked off the stage. The band started up
"Happy Days Are Here Again," but the applause and cheering
drowned out the music. The Hawaii delegation enthusiastically
waved their signs high above their heads. Delegates jumped up
and down and hugged one another.

Tom Bankhead's chest puffed with pride as he beamed at the TV
screen. *That was exactly what we needed. We've changed the subject. The election is no longer about our war-mongering candidate.
Instead, the bull's-eye is squarely on our out-of-control opponent
who'd stop at nothing to advance his candidacy.* Sitting in his hotel
room, Tom leaned back on his sofa, took a sip of bourbon, and
waited for the response from the pundits.

CHAPTER CIX

Wednesday, August 22nd

Honolulu, Oahu

On Tuesday, the delegates were still buzzing about Mitsunaga's speech. How they had turned the tables on the Republicans. All day long, DNC leaders huddled with the congressional leadership. Smith's campaign staff was kept out of the meetings by DNC Chairman Jones, an Andrews holdover, and Charley Johnson's allies. But they couldn't agree on what to do. Many felt that rallying around the vice president was the right strategy. Andrews controlled the California delegation. He wanted them to vote for Roy Green, the sitting governor of California, even though Roy had no desire to be a candidate. The senior senator from Colorado was doing the same thing. He'd worked his delegates to vote for the mayor of Denver instead of Smith.

Throughout Tuesday and into Wednesday the revolt was building. Andrews's surrogates worked the phones. They collared delegates on the floor to turn them away from Smith. The problem was they had no candidate. Charley Johnson agreed to run, but no one wanted him to. The big-state governors all bowed out. No serious candidate wanted to start a campaign in September, only nine weeks before the election. Smith had run for the nomination virtually unopposed. He was sitting on a mountain of cash poised for the sprint to the election. They couldn't see a viable alternative. The leaders decided to let the delegates vote their consciences. The Andrews staff worked the phones furiously to get enough states to vote for their favorite sons. They'd stop Smith from winning on the first ballot. What would happen after that? God only knew.

Late Wednesday afternoon the voting began. Alabama started by casting all sixty-seven votes for Larry Smith. Smith had won the primary, and there wasn't a Democratic favorite son to rally around. The Andrews supporters had pushed the mayor of Birmingham as a favorite son, but the delegates stuck with Smith.

Alaska voted fourteen votes for Smith and seven for its senator, Hank Beech. The Andrews staff whooped it up when they heard the vote.

Arizona kept the ball rolling away from Smith casting twenty votes for the vice president and sixty-eight for former Governor Hackman. Smith had pleaded with Governor Hackman to stick with him, but the former governor and close friend of President Andrews told him to 'go to hell.'

California voted all 535 delegates for its favorite son, Governor Roy Green. The convention band played raucous choruses of "California Here I Come" as the Golden State delegates engaged in a five-minute noisy demonstration on the convention floor.

The roll call continued with Smith gaining 30 to 40 percent of the delegates. But, in most states, favorite sons were getting a majority. When it was Hawaii's turn, the young governor, Danny Leong, announced that the Aloha State proudly cast its thirty-four votes for Hawaii's most favored son, the former senator from Hawaii, Ken Mitsunaga.

A hush fell over the convention hall as the Hawaii delegation jumped and hollered. They hugged each other while raising and lowering signs bearing the countenance of the former senator. A low, growling murmur began to grow in the chamber until it built to deafening cheers and applause throughout the hall.

Tom Bankhead was sitting with the Kentucky delegation and said, "Well, I'll be damned. Listen to that."

Indiana cast 2 votes for Smith and 59 for the former senator Evan Culver. Iowa cast 20 votes for Smith, 35 for the junior senator from the state, and 4 for Mitsunaga. The second surprise of the evening came when the Illinois delegation cast 150 votes for the mayor of Chicago and 65 for Mitsunaga. And then New York cast 100 votes for Governor Johnson, 60 votes for Smith, and a whopping 150 votes for Mitsunaga.

With each vote for Mitsunaga, the convention hall erupted in cheers. At the end of the first ballot, Smith had 1,200 votes, Mitsunaga had 1,000 votes, and the favorite sons had 2,983 votes. Smith had fewer than half the votes he needed in order to be nominated.

Charley Johnson called Tom Bankhead. "Tom, what the hell are we going to do? We can't nominate Mitsunaga. Can we?"

"Why the hell not? The delegates are cheering every time someone says his name. If he wins the nomination, there'll be pandemonium in the hall. If we rally around Smith, Andrews will go on an all-out jihad that'll rip the party in half. Not only will Parker take the presidency, but all our candidates will be torn, trying to figure out who to align with. This could end up being worse than Carter versus Kennedy in 1980. The delegates have already figured out we don't trust Larry Smith, and they don't trust him either. Imagine what ordinary Americans are thinking. We need a fresh change, and Ken Mitsunaga sure is that. Seriously, Charley, what've we got to lose at this point?"

"But Tom, just because Rebecca DeLaurio was colluding with Parker doesn't prove he wasn't taking Chinese money. And even if the public can be convinced he didn't take contributions from the Chinese, how do we deal with his affair with Rebecca? He never denied that relationship."

"Hell, Charley, after Monica Lewinsky, an affair is little to worry about. Besides, all of America has seen Rebecca sneaking out of Parker's door, not Mitsunaga's. If anyone has an Indian Affair problem, it's Parker. His camp can't bring up the Mitsunaga accusation. They'd have to answer questions about what Parker was doing with Rebecca alone in his hideaway. That's a non-issue. As far as the Chinese money, who knows what really happened? The Justice Department never found it in Mitsunaga's accounts."

"You heard his speech. He sounded pretty sour on politics. Do you think he'd do it?"

"If I know Ken, he's watching right now, flabbergasted. I don't know if he'd do it. But I think we could convince him to, if for no other reason than to have a chance to stop Parker. Will Andrews go along with that? You better give him a call and find out because it sure looks like the delegates are leaning his direction."

"Andrews suggested he'd support Homer Simpson if it would stop Parker and Smith. I'm sure he'd welcome Mitsunaga."

Tom looked back at the stage. The chairman of the convention decided that the best thing to do right now was to stall. Hawaiian musical star Kane Adams began a medley of patriotic songs in Hawaiian.

Tom walked out of the hall to call Ken Mitsunaga, rehearsing in his mind how he was going to convince him to run.

Ken Mitsunaga sat in his recliner in his office at home watching the convention on TV when the phone rang.

"Ken, it's Tom Bankhead. You watching this?"

"Tom, I don't know what you've done, but the delegates have gone nuts. I want you to know I had no idea Governor Leong was going to cast Hawaii's votes for me. That was crazy. And the rest of them make even less sense."

"I don't know about that, my friend. I think they're making a lot of sense. That speech of yours hit a nerve. Many of us have been thinking the same thing, but we're all so deep into the process we didn't think to say it. Let alone try to live it. They think you're the right man for the times, and I sure do agree with them."

"Tom, stop hitting the booze. I was tossed out. I'm damaged goods. The party would be crazy to nominate me. I'm done with politics, Tom; that's what my speech was about."

"Ken, today everybody wants to be done with politics. But we still want someone to lead the nation. We need someone who is willing to work with both parties. Look at your relationship with Sam Jackson. That was a model for bi-partisanship. We all envied how you two worked together on defense policy. How you worked on things affecting your states and the Pacific. We want you to take that model and put it into practice running the country. In your speech, you told the delegates to find someone who would work for the whole country. They found him, Ken. You."

"Tom, you can't be serious. I don't have staff. I don't have a campaign. I don't have money. I don't have any of the things you need to run a campaign. It's nuts."

"Ken, you have what you need—the confidence of the American people. Americans love an underdog. They love to vote for the guy who was wronged, dusted himself off, and got back in the fight. This is your chance to be that guy. Ken, this is your chance to be president. Think of all the good things you could do for the country. And besides, I know you can beat Parker. I'm sure the RNC is wondering how to back away from him, but it's too late for that. They rallied around him and put him forward, and now they're stuck with him.

"We were almost in the same boat until President Andrews went on TV and turned on Smith. If we don't follow the president, if we nominate Smith, Parker has a real good chance of becoming president. I know you don't want that. Ken, you're our best hope of stopping Parker. You've got to believe me on that. The delegates, the heart and soul of our party, are screaming for you. You need to answer their call and pick up the gauntlet. We need you to accept the nomination. I'm confident if you agree, we'll have more than three thousand delegates cast their ballot for you on the next vote. What do you say?"

Tom waited for an answer. He was pretty sure he'd punched all the right buttons. Duty, honor, country, and opportunity—not to mention squashing Parker. He hoped it was enough.

"Hold on for a second, Tom." Ken put down the phone and went to talk to Rosie. "Sweetheart, you won't believe this, but Tom Bankhead is on the phone."

"Well, I figured it was either him or Charley. Ken, I'm watching the convention. It's obvious they want you."

"Rosie, this is the heat of the moment, the passion of the crowd. They don't know what they want."

"Oh, Ken, I don't agree. I think they know. They want what you told them last night. They want a leader, Ken, and they think that leader is you."

"What do you think?"

"Ken, I've known all along you were the right man for the job, but it's up to you. You know the stress and the strain that comes with a job like that. There'll be challenges that'll test every ounce of strength you have. You have to decide if you have the fire to accept the challenge."

Ken walked over, reached down, and clasped her hand. "But you told me how glad you were I retired and returned home. If I say yes, and somehow we actually win, we'd be back in Washington with a schedule much crazier than I ever had in the Senate."

"I'm aware of that. But Ken, there's no way I would put my selfish desires to have you here in Hawaii with me over the good of the nation. And something tells me you'd put the needs of the nation above your own selfish desires as well." Rosie smiled down at him. "That's who you are. That's the Ken Mitsunaga who I fell in love with and married."

"So you think I should do it."

"Ken, you should do what your heart tells you." She gave a lopsided grin. "But . . . you'd make a great president."

"OK, Rosie, I'll tell him yes. I hope you're ready for a wild ride."

"As long as you're driving, I'm ready."

Ken walked back into his office and picked up the phone. "Tom, if the delegates nominate me, I'll accept the nomination. But I'm picking my own running mate. No one gets any say in that decision. Is that a deal?"

"Ken, my friend, you've got yourself a deal. Let us know who you're choosing, and we'll find someone to nominate and second him—or her—tomorrow night. Ken, this is wonderful news. I'm happy for the party, but most of all I'm thrilled for the country. I can't think of another American who would make a better president."

"Thank you, Tom. I'll be in touch when I make my vice presidential selection."

Ken sat down in his chair. He'd muted the TV and was watching, but not listening, to Kane Adams serenading the convention. When the camera panned to the crowd, he could see the delegates huddling around their state chairmen. Occasionally he'd see someone on the phone trying to hear over the music. He couldn't believe this was happening. After a few minutes, the chairman gaveled the convention to order and started the roll call. Alabama cast its votes for Guy Edwards the mayor of Birmingham, but from there the tide began to roll the other way. Arizona cast 68 votes for Mitsunaga. California's governor Roy Green announced that the Golden State cast all 535 votes for the next president of the United States, Ken Mitsunaga. The convention erupted. By the time Pennsylvania cast its votes, Mitsunaga was the nominee. In total, he received 3,864 votes. Larry Smith had 800, and the rest were spread among favorite sons from various states.

Rosie made sure she was the first to congratulate him with a victory kiss. He thanked her and said, "I hope we know what we are getting into."

She smiled, wiped back a tear, and said, "Whatever happens, I know you'll come out victorious."

Ken smiled at her and said, "Now I have to find a vice president." He picked up his phone and scrolled through his contacts looking for a number.

CHAPTER CX

Honolulu, Oahu

"It's Ken. Are you watching the convention? As you can see, the crazy fools nominated me. I told them I'd only accept if they'd let me choose my vice president. There's only one person whom I can imagine serving with, and that's you. Sure, I know this could create some problems, but I believe this is exactly what the country needs. Can I convince you to agree and serve with me if the people choose us over Parker?"

Ken listened to the voice on the other end and responded. "I understand all the reasons not to do this. But you know as well as I do, this is the type of thing the American people need. And I know you're the person for the job. Don't tell me 'no.' After all, I might be president soon." He chuckled a little. "Are you with me?"

Ken smiled and said, "That's wonderful. Now I need you to get on a plane and get here by tomorrow night. With the time change, that shouldn't be a problem. And thank you. If indeed I'm going to be president, I'll need your advice, counsel, and friendship to support me. Get some sleep tonight, and I'll see you tomorrow. Now I have to put on my best suit, and Rosie has to dress so we can get to the convention center and accept the nomination."

An hour after the delegates voted, their candidate took the stage with Rosie. Tom Bankhead introduced him to roars from the delegates. Mitsunaga quieted the crowd and spoke. "My fellow Americans, two nights ago I came to this auditorium. I urged you to find a new candidate to change 'politics as usual.' I had no idea you would think I was that man. I have no speech to make. I never thought I'd be invited back. I can only say this. I am honored and humbled that you've selected me as your nominee, and I'll try to live up to your expectations. Therefore, I accept your nomination for President of the United States."

He motioned for Rosie to join him from the back of the stage and asked Tom Bankhead to come over as well. Together the three of them joined hands and raised their arms in a salute to the delegates. The delegates roared with approbation. Ken kissed Rosie and shook Tom Bankhead's hand. Waving to the crowd while gripping Rosie's hand, Mitsunaga walked off the stage.

CHAPTER CXI

Pearl Harbor, Oahu

Stu Lockwood sat alone on the patio outside his quarters. He'd dismissed his aides for the evening. He was reflecting on the events of the past few weeks: the attack on North Korea, the saber-rattling over China, the political upheaval over Parker, the president's call, and now Smith and Mitsunaga. Most of all, he thought about Marge and the grandkids. The events of the past week hadn't afforded him the opportunity to grieve. He'd been too busy as the world teetered on the brink of calamity. Now alone, as dusk turned to darkness, his loss finally hit him. He was nearly sixty. Most likely in his last navy job. He and Marge had planned to retire to a condominium northwest of Seattle in Friday Harbor. From there Marge could keep close tabs on the grandchildren while he enjoyed sailing and the natural beauty of Washington. Now, that was gone.

For the first time in his adult life, he felt adrift. The phone rang inside, and he walked through the screened porch into the living room to get it.

"Dad, it's Tom. How are you?"

"Tom, I'm OK." Even as he said it, he felt his throat tightening and his eye tingle with unshed tears. He dropped into a nearby chair. "Actually, I'm feeling a little lost right now as I finally have time to think about your mother and the kids. You know I'm so sorry for you and your loss, for all our losses. I'm not sure how we'll ever recover from the tragedy. How are you, son? How's Susie?"

"Dad, it's hard right now. We're taking one day at a time, but there's one thing I wanted to tell you. We've just come home from the doctor's office. It's still early, but we found out for sure. Susie's pregnant. We're going to have another child. I know she won't replace Tommy or Sally or Henry, but at least we're being blessed with another child."

"Tom, that's wonderful. You said *she*. It's a girl? Susie's OK?"

"Dad, Susie's fine. In fact, she's terrific. And yes, Dad, it looks like we're going to have a girl. If it's OK with you, Susie and I would like to name her Marge."

Stu gulped back the rising tide of emotion and wiped at the tears welling in his eyes. "Son, I think that's wonderful. That's great news. I'm so happy for you, and for Susie. And Tom, actually, I'm happy for me. You've given me a lift, a little hope in this difficult time. Thank you so much for calling. Give my love to Susie and take care of her, Tom. Life is fleeting, as we both know. Take care of her, and take care of yourself."

"I will, Dad, and you take care of yourself. You proved the nation needs your steady hand on the rudder."

"I will, son. I will. Thanks for calling. It must be late there. It's getting late here. You better get some sleep. We have better days coming, Tom. We're going to be fine."

"I know, Dad. Take care and good night."

CHAPTER CXII

Thursday, August 23rd

Honolulu, Oahu

The decision had been made. Hawaii's Governor Leong would nominate Mitsunaga's choice for vice president. Clarence Channing, the retired senator from Maine who'd served in the chamber for nearly fifty years before stepping down at the age of eighty-five, would second the nomination. The choices would show that the nominee was clearly Mitsunaga's selection and was supported by party elders.

At 3:30 p.m. the chairman gaveled the convention back to order. Danny Leong was recognized. "Mr. Chairman, today, as governor of the fiftieth state which has welcomed all the delegates to our home to be part of our Ohana and to share the richness and warm embrace of the Pacific, at the request of our nominee and next President of the United States, our beloved Senator Ken Mitsunaga, I am proud to nominate a great friend of the state of Hawaii, the senator from Washington who has worked so closely with our nominee for more than thirty years—Senator Sam Jackson."

There was a moment of stunned silence in the room as the delegates realized they were being asked to approve a Republican as their vice presidential candidate. The Hawaii delegation cheered, but mostly the room was silent.

At that point, the chairman recognized the governor of Maine, who called upon former Senator Clarence Channing to speak. Using two hands to help raise himself from his seat, Senator Channing stood and grabbed the microphone. "Mr. Chairman, fellow delegates, it is my distinct honor to second the nomination of one of the finest gentlemen who has ever served in the United States Senate. A man of the highest moral character, who has crossed party lines on countless occasions to do the right thing for this great nation. Mr. Chairman, I second the nomination of the senator from Washington, my former colleague, very good friend, and the next Vice President of the United States, Senator Sam Jackson."

The chairman banged his gavel and asked for a voice vote on the nomination. The delegates, some still in shock, voiced their tepid approval. The chairman affirmed the vote as an approval of the nomination and instructed the band to play.

Less than a minute later, Senator Mitsunaga appeared on the stage.

"Ladies and gentlemen, friends and delegates, some of you might be surprised by my selection of Senator Sam Jackson. I can assure you he's the best choice to serve as your vice president. Sam Jackson and I have worked together in the Senate for more than thirty years to protect our nation's defense and to safeguard democracy. We promise our actions will not be guided by party or partisanship, but by what is best for the American people. I thank you for accepting my recommendation. And now I introduce to you my friend and colleague, and your next vice president, Senator Sam Jackson."

Sam Jackson walked onto the stage to sustained applause, albeit not as raucous as the reception afforded the nominee. He waved to the delegates, hugged the candidate, and together they saluted the crowd with locked arms.

Rosie led Senator Jackson's wife and son Tad onto the stage, and the candidates turned to embrace their families. They all waved to the crowd as the band played "Happy Days Are Here Again." The Hawaii and Maine delegations ran to the front of the convention in a spontaneous demonstration. They were joined by the Washington State delegation and various others.

Senators Mitsunaga and Jackson enjoyed their moment and then departed the stage. Shortly thereafter, the chairman gaveled the delegates to order. After concluding final housekeeping business, the convention was adjourned.

CHAPTER CXIII

Washington, DC

Harris Ward hadn't traveled to Hawaii. *Roll Call* wouldn't foot the eight thousand dollars it would have cost to send him to Honolulu and put him up in even the cheapest hotel. Instead, like millions of other Americans, he watched the drama unfold on TV. He'd been able to reach out to a few members, like Charley Johnson and Senator Bankhead, for comment early in the week. Without face-to-face contact, however, he had been rendered a bystander for all intents and purposes.

He somewhat enjoyed that role for a change. He relaxed on his couch and watched gavel-to-gavel coverage on PBS. But as the tension built, he grew increasingly frustrated at his inability to get the behind-the-scenes action. Still, he was fascinated by the drama. First, Mitsunaga was called back from the grave to offer a stunning rebuke of politics, politicians, and the media. Ward's story on Monday's activities described the scene as if it were a Greek tragedy. The hero rises from the dead to avenge his murder and destroy his murderer. The delegates served as his Greek chorus, offering comic relief and choreographed demonstrations.

His description of Wednesday was a biblical metaphor. The prodigal son returns home. The family dines on the fatted calf. The other son is shunned for not living up to his father's expectations.

After Thursday night's viewing of must-see TV and the last bombshell—the selection of Senator Jackson—Harris was at a loss for an appropriate metaphor. The jaundiced journalist was genuinely excited. The pairing of these two old bulls who had persevered for so many years under difficult conditions might actually offer America change. The callous and calloused reporter, who had seen every story from every angle, thought he actually saw something new, something genuine. He wrote:

> For thirty years, this reporter has walked the halls of Congress and reported on the news of the day. He's watched as good men and women advocated policies they viewed as beneficial. But in this time of intense partisanship and ideological divide, it would be nearly impossible for any reporter not to become skeptical that anything good could be done. And yet, on occasion, friendships and partnerships flourish. In difficult times, unlikely actors rise above the disputes and the rhetorical belligerence that mark most days in Congress.

> No partnership has been more fruitful in crossing party lines and accomplishing the nation's business than that of the senior senators from Washington and Hawaii. Their successes don't make *Roll Call* headlines. They are completed without political showmanship and grandstanding. But together they've done the hard work of moving legislation through committees, through

the Senate, and onto the president's desk. If ever there was a partnership which could steer this nation onto a less partisan path, I can't imagine a more likely one than Mitsunaga and Jackson.

Harris read the words again and again. The Parker camp would cry foul. They'd complain that *Roll Call* was editorializing the news. Today he didn't care. He'd let his editor make the call. Harris hit send, felt a slight tingling and an almost eerie sense of wellbeing. He turned off the computer and headed for bed.

CHAPTER CXIV

Tetiaroa, Tahiti

It was Thursday evening. Rebecca DeLaurio succumbed to the temptation and walked down to the hotel bar for happy hour. She normally avoided the tourists and particularly happy hour. In the hotel's tiki bar with its thatched roof and dried-grass parasols over the tables, tourists gathered between 5 and 7 p.m. for cheap drinks along with the Tahitian version of Hawaiian pupus. On some weeknights, they even had Tahitian dancers to entertain the tourists. Rebecca hoped that, since it was almost the weekend, the bar would have fewer customers. But on Tetiaroa there wasn't much to do after dark. This close to the equator the sun set around 6 p.m. every day, so there was bound to be a crowd.

Rebecca sat at the bar a few minutes before 6 p.m. in clear view of the television. There was only one TV on the island, and it was in the tiki bar. That single TV received a video feed from Papeete, the capital city of Tahiti. Most of the time it showed American sitcoms, a few French TV shows, and local news and weather. But on Thursday evening at six o'clock, the feed was from CNN International. It offered a one-hour roundup of news, mostly from the States but with occasional highlights from other places. Rebecca remembered that the Democratic convention was this week, and she was curious to see how it turned out.

The program began with the classic "This is CNN" voice-over, and then the anchorman started. "Good evening, ladies and gentlemen. The political bombshells continue to fall in the American presidential campaign. Last week the country was shocked to learn that Republican nominee, Senator James Parker, conspired with former Senate staffer Rebecca DeLaurio to bring down former Hawaii Senator Ken Mitsunaga."

Rebecca's head shot up as she heard her name, and she glanced nervously around. She drained her glass in one gulp, put on her sunglasses, and stood up to leave. She froze as she saw the grainy video of herself emerging from Parker's office. *How in the hell?*

"And now, we have even more startling news. Last night the Democratic delegates shocked the nation by rejecting the sitting vice president, Larry Smith. Instead, in a scene from a Frank Capra movie, they nominated the man shamed by Senator Parker, the disgraced former senator from Hawaii, Ken Mitsunaga."

Rebecca gasped as she heard the news. She watched the shots of Senator Mitsunaga raising his hands on stage in the traditional victorious salute with his running mate. *Holy cow, that's Sam Jackson. What the hell is going on? I don't believe any of this. Parker was caught? Smith is out. Ken is the Democratic nominee with Sam Jackson, of all people.*

She really, really wanted to stay and watch but couldn't risk the possibility of someone recognizing her. And knowing CNN, it was likely they'd be endlessly repeating that same clip of her. She lowered her head and left the bar. As she walked out, she stopped for a second, looked back at the TV, and began to laugh. She took the beach route back to her cottage, allowing the warm ocean waves to lap at her feet and ankles. She couldn't stop laughing.

CHAPTER CXV

Honolulu, Oahu

Paula sat on her couch in a state of disbelief. First Parker, then Smith, then Mitsunaga, and now Jackson. It was too good to be true. She laughed and clapped her hands. She cried a little as she watched the two senators—her two former bosses on stage together. She was excited, but mostly deliriously happy for Senator Mitsunaga—now lifted from pariah to messiah. The delegates were convinced he'd lead them to the Promised Land, and who was she to doubt it. If anyone could do it, it was those two.

She put her feet on the coffee table and finally turned off the sound. Chauncey had called, but she was more interested in watching the coverage than talking to him. So, the conversation had been brief. It had been hours since the convention ended, but she sat glued to the TV.

She'd watched the reaction from the Republican hired guns. They argued America was fed up with Democrats leading the country. They branded Mitsunaga an Andrews clone and continued the mantra of "No more years." Speaking for the Republican nominee, Steve Simpson congratulated Senator Mitsunaga. But he made it clear he knew the country was sick and tired of big-spending liberals. He was certain Americans wanted a change that only Republicans, and specifically Senator Parker, would provide.

Democratic pundits were smug and confident. They gushed over the new ideas coming from Senator Mitsunaga. They embraced the notion the Mitsunaga-and-Jackson team was a new unity ticket. They guaranteed this would end the politics of bickering and stalemate. In essence, the fall campaign had begun.

CNN was running the same video clips. Rebecca was shown leaving Parker's office. That was followed by Parker attacking her at the Mitsunaga hearing. Finally, they cut to the image of Mitsunaga and Jackson on stage together with arms raised in salute. This endless loop continued to play while a stream of reporters and experts voiced their opinions. She yawned a few times and realized it was after 11 p.m.

She grabbed Bo and gave him a big hug. He returned the affection with a thump of his tail and a lick that covered her entire face. She laughed, wiped her face, and kissed him on the head. She thought for a minute about all the good President Mitsunaga could do. He might resuscitate Hawaii's economy. He could restore all the projects that he'd initiated and Parker had killed. The phone rang. A familiar, melodious voice spoke.

"Paula, it's Ken. I need you."

To the Reader

Vigilante Politics is a work of fiction. Many of the institutions and programs described are real. The Daniel K. Inouye Asia-Pacific Center for Security Studies, Pacific Disaster Center, Maui High Performance Computing Center, and AEOS telescope are defense entities located in Hawaii. The SBX barge, F-117 aircraft (retired), and Massive Ordnance Penetrator (MOP) are in the DoD weapons inventory. But, to the author's knowledge, the F-117 and MOP variants do not exist.

Several of the events mirror actual occurrences. However, the characters, and incidents described in the book are the product of the author's imagination. Any resemblance to actual individuals or events is coincidental.

I am grateful to friends and family who suffered through many drafts and offered constructive criticism. They greatly improved the work. I also want to thank the editors at Quill Pen Editorial Services. Their creative insight and talent shaped the author's manuscript into a final product. I, alone, am responsible for all errors.

About the Author

C.J. 'Charlie' Houy is a veteran of Washington D.C., having served for thirty years on the staff of the Senate Appropriations Committee. Senators have praised him in the *Congressional Record* as "a model of responsible and enlightened public service" and "a consummate expert on defense issues." He is a recipient of the Navy Distinguished Public Service Award and the Secretary of Defense Medal for Outstanding Public Service. Charlie splits his time between Washington D.C., and Pacific Grove, California.